THE 20'S GIRL

THE GHOST
AND
ALL THAT JAZZ

JUNE KEARNS

In Memory
of
Nell, Doll and Kath
The wonderful Little sisters

CHAPTER ONE

'A MILLION WOMEN TOO MANY!
1920 HUSBAND HUNT!'
Daily Mail

Summer 1924. Southwest Texas

'A word, Coop? Before I go.'

The funeral and wake was almost over when Orin Ewing, the family lawyer, drew him aside. A matter, he said, that needed attending to.

It had been a big affair. A gathering of the cattle clans. Mahogany-faced men in starched collars and neckties, standing soberly at the graveside, as a hot Texan breeze flattened dry grass and blew the preacher's words clean away.

Then Orin's hand on his shoulder, Orin's voice low and serious, and Coop led the way through clouds of cigar smoke to a quiet spot, all the while thinking, some simple land ownership matter, boundary dispute.

Afterwards, more in bewilderment than anger, he asked, 'Why, Orin? What the hell was he thinking? Did he *ever* mean to tell me?'

Orin had no answers. 'Reckon he just ran out of time, boy.'

Later, driven by demons, Coop rode a horse hard to the horizon and brought him back, trembling and in a lather. He'd had hours by then, to get over the shock. Anger had been laid aside; he knew what he had to do.

'Orin? What'd you say about me going to England?'

'I'd say don't do it, boy!'

'I'm doing it.'

Autumn 1924. The English Shires.

She would. She wouldn't. She might.

Pushed down the lane by a wet wind, Gerry held onto her hat and her bicycle. Hedgerows, trees, fields, flew by in a blur. It was weather for woollies and wellies, but she hadn't got either of those.

Instead, she was drenched in scent and in something crêpe-de-chine with flapping skirts from the bottom of her aunt Leonie's trunk.

Why? Because she hadn't decided what to do yet.

What was wrong with her? Anyone would think she was feather-headed, the number of times she'd changed her mind. Goodness knows there were few enough men to go round anymore, and how many of those were beating a path to her door? She should be grateful.

Squishing bicycle wheels through leaves at the side of the road, she chewed the knicker-elastic under her chin, there to stop her hat from flying off. A gang of rooks in gothic black rose up - *caa caa* - to swirl over ploughed fields behind the hedge.

If only the invitation had been for something else. Afternoon tea with Archie's parents? Just thinking about it made her twitch.

So what if she was pushing thirty, with the chill wind of spinsterhood gusting round her ears? She wasn't ready yet, for trial by Major and Mrs Dutt-Dixon-Nabb. Nowhere near.

'All right, Miss-Change-Your-Mind,' Prim had said. 'What's wrong with Archie?'

Nothing. Engaging good looks, a winning way. The sort of suitor to bring a grateful tear to any mother's eye. It wasn't him, it was her. Small, unexceptional, Gerardina Mary Chiledexter.

'He's nice,' she'd said. 'I'm flattered. But what have we got in common? A sort of junior squire from a county family, who hunts and shoots things - and me.' She had paused. 'D'you think it's money?'

A snort from Prim. 'You haven't got any.'

'Archie doesn't know that, does he? We don't talk about those things, we don't even *laugh* together much.'

Prim had enquired, rather sourly, what there was to laugh about. 'Look at me,' she'd said. 'I'll never bag a husband now, the competition's far too cut-throat. It's not fair; I've been cheated. My destiny, whoever he was, is probably under the mud of some awful French battlefield.'

'Is there such a thing,' Gerry had murmured, 'as destiny?'

'Your aunt believed in it. Did she have an opinion on

Archie, as a matter of interest?'

'Erm …' (*Well-bred, but weak, darling. A mother's boy. Fingernails too clean. And that name! Hardly trips off the tongue, does it?'*)

Of course, Leonie had an opinion on most things, and hadn't been shy about sharing them, either. Physics, fortune-telling, foreign money. Not that her views had always been reliable. Who cared though, when she'd taught you to dance the hoochie coochie and the turkey trot, wearing ostrich feathers and waving an Egyptian cigarette in a long black holder?

Wild, wonderful Leonie. Why did you leave us in such a mess?

Gerry careered down the hill to the higgledy-piggledy part of town, past Peagrams Drapers and Outfitters (*Dresses for all seasons*), and Hazeldine's Bakery (*Bread with purity and nutty flavour*).

Clattering over cobbles to the saggy frontage of Bent's Fine and Rare Books, she came to an abrupt halt.

'Igor! Move.'

A scar-nosed, frayed-eared hooligan tomcat, big as a small bear, sat in the doorway, eyeing her coldly.

'Shoo!' She rang her bell, stamped her foot. 'Shoo, shoo!'

Turning his head with infinite disdain, Igor didn't budge an inch.

After some complicated manoeuvring of wheels and cat's tails, Gerry banged up the steps into the narrow three-storeyed building that housed the bookshop. The bell over the door jangled its annoyance.

'That cat,' she announced, 'is scary! A witch's cat. Not a whisker of loyalty to anyone.'

From behind a pile of catalogues, business letters, bills and receipts, Prim peered over her spectacles. 'Did you look in a mirror before you came out?'

'It was windy.'

'Well, a *man* called to see you, apparently. Left a note on the door. Better smarten up a bit before he comes back. That's not a suitable dress to ride a bicycle in.' She held out a handkerchief. 'And there's oil on your nose.'

'Which man?' Rubbing her face, Gerry noticed Prim's tight bun unravelling. Always a bad sign.

'Name of …' Prim rummaged for the note, 'hmm … let's see. Yes, Cooper.'

'Who? Do we owe him money?'

'Gerry, dear, we owe everyone money.'

Almost everyone. They were sliding out of control, that was for sure, and it was Gerry's responsibility now, all down to her, and the reason for the layers of bags under her eyes.

Debt, they were in debt. Aunt Leonie's bookshop sinking under a huge wave of bills and final demands, and Gerry couldn't sleep because of dreams of being dragged off to debtor's prison by crowds of baying creditors.

'Can't we at least ask Cyril to mend that window?'

'No.' Prim tapped her teeth with a pencil. 'Even Cyril and his ladders are beyond us now. I wouldn't take your coat off either, if I were you. There's no more coal for the stove.'

The few early customers in the shop weren't likely to save

their bacon either - someone from the Light Opera Group looking for music and one of the Miss Webbs after the new Ethel M. Dell.

Mid-morning found Gerry, still irritable with worry, on her knees with swirling skirts bunched up.

She'd measured the broken window and cut brown paper to size, but nothing had been in the thingummy drawer where it was supposed to be - the sharp knife, the tacks, the hammer - and rummaging round for them had taken ages.

When the bell over the door clanged again, she turned to see someone tall and well-built with considerable shoulders duck through and stand there, filling the frame.

A whirl of dust and leaves blew in after him.

The collar of a calf-length coat was turned up, the brim of a hat pulled down. Narrowed eyes assessed the shop. 'Okay if I take a look round?'

Unmistakeably American. Voice a slow, dark drawl. And something about him that said trouble. The coat and hat gave him a menacing gangsterish sort of look, more suited to the mean streets of Chicago, than Lower Shepney Market.

Gerry and Prim exchanged glances. Oh Lord. They didn't owe money across the Atlantic as well, did they? Was this the beginning? The wolves had smelled blood and were gathering, ready to rip them apart?

The man wandered round, a dark, brooding presence. With everyone else trying to ignore him and pretending to be busy, he pulled a few oversized volumes from the Military

History section, (Battle plans! Tactics!), flicked idly through, then slotted them back.

There was a moment's distraction when a vision in dangling two-headed fox-fur and hat moulting feathers wobbled over the threshold. Singing something about 'rescuing the perishing' in high falsetto, she waved a book that she wanted to swap.

'Swap?' Prim said loudly, for the benefit of anyone listening. 'No, no, Mrs Applegarth. This is a bookshop. We sell, we don't swap.'

'Eh?' Mrs Applegarth cupped a hand to her ear. 'I can't finish this, dear, it's too thick. Mr Applegarth keeps distracting me with his euphonium playing.'

'Come over here,' Gerry hissed from her dim corner. 'I'll find you a nice thin book.' Turning blindly back to the long oak shelves, her mind was now blank. Did L come before M? Or after P?

Minutes later, with the man still loitering but clearly paying attention to everything going on, she went back to the broken window. Banging the last tacks in, she rocked back on her heels to admire her handiwork.

It was no good. The day had been ruined. Was this what they could expect from now on? Was that what debt collectors looked like? Towering, silent?

'Excuse me?'

Her ears pricked at the low southern drawl.

'Name's Cooper. And I was hoping to meet with Mister Chiledexter. Mr Gerry Chiledexter?'

'Ah.' Dropping the hammer, Gerry scrambled to her feet. As her heart sank to her boots, she felt her breakfast kipper start to come back up. 'Um, that would be me.'

Ducking under a swinging bucket, strategically placed to catch drips, the man edged towards her.

'You?'

She nodded.

'*Gerry* Chiledexter?'

'Well. It's Gerardina, actually.'

He just stood, stared.

'Gerardina Chiledexter?' A weak smile, and she pulled at her dress, which had somehow become all tucked up. 'Can I help?'

As her words trickled out, a blur of black fur burst through the newly-papered window like a circus dog through a hoop, crash-landing on all fours. Igor, wearing a pleased expression and looking as if he expected applause.

Deaf to Gerry's shrieks, he stepped fastidiously over a line of books set aside for the Lower Shepney Market Literary and Philosophical Society and proceeded to cough up a fur-ball on the cover of *What To Do Until The Doctor Comes.*

Wrenching her attention back to the man, Gerry was met by another unblinking grey stare, as dark and intense as Igor's when he was watching a bird.

They regarded each other in silence. A long silence.

'The owner?' He was unable to hide a flicker of disbelief. 'They said, Gerry Chiledexter. I thought …'

Gerry knew what he thought. Now, he had the air of

someone faced with country bumpkins who dealt in groats, and bartered with hens and cabbages.

'I was expecting a man.'

'Yes. It's *Gerardina*, you see. After Saint Gerard Majella? The patron saint ...' she stopped herself.

'Right.' His expression unreadable, the American looked pointedly at the clock. 'Well. I've some business to discuss. And time's kinda short. When would be convenient?'

At that moment, Gerry experienced an overwhelming urge to bolt, shut herself in a cupboard and shout through the door. *'Take the money, yes, yes, take whatever's in the cash drawer! So sorry! Sorry! Sorry!'*

Clearing her throat, she tried to construct an excuse. 'Ah. Well, any time, really. Except ... unfortunately, this afternoon. Yes, an appointment. So, anytime ... after perhaps, the weekend?'

'How about now?'

'Now?' A nervous sidelong glance caught Prim, from her ringside seat, signalling frantically. 'Erm, no.' Gerry said. 'Not just now.'

'Why not?'

'I'm afraid ...too busy.'

Another pause. The man took off his hat.

Staring at shoulder-length hair and an unshaven face, browned by wind and sun, Gerry was reminded again that this was not the sort of look often seen in Lower Shepney Market. Poker straight partings and regimented haircuts were the mark of a gentleman here.

In other circumstances, she would have crossed the street to avoid this person. Crossed the desert, the Kalahari.

'You don't look too busy.'

'We're … ah, expecting … expecting to be busy.'

The American's eyes flicked round the empty shop, past wide gaps in the shelves to the paper, now hanging by one tack over the broken window.

'Mizz Chiledexter?' He sounded pained. 'Listen, I'm kinda tired. I've come half-way round the world to discuss a business matter, it's been raining since I got here and I want to go home. Real bad. Y'know how that feels?'

A bonfire began in Gerry's cheeks.

'Yeah, it feels lousy.' Glancing back at the clock, he sent her a glint of a look. 'And you need to do a helluva lot better, pardon me, than a week Saturday, or whenever it was.'

Why did this person's dislike seem so personal? Gerry took a nervous step back, visions of unpaid bills floating in front of her eyes.

'What's this?' Mrs Applegarth's hat, quivering with the assorted feathers of several dead birds, bobbed suddenly between them.

It was the man's turn to look startled.

'This book you gave me, dear.' She waved a slim volume under Gerry's nose, *The Study Of Mosses and Liverworts*. 'I like a nice murder mystery.'

'Oh! So sorry, Mrs Applegarth, I - '

'Or something more … mystical.'

'I … beg pardon?'

'You know, dear.' Her voice dropped. 'Wraiths, apparitions. The other side?'

'What! One moment - '

Dredging up a smile, Gerry turned back to the man's unflinching gaze. 'Where were we?'

'You said, come back next week; *I* said ...' a pause, coated in thick black ice, '... no thanks, better think again.'

'All right,' she said, and heard a dull thud in the background, possibly Prim's head hitting the desk. 'Later, then. Perhaps this evening?'

'What time?' Quick as a flash.

'Six-o-clock, at Tally-Ho Lodge? Left past the church, follow the high wall to the top of the lane, then just past the big iron gates to the Hall.'

Another critical, summing-up stare seemed to cut straight through her.

'We can discuss your ... um, business then,' she persevered bravely.

This lame remark was met with a somewhat imperious arching of the eyebrows and a brief nod. No effort wasted on pleasantries or handshake. Then the hat was back on, the brim pulled low over his eyes.

As he turned to go, Gerry rolled her eyes at Prim. How had she managed to turn this into such a combination of dog's breakfast and pig's ear?

Barely avoiding the hanging bucket, the American ducked back through the open door, followed by Igor, who turned his back and stalked out, tail erect, on the visitor's heels.

Traitor, Gerry thought. *Wretched animal.* From the back, those puffed furry breeches made him look like some sort of eighteenth century rake.

She hadn't wanted a cat, especially not some huge brute who sat and stared at her all the time, then disappeared for weeks on end only to turn up in unexpected places.

But Igor had belonged to Leonie. Never the sort to roll over and have his tummy tickled, he'd gone missing after her funeral, and had only recently returned, to slap and scratch at the front door.

Apparently, it wasn't enough to cut Gerry dead in front of her friends. Now, he was hobnobbing with her enemies.

She suspected a witch in the neighbourhood.

CHAPTER TWO

'If you're hoping for a husband, be warned!
Nice young men have no time for jazzing flappers.
They prefer a home-made girl.'
A Woman's Way, 1923

'According to this,' Gerry tapped the oversized volume on her knee, 'Booksellers used to be rich.'

Prim rolled her eyes. 'When was that!'

They were huddled over a pot of tea, munching penny buns.

'1830's. They lived in luxury, apparently, and ate turbot for supper. You see? How have I managed to get everything so wrong? '

'Not your fault, you've done your best.' Refilling chipped teacups, Prim looked over the spectacles, now half way down her nose. 'Anyway, what did they say at the bank?'

'Same old thing. It was Mr Grewcock, back from the navy. The ship's been scuttled, he said, and we're sinking.' Gerry blew on the tea, warming hands round the cup. 'Leonie just left too many debts. He used a lot more words though, and kept tut-tutting. In his opinion, women shouldn't be left in charge of anything. All very strict and shiver me timbers.'

The gist of it, was that her safe little ship of a life was in danger of slipping its moorings. And now, it seemed, about to be scuppered by a great big American battleship.

'That man,' Prim murmured, 'the American. Where do you think he sprang from?'

Cooper? Gerry didn't want to think about Mr Cooper. Clearly, he was going to be difficult. 'I've no idea. Did he have to be so disagreeable?'

'We owe him money, Gerry. I daresay some situations call for it.'

Gerry bit her lip, recalling candid conversations behind closed doors at the bank, when Leonie's adventures had been discussed. Travels to far-flung places like Madagascar, Peru. Bills and bank debts were even now drifting back, apparently - costly pigeons coming home to roost.

That was quite apart from all the other IOU's that she'd found languishing in the depths of her aunt's Hermès handbags.

Trouble was, her aunt just hadn't understood money.

'I did my best, you know, Prim, to get Leonie to talk about finances. The last time, not long before she died.'

'Oh? How did she respond?'

'By trilling, 'Not now, dulling,' and skipping off to London to see *Chu Chin Chow*.' Another gulp of tea.

'Did she leave you *anything*, apart from her debts?'

At Prim's tone, Gerry shot the other woman a quick look. With her plain black silk, sensible shoes and hair scraped back into that wispy bun, a person would never guess that she was only thirty-two years old.

But Prim understood only too well the strain of watching her purse and scraping for money. Having looked after fractious and ailing parents until they'd died, she'd been left with barely anything to live on herself. Until Leonie had sailed to her rescue, offering paid employment.

'Her clothes.' Gerry flexed fingers, still blue with cold. 'Her glove stretcher, some silver-trimmed scent bottles. That was about it. Most of the jewellery was sold for spending sprees in Paris.' She chewed her lip. 'I expect that American's rich as Croesus, too. Probably doesn't even need our money.'

'We can't hold that against him, can we? I don't suppose he can help those cheekbones, either.'

Gerry frowned. 'If you ask me, there's something objectionable about really handsome men. They're too used to being admired; it makes them far too pleased with themselves.'

'You wouldn't want to wake up with a smouldering Heathcliff beside you on the pillow, then?'

Gerry had the grace to blush. 'I think passion should start with great conversations, that's all. Not just ... appearance.'

'Well, bully for you, Miss Particular.'

'I don't trust men like him. They bring me out in hives.'

'Then why invite him to the cottage? It's dark by half past five. You'll be all on your own.'

'There's Sully next door, within screaming distance.'

'Ha, and what'd the likes of old Sully do to whatshisname? Throw a few turnips at him?' Folding her arms, Prim eyed Gerry thoughtfully. 'Gerry?'

'Mmm?'

'Don't let this ... Mr Cooper ... intimidate you.'

'I won't.'

'And, well ... try to make a good impression. At least make him *think* we know what we're doing. Wear something ... you know, presentable.'

'Aren't I always presentable?'

Prim coughed and adjusted her spectacles.

Later, Gerry found herself going over and over things in her head. People were forever offering hints, tips, advice. Try this, do that. Sell up! Stick it out. Which was best? No idea.

So when Archie arrived at the bookshop door, attentive and immaculate in patent leather shoes, well-cut coat and crisply waved, silky-yellow hair - she heard herself say *yes*, when she should have said *no*.

Tea with the Dutt-Dixon-Nabbs. Why worry about that?

Archie had been dropping hints. About ... what was it? Clothes etiquette.

Certain standards of dress would be required for this tea-party, apparently. None of that haute-couture in mothballs, thank you. Especially - and this with a shudder - nothing with tassels or feathers.

Gerry had known just what he meant. It wasn't any old lace rag reeking of lavender from the back of the wardrobe, either. Oh, no. Leonie's precious cache of Patou and Poiret - *that's* what Archie had been referring to. Her Charles Worth and Molyneux, her Madeleine Vionnet. Four bursting wardrobes, and trunks stuffed to their straps with wildly expensive couture cast-offs.

The thing was, Leonie hadn't cared one jot about dressing appropriately. She'd worn things in the middle of the day that most people wouldn't risk after dark.

Fashion had been her passion. And these were love-affair clothes. Fragile silk velvets and guipure lace, beaded tulle, and satin scattered with tiny seed pearls.

Gerry adored them, every one. Dresses that crackled and rustled. Wraps and squashy furs. Pretty, desirable things that lifted the spirits and made life seem so much more bearable.

Wearing them kept her aunt close. Threads of connection.

One of Gerry's earliest memories of arriving from India, en route to boarding school, was of an appalled Leonie holding up vests and belts, bodices and bloomers, over-stockings, garters, gaiters. 'They're trying to *bury* you, my darling!' she'd said. 'In heavy wool!'

And that was how it had all started. That day marked the beginning of her own education, in the magic of fashion. Years of playing dress-up, and the start of conversations such as: 'We're not allowed to wear shiny shoes like these ones, Leonie.'

'*Gorgeous* patent leather. Why ever not?'

'Well. Because they may reflect, you know ... our under-thingies.'

'Perfect reason to get rid of those wretched woollen bloomers, darling.'

Of course, Leonie, had been a standout in any crowd. She'd just had that ... thing about her; something that made people look twice.

Gerry, on the other hand, had needed all the help she could get. Until one day, her aunt had narrowed her eyes, and said, 'Why, Gerry! Look at you. Who put that outfit together, who altered it for you?'

'Me! I did it myself.'

'Well, well. From the cocoon, a butterfly!'

Even so. Tea at the Dutt-Dixon-Nabbs? Sigh. That required extra special consideration.

She'd found gloves and hat to match the tissue-thin tea-dress, fastened two loops of Leonie's seed pearls at her throat and tried twenty-two ways of pinning up her hair, before piling it high with combs and pins to stop it disintegrating into a tangled nest.

'How do I look?' she'd asked Prim that afternoon, pushing feet into strapped lizard-skin shoes.

'Quite the pip. Perfect for cricket club teas and making up a four at tennis.'

'Oh, Lord.'

'Well you're making a statement, aren't you? Saying, I don't give a *fig* for warmth or practicality. Oh go, just go and set those china teacups a-rattling.'

So now here she was, on the edge of a cracked leather armchair, balancing bright smile, cup, saucer and Crown Derby plate, while being eyed by Mrs Dutt-Dixon-Nabb - ('*Call me Dephne*') - in a way that made Gerry feel like a piece of prime beef. 'How unusual you look, my dear. Is that dress an old favourite?'

A chilly start. Why, wondered Gerry, hadn't she worn something simpler? Plainer, heavier - a burlap sack, perhaps.

There wasn't much comfort in the conversation, either. Archie's mother had something of the dowager about her. Holding her teacup, her little finger stuck out at a perfect ninety-degree angle, and when she spoke, it made you sit up straight and pay attention.

The house, too, was rather cold and grand and eighteenth century. Crusty oils lined the walls, interspersed with prints of beady-eyed game birds and faded photographs of the Major. Gerry counted nine.

The Major by a tent, in uniform; the Major with foot on felled lion. Here in pith helmet with smiling natives, there astride a camel.

She looked nervously around for something else to stare at. 'What a wonderful piano.'

'Do you play, Miss Chiledexter? My children are all accomplished musicians.' Mrs Dutt-Dixon-Nabb gestured toward a photograph showing a set of small children, in descending order, in matching coats with velveteen collars. 'Perhaps Archie would oblige us with a recital later.'

Catching Gerry's eye, Archie pulled a face.

'Do you sing? Archie has a particularly broad *tessitura*. He's often complimented. Last year, the Gilbert and Sullivan Society were quite transported by his Nanki-Poo. Isn't that so, Archie?'

The Major, all bristly tweed and George V beard, was a shouty sort of a person, who tended to boom in capital letters. When Gerry mentioned the bookshop, a vein began to throb in his forehead.

'YOUNG WOMEN TODAY! THINK THEY CAN DO THE SAME AS A MAN? HA! CRACKPOTS AND BUSY-BODIES SHOUTING FOR THE VOTE!'

At that toe-curling moment, Gerry's mouth was full of macaroon and she couldn't have responded, even if she'd wanted to.

Just as well. Conversation had already suffered a bit of a hiccup, when she'd told the Major that she didn't hunt. Worse - oh, Lord - that she didn't really *care* for blood-sports.

Every question seemed to set a trap. And she knew, very well, that she was being looked over, measured up, or what-ever you wanted to call it. Archie had admitted as much. The Major, he'd said, perfectly seriously, recommended thorough reconnaissance before making a match.

And the Major's views were clearly as firm as his wife's Marcel Wave

'But don't worry your head, my little kitten,' Archie had added. 'The parents will dote on you.'

Gerry didn't want to be doted on. She wasn't absolutely sure that she wanted to be matched, either. With Archie, or anyone else. What she wanted … oh, she didn't *know* what she wanted.

Lately, she'd found herself dreaming of risk, romance, adventure. A trip up the Amazon, slow boat to China. Exploring lost cities ruled by legendary Mesopotamian kings, that sort of thing.

Not life as lady-of-the-manor. All Boxing Day meets, stirrup cups and yoicks tally-ho. Because, there'd be no avoiding it. As well as being Lord Lieutenant of the County, the Major was the local MFH - to the hunting-pink fraternity and their hunting-pink complexions.

Anyway. However hard she tried, she just couldn't imagine staggering under the weight of that surname. Wasn't one hyphen enough for anybody?

It wasn't until conversation turned to her aunt though, that good relations really started to unravel.

It started innocently enough. Having been treated to a trot through the Dutt-Dixon-Nabb family history, Gerry was asked about her own. A *when-did-you-last-see-your-father* sort of inquiry.

The answer to that, of course, was not for some time. She was a child of the Raj, Gerry explained, and with her father a government administrator in India, she'd been packed off to England at a very early age. To be passed round the relatives, she might have added, but didn't.

Her mother had considered herself far too young and glamorous to be saddled with the responsibility of a child. She didn't say that, either.

Hardly the time to go over the sad story of her birth. How her mother had refused to name her and screamed at the Saved Mary Magdalens, to take the wailing brat away.

Hence, of course, Gerardina - chosen by the nuns from a book in the *Six o'Clock Saints* series. Fortunately, when none of the other relatives could be bothered, Aunt Leonie, her mother's sister, had taken her in.

'Ah, yes.' Mrs Dutt-Dixon-Nabb fingered her pearls. 'I have to say, my dear, one has always felt a great deal of sympathy for your situation.'

'I beg your pardon?'

'For someone so young and impressionable to be left in the care of, well … such a very *unreliable* person. Far be it from me to speak ill of the dead, but wasn't your aunt rather … bohemian?'

No better than she ought to be, was the suggestion - and it was those weasel words that brought Gerry to the brink of a tantrum.

She couldn't deny that Leonie - with her exotic glamour and dancing all night at the Ritz - had never been cosy, like other people's aunts. No sober tweeds, stout brogues or tea at four-thirty there.

Wild and free, she hadn't given two hoots for reputation. Of course, she'd excited gossip, of *course* she had. Without her, though, without Leonie's warmth, love and laughter, Gerry knew that she would have been deeply scarred.

Throwing a glance at the plumply-corseted Daphne Dutt-Dixon-Nabb, she heard Leonie's voice in her head: '*What on earth is the point of getting the vote and shorter skirts, my darling, if your husband still keeps you in corsets?'*

'Of course, you must have been so awflegh unheppy.' The accent was impeccably clipped. 'The entire county was aware of your aunt's scandalous behaviour. And what your poor dear parents thought ...' Mrs Dutt-Dixon-Nabb patted her pinched waves. 'Well, one simply can't imagine.'

'Now, Mother-'

'Please don't interrupt, Archie.' A derisory sniff. 'You see, one's afraid this is the trouble with these ... feshionable people. They know nothing of our country values.'

There was a harrumphed 'hyah, hyah,' of agreement, from the Major.

At that point, Gerry's face grew hot and she wanted to shout and stamp her feet. She wished now that she'd worn something outrageous and *really* given these people something to sniff about.

'There was no need for anyone to feel sorry for me,' she said, as evenly as she could. 'Aunt Leonie took me in, when I was very small and very scared, and never ever let me down. I adored her.'

We had fun, she wanted to shout. We danced to rag-time! We played the kazoo and the swanee whistle! 'As for those poor parents, well ... I hardly knew them, barely saw them, for years at a time.'

And snap! Just like that, she was caught. The trap had been sprung and there was no going back. Her words were left hanging, while Archie's mother looked as if she was chewing a wasp.

Somehow, Gerry knew that she had lost the battle. One that she hadn't really been aware that she was fighting.

A long stretch of silence followed. Just the clink-click of cup on saucer, the sonorous tock of the long-case clock, and rain spitting spitefully against the windows.

With Mrs Dutt-Dixon-Nabb apparently rendered speechless and the Major's eyes raised to the intricately plastered ceiling, Gerry looked to Archie to come to her rescue.

Help, she tried to signal. *Please, Archie! Help me out here.*

No response. Avoiding her gaze, he busied himself pinching the knife-edge creases in his immaculate trousers, admiring the shine on his handmade shoes. The message was unmistakeable.

Gerry watched him stand and sidle over to the window, apparently fascinated by something in the garden. As he fiddled first with gold cufflinks, then his Old Etonian tie, he seemed to be sweating slightly.

She, on the other hand, had started to shiver and hearing the panicky rattle of cup against saucer, realised her hand was shaking. What was she *doing* here? Cold house and now, cold shoulders.

Seeking escape, she left the room to powder her nose. Even before the door closed, she heard the explosive hiss of conversation.

'Really, Archie! Why didn't you tell me she had a speech impediment?'

'Oh, come now, Mother. She's a little shy, that's all.'

'Shy! The gel can barely string two words together! She has absolutely no conversation. No, I'm sorry, Archie. It won't do. Running a shop with her chum? My dear, she's in *trade*.'

And that, Gerry thought, said it all. No flowery silk tea-dress and set of her aunt's good pearls would ever change it, either.

Coming back into the room, it took a huge effort to keep her social smile in place. The temperature had now dropped several more degrees.

Conversation continued in a rather desultory way, but the parlour maid carrying more tea was waved away, 'No thank you, Margaret. By the way, that last pot wasn't scalded,' and the tea-party brought to a brisk conclusion.

To give him credit, Archie quickly rallied and did his best to make amends. Catching Gerry's eye, he shook his head and mouthed some sort of weak apology.

Too late.

Gerry insisted, absolutely insisted, on walking home alone.

Yes, she knew the light was beginning to fade.

No, really. She liked walking in the rain.

CHAPTER THREE

'Women approaching thirty may have lost all chance
of inspiring affection.'
Advice to Miss-All-Alone, 1924

Two and a half miles. Unsuitable, too-tight shoes. Drenching rain.

Gerry kicked off the shoes, tore off wet dress and stockings with bloodless fingers, and left everything in a sodden heap on the floor.

Then cried, in frustration.

It wasn't the Dutt-Dixon-Nabbs' fault. They'd helped her to see, that was all. She didn't fit in anywhere, didn't belong. What was she going to do with herself? With her life! She was cold, she was wet, she felt sick.

The bookshop? A dead horse, even before she'd started flogging it.

Marriage? Not a hope. All gone. Young men fallen in their thousands. The butcher, baker, candlestick maker. She'd end up a dried up old twig of a spinster with an arthritic cat -

unravelling wool, bottling beans. One of the surplus women, doomed to maiden aunt-hood.

Teaching? Don't think so. Talents? Um … training?

Hadn't she always been an outsider? Too shy and plain for India. '*My dear! So mousy. Dull as a button. Not a bit like her mother.*' Too gauche for her English boarding school. Even here, in the village, she was a fish out of water.

Lately, she'd been wondering. Who, exactly, *was* she? How had she ended up like this?

She lit the fire, but the logs were still damp, and smoke refused to go up the wet chimney and billowed back. Soot on her nose. Dry rot in the roof and splodges of damp creeping up the walls. A metaphor! For her life!

She cried some more.

What was happening, what was the matter with her? Until a few months ago, she'd almost never cried. Hadn't she been resolutely dry-eyed all through her lonely childhood and those awful school days? Suffering in silence.

Then Leonie had died. And grief had hit Gerry like a stone. The dam had finally burst.

Shrugging on her aunt's peignoir - scarlet silk, hand-painted with exotic blue birds - she buried her face in its folds. It still smelled faintly of Leonie, and something exotic, vanilla-laced.

There were ghosts here. Oh, yes. Leonie's room, her furniture, pictures and ornaments. Sometimes, she found these ghosts comforting. But, not tonight.

'What am I going to do, Leonie?' she wailed to the air,

then flung herself across the hearthrug, crumpled up and fell asleep.

Bang. BANG BANG! Something pounding the door, rattling the letter-box.

Staggering into the hall, Gerry opened the heavy oak door a crack.

'Yes?' The force of the wind flung it violently back.

A figure loomed menacingly out of the darkness, about ten feet tall and very wet - its head covered by a brown leather helmet, its eyes invisible behind huge goggles.

Gerry shrank back, from this eyeless apparition. Like something out of the *House Of Usher.* Shouldn't it be chained up? Driving rain and wind buffeted it sideways. Drips from the ivy splattered its long leather coat.

'Who lives here? Hansel and Gretel?'

The American? Drat. *Drat*! She'd forgotten all about him.

'Can I come in?'

A flash of lightning lit up the overhanging trees and empty lane. Tightening the thin robe, Gerry overcame the temptation to slam the door in his face. Almost naked under the silk, she felt cornered. 'I'm not dressed!'

Ducking in, he pushed past her. 'Don't worry,' he said, with a cursory glance, 'you won't need protection. We have to talk.'

As a wet Igor shot in behind, she put her weight against the door, wincing at the sight of herself in the hall mirror. Oh, Lord. Red-nosed and rumpled, eyes swollen from weeping and witch's hair - half-up, half-down - drying in a frizz round her face.

The man had already taken off helmet, goggles, gloves, and was now shaking out his hair like a dog and dripping puddles over the flagged floor.

'You *did* say six?'

'Yes. Yes, I'm sorry.' Gerry put a self-conscious hand up to her own hair. 'It's a bad time for me, that's all.' Hadn't she had enough embarrassing social encounters for one day? 'I wonder ... could we *possibly* rearrange?'

'Not now, no. This has waited long enough.' He didn't look open to argument.

Pointing to the parlour, Gerry didn't offer to take his waterlogged coat. 'Mister ... ?'

'Cooper, just Cooper.'

'One moment then, please, while I put on some clothes.'

'Oh, don't bother on my account. I'll do my best to keep my manly passions under control.'

Ha! Scarlet-faced, Gerry trailed after him into the parlour. Marie Antoinette on her way to the guillotine. Was there *any* chance, she wondered as he turned to face her, that this would go well? Might they be able to have a chat and get it out of the way without blood on the carpet?

Deep breath. She decided to launch straight in. No pretence, no excuses.

'Look, Mr Cooper,' she shook the words loose. 'I don't want to waste your time. We've been through a bad patch, I'll admit that ... but ... well, I'm determined to work things out.

Whatever the debt, I'll pay you back.'

There. That was about as much humble pie as he was going to get.

'Somehow. You have my word …'

The man's frowning stare didn't bode well. He'd unbuttoned his wet coat, but the collar was still up and he was now dripping over the Persian rug.

'Erm, of c-course,' she muttered, as wind shrieked round outside and squally rain pelted the window panes, 'it may take some time …'

There was a pause, as she tried to kick wet clothes, darned stockings and an old apple core coated in drifting fluff, under the ottoman.

' … to pay off *all* our debts.'

Cooper glanced at his wrist watch and swore gently. 'Mizz Chiledexter …'

'But, please … rest assured -'

'You don't owe me any money.'

She stared, with suspicion. 'Pardon?'

'It isn't money.'

His eyes roamed round, taking in the solid Victorian furniture, high-backed chairs and huge painted dresser crammed with china, exotic knick-knacks and signed pictures of actors and important-looking royal personages.

As sulky smoke billowed back into the room, Gerry frowned. 'What, then? Have I done something wrong?'

'Probably.' He stooped to peer at hand-tinted photographs of Leonie in a variety of elegant and extravagant poses. 'But that's not what this is about. Who *is* this?'

'My aunt. Aunt Leonie.' Limpid-eyed, reclining on a tiger skin. Wearing a wisp of gauze, her best diamonds and very little else.

Ducking the beams, the man moved to the window, parted the curtains and stared out. He had the look of someone who wanted to smash something. Or hurt somebody.

Like Igor stalking prey, Gerry thought. *Not* money? Well, something was coming. Why didn't he just spit it out then, and go away?

But when he'd sneezed several times, and his feet started to squelch, she couldn't help suggesting he take off his coat. And when she came back into the room, he'd stopped pacing and propped his whole big, exasperating personage up against the wall.

He looked too big for his clothes. Perhaps they'd shrunk. Faded shirt clung damply to his body and the bottoms of his trousers were soaking wet.

And in spite of his skin being a healthy outdoors sort of colour, closer inspection now showed him to be bleary-eyed and exhausted, with a streaming cold.

Normally, she would have been more sympathetic. 'Would you like a hot drink?'

'No, thanks.'

Sliding from the wall, he jack-knifed into an elderly horse-hair armchair, and sneezed again. 'I've had enough English tea to last me a lifetime.' The chair, having never experienced anything like it, groaned in protest.

Gerry's eye was caught by his boots. High cut, elaborately tooled and stitched in coloured thread. She couldn't help staring. 'Brandy, then? Scotch and soda?'

'Would be …very good.' He sat slowly back, sizing her up.

Steadying her hand, Gerry poured two fingers of her aunt's best malt into a tumbler, splashed in soda, and for a few moments they sat in silence, either side of the spitting fire.

Igor, his coat fluffing out as it dried, sat on guard between them.

How long had it been, she wondered idly, since a man like this had been in this room? Someone so large and ruggedly masculine and self-possessed. A year? Another life-time. He'd completely altered the atmosphere.

Not that it was the least bit companionable. At close quarters, he seemed even more menacing. Elbows pressed primly against her sides, Gerry felt filled with foreboding.

Mr Cooper, on the other hand, had downed most of his whisky. Leaning back in the chair with its lumpy stuffing, eyes half-closed, he seemed in danger of drifting off.

As the fire sparked and rain hammered the roof, Gerry's own mind wandered away to water that was surely even now, pouring in through the bookshop's broken windows. *Life*, she thought wearily, *chez Miss G. Chiledexter*.

'I didn't reckon on monsoons in England.' The American swirled the dregs of his drink round in the glass. His fingers were long, skin brown.

Gerry didn't smile. She refused to be charming. This was

like being back at school, waiting to have your knuckles rapped by Matron. Any minute, he would drop that soft drawl, and start shouting at her to pay attention.

'Better tell me why you're here, Mr Cooper. I can't think it's to discuss the weather.'

'I thought it was customary with you Brits,' he said, wearily. 'And it's not Mister, just Cooper.'

'But … is that your first or your second name?'

'No idea.'

'You don't *know?*'

'Nope.'

She waited for an explanation. None came. For goodness sake! She stood up. Whatever this turned out to be, she had no intention of taking it sitting down.

'You said …' What *had* he said? She could barely remember. 'You said we didn't owe you money?'

He set his glass back on the table. 'You'd better sit down.'

'I can hear perfectly well standing up, thank you.'

A long pause did nothing to ease the tension. There was something watchful and controlled about him. Then suddenly, 'Why Tally-Ho? Tally-Ho Lodge?'

Gerry shrugged. 'This is hunting country.'

'Do you hunt?'

'No.'

'Ride?'

She shook her head. 'Not anymore. I used to jog around a bit, but there aren't as many horses as there used to be. They were all shipped to the western front.'

He gave her a narrow-eyed look and seemed to be mulling something over.

'And, you're not married?'

'No.'

Another pause. 'So, this aunt. Leonie? When exactly did she pass away?'

'Eight ... no, nine months ago now.'

'See, here's the thing, Mizz Chiledexter. Since I was eight years old, I've been working a ranch in south-west Texas, finest spread in the valley.' The drawl was soft and low now, almost musical. 'Rearing cattle for beef, breeding horses. It's been sweat and blood my whole life, all I've ever known.'

He paused, shifting in the armchair.

'Until recently, I believed that ranch was all mine. A while ago, I learned the truth. Only half belongs to me. The rest was left to someone else.' He let out a long, slow breath. 'Behind my back.'

Gerry made what she hoped was a sympathetic sound, and murmured something about a shock.

'A damn nuisance is what it's been! I'm in a hole. Can't plan, can't build. Land, water, mineral rights. I want it all back.'

'Ah.' Gerry's expression grew wary. 'So ... who owns it?'

Another pause.

She waited.

'Mr Cooper? Who owns the other half?'

There was a highly-charged silence.

Then, 'You do, Mizz Chiledexter,' he said, with a hard stare that managed to suggest that it was all her fault. '*Apparently.*'

CHAPTER FOUR

'Marriage can't be every woman's destiny. Why not
concentrate your mind on good works?'
The Bachelor Girl's Handbook, 1924

'Of course,' the American narrowed his eyes, 'my lawyer
thought you were a man. You know … Gerry?'

Gerry wasn't listening. After his first dramatic announcement, she'd slumped back into her chair - for a moment, quite
speechless.

'But, this is ridiculous.'

'Damn straight.' Cooper shrugged. 'But it was Frank
O'Rourke's last will and testament, and by God, I'm obliged
to honour it.' He shot her a pitying look. 'Are you saying you
had *no* idea?'

'Of course not! I've never been to America. And I barely
know one end of a cow from another.'

'Pretty much what I thought. That's why I'm here, offering
to buy you out.'

'Wait.' She leaned forward. This was mad, quite mad. 'Are

you quite sure you've got the right person? Who *is* this ... Frank O'Rourke? Why would he leave his ranch to me?'

'It was left to your aunt. With the proviso that when she died, it would pass to her heirs. She never mentioned it?'

Gerry racked her memory and drew a blank. Leonie had never been much of a letter-writer. There'd been picture post-cards, from time to time, that was all. Foreign stamps. Lots of exclamation marks.

'She never bothered much with business. Bills and ... you know, papers, money. Anyway, I didn't ...' She bit her lip. 'When she died. It was sudden, you see. Unexpected.'

Shock, sadness, nights without sleep. Days that were almost unendurable.

Loosening his collar to reveal some sort of beaded leather cord thingy round his neck, Cooper growled his way through his own tale, his voice dipping and rolling.

Leonie had been travelling America, west to east. Gerry knew that much, at least?

She nodded.

Well, somewhere along the way, she'd met ranch-owner Frank O'Rourke and- surprise, surprise - discovered a distant connection. Some English great-aunt of hers turned out to be a cousin of a relative of his. Cooper waved a dismissive hand. Something like that.

Yes, thought Gerry, that was Leonie. Been everywhere, knew everyone. 'It was just chance that they met, then? Pure chance?'

'Oh, yeah,' he said, with heavy sarcasm. 'Call it Kismet. I

guess Heaven must have brought them together.'

'And because of that ...' she was still staring in disbelief, '... just because I've turned out to be some distant twig on your family tree, I now own half of your father's ranch?'

He shook his head. 'You're no relative of mine, Mizz Chiledexter. Frank O'Rourke wasn't my father. He took me in when I was eight, raised me as blood kin, educated me. Your aunt,' he said, 'must have charmed the high-class boots right off him.'

'That was just how she was,' Gerry murmured. 'She charmed everyone. Did you meet her?'

'No. Long-lost relatives ought to stay lost, in my opinion. Anyway, main thing now, I can give you a real good price for your share of the property. Enough to get you out of trouble, and still some.'

Gerry frowned. Had there been a list of her debts in the newspaper?

'One visit to the bookshop was all it took,' he said, apparently reading her mind. 'Sell to me and you could do some work on this place, too.'

'I don't *own* the Lodge. Lord Evelyn just allowed my aunt to live here.'

A lip curl of contempt. 'She charm him, too? Anyhow,' he pulled a damp manila envelope from his shirt pocket. 'I took the liberty of bringing papers along with me. If you sign now, it will save me a whole heap of trouble.'

Now? This minute! 'Wouldn't we need a witness, or something?'

'I understand there's a neighbour?'

He'd thought of everything. 'Sully.' Gerry looked round, vaguely. 'Well, yes. He'll be here, presently. With supper.'

'He brings you supper?' He somehow managed to make it sound unpleasantly compromising.

'He catches it,' she said, not bothering to mention that 'it' usually came in a bucket, and could be anything within Sully's range that wriggled, swam or flew. 'I cook it.'

'Well, while we're waiting on Sully, take a look at these.' Seeming in better spirits than he had all evening, he straightened the dog-eared roll of papers and passed them over.

Gerry peered, suspiciously. As squiggles of text swam in front of her eyes, she felt like a small child, dragged along in a direction it wasn't at all sure it wanted to go.

'Is this a *legal* document?'

'Rough draft. My lawyer was out of town. You have my word on those terms though, Mizz Chiledexter. I'm offering top market price, and then some.'

Maybe, thought Gerry, still reeling from his brisk spit-on-hands manner. Sign, sell? Well, she supposed so. What else would she be likely to do?

'If we shake on it now,' he said, 'we can go get on with our lives.'

'But, when did your ... when did Mr O'Rourke die?'

'Five months ago? Just over.'

'Aunt Leonie's solicitor never said anything to me about a ranch.'

He shrugged. 'That's lawyers for you. Too slow or too

slithery.'

Slithery? Mr *Peale* of Peale, Smedley and Pole? Stone-deaf Mr Peale, who grew prize-winning calceolarias? Wait. Hadn't he sent a message asking to see her? When *was* that? Weeks ago. Maybe, a month.

Oh, Lord, and she'd put it off, hadn't she, convinced it was something more to do with money and debt, and not wanting to face up to it. Head in the sand.

Dragging her mind back, she tried to concentrate. What could be better than saving the family bookshop? Hadn't she always loved it? The smell of leather, new paper, ink. Memories of sitting in its dusty corners, reading and drawing, when she was small.

It was her living now, and this man seemed to be offering a lifeline. So, what was holding her back?

A feeling of unease, that's what. The kind she couldn't quite put her finger on. Just bear in mind, she reminded herself, that you're practically penniless.

While she wrestled with that thought, a gust of wet wind blew Sully in. 'Some daft eejit's left a motorcycle by that there blocked drain. Damn near broke me ankle on it.'

He shambled across the threshold, a small thick-set man with trousers held up by a piece of baler twine.

Sully kept pigs - prize Large Blacks - and judging by state of him, shared the sty with them, too. He wafted in now, bringing a smell that would fell a cat. Gerry was used to it and had learned to breathe through her mouth. Visitors, on the other hand, tended to recoil.

She risked a look at Cooper. He seemed to be holding his own and even managed to gamely shake hands without staggering back. Unlike Archie, who always stayed well downwind and called Sully a malodorous peasant.

'Reckon that'd be me,' the American said.

'Your ve-hickle?' Sully pulled at his cap. 'Tch. Wash-brook's over its banks agin. I just seen coots paddling round them wheels. Staying local are you then, mister?'

'The French Partridge.'

'That's nice,' Gerry murmured. 'Charles the Second stayed there.'

'I hope he got better service than me.' Cooper sounded sour. 'I tried exchanging money for food, but apparently Cook is indisposed. I haven't seen red meat for a week.'

Gerry wondered if he took it raw. That might explain how he was. Big, brutish, muscular. Probably been raised by wolves.

Sully nodded. 'Thet's Mrs Bellchambers, that is.'

He and Gerry exchanged a look. Mrs Bellchambers of the heaving bosoms, the crossover pinafore and gouty foot.

'You 'aven't missed much,' Sully said. 'Better off having supper here, with me and Gerry. Plenty 'ere.'

As Gerry tried to aim a surreptitious kick at Sully's shin, Cooper's eyes went to the bloody dripping sack dangling from his hand.

'What's in the sack?' he said, evenly.

'Sheep's head, pig's snout. Entrails.'

'Sounds tempting.'

'Nah.' Sully gave his gummy grin. 'For 'is Lordship's dogs, thet is. These is ours.' He pulled three shocked-looking trout out of his trousers. 'Gerry's a real good cook.'

This was true. Gerry could cook and she could sew, because Leonie hadn't been the least bit domesticated. At that moment, though, she wanted rid of this American person, as quickly as possible. Hadn't her day been blighted enough?

Thankfully, he didn't seem very enthusiastic about sharing supper with them, either.

'Well, that sure is kind of you, err … Sully, but I'm a little short of time. There's something else you can do for me, though. Witness Mizz Chiledexter signing these papers?'

'Eh?' Sully lifted his hat, revealing bristles of hair that looked as if a pitchfork had been dragged through. 'Sounds a bit legal-like.'

'Just to say she signed of her own free will, that's all. If you wouldn't mind.'

No question, Gerry thought, as to whether *she* minded. No *of-course-you-may-want-time-to-consider* kind of thing, no namby-pambying around. The visitor was on the alert, moving them briskly on.

'Right. Shall we make a start?'

'We' didn't seem to have much to do with it.

High wind moaned round the chimney. Rain raced down the steamed-up windows, dampening rolls of newspaper that Gerry had crammed into the ill-fitting wood frames with their spidery corners.

She looked vaguely round. Ink? Pen?

From somewhere, Cooper produced a fountain pen and straightening up, hit his head on a beam for the umpteenth time and mouthed an oath. 'It's like a rabbit burrow in here. Ready then, Mizz Chiledexter?'

Gerry glanced up, trying to read his expression. To her jaundiced eye, it seemed to be saying: *Oh, come on, come on! Five minutes, a couple of signatures, and I'm out of here!*

Rabbit burrow? Well, that was how *she* felt - like a rabbit in a burrow, with the wily old fox outside, waiting to pounce.

Sifting the papers again, she pretended to read. 'This place. Your ... um, ranch. It's in Texas, you say?' Whoa, her instincts seemed to be saying, slow down. 'You know, this all feels a little ... rushed?'

Looking up again, she ran into that disconcerting grey stare.

'I don't like to sign anything I haven't read thoroughly. I need more time, I think. You know, to go through it all again'

'Right.' Glancing at his watch, he seemed to be keeping a tight hold on his feelings. 'Okay. I'll wait.'

'Oh. Well. Actually ...'

Actually, why hadn't she taken the time to get dressed? A thin peignoir with blue parrots and holes under the arms, didn't make a person appear very convincing. Especially now, with her blue goose-bumps matching the parrots.

'I'd rather read these through, in my own time.'

'Come again?'

'If you don't mind.'

'I do mind. Yeah. Day after tomorrow, I'm headed for Scotland to look at cows. Then, an eight-week trip home. Does that sound like someone at a loose end?'

A stiff silence. Sully shuffled his feet, before trailing off to the kitchen, with his sheep's head, his smelly trout and a tuneless whistle. Traitor.

Gerry's mind wandered. 'Cows?' she said, clutching at straws.

'What?'

'Why are you going to look at Scottish cows?'

'Selective breeding.' He held her gaze, his eyes cold. 'Bull semen?'

She blinked. Enough. 'Well,' she said. 'Perhaps I could meet you some other time. Before you go?'

'Now, hold on.' The American stopped being patient and started to sound exasperated. 'How long can it take to chew this over? It's not the Magna Carta, is it? Look, I get my ranch back, your bills get paid. Sounds clear enough to me. Let's get on and get this done.'

'No.' Feeling her face heat up, she folded the papers and held them out. 'There are parts of this I don't understand.'

'Show me. Which parts?'

'All of them. I'm just not comfortable signing anything now.'

'Lady, I've run way out of time for comfortable.'

Oh, watch out, Gerry thought. Here was someone used to getting his own way. He'd come here to get something done and didn't like failing, did he? Understandable, of course. But bad luck. She had no intention of being bullied.

'I'd like to speak to my solicitor first,' she said, 'Mr Peale. Before I sign.'

'You don't trust me.'

She tried a light laugh. 'I barely know you.'

'Then, don't open your door at night to people you don't know.'

Gerry's voice stopped working. This was getting silly. When had it stopped being a conversation and turned into a series of challenges?

'All right.' Another flash of impatience. 'I can give you one week, one week only. Meet me next Friday at the French Partridge. Better make it early. Here,' he handed back the envelope of papers, 'just be sure these are signed in all the right places. And I mean, damn sure.'

Gerry went to collect his coat, helmet, goggles and gloves, and led the way into the hall in silence. Igor followed, and she felt two pairs of eyes boring into the back of her head.

As she loosened the latch, the wind snatched the heavy oak door and banged it back.

Outside, all was pitch black. No sign of a light anywhere. Just the steady hiss of rain, wildly swaying trees and faint sound of bells on the wind. It seemed operatic, eerie. Almost Gothic.

The sort of night that made a person wonder what was out there.

Cooper frowned. 'What's that noise?'

'Bell-ringers.' Gerry shivered. Only phantoms and bats

were missing.

He turned up his collar. 'Are we being invaded?'

'They're practising, at St Cyriacs.' *Ignorant oik.* 'That church at the end of the lane? It's very old. You may have noticed it. Probably Anglo-Saxon.'

His eyebrows raised. 'Wouldn't the name and that central tower more likely make it Norman?'

An odd look from Gerry.

Mister Clever Clogs must have been flicking through the guidebook. She couldn't imagine him going in to admire the rood screen or enduring Mrs Pratt-Steed at Evensong, battering Bach on the organ with all the stops out.

'The main church is Norman,' she said, firmly. 'The original building was Saxon.' *So there.*

He pulled on the leather helmet, the huge gloves and paused again.

'Gerry,' he murmured then, half to himself. 'Gerry Chiledexter?'

'I beg your pardon?'

'That name. Odd, isn't it?'

'It's Ger-ar-dina,' she repeated, tightly. How many more times? Something else, of course, that Leonie had been responsible for.

At their very first meeting, she'd narrowed those limpid violet eyes, and said, 'Such a long name for such a very small girl. I shall call you Gerry. Less of a mouthful. What do you think?'

Thus, Gerry had joined the massed ranks of Leonie's friends

with their pet names - Toots and Rollo, Isie and Sapphy.

'Ah, yes,' the American drawled. 'After the patron saint of ... what did you say?'

Gerry hadn't said. She glared. 'Expectant mothers.'

The helmet hid any expression as he turned away, ducking to get out of the door. For some reason, best known to his inscrutable cat-self, Igor slid out after him. Darkness and a heavy curtain of rain swallowed them both up.

Shutting the door against the force of the wind, Gerry gave it a petulant kick for good measure. As she trailed back to the kitchen, she heard a motorcycle kick into life and roar hell for leather down the lane.

'Fair old pair of boots that feller had.' Sully waved hands slimy with fish guts in the air. 'Yessir. Pr - etty fancy. Do that make him some sort of cowboy, then? One of them there Yankee buckaroos?'

Gerry shrugged.

'A man's man, he is. Not like that Archie Dee-Dah-Do-Dah. He aren't right for you, y'know, not right at all.'

'Oh, really. And how would you know who's right for me and who isn't?'

'Because I've known you since you was a nipper, Miss Smartie-Pants, that's how. As for that Archie feller. He wears gentlemen's *lounge* slippers, Margaret says. Monogrammed.' Sully spat towards the door. 'With 'is initials on.'

Gerry shifted uneasily. She didn't want to think about Archie, or his clothes, or his condescending family. For that matter, what did that American's boots say about *him*?

Peacock? A dandy? Not when the rest of him seemed to scream red-blooded masculinity.

She poked fish fiercely round in the pan. She didn't like anything about that man. She especially resented him knowing about Norman saints and church towers and the finer points of fly fishing. Why couldn't he just be boorish and ignorant, and confirm all her rotten prejudices?

Sleep didn't come easily that night. As the church clock chimed the night hours, strange thoughts and images danced through Gerry's mind, making her toss and turn.

Ghosts. Ghosts everywhere.

CHAPTER FIVE

'In times such as these, highbrow girls and bluestockings
are bound to stay single.'
A Modern Girl's Guide to Love, 1923

'So this Cooper person,' Prim said. 'He wants to *give* you
money, not take it away. Is that really what you're saying? Are
we actually going to be solvent?'

'Well, we could be.' Still swaddled in scarves and coat,
Gerry nodded. 'At least, I think so. Nothing's settled. I've got
to talk to Mr Peale and ...'

'We'll be able to pay restorers and binders? Mend windows,
that sort of thing?'

' ... make sure that everything's legal and above board.
Then I'll have to sign my share over. To ... you know. What?'

'The leaks? The collapsed ceiling?'

'Well, yes. Mister ... um, Cooper seems to think there'll be
more than enough for all of that and he's mustard-keen to get
things settled.'

Drifting over to the wind-up gramophone, Gerry shuffled

through Leonie's records, and minutes later, the bookshop filled with the strains of *Hitchy-Koo*.

'Hmm.' Prim drummed fingers. 'Sounds too good to be true, doesn't it?'

'Like a fairy godfather turning up with a leather bag full of gold sovereigns?' Gerry side-stepped towards the desk. 'Ooh, is that seedcake? I'm starving.'

'We haven't had money since Leonie persuaded her financier friend to ... what was his name? You know, the one with the blue ... '

'Nose? Eyes.'

' ... that car.'

'The Bugatti.' Gerry swallowed some cake. 'Well, Leonie wasn't interested in the bookshop, was she? Not really. All that rare, antiquarian stuff. Too dull, she used to say, too dusty. She preferred romances, *The Captive Heart* and such.' Sigh. 'I daresay Grandfather left it to her, in the hope it would slow her down.'

'Didn't work, did it? She barely ever set foot in here.' Prim nodded towards the portrait on the wall. 'He'd be twitching in his grave if he could see what she's done to it.'

'Oh, Prim, how can you criticise, when she was so ...'

'Wild and wilful? Didn't she sell everything off? Everything worth anything. Illuminated manuscripts, those rare limited editions. Furniture!'

'But she was so *generous*, such razzle-dazzle company. She lived for the moment, that's all. Wasn't Mother the same? Until she married, anyway. People still sigh about the Bent girls, always rushing giddily around, having a good time.'

'I know, Gerry, I admired Leonie, too. But, really ... the Aubusson rugs? All to fund that lavish lifestyle.' Prim finished on a sniff and several things happened, almost simultaneously.

The music croaked and died. A sudden hard gust of wind set windows a-rattling, and Igor, who'd been lounging around licking his stomach, sprang up, fur staring.

Then, before their disbelieving eyes, a line of heavy books began falling to the floor, one by one - each appearing to fling itself from the shelf to land with a dull thud on the floor.

Not the easily replaceable volumes, either, ho, no - some were first editions, with cracked, embossed spines; a few actually bound in shipwrecked leather.

When the shelf was empty and books strewn higgledy-piggledy, they sat shocked and silent, Igor stiff to attention beside them.

An intake of breath from Gerry.

'What,' Prim shivered, 'was that?'

They trailed fingers over the bookshelves to examine them - front, back, sides. Nothing. Against every law of physics. No broken fixings, sagging wood, just a few dead bluebottles amongst the dust balls.

The clock ticked. Wind rattled broken windowpanes and there was a distinct icy chill in the room.

'Can't we light the stove?' Gerry murmured.

'D'you know the prize of coal?'

After a long, puzzled silence, when they both kept their

thoughts to themselves, Prim cleared her throat. 'So, you *have* reached some sort of understanding, with this person, this Cooper?'

Oh yes. Gerry dragged her mind back. *We understand each other, all right. I don't like him; he doesn't like me. Hate at first sight.* 'I just want to read everything through again,' she said, 'before I go to see Mr Peale. You know, to be absolutely sure ...'

'Better be quick then, in case he changes his mind. D'you hear, Gerry? We can't go on like this.' Prim nodded at the bookshelves. 'Everything falling apart; scrimping and saving and worrying all the time.'

Gerry didn't respond. If Prim only knew. Books hurling themselves to the floor was only part of it. Too many things had been happening lately, without a hint of rational explanation. Poltergeists? Malign spirits?

In fact, this sort of hocus-pocus was becoming so common, that Gerry had developed a rash on her neck. She'd kept it to herself, of course. Prim would have said it was just imagination.

Leonie had trusted signs and portents. Well, she would have, wouldn't she? Palms, tea leaves, tarot cards. And she'd consulted the I Ching, *and* believed in angels, *and* prayers to ancient saints. Every mystical angle covered.

One thing Prim was right about, though, was money. It was all Gerry thought about now. Money due, money owed.

'It's not just the bookshop, Prim. There's something else. Lord Evelyn wants the lodge cottage.'

'He's not turning you out!'

'He needs it, he says. For an estate worker.'

'That heartless swine! He's got *eight* cottages, for goodness sake. He's got nine thousand acres!'

'He didn't tell me himself, just sent that creepy lickspittle of a steward.'

'Gimson?'

Gerry nodded. 'Rents are down, he said, and there's the upkeep of the Hall and that huge estate. Anyway, I suppose it always was a grace and favour sort of arrangement.' She sighed. 'You know ... with Leonie, after ... well, she was forced to sell the family home.'

'Ha!'

'Anyway, he wants me to leave, as soon as possible.'

'You seem curiously serene about all this.'

Numb, actually. Could things get any worse? Unattached, unsupported, and soon to be a homeless pauper? 'Oddly enough,' she said, 'I've been invited to dine at the Hall tonight. A sop to Lord E's conscience, I suppose.'

'Tell me more about this American then,' Prim said. 'Tell me what happened, tell me *everything*.'

Gerry had already made herself late.

First, by having her nose deep in *The Return Of Dr Fu Manchu* and forgetting about going out. Then, being reluctant to drag herself away from the fire.

Bitter experience of the Hall's decaying grandeur had taught her there would be no fires in any of the rooms, and all the guests would be blue and goose-bumpy.

So, why bother? Why go to all this trouble just to salve Lord Evelyn's guilt at turning her out into the snow? She could just gibber an excuse and wriggle out of it. A headache? Only a little white lie.

'A lie is a lie, whatever colour it's wearing.' That wretched voice in her head. It seemed to get louder every day. Where on earth, was it coming from?

Yes, no. Stop, go.

'Oh, don't look at me like that,' she said to Igor, who'd been staring at her in that baleful way, his pupils all dilated. 'I'll go. I am going! All right?'

Talking to the cat? Another very bad sign. And by then, oh dear, she was very, *very* late.

It was pitch black when Gerry finally trudged up the long drive to the Hall. The skies had been leaden all day and there was no moon. In one hand, she held a duck-handled umbrella; in the other, the hem of her velvet evening coat, to keep it clear of mud and squelching leaves.

For some reason, Igor chose to accompany her half-way.

All Hallows Eve. Birds had all gone and drifts of mist closed in, dampening her hair and transforming the landscape. She had that eerie feeling again, the one that gave her the shivers.

Something behind, something gaining on her!

Oh, stop. Pull yourself together.

What did she expect to loom out of the darkness? Werewolves? *Where there is no imagination, there's no horror,*

Sherlock Holmes had said. Yes, well. She didn't *want* to believe in omens, signs or premonitions. But it was hard not to, after all that had been happening lately.

A shotgun sounded, out of the mist, making her even more uneasy. Stupid. Someone out on the hunt, most probably, on the prowl. Then the muffled scream bark of a fox. At least, she thought it was a fox.

Stopping to listen, she didn't turn round. A dangling twig slapped her face. No movement, no shuffle of steps. Just ghost trees creaking, sighing, and a faint wind through leafless branches.

A quick look in the direction of the lake - all veiled and mysterious - and she hurried on, her own breath loud in her ears.

Under a canopy of ancient dripping oaks, past wet lawns and moss-covered statuary, and now here she was, at the steps of the terrace - ghosts and ragged wraiths, hopefully all behind her.

The great house loomed importantly up, with its carved portico and lights flickering in high arched windows. It looked grand enough from out here, but anyone inside for more than a few minutes could see that it was a run-down, ramshackle pile, in desperate need of repair.

Lord Evelyn may have been the umpteenth baronet in a line stretching back to Charles the First, but since the loss of son and heir in the war, he'd lost interest in everything else, too.

Except his beloved huntin', shootin', fishin', of course. (If it moved and breathed, Lord Evelyn believed in shooting, snaring, plucking or skinning it.)

Adding to the Hall's air of neglect was the wing that had been used to house the gassed and maimed, shipped back from France, years ago. Those sad convalescents with rotting feet and shaky hands and empty, staring eyes.

Gerry remembered reading to one young man, his face horribly scarred by sniper fire. 'Jane Austen,' the brisk nurse had declared. 'That's what we recommend for hysteria.'

Her aunt hadn't been able to bear it. 'Too awful,' Leonie had said. 'The nurses fierce as men, and the men ... *crying*, like children.'

Those bleak rooms were still shut off; the furniture swathed in dust sheets.

As she trudged up twenty or so stone steps to the front door emblazoned with the Evelyn coat of arms, several small dogs rushed out, barking shrilly.

The clock on the stable block behind the house struck the hour and she counted the strokes. Oh, dear.

'Good evening, Miss.' She was greeted by an ancient in tails.

'Evening, Borely.' She bent over to pat the dogs. 'I'm afraid there's mud all over my shoes.'

'Don't worry, Miss Gerry. Leave 'em to me.

'I'm ever so late. Could someone bring them to me in the library?'

'Erm ...' Borely began, delicately, 'if I *might* just suggest, Miss ...' and taking charge of leaking shoes, coat, hat and umbrella, he led Gerry to a tiny cloakroom hidden behind the double staircase.

She peered into the speckled mirror. The Wreck of the Hesperus stared back. Wild hair standing on end, and that tint she'd put on her lips smeared like jam.

Her dress was French, a Madeleine Vionnet, its sculpted skirt ending just short of the ankle. A present from Leonie, ordered from Paris, not long before she died. Gerry recalled unwrapping it, the layers of soft tissue, the ribbon.

Utterly gorgeous, of course, a dream dress, but was it right for tonight? Too bold, perhaps? Too Parisian? Would that hole under the arm be likely to show?

Leonie would have known at a glance. *'Perfect, darling. Très, très chic.'*

Stabbing her wayward hair with pins and anchoring it with a diamond clip, Gerry leaned forward to peer at herself in the glass and practise a few happy, party expressions.

For pity's sake, she asked herself again, *why bother?*

Why not just slip through that baize door into the servants' quarters for cocoa and crumpets in front of the fire? She could help Mrs Borley wind her wool, while Borley went in and out to the call of the bell.

Another huge sigh. Adjusting her yard of pearls, Gerry padded bare-footed across the echoing marble-floored hall, past the line of Reynolds and Rubens, lacquered Chinese cabinets and huge rococo mirrors, through a series of rooms towards the library and a distant thrum of conversation.

On the threshold, she hesitated.

Beyond the arched doorway, an oak-panelled room with walls of precious books, lit by low lamps with fringed silk shades. Thirty or so people were milling politely about on worn oriental rugs, while Madeira was passed round on silver trays.

It wasn't a white tie and tails affair, but Gerry spotted some heavy lace and pearls, so perhaps her dress wouldn't stand out too much. Although, you could never fade into the background wearing anything that Leonie had chosen, and she *was* showing more than just a flash of ankle.

Mercifully, there was no-one at heel to announce her. These days, Lord Evelyn dispensed with formal introductions and just flung everyone in together. Every man for himself.

Hey-ho.

Taking a deep breath, Gerry plunged in and got her first nasty surprise of the evening, when a party of people inside the door turned to gape. Major and Mrs Dutt-Dixon-Nabb and friends, scattering hyphens in their wake.

She found herself confronted by a line of raised eyebrows, a smile that didn't quite reach Mrs D-D-N's eyes, and one of her supercilious up and down looks. One that said not-right-clothes, on a not-top-drawer-person..

Dismissed by shaking heads, she edged away, downed a thimbleful of Madeira and tried to ignore the whispers behind her back.

'Bare feet ... too, too far! *And* no gloves.'

'The mother, I understand, was perfectly respectable.'

'Dead?'

'Cholera. One does one's best to be civil, of course, but really ...'

Oh. Oh. Too late, to turn tail and go home? Because enjoying herself was clearly out of the question. Ha, bad luck. No time for excuses, no escape route, either. Have to stick it out.

She shivered. The room was chilly as a morgue.

So, was Archie here? Edging round, she positioned herself behind a lamp-stand with deep parchment shade. Oh, dear, oh, yes. Over there, by the Adam fireplace. Elegant as ever in evening black with a white wing collar. The first time she'd seen him since that grisly tea-party.

Lord. How much embarrassment could a person be expected to stand in one evening?

Trying to adopt a nonchalant expression, she moved on into the fray. Like every social gathering, it revealed a distinct lack of young men.

Local gentry and bigwigs, with their Horse and Hound complexions. A few intimidated underlings - gamekeepers, beaters, shooters - who'd been out all day popping and banging at pheasants. Plus, some poor beleaguered womenfolk huddling together to keep warm.

Ah, thought Gerry. So, that was why the Dutt-Dixon-Nabbs were still at the library door, like bulldogs guarding a gate. They didn't care to rub shoulders with the hoi polloi, did they? It was only since the war that the lower orders had been allowed across this hallowed threshold.

Not so long ago, this great house had been a little kingdom, with hierarchy upstairs and down. All gone, together with many of the servants, footmen and between-stairs maids.

This was more like being in the middle of the hunt, but with canapés.

Conversation swelled around her. She was recognised, greeted.

'Wonderful to see you!' Colonel Dudley brayed, pumping her hand, while crushing her bare toes with his gouty foot. 'Been meanin' to patronise your establishment, me dear. A book I'm after. The one by that otter huntin' cove. D'you know it?'

Tally Ho. Someone offered a sherry. Someone else, with a bristly moustache, kissed her cheek. All that high colour. From being out so much in fierce, wet winds.

Who was Archie talking to? Gerry wondered. Hopefully someone who would keep him busy for a long time. She shuffled round, standing on tiptoes for a better look. Drat. Still couldn't see.

'Ger-ar-dina!'

Lord Evelyn, florid-faced and smelling of cigars and old dogs. 'You look like a nymph. Sight for sore eyes, m'dear.' Tonight, he was all hostly noises and purring charm. The charm, Gerry thought, of the sabre-toothed tiger. 'Now then, feller for you to meet.'

Clamping a hand round her wrist, he shouldered his way across the room. 'Over here. Says he knew Leonie.' People fell back respectfully. 'C'mon, come along. So glad you came.'

Towed along, muttering that she wouldn't have missed it for the world, Gerry didn't pay much attention to where she was going. Her main concern was to avoid Archie.

'Now, then. Yes.' Lord Evelyn let go of her wrist. 'Here we are.'

Flexing her fingers, Gerry turned round with a bright party smile.

It quickly faded.

CHAPTER SIX

'For a young woman to approach a man, is most
definitely taboo. One must always be introduced'
The Single Girls' Guide to Matrimony, 1923

Cooper!

Gerry backed into the Hepplewhite sofa. For goodness
sake! Why hadn't she noticed him before? Six foot something,
without a rag of formal dress to his name? He stood out a
mile.

Their eyes met, and as Lord Evelyn galloped merrily
through introductions, Gerry completely lost the thread of
what he was saying.

A fractional nod from Cooper. 'Mizz Chiledexter.' Very
formal, stiffly polite.

'You've met?' Lord Evelyn eyed them, curiously.

'Oh, yes.' Gerry's throat was dry. They certainly had. Met,
crossed swords and parted. And he looked even taller and
more forbidding than the last time. 'Yes, we have.'

'Good show! Capital, capital.' Duty done, their host swiftly
turned and left them together.

An awkward silence. Cooper leaned against sombre wood panelling and watched her, with that odd intentness.

'Mizz Chiledexter?'

'Yes?'

She didn't like the way he was looking at her. He wasn't going to ask for a decision on those papers now, was he? Tonight? She felt herself flush. Too soon! Too late, on the other hand, to make a run for it. She was cornered.

'You appear to have bare feet.'

'What? Oh … yes, mud. On my shoes. Someone's cleaning them for me.'

There was a slight arching of an eyebrow, as he coolly appraised the rest of her.

He was on his guard, alright, Gerry thought. So what? She was on hers, too. Oh behave, she told herself. He's a stranger far from home, isn't he? Do unto others, blah, blah. Come along now, best party manners.

Taking another sherry from a passing tray, she gulped down a warming mouthful, and said, as sympathetically as she could manage, 'How is your cold?'

'Developing nicely. Will it ever stop raining?'

'Oh, this is just a sprinkle.' She found herself rushing breathlessly to the defence of the English weather. 'And why everything is so green, of course.'

'Yeah, I'd noticed. Green and drenched and dripping.'

'A pity for anyone visiting though, because …'

'We may drown?'

'Because, there's some beautiful countryside here. Woods

and hills and … yes, it's quite … quite lovely in the spring.'

'Well, come spring, when I'm back in hot Texan sun, guess I'll be kicking myself.'

His voice was deadpan, and as another burst of rain splattered the windows, Gerry sighed. If he was waiting to be amused, she was already failing miserably. How had he managed to weasel his way in here, anyway?

'So, how do you … um, know Lord Evelyn?'

'You mean, what's a feller like me doing in a place like this?'

'Erm … ' She shifted her feet.

'Guess there's no fooling you.' He stretched out the vowels, laying on, she suspected, a really thick drawl. 'We're real plain folks where I come from. But me and Lord Evelyn … we got a lot in common.'

'You have?'

'Sure. Country estates. Chippendale staircases.'

'Really?' Eyes widened.

He raised an eyebrow. 'More like common interests. Livestock and breeding. Cattle, horses?'

'Ah, yes. Yes, I see.'

'He's real hospitable.'

'Oh.' She shifted to the other foot. 'He *certainly* is.'

His turn? The silence stretched on. And on. Apparently, he didn't want another turn. *It's called a conversation*, Gerry wanted to say. First I speak and you listen, then you do the same. Keep up, man!

She said, 'Were you out shooting today?' but didn't really

require an answer. Here was a merciless dead-eyed shot, if ever she saw one. How had he got that thread of a scar on his face? The one showing up so white against his skin? Wrestling with bears?

'Do you shoot?' he asked, and she shook her head.

She didn't ride to hounds, didn't stalk or shoot and couldn't cast a line, either, without taking someone's eye out. 'Men with big guns shooting small birds has never appealed very much to me.'

There was a dry pause.

'Guess you won't be eating any of the results, then. P'raps you'd rather we used catapults?'

'I've nothing against *game* as such, just birds being reared to be shot for sport. Some are too fat to even fly.'

'That's life, isn't it. Far as I know, no game's ever been born plucked and in a puddle of gravy.'

Touché. Feeling foolish, un-sporty and utterly charmless, she picked at a nail, and polite conversation dribbled away again. What had Sully called him? A man's man. A man for livestock, shooting and the saddle. Not, apparently, one who felt the need for small talk. Not with her, anyway.

Another sherry.

Glancing over her shoulder towards the door, she intercepted a look of unwavering dislike from Mrs Dutt-Dixon-Nabb. Slings and arrows, from all sides.

Minutes passed by, dragging their feet, and noise rose to a crescendo around them. Gerry found herself rendered mute, and there wasn't so much as another squeak from the

American.

If only, she thought, they had something in common, *anything* in common. Oh, don't be stupid! The only reason he was even condescending to talk to her, was because he needed her signature on a piece of paper. Not that he seemed to be making much effort to win her over.

Rooted to the spot like some faithful spaniel, she couldn't help noticing that his very presence was sending certain other parts of the room into a deep swoon. Heads were turning, wondering who he was, hoping he would chance to look at them. You could almost hear the female knees a-trembling.

Oh, really! So … *irritating.*

'Sherry, Miss?'

'Oh, yes. Thank you.'

Her gaze drifted to a gilt-framed portrait behind the American's head, a family group in Arcadian setting, flanked by well-bred hunting dogs. Ancestors of Lord Evelyn, with their Plantagenet faces.

An arrogant lot, those blue-blooded rakes. Adulterers, gamblers, sportsmen. Come to think of it, their expressions were very like Cooper's. He had that same air of bored irritation about him, Lord and master of all he surveyed.

With an immense effort, she brought her eyes back, to a point somewhere near the second button on his shirt.

'When are you …' dry cough, to get his attention for her next piercingly interesting question, ' … travelling up to Scotland?'

His gaze drifted absent-mindedly back. 'Soon as I can get

enough clothes dry.'

'Whereabouts? Where in Scotland?'

'Way up.' He waved a hand. 'The Highlands?'

'Oh. That's …'

' … wonderful country?' Eyebrows lifted ironically.

'Spectacular, *actually*. Wild and … and empty and quite breathtaking. Good fishing, stalking and shooting. If you like that sort of thing.'

'You're talking to a Texan, Mizz Chiledexter. We reckon we've just about got sole rights on spectacular and breathtaking.'

Gerry stared. 'Isn't that rather narrow-minded of you?' *Ignorant*, was the word she would've liked to have used, the one she bit back.

'Everything seems pretty much small-scale here.'

'Big isn't always better though, surely. After all, much of Texas is still wilderness, isn't it?'

'Better find yourself a new geography book and atlas, ma'am. Texas has every sort of climate, every type of terrain. Desert, mountains, prairie.'

A dark stare, through narrowed lids. Not even the faintest flicker of a smile.

As a draught from the window stirred the faded brocade curtains, dislodging a moth or two, Gerry fingered her long strand of pearls, and felt about two inches tall.

This wasn't anything like polite social chit-chat, more an exchange of gunfire. Was this how he behaved with everyone? Like someone squaring up for a scrap.

He had his reasons, of course. She'd become some sort of threat to his livelihood, apparently. A thorn in his side. And he didn't like it, did he? Didn't like being challenged, not one bit.

Another nod to the person with the sherry tray, and Gerry found herself wondering if all those 'yes, pleases' would be the most meaningful exchanges she'd have all evening.

'Are those for real?' Cooper said suddenly, frowning at the nearest wall of morocco leather and calfskin-bound books, with gold-titled spines.

'Real *books*? Of course they are.' *Ignoramus.*

'Have you read many of 'em?' His eyes bypassed memoirs of turf and field, histories of the thoroughbred, stacks of Horse and Hound. 'What about those …'

'Dickens?' clipped Gerry, in her best Oxford English. 'Dryden, Trollope?'

Of course, men like him didn't read, did they? Too busy poking things with sticks and hunting them down and shooting them.

'Guess you were brought up in these sorts of surroundings, huh?'

'I wasn't, actually. Not at all.'

No point saying more.

Why bother telling him about India? The polo, the pig-sticking, tiger-shooting. Being bounced between there and the dreaded boarding school. Waste of breath. He was bored with her company. The last thing he wanted was her life history.

Another epic silence. Gerry stared up at the Grinling

Gibbons carving, then down to the Turkish rug, worn to the weave, at her feet and considered throwing herself down on it, drumming fists and screaming.

Aeons passed, dinosaurs died out.

Lifting her chin, she looked him straight in the eye. His face seemed a bit wavery. It appeared to be … oh, Lord, to be actually *dissolving* round the edges. How many tots of sherry had she actually had? She was becoming all bleary.

'Well, Mr Cooper.' With a huge effort, she adopted a breezy tone. 'We seem to have discussed the weather and geography and … you know, hobbies and pastimes and everything. And it's been *so* interesting. I mustn't be selfish though, must I? I really ought to allow you to charm someone else, with your … your company.'

His lip twitched and for one moment, Gerry actually thought she saw a glint of humour, perhaps the stirrings of a wintry smile. But, no. He wasn't going to smile just to oblige her, was he? That might show some sign of genuine human warmth.

He said, 'Guess we're done, then,' and sneezed. His voice was raw and husky. Another bout of coughing ensued.

English germs, thought Gerry, with satisfaction. There was something about this man that made her completely forget good manners. And what really stuck in her craw, was that sooner rather than later, she was going to have to do exactly what he wanted, and sign his wretched papers.

Luckily, at that point someone appeared, carrying her shoes. Feeling quite queasy now, she tried standing on one leg like a stork, to put them back on, but the leg gave way and she wobbled precariously.

An iron hand shot out. 'Better lean on me.' Caught by Cooper, she was pulled in close. 'Well ah declare, Mizz Chiledexter, you appear to be an itty bit tipsy.'

Mortified, Gerry arched herself backwards.

'Aw c'mon.' He tightened his grip, 'force yourself. Or break your neck.' Cupping one of her feet, he slipped it into a pointy-toed, beribboned satin evening slipper. 'You walked here in *these,* in the rain?'

Gerry couldn't speak. Something else was happening. Leaning against him, feeling the unfamiliar warmth and closeness of a muscular male body, a shameful weakness was creeping over her.

Her body was beginning to react, without any permission at all from her brain. *Steady, steady*, she thought, breathing in faint scents of wood-smoke, soap, leather. But her brain flatly refused to cooperate.

Drat. Drat, drat!

'There's isn't going to be dancing, is there?' Cooper's voice over her head, as she disentangled herself and stooped to tie the silk bows on her shoes.

'No.' He was still too *close*. 'These aren't dancing slippers.' She kept her head low to hide a hot blush, and for a few truly terrible moments, thought she was going to be sick all over his boots. 'No, they're ... don't you like dancing?'

'Me? I'm a quiet-living feller. I reckoned all you English girls would be blushing behind your fans.'

Gerry straightened, another rush of blood to her head. 'There may,' she said, swaying unsteadily, 'be hunting horns. And shooting.'

'In the *house*?'

'It has been known.' Self-conscious, furious with herself, she felt a strong inclination to hit something. Or somebody. When was this hell going to end?

'*Gerry*, Gerry!' A tug on her dress, a fierce hiss in her ear. 'You sly, sly thing, keeping this to yourself. Quick, before Fa sees! Introduce me.'

Kitty Dudley, the Colonel's youngest daughter, who'd already been causing a stir, with her bare arms and oh-look-at-me skirt barely skimming her knees.

You'd never find Kitty blushing coyly behind a fan, the girl whose pupils were now dilating at sight of the striking figure in front of her. Rather like Igor, when he spotted a fish-head in his dish.

Gerry did as she was told, then stood back. Could she just slink away now, while those two stood there exchanging pleasantries and doing whatever else they were doing? Admiring each other. Would they even notice?

Dinner? Oh, yes!

When someone came in to make the announcement, she turned towards the dining room, in relief. Thank Heaven.

The ordeal, however, was far from over.

First a snatch of conversation wafting over from an aggrieved-sounding Major Dutt-Dixon-Nabb, on his way to the dining room.

'Big, blue-chinned fella? *Brown* boots! I ask you!'

'Some ghastly foreigner or other. Colonial, I think.'

'Good Lord! Least he's not French.'

Then, searching for her place at the vast table, glittering with silver and candles and crystal, Gerry found herself flanked by a rock and a hard place. On her left, the vicar; on her right, Archie Dutt-Dixon-Nabb. Her reluctant hero.

That was problem enough.

But directly opposite, across the crisp white linen and only partially obscured by an arrangement of bronze chrysanthemums, twigs and berries, was Cooper.

Oh. Pass the hemlock, she thought, wearily.

Fortunately, she was saved from further conversation with him by Kitty, who having most probably finagled the seating arrangements, was now glued to his side at the table.

And they appeared to be getting on famously. Oh, yes. Gone was his air of bored indifference, he was even laughing … *laughing*, while Kitty, all crimson pout and kiss-curled hair, hung onto his every word, with breathless interest.

What's more, their voices had sunk to a confidential murmur, cutting them off from everyone else.

Granted a front row seat to this mutual admiration society and distracted from her soup by fluttering eyelashes and mews of delight, Gerry sat across the table, stony-faced and stiff as any maiden aunt.

Cooper, of course, his profile dark against the candlelight, didn't throw so much as another glance in her direction. Well, good. Yes.

How on earth though, had Kitty managed to make him so mellow? Because she looked so pert and pretty, with her polished shingle with a bow in it? Or something to do with that outrageous décolletage, as she leaned over with a coquettish whisper?

Who could say? Gerry gazed furiously into space. Anyway, who cared? They were probably discussing the blood lines of his precious prize breeding stock, or something.

Well, good for you, Kitty. Reaching for her wineglass, she emptied it with one careless swallow. Just take care, that's all I can say. He's from Texas, you know. They do things differently there.

Archie? Oh, Lord. That was another matter.

Having been concentrating so hard on the flow of conversation from the other side of the table, Gerry had barely heard a word Archie had been saying. At one point she'd been tempted to hiss, 'Oh, shut up! I'm trying to listen!' How rude.

Because, in spite of everything, she still liked Archie. Didn't everyone? Easy to get on with, smart and well-groomed with impeccable manners. He couldn't help his parents, could he?

So why did he suddenly seem so … oh, so weak and effete, somehow. She had to abandon him, didn't she? Simply had to. It was only fair.

But over the fish, before she had a chance to mention anything, Archie said he was sorry. My word, was he sorry. About what had happened at the tea-party, for not defending Leonie to his parents and not galloping, white-knight-like, to Gerry's rescue. Sorry, sorry, sorry.

'Don't worry about it, Archie. Your parents have got your best interests at heart, that's all. We can still be friends, can't we?'

Friends. There. Couldn't they leave it at that?

Next, the pheasant.

Another covert glance at Cooper, who still seemed to be having a fine old time with Kitty. He had, Gerry couldn't help noticing, perfect table manners. Pity. She'd hoped to see him blowing on his soup or gnawing bones.

She herself, could find absolutely no taste for the nasty-looking mess of pimpled bird on her plate. Pheasant? It wasn't much bigger than a canary. Prodding it round with a fork, she looked up to catch Cooper's challenging stare.

Raising his glass - in mockery, of course - he managed to hold her gaze with those glittering eyes, like a snake with a rabbit. Then, just as suddenly, he gave a broad wink, before turning solicitously back to Kitty.

Dazed, she dipped her head, the pheasant turning to ashes in her mouth. What was *that* all about?

'Who *is* that person?' Archie hissed.

'Oh. He's American.'

Dessert?

Gerry wished that she could.

This was so unfair. Why had she bothered to stay? Hadn't she known from the beginning that it would be awful?

After that, she wasn't much in the mood for food *or* conversation. In fact, she was feeling more than a little green around the gills, and having trouble following things.

But she talked to Archie, talked to the vicar, talked and smiled and talked and smiled until her face ached with the effort of it. For an eternity, it seemed.

Death by droning.

And when the men left for their port and brandy and cigars, she had to listen to Kitty, twittering on in a thoroughly besotted way about Cooper, as they powdered their noses.

It was late, very, very late before she could even consider escaping.

At the end of the evening, as she swayed under a chandelier dripping with crystal beading, Lord Evelyn said not to worry about moving out of the cottage for ... oh, at least a few weeks.

Then he asked her, in a fruity drawl, to please remind that rascal Sully that William the Conqueror had blinded and castrated poachers caught on his land. Would she do that?

Oh, she would, yes. She certainly would.

Then, down the stone steps into a disheartening drizzle, to trudge home. Alone.

Silent inky blackness.

Owls, bats, ghosts.

And something clawing through the branches.

The witching hour.

Outside the cottage door, a silent watcher.

Igor, awaiting her tipsy return.

CHAPTER SEVEN

'Try not to become shabby, shallow or sour.
Rather, read improving books and drink cocoa.'
Advice to Miss-All-Alone, 1924

Peale, Smedley and Pole, declared the brass nameplate, on a lopsided building between Geo. Wigley & Sons, Auctioneers and Odells, Ironmongers.

Gerry didn't bother making an appointment.

Propping her bicycle against the wall, she negotiated her way past the formidable Miss Perkins thrashing a typewriter inside the front door, and climbed two flights of rickety stairs to the cramped eyrie that was Mr Peale's office.

A stuffy room, littered with papers and smelling of dust and cigars, its legal-green walls were lined with tier upon tier of fat, calf-bound books.

'Ah, Gerardina!' Getting up from his desk, Mr Peale looped gold-rimmed spectacles over his ears. A huge portrait of his father, the man who'd started the first legal practice in the market town, dominated the wall behind him.

There was a marked family resemblance.

'Come in, come in. I was wondering when you'd come to see me.' He waved her vaguely towards a sagging armchair. 'Now. New developments!'

Gerry sat down, pulling at her gloves. 'Mr Peale?'

He flicked snuff from his sleeve, before looking over his spectacles. 'Beg pardon?' He pointed to his ear. 'You'll have to speak up, my dear.'

'Before we discuss anything else ...' raising her voice, Gerry fumbled in her bag, '... would you please look at these for me?'

As Mr Peale flattened the roll of creased papers, Gerry felt fidgety and uneasy. Her head hurt from lack of sleep and too much sherry, and her last time in this room had been for the reading of her aunt's will.

'Interesting.' Mr Peale leaned back in his chair. 'Most interesting.'

'So, what are your thoughts, Mr Peale? Sorry ... THOUGHTS? Mr Cooper came all this way to arrange a quick sale. Is there any reason ... no, no, REASON ... for me to delay? The bookshop needs capital, and ... well, things have been rather difficult, lately.'

Mr Peale pursed his lips. 'I could certainly oversee a sale for you, if that's what you want.'

'But, what do you *think*?'

'I think, you should look at this before making any decisions.' He sifted a stiff ivory-coloured envelope from a file and offered it to Gerry.

Staring at Leonie's handwriting, all loops and swirls and

curled tails, sent a shiver down Gerry's spine. For weeks, her head had been full of ghosts and spirits, signs, portents. Now, this. A *letter?*

'Your aunt requested we file it with her will, and pass it to you, only if a certain set of circumstances should occur.'

'I don't understand.'

'That letter should clarify things. Why, you're white as a sheet, my dear. Tea? I think some tea might be in order.'

While he went out to summon Miss Perkins, Gerry opened the envelope and drew out a single sheet of cream vellum. Leonie's letter, typically short, was full of crossings out, with scribbled notes in the margins.

The main part:

My darling Gerry.

When you read this, it will mean that a close friend of mine has died, and left you, dear heart, a share of his estate, in the American southwest. It's the most heavenly place ,Gerry. I've spent some wonderfully happy times there.

Now. Goodness knows, I've never been sensible with money nor the least bit bothered about keeping accounts. Apart from the bookshop, I suspect my worldly goods will amount to precious little.

So, selling your share of this Texas property might, I suspect, settle all debts and even leave a little bit over. That's why, darling girl, the request I am about to make, may seem just another of my ridiculously selfish whims.

Nevertheless, here it is.

I would like you to consider holding onto this estate, for a short time - six months or so - before agreeing to any sale. More than anything in the world, I would like you to visit the place for yourself. If lack of money proves a hindrance, Mr Peale may be able to make some suggestions.

Loose ends, darling, that's what this is about. I don't want to go into the whys and wherefores now. Hopefully, all will become clear, in the fullness of time! Trust me?

Sorry to sound so mysterious.

Love for always and for ever, Your own, Leonie.

Gerry's hand shook. She read the letter once, then once again, trying in vain, to decipher scratchings out in the margin.

'Miss Chiledexter?' Miss Perkins hovered with a tray. 'Tea and shortbread. Shall I pour you a cup?'

Gerry's hand, holding the letter, fell to her side. *Loose ends, everything will become clear.* What did *that* mean? Why hadn't Leonie ever told her about any of this?

A cup of tea was placed gently beside her.

There was a story here. Glancing back at the sheet of paper, she tried to find it, to shake out her aunt's reasoning. No good. Unpaid bills kept swimming before her eyes, a balance sheet lined with figures - all red, none black.

She had to sell. Didn't she? What else could she do? Still brooding, she went to the window, barely noticing the weather or figures scurrying across the busy market square. Her mind was too busy.

She was still staring into space, when Mr Peale came back.

'Mr Peale? Did you know what was in that letter?'

'What say? Yes, my dear. I did. Your aunt took me into her confidence.'

'But, what was in her mind, have you any idea?'

A long pause. Unhooking his spectacles, Mr Peale rubbed his nose. 'She was a fascinating woman, my dear. A woman of secrets.'

'She certainly was. But, I *have* to sell.' Gerry's eyes watered, and she bit her lip, angrily. 'Don't I? Everything's going out, Mr Peale, nothing's coming in. We owe far too much money.'

'The last thing your aunt would have wanted, Gerardina …' Mr Peale paused and seemed to be debating with himself, '… the very last thing, would have been to make things difficult for you. Although it was clear to me at the time, just how much that request meant to her.'

'It may have been clear to you, Mr Peale, but she never mentioned her American friend to me, not once. Not his land, nor … that ranch.' Gerry stopped to blow her nose. 'When did she write that letter?'

'After her last visit to that part of America, I believe.'

'Her *last* one! How many visits did she have?' Another thought. 'Mr Peale, have you ever met Mr Cooper, the other beneficiary?'

'Not personally, no. I've corresponded with his lawyers, of course.'

'Would he be likely to know about any of this? He seemed very impatient to arrange a quick sale.'

'Say again? Ah well, that may be so. And it could still be

arranged, if you wish. I could put everything in place for you.'

Confused, Gerry gazed at the portrait behind the leather-bound desk. Josiah St John Pomeroy Peale, in sombre palette of burnt umbers, greens and greys, stared steadily back - his expression kind, but distant. He didn't offer any help.

She turned back. 'Would it mean that I could have some of the money straight away?'

'If that is what you want.'

'But it's not what Leonie wanted, is it? What did she mean by loose ends? Which loose ends?' Gerry's voice wavered. 'Help me, Mr Peale. I'm so muddled. I don't know what to do, anymore.'

'No need to do anything, not yet.' He patted her hand. 'Take the letter away and have a good think about it. Come back to me when you've made a decision.'

Pale-faced, Gerry clattered down worn stairs, past Miss Perkins and her furiously clacking typewriter, out into the cobbled market place, where she stood for a moment, oblivious to drizzling rain and market-day bustle all around.

If that's what you want. Huddling into her coat, pulling her hat over her ears, she pushed her bicycle towards the bookshop. That's what Mr Peale had said. *Tell me what you want.*

What *did* she want? She'd rarely been asked that before. She didn't make things happen, she mostly did what was expected. Small wonder she could never make up her mind about anything.

Apparently, then - as Hazeldine's errand-boy swerved by

her on his overloaded bicycle, wafting smells of hot bread, she turned back towards the baker's - *apparently*, according to Mr Peale, this could all be perfectly straightforward.

A simple monetary transaction, a firm handshake, and all over. The ranch back in its rightful hands. Bents Fine and Rare Books saved. The answer to a prayer and end to sleepless nights.

Best of all, goodbye and good riddance to Cooper. She pictured herself skipping happily away. But, what about Leonie and what Leonie wanted? Would she ever be able to stand the guilt?

Lost in thought and nibbling a floury bread roll, she was almost deafened by the sudden ear-shattering din of a motorcycle at full throttle.

Shattering the morning's calm, spraying water from the puddles, the vehicle blasted its way up the main street like a bat out of hell, its goggled and leather-helmeted driver crouched low over the noisy machine.

Gerry reeled back, into a shocked woman pushing a perambulator. As she turned to apologise, he roared past with a cloud of oil vapour and rude *parp-parp* on a two-note horn.

The American! Of course. For all the world, like Mr Toad out on a spree. What a show-off.

Leonie, of course, would have heartily approved. A great fan of horseless carriages, she'd adored chugging and honking along, all goggled-up and hatless, her hair blowing out behind her.

As for Gerry, hadn't she gone to bed with that man on her

mind, tossed and turned all night, and woken up with him still there? Now, here he was again.

Had he ever felt the need to play safe and make excuses? She wiped the grit from one eye, as he disappeared into the distance. Ho, not him - probably never experienced a moment's self-doubt in his entire life.

So, what to do? With rain trickling down the back of her neck, she stood perfectly still and once more, asked herself that question.

'Go and see! Go to America, go to Texas!'

And, lo. Quite suddenly, she had an answer.

Strange, really. How the idea seemed to have come into her head without her brain having had very much to do with it.

CHAPTER EIGHT

'Take heed. The feather-brained, thoughtless girl will
always be last left on the shelf.'
Heart-to-Heart column, 1922

'I still don't understand.' Prim poked a hairpin back into place
with a pencil. 'Why can't you just sell to old Thingy and be
done with it? Good Lord,' as Gerry shrugged off her soggy
coat. 'What *are* you wearing?'

Gerry looked down. 'Um … Molyneux, I think. Don't you
like it?'

'It's an evening dress. Isn't it?'

'Is it? I was distracted; I just pulled something out. Anyway,
listen, Prim. Leonie left this letter, asking me not to dispose
of land or property for … oh, at least six months, I think she
said.'

'Leonie! She was the last person in the world to bother with
things like that.'

'I know, all very confusing. Here, have one of these while
they're warm.' Offering up the bag of bread rolls, Gerry cast
herself into a chair. 'I mean, what would make her do that?

What's going on? I've got the strangest feeling she wants me to find out.'

'Well, Sherlock, the only people who can shine any light on that are dead. So what will you do? Use a ouija board?'

Gerry brushed crumbs from her mouth. 'Have you ever … do you believe in them, Prim? Spirits, I mean. Because …'

'Ghoulies, ghosties and long-leggety beasties? Noo. You do, I daresay.'

'Well. Lately, I've been *sensing* something. Don't look at me like that. Nothing that announces itself, just a sort of … presence.'

Hard to explain. It didn't sound much. Just the creak of floorboards, the cottage shivering and whispering. Something indeterminate - half-sensed, half-glimpsed - but more and more difficult to ignore.

'Mice.'

'Mice don't breathe heavily. I just … I had to tell someone.'

'You're not getting enough sleep, then. Unless you've taken to Sully's sloe gin.'

'P'raps, I did have a tot of sherry too many last night, but I don't *see* anything, just feel it. A sort of fluttering in the air, a wisp of something. Then a voice, in my head, that's not my own.'

'Oh, stop!' Prim drew back, as if Gerry had suddenly become infectious. 'Much more of that and I'll recommend you to the Temperance Society.'

Whose voice was it? Gerry had no idea. Armed with a

poker, she'd searched the house. Sitting room, parlour. Up the staircase to her low-ceilinged sloping bedroom. Nothing. She'd even looked under the bed.

And she'd tried really hard to ignore whatever it was, but it hadn't gone away. Then, there was …

Igor.

That cat definitely had an aura. She looked down towards her feet and he stared back, in his unblinking contemptuous way.

Sometimes, when he sidled in, she caught a really heady waft of perfume. As if he'd walked through a spilled bottle of her aunt's best scent. That *was* strange. Where had he been?

Once or twice lately, she'd even found herself checking him for signs of a champagne hangover. Nonsense, all nonsense. She knew that.

'Anyway,' she mumbled, through another mouthful of warm bread, 'I can't help thinking it's some sort of omen. You know the kind of day, Prim, that can change your life, forever?'

'No. And stop spitting crumbs on these accounts. They're in enough of a mess already.'

'Well, this is one of them for me. I'm tired of doing what everyone expects, all the time.'

Prim chewed the end of her pencil. 'So, what do you … oh, footle. Look, another wretched drip. Just push something underneath, will you.'

'I've decided.' Gerry nudged the bucket with her foot. 'No more being sensible. It's yes to adventure! I'm off to America!'

'What … whoa, there! Hold your horses. What's brought this on, all of a sudden?'

Pushing back her chair, Gerry went over to the gramophone, lifted the lid.

'I've been thinking about it. Going where Leonie went, seeing what she saw. Finding out about this Frank O'Rourke. I'm sure now that's what her spirit, or whatever it is, is asking me to do.'

'Wait! A *ghost* is telling you? You're doing this because of some message from the other side? What's got into you?' A pause. 'Gerry! Must you keep playing that awful jazz music?'

'It's Leonie's. I just … ' Heavy sigh. 'Anyway, didn't someone cancel their passage on the Titanic, because of a premonition?'

'But, you're not the adventurous type. You may sometimes dress like a pirate, but it doesn't make you devil-may-care, does it?'

'Prim, that's just the point. The pencils in that pot are more unpredictable than me. For once in my life, I want to take a risk!'

'What about Archie?'

Don't ask. Gerry shrugged.

'For goodness sake, what's wrong with you, Gerry? We've more chance of being flattened by marauding elephants than finding a husband. And you turn up your nose at Archie.' The shop was empty and quiet. The only sound, the drip-drip of water into the bucket. 'What would your mother have said?'

'My *mother?* Her only advice was never to marry a foreigner.

Anyway. Archie doesn't want me, Prim, not really. I don't know what he wants. And *his* mother can't stand me. Anyway, there's never been even the faintest whiff of a proposal.'

'Well there won't be, will there, if you go off to America? No point hanging around waiting for your heartstrings to go zing, zing, zing.'

Gerry chewed the side of her thumb.

She'd never managed to stop blushing or tame her own hair. She'd been kissed a few times, but never ever - except for a slobbery old Border Terrier of her aunt's - with any sort of passion. She had never been loved.

The only time Archie had made a sweaty lunge, it had been such a surprise that she'd almost hit him in the eye with a swinging right cross. There'd been no preliminaries. No long glances, no touch or caress. Just a quick hard collision of bodies and nauseating smell of brandy.

She still turned red at the thought of it.

Worse, Archie had left her with the distinct impression that it was all her fault. Another test failed.

There were rules. She knew that. Rules that the better class of virginal spinster, such as herself, found it hard to get the hang of. Like learning a foreign language.

She was familiar with 'The Facts', of course. The gynaecological bits and pieces. After all, she'd lived with Leonie for years, and flicked through that well-thumbed copy of *Married Love* by Marie Stopes at the back of the bookshop shelf.

But, what was love like? That was what she wanted to know. How did it feel? That frisson, the magic? A mystery.

An unsettling thought wormed its way back into Gerry's mind, one that she'd been finding surprisingly difficult to dislodge. Her own body's reaction to that of the American. Someone she didn't even *like*, for goodness sake.

How he'd touched her, the instant charge that she'd felt. His jutting hip and hard body, the assault on her senses. Was that the zing? The one Prim was so dismissive about?

If only there were dictionaries to explain these things! *Zing: a reaction to being held tight in a man's brawny arms with his breath on your neck.*

Well, whatever it was, it had bypassed her brain, made a bee-line for her emotions and left her with an unexpected ache. One that she had no intention of discussing with anyone else. Ever. These stupid thoughts were taking hold.

If she wasn't careful, she'd end up like that relative of Prim's. Marjorie somebody or other? That poor creature, who after years of yearning for the touch of a man's hand, had made a desperate pass at the piano tuner - the one with bad breath, who suffered from dropsy - and for this one terrible slip, poor Marjorie had been carted off to the asylum, never to be seen again.

I want more, brooded Gerry, *that's all*. Not turtle doves and cooing and those sorts of things. But, excitement, a proper meeting of minds. Was that so wrong? Well, whether it was or whether it wasn't, she had to stop thinking about love and start thinking about money.

Prim, of course, was in no mood for any of it.

'You're not still looking for the fairy-tale,' she said, 'are you? You know, the white knight? Anthony and Cleopatra? Because, if *that's* what this is all about …'

'I just don't want to settle. I'd rather not marry at all.'

'Oh, Gerrygerrygerry!' Prim raised eyes to the cracked ceiling. 'So young, so naive. You're looking for something that doesn't exist. Real life isn't like books, you know.'

A very good reason, Gerry thought, *for reading books in the first place.*

'Anyway, you know nothing about this Cooper, do you? Nothing that matters.' Lips pressed together, she turned away.

Gerry slumped. Were they quarrelling? They never quarrelled. 'Six months,' she said, without much conviction. 'That's all. I'd be away for just …'

'You've made up your mind, then? You're quite set on it?'

Gerry hesitated. The idea *had* got a grip, one that she was finding harder and harder to shake off. She couldn't get it out of her head.

A sideways look at Prim. The other woman's high-collared blouse and simple skirt were plain, neat and spinsterly, emphasising bird-bone wrists and ankles. No brooch or trimming, no ornament. Nothing extra.

Prim could never risk everything on a whim like this, could she?

As the slow rhythmic drip of water into the bucket became a more urgent splash, Gerry thought, *I'm being reckless, aren't I? Selfish. I should be concentrating on mending the roof.*

'Prim, I know you don't think -'

'Oh, don't worry about me.' A smart tap from Prim's pencil. 'Off you go on your voyage of discovery and leave me here, stuck up this gum tree. No help, no money and a dripping roof. Unless you've got any other rabbits to pull out of the hat.'

Rabbits? Gerry hadn't even got a hat.

'Look,' she said, suddenly contrite. 'I'll go back to Mr Peale. And - oh, Lord - I suppose I'd better go to the bank.'

'It's, um ... rather a long story, Mr Grewcock.'

'Close the door, please Miss Chiledexter. And make it short, if you will.'

Long or short, Mr Grewcock didn't like Gerry's proposition. His face puckered, as if she'd waved a week-old kipper under his nose.

He had all their bank records spread out in front of him, bills, receipts. Rather a mean-spirited, penny-pinching way for a bank manager to begin an interview, in Gerry's opinion.

Anyway, as far as the bookshop was concerned, the bank's purse had been snapped shut. No more credit, none. Zilch.

'Under no circumstances,' he said, 'can huge debts like these be allowed to continue. My father may have tolerated such shortcomings, but times have changed. Attitudes, y'know. We're recovering from a war!'

He sat back with a self-righteous air. Not, Gerry admitted to herself, that it wasn't deserved. He didn't leave it there, either.

'Y'know, this is just the sort of recklessness, Miss Chiledexter, that my father used to put up with from your aunt. This is *exactly* what she would have done.'

Oh no, it wasn't, thought Gerry. When Leonie had no money, she went shopping. By now, she would have disappeared on a Grand Tour, or been seen boarding a small bi-plane for Paris, in search of designer frocks, furs and fabrics from Le Bon Marché and Chanel. To make herself feel better.

What she *wouldn't* have done, is don a beetroot-coloured cardigan and come begging to the bank. *Pouf*, she would have said, to all that.

It occurred to Gerry then, to give the whole thing up. Perhaps the idea *was* utter folly. But even as the thought entered her head, she rejected it.

Instead; 'I understand your reservations, Mr Grewcock, really I do, but won't you please reconsider? The money from the sale of this property will eventually come to me. Six months' grace is all I'm asking.' She paused. 'And as Mr Peale has already agreed to support me in this venture, I wonder …'

Gerry held out a large box of rose and violet creams.

'I'm sorry, Prim. I've been thoughtless.'

'Hmmm.' Prim lifted the lid. 'Go on, then. Was Mr Grewcock helpful?'

'No, it was like pulling teeth. He was very rude about Leonie, too. He said she was feckless.'

Prim arched one eyebrow.

'Oh, all right, but he didn't really know her, for goodness

sake. Anyway, mostly because of Mr Peale's support, he's *reluctantly* agreed to six months' grace. The bank will honour all pressing bills and debts in that time. After that, I have to sign over my share of the American property and settle up. If I don't, he threatened consequences.'

'Dire?'

'Oh, yes. 'Woe betide' ones.'

'What about the cottage?'

'Sully says I can store my worldly goods with him. It's not as if they'll take up much room.'

'Sully!' Prim let out a squeak. 'His cottage needs fumigating. All that nasty stuffed wildlife in glass boxes, the stoats and badgers! Ugh. And dead birds hanging from his larder ceiling? No, no. Better move in with me.'

'Are you sure? Is there room? Oh, thank you! Thank you, Prim.'

At this point Igor, who never demeaned himself to sit on anyone's knee, sprang up onto Gerry's lap. Turning round and round, he settled himself comfortably into the dent on her dress, and started to purr like a powerful treadle sewing machine.

As if he approved.

'Ridiculous creature.' Gerry frowned. 'Do you think he's psychic? Do psychics eat beetles?'

Prim wagged a finger, Cassandra-like. 'Just leave Igor out of it. Because, there'll be no happy ending to all this, Gerry, mark my words. It will end in tears, I feel it. In my bones.'

'I have to do this, Prim. That place, in Texas, it's ... yes, it's calling me.'

'The bank and bailiffs will be calling you too, unless you bring back enough money to pay the bills. It's not that I *mind* looking after things. It's you going off into wild frontier country, that I'm really concerned about. By yourself, with this whosit … Cooper.' She paused. 'Does he have *any* idea at all what you're planning?'

'No.' Gerry paused to pick the cat hairs from her dress. 'Not yet. He's in Scotland until the end of the week.' A small mercy. For which she was very grateful. 'I'm meeting him on Friday, at the French Partridge.'

'Well, good luck with that! There'll be a devil of a row.'

CHAPTER NINE

'Don't be too 'clever' or talk loudly in public.
Rather, be womanly and modest.'
How to Attract a Man, 1923

'He's back,' Prim said.

'Who?'

'Six feet four with a hint of cold steel, that's who! Your Mister Cooper caused quite a stir in the High Street today, turned everyone's head, even mine.'

'He's not *my* Mister Cooper! Haven't I told you how horrible he is?'

'Oh, be fair. An interesting stranger, a town full of unmarried broody hens. How can we help ourselves?'

Proofed against wind and weather in ancient fur coat and oversized boots, Gerry steered her bicycle up the sweep of gravel, through dripping rhododendrons, to the door of the French Partridge.

The sky was pearl grey, mist had barely lifted. It was still drizzling with rain. Two fat spaniels lolloped out to greet her.

Stepping round luggage stacked in the porch, she found Cooper pacing the draughty reception hall, like a caged animal. A week since they'd last met, and she'd forgotten how large and intimidating his physical presence could seem.

In these surroundings - sixteenth century coaching inn, with flagged floors, wide oak staircase and fireplace big enough to roast an ox - he stood out more than ever.

A race apart. The advance guard of a marauding horde, perhaps - sent to frighten the natives. Vlad the Impaler came to mind, back from savaging someone, somewhere.

It wasn't only his clothes. They were hardly English country gentleman and he was sorely in need of a haircut, but not just that. Something else, something rougher, more dangerous. Trouble waiting to happen?

Once again, he unsettled her.

'You're late,' he said, and sneezed twice. As if her mere appearance was an irritant, soon to bring him out in spots or set off a bronchial wheeze.

'Sorry.'

Neither of them wasted a smile.

'How was Scotland?'

'Wet.' His voice, now raw and husky, was almost down in his boots. 'Wet and cold. Have you got the papers?'

Gerry patted her pocket. 'Could we … um, sit down for just a minute?'

He led the way to the oak-panelled lounge - deep armchairs, shabby chintz - and turned to confront her, eyes travelling slowly from the ankle-length fur down to her boots, hobnailed and borrowed from Sully, who'd worn them in the trenches.

His look seemed to suggest she should be standing in a field somewhere, as a bird-scarer, and she was suddenly struck by an uncomfortable memory of that party. Had she really almost been *sick* on his shoes? Oh, Lord.

'Please tell me you've signed,' he said, without expression.

'Not, exactly.'

'Don't start fencing with me, Mizz Chiledexter. Have you or haven't you?'

Peering out from the brim of her hat, she shook her head.

'Why the hell not?'

'It's ... a little hard to explain.'

Sprawling into a chair, frustration evident in every muscle, he passed a hand over his eyes.

Gerry took off her hat, sending hairpins flying, and shrugged arms out of her coat. Spread over a chair, it resembled a huge furry animal, ready to rear up and maul someone.

The American's expression gave her the same feeling. Perched nervously on the edge of the opposite chair, she prepared for his attack.

'Ten minutes,' he said, squinting suspiciously at the fur. 'That's all you've got.'

'Erm ... did you buy your cow?'

'Bull, it was a bull.'

'Oh. Well, was the trip worthwhile?'

'It'd better be. The animal cost enough.' He named a sum bigger than the bookshop had managed to accrue in the last two years.

Gerry gulped. There was a fire in the room, but her hands felt icy. Ten minutes? She'd been practising all week, but still hadn't worked out *exactly* what to say. The gist of it, she told him, unwinding her scarf, was to do with Leonie.

'I mean, how did she meet Frank O'Rourke? What made him put her in his will? There must be more to it than ...' Her voice trailed away. 'I have this urge to find out.'

'And how d'you reckon on doing that, when they're both dead? No.' He held up a hand. 'Don't tell me, I don't want to know.'

Ghosts? Having opened her mouth to bring up the subject, Gerry closed it again. 'Aren't you the least bit interested in knowing why your Mr O'Rourke did what he did?'

'No. I'm still waking up in a cold sweat every night, wondering how to put it right.' He sneezed again, several times.

Sooner or later, Gerry thought, she'd have to tell him that she wasn't going to sell. She had intended to confide exactly how she'd arrived at that decision, but nothing in his manner invited it.

Anyway, how could she explain what she didn't understand? She'd been worrying away at Leonie's letter, like a dog with a rabbit, to no avail. Did this man believe in Fate, she wondered? Did dreams lie?

'Look,' he said. 'Here's the situation. I have a ranch; you've been given a share of it. You need money; I'm offering to buy you out.'

'And, I accept, I accept your offer.'

'You do!'

'Yes. I do. Just … not yet.'

A door slammed. Someone's feet creaked heavily on the stairs.

Cooper leaned back, clasped hands behind his head and regarded her, coldly. 'Okay,' he said, heavy-eyed. 'Let's cut right to the rat killing, shall we? How much?'

'I beg your pardon?'

'Granted. How much d'you want?'

'Not everything's about money,' Gerry said, loftily.

'That's the stupidest thing I've heard. You've got one hell of a problem here, lady, almost as bad as mine. Right about now, someone's planning to foreclose on your bookshop.'

'And you're the person, I suppose, who can save me from squalor and penury?'

'Right on the money.' He stopped, turned, and coughed violently into a handkerchief. 'How else are you going to pay off your debts? With buttons? For pity's sake, go see your lawyer and get some proper advice.'

'I've already -'

'Wait, hear me out! I didn't travel thousands of miles to a speck on the map to get pneumonia and go round and round with you. Last week, this seemed a small hitch. For some reason, you're turning it into a real big problem!'

His voice rose. One of the spaniels came in to see if it was worth raising a woof, then waddled off again, Gerry's eyes following.

'Are you listening to me?'

'It's hard not to, you're shouting.'

'Look, it's my life we're talking about here, and you don't know a halter from a hind leg! You've no interest in cattle or ranching, have you? You don't even ride. So what the hell are you playing at?'

Pushing an errant pin back into her hair, Gerry started to feel like one of those pheasants winged by his double-barrelled blast. Bang, bang.

He'd come to England with something to prove, hadn't he, scores to settle? But why go tooth and nail for her? The people he needed to shout at were dead. Blame Frank O'Rourke, she wanted to say. Blame Leonie. Don't try pinning this on me.

'So, that's all you're giving me?'

'Yes.' She pulled down her cuffs, fiddled with her gloves. 'That is … no.'

'Yes-no? What is this yes-no?'

'I *can't* sell you my share of the ranch, not for six months, anyway; that was my aunt's last wish.'

A stunned silence, and she rushed to fill it - pulling papers from her pocket and handing them over.

Cooper frowned. 'She put that in her will?'

'She left a letter with her solicitor … you know, Mr Peale?'

'Saying what, exactly?'

'That she didn't want me to sell, straight away.'

Her words bounced off his stunned expression. He stared at the papers, then tossed them down on the low table between them. 'Why in the world would your aunt do that?'

'I've no idea.'

Soot fell down the chimney, making the fire sizzle and smoke puff out in a cloud.

A cough, then Cooper leaned forward. 'Wait. This was just a whim, is that what you're saying? Not some rock-solid legal condition that has to be held to, no matter what.'

'Well ...' She frowned.

'So, if you wanted, you could ignore it.'

'I could.' Deep breath. 'But, I won't.'

'You got a good reason for that?'

'Because I loved my aunt, because it was her dying wish! Look, I've made up my mind.' Gerry spoke in a rush. 'I want to see your ranch, talk to your people, and find out first-hand what happened between Mr O'Rourke and my aunt.'

'Whoa! Let's work out a compromise here. Look, who's advising you, who do I need to speak to? Give me names!'

'It's just something I need to do. Six months, then I'll sign my share of the ranch over to you, I promise. Trust me.'

'Lady,' he said, his eyes a particularly flinty grey, 'I don't trust anyone.'

Another long silence. He slouched deeper into his chair.

Now what, Gerry wondered? Sitting up, ramrod straight, she crossed her fingers.

The clock in the hall chimed the half hour. Someone passed by the window, bent double against horizontal rain, pushing a barrow with a squeaky wheel.

Just when the silence had started to feel oppressive, Cooper began another terrible fit of coughing and wheezing, and Gerry briefly considered suggesting Sully's remedy of rubbing goose grease on your chest.

Perhaps not. Sometimes Sully and those old wives were right; sometimes they were wrong.

Thoughts drifted treacherously back to that party at the Hall, and the tingle she'd felt at the back of her neck, when this man had touched her. Ha! Long gone. And clearly, Prince Charming here had no memory at all of any closeness or slight melting of the ice-cap.

'All right,' he said at last, clearing his throat in a pessimistic sort of way. 'I don't give a damn for your reasons, but I'll wait. Yeah. I'll wait the six months for you to sign your share over. There's no need for you to come out to the ranch.'

'Wait.' Gerry kept her voice low. Unlike him, she hadn't been brought up to shout at strangers. 'Mr Cooper, you're missing the point.'

'The *point*?' he said, taking the word by the scruff of the neck and shaking it. 'The *point*, is that the last thing on God's earth I or any of my 'people' need now, is some English lady bountiful, looking for excitement in her boring small-town life, coming to meet the natives. Hear what I'm saying?'

Staring down at the table, Gerry felt like breaking it over his head.

He hadn't finished, either.

'Think you can just waltz into my life, pretty as you please, messing up everything I've ever worked for? All right, I wasn't born to it, but I'm connected. It's in my blood.' He paused. 'The Circle-O needs one person in charge, not two.'

Well, guess what, Gerry wanted to hiss, *I don't want to be* in charge, thank you. I just want to come and have a look, that's all.

'If it's a vacation you need,' he went on, 'do everyone a favour, will you? Go to France. Or Italy. Or some other place where starry-eyed women go to find adventure. Why waste your life on this? Seems to me, lady, you've got too much damn time on you hands. Why aren't you settled and married?'

Cheek! 'I'm an Englishwoman, Mr Cooper. Between the war and the septic flu epidemic, most prospective bridegrooms were wiped out.'

'Missed the boat, huh? There must be *some* fish left in the sea, surely.'

Feeling as dull and frumpy as an unpromising pig that a farmer would have a hard time selling at market, Gerry pushed back another errant strand of hair. 'Unfortunately, I don't want to marry a fish. What about you? Are *you* married?'

'Never found anyone I liked the look of enough.'

Now, *there* was a surprise. 'Well. I'm sorry you're so much against this, but I've made up my mind. So, please. At least, take time to consider.'

Standing up, she went to stare out of one of the tall windows, swagged, looped and draped in dusty, faded brocade. She'd completely run out of things to say.

There was a spiteful splattering of rain against the glass. A bout of frenzied barking outside.

'Perhaps,' he said, coolly, 'we should go argue this out in court.'

She was too angry to turn and face him. 'You haven't got

time for that, have you? It might moulder on for years.' Staring fixedly out at the wet terrace and tightly-clipped hedge beyond the balustrade, she muttered, 'Like Jarndyce and Jarndyce.'

Not that a philistine like him would have read any Dickens. Deep breath. 'Of course, it will be some time before I can think of travelling.' She looked round. 'Perhaps we could meet once more, before you go back.'

'Meet?'

'Yes. To discuss my …'

'What for?'

' … arrangements, my travel arrangements. It might help.'

'I don't think so.'

'Well, how should I … you know, communicate with you then, let you know when I'm arriving.'

'Do you know anything about Texas?'

'It's in the south, isn't it, near to Mexico. Its history, well … um, it's big?'

'About a thousand miles from one end to the other. So I guess natives will have to run between us with messages on forked sticks.'

Silence.

'Would it be possible for you to be any *less* helpful and understanding about this, Mister …'

'No, I don't think it would. Because you're making a mistake here, Mizz Chiledexter, a big one.'

'Six months,' she said, obstinately, 'and then I'll sign everything over.'

'Oh, you'd better. Because if you don't, I'll have lawyers

crawling out of your ears. See, I'm prepared to die to keep this ranch. Would you do as much to take it away?' He stood up, abruptly.

They were eyeball to eyeball now. Her mouth dry, Gerry felt herself retreating. 'So, when will you be leaving England, Mr Cooper?'

'Just as soon as ever I can. And it's Cooper,' he flung over his shoulder, on his way out of the room. 'How many more times! Drop the damn mister.'

Gerry braced herself for the shudder of a slammed door. Other voices came to join his deep southern rumble, in the hall.

Minutes later, her straining ear caught the sound of a starting handle being cranked, then gravel crunching and shifting under wheels outside. Dogs barked and a motor vehicle chugged away, leaving a cloud of white smoke to billow by the window.

A hush settled. He'd gone.

She felt herself slowly shrink, like a deflating balloon. Well, the words had been said, and she'd survived, hadn't she? Just. Brow-beaten, threatened and compromised, yes. But still alive.

'So far,' she told the silent room.

Bundling herself back into her old fur, Gerry waited until the clock struck the hour. She wanted to be absolutely sure that Cooper had gone. In fact, not just gone, but completely disappeared, out of sight.

The two wet spaniels paddled in and sat steaming in front

of the fire. One of them came to push its wet nose into her hand, sniffing suspiciously at her coat.

'Miss Chiledexter.' A sharp tap-tap on the window. She jumped and looking up, saw her own startled reflection in the glass.

'This your bicycle out 'ere, Miss?'

Fred Longmarsh, the gardener.

'Yes.' A heavy sigh of relief. 'Yes, it is.'

'You got a right bad puncture then, Miss. Back wheel.'

CHAPTER TEN

'Be a home maker and home lover.'
A Woman's Way, 1923

'Cross? He was hopping mad. All blood and guts and thunder. He thinks we're a stunted race who live in doll-sized hovels and talk in funny voices.' Gerry sighed. 'Well, to be fair, that's just his opinion of me. I'm not sure what he thinks about anyone else.'

Prim pulled a face. 'Understandable, I suppose. He's come thousands of miles, apparently for nothing, and you're the one standing in his way.'

'I don't think he's used to anyone saying no, that's all it is. He's used to making a lot of noise and shoving people around. Like a ... rutting elk.'

'Some people around here think he's rather nice.'

'Well, *some* people are wrong! Do you know, I've met him three or four times now, and never even seen him smile. Is that normal? Not once, not even the faintest twitch of his lips. He probably thinks it's a sign of weakness.'

Gerry ignored the little voice in her head that said: *Of course, he smiled at Kitty Dudley, didn't he? Oh, yes. Even laughed. Out loud!*

'Anyway, he's completely against the idea of my visit and when I asked for advice on how to get to … oh, wherever it is … he was really rude and said that I've *sure* got a problem, but it's *mah* problem.'

'He's put you off, then?'

'Aren't I entitled to go and see what I've inherited? No, I'll make my own way there. It's not uncommon nowadays, is it? Women climb mountains and cross deserts, by themselves. Look at Leonie.'

'Ducky,' Prim said, 'Leonie was *never* on her own. Not for long, anyway.' She paused. 'It's not too late to change your mind, you know. Are you sure about all of this?'

'Listen, Prim. Where's the danger? Tell me that. Where's the danger in me doing this?'

With Christmas approaching and snow lying in drifts, a telegram arrived, from Texas. Turning it over, Gerry half-expected to see smoke seeping out of the envelope.

The message was stark and to the point. It didn't bode well.

IF YOU'RE STILL DEAD-SET ON VISITING, I NEED NOTICE. PLEASE TELEGRAPH JERICHO WELLS WITH DATE AND APPROX TIME OF ARRIVAL. COOPER.

Not one single, kind conciliatory word. Could you shout

in a telegram?

'That's the worst invitation I've ever had,' Gerry said.

Not that she'd have expected any sort of apology. It would probably have taken a fish hook to drag one of those out of him. Still, this was better than nothing, wasn't it?

Dead-set? Oh, she certainly was.

A flurry of packing followed. Initialled cabin trunks with brass bands all around. Leather suitcases, portmanteau, hat boxes, dressing-case.

'Will you wear all of these?' Prim asked, as Gerry sat altering the neckline of a dress, with small, neat stitches. For days, she'd been snipping sleeves, discarding ribbons.

'No idea.' Gerry snapped off a thread with her teeth. 'What do people wear in the middle of Texas? You can never take too many clothes, that's what Leonie used to say, wasn't it? Ensembles for everything. Beach and mountain, dining, dancing.'

'Those, dear girl, were for Deauville and Cannes! How many *ensembles* do you suppose you'll need on a cow farm in the middle of nowhere?'

'The beaded voile?'

Prim rolled her eyes.

'The Japanese silk pyjamas, then.'

'You'll frighten the natives. And remember, Gerry. It's burning hot there. And you ... *freckle*!'

Then, there was Archie - sleek and smart in heavy coat, suit and spats on that fiercely cold day and topped by a velour hat, at a particularly rakish angle. His precious dogs - 'desperate for a run, poor chaps' - at his side.

'Let's not go over all this again, Archie.' With sheep's cries in the distance, and skies still leaden with snow, they trudged past crumbling greenhouses in the Hall grounds. 'I would never fit into your life, would I? We're agreed on that. And your parents ... well, they could see it long ago.'

'I'm tired of pleasing the parents,' Archie said. 'I don't like the gels they like, not one bit. I'll make my own choice.'

Gerry was still confused. Surely, that was only part of it. There he was, the right family, right school, right regiment. Good breeding clearly stamped across his forehead.

Weren't there masses of single women in the county, all with four or five rows of pearls, desperate for such a prize? All much more able to comport themselves prettily at any Dutt-Dixon-Nabb tea-party, too.

Smelling the brandy on his breath reminded her of their one disastrous, thin-lipped embrace. She was convinced that Archie hadn't enjoyed it any more than she had.

To be absolutely, scrupulously fair, hadn't he always been a bit of a cold fish? Buttoned-up, fastidious, with no visible emotion? Only his beloved dogs seemed able to make him unclench.

'Are you certain, Archie,' she said, with sudden clarity, 'that you want to settle down, at all?'

He stopped to stare at the ground, his face half-hidden by

the hat.

Shifting from one chilblained foot to another, Gerry peered over at him. In spite of the biting wind, his face was quite red. Goodness, she thought, he's *blushing*!

A sudden gust of bitter north-east wind set the ravens yakking and brought stinging flurries of snow. Heads down, they walked on, leaning into the wind. The dogs, tails up, noses down, led the way.

'It's expected,' he said, at last. 'Stay quiet and show willing. For the sake of Good Blood.'

His voice was so quiet, that Gerry wondered if she'd misheard. She held her breath, expecting some heartfelt confession. None came. Instead, she found herself thinking back to a recent conversation, with Prim.

'Odd, really,' Prim had said, 'for someone of Archie's age not to be already attached, don't you think? You know, considering the competition here for every available man.'

'I thought you liked him.'

'I do. Yes, I do. A fine looking chap. A little soft, perhaps, around the edges. You know, not very ... athletic.'

'He hunts! He's an excellent shot. You *told* me ... you said yourself he's the answer to any maiden's prayer.'

'Mmm, yes. Maybe.'

'Maybe what? Just because he dresses well and likes good accessories ...'

And suddenly, a flash of memory. Beautiful young men friends of Leonie's who'd stayed with them from time to time. They'd arrive in pairs - in flowing Oxford bags, silk socks, hats at an angle - and were always great fun and devoted to one another.

'I'm sorry, Gerry.' Archie interrupted her train of thought. 'Because, you know ... well, you're different.'

What did that mean? Gerry didn't know and wasn't sure that she wanted to, either. Oh, well. It didn't matter anymore, did it?

The air was now thick with falling snow, fat, determined flakes. Clapping frozen hands together, her breath blowing white smoke, she told Archie what she was planning to do.

'America! What on *earth* for? Never cared for Americans, don't like their attitude.' He paused to call the dogs. 'And that ... Cooper cove, with his damned mask of politeness, swaggering around as if he owned the place! Bit of a bounder, if you ask me. Mean sort of brute. Needs a haircut.'

Mean? Gerry blinked feathers of snow from her eyelashes. It wasn't the first time she'd heard Cooper described in that way. Mesmerised, she stared at the dancing flakes.

No-one could deny that he had a short fuse, a rough, brooding sort of quality. *And* he'd threatened her, hadn't he, at the French Partridge? Or had that just been bluster?

Not that Archie's opinion was going to make a pin of difference now, nor anyone else's. Because they were all against her adventure – the Vicar ('but is there an *English* church there, dear?'), the postmaster, Prim. Everyone, that is, except the wonderful Mr Peale, who had somehow managed to extricate enough money from the bank to fund the whole expedition.

Anyway. She was tired of trying to justify herself. It was too late. She was going to America, and that was that. The lure of adventure had become too strong.

For weeks, Gerry had been dreaming about Texas, her mind full of Mexicans and conquistadores, Spanish missions, Jesuit priests. It sounded wild. That was what excited her. Untamed. A corner of the country where restlessness and wildness still lingered, in every kind of scenery, every sort of weather.

Apart from that, she was hearing the voice again. *'Go, you must go',* it had said, outside Mr Peale's office. *'Go to America, go to Texas.'* A message in her head so strong and clear, that she'd been quite unable to ignore it.

She wiped her cold and watery nose. Snow was spreading softly, silencing everything. No birds, voices, footsteps. Just a still silence, cutting them off. The world seemed to be holding its breath.

'When you come back,' Archie said, sounding slightly embarrassed, 'let's try again, eh? What say, Gerry?' Eyes sliding away, he stooped over the dogs, his kid-gloved hand caressing panting, snowy backs. 'Fresh start?'

'Four months is a long time, Archie.'

'I'll miss you,' he said.

No you won't, Gerry thought. Not for long, anyway.

Next, the transformation.

Taking off her hat, shaking her head, Gerry caught Prim's stunned expression.

'Oh! Your beautiful hair! What have you done?'

'Cut it off.'

Prim stared. 'Is that a bob?'

'Actually, it's a shingle. A symbolic shearing, for my American adventure. What do you think? Isn't it chic?'

'Too chic by half,' Prim said, drily, 'for where you're going.'

Still a million things to sort out. The bookshop, the cottage. Her furniture in piles, ready to be moved. Hadn't Hannibal taken elephants over the Alps with less trouble?

Then, just before Gerry was due to leave, Igor disappeared. As quickly and unexpectedly as he'd once arrived, he was gone. Gerry wasn't too concerned. Hadn't he always been independent? And Prim and Sully would keep a weather eye, if he deigned to return.

As for the spirit or ghost or whatever it was. The voices had stopped, just like that, all of a sudden. But *something*, that haunting sense of Leonie pressing close was still there. Gerry was struck by the strength of that feeling. Her aunt's presence was everywhere. Drifting through dusty rooms, wafting, shimmering, dancing.

On her very last day at the little cottage, she raked out coals in the grate and spread the ashes over the garden. Then, closing the door to leave her cat-free home to the mice, she distinctly heard the soft whisper of silk dragged over a stone floor.

A chill at the back of her neck.

No matter what common sense or anyone else said, it was hard to believe that Leonie was not still around. Had she ever really gone?

Unlike her aunt, who'd been able to set off on a mule in some dangerous foreign place, without any knowledge of geography or sense of direction, and still somehow arrive in the right spot, looking glamorous - Gerry was not a good traveller, never had been.

Leaving England, she sailed from Liverpool on a majestic Cunarder, with the Atlantic in a very bad mood. Thunderous waves crashed the ship, sending clouds of spray over the sides and flooding the decks.

For days and days after landing in New York, Gerry was still walking with the pitch and roll of that sea.

Then, weeks living out of a suitcase. Hundreds of miles, with different railroad companies - *'Welcome Aboard!'* - and hectic changes of Pullman, scraping and jerking at every fly-blown stop.

And Texas not even in sight, the friendly Pullman conductor with the gold stripes on his sleeve told her, as she gazed out at passing scenery.

The train got hotter, the landscape larger - flying by in a blur. Advertisements started flashing by, for cattle feed and chewing tobacco. Too much travelling. Would her muscles ever stop complaining? Would she *ever* sleep through the night again?

And, Jericho Wells?

She'd tried finding it in railroad folders, tracing the length and breadth her route with one finger. No success, not even a splotch on the map. A nowhere place.

Where *was* it, then? Her dream spot, her destination. Where was it even *near?*

Chin sunk to her chest like a roosting bird, Gerry drifted in and out of sleep, cloudy images floating through her mind.

Herself at four or five with wispy pigtails, all dressed up and on her best behaviour. Under the clock at some port or railway station, hunched on her luggage with a label round her neck and chilblained toes. Missing the perfumed air and colours of India, missing her ayah, missing her dog.

While other tiny travellers were kissed and borne away, Gerry knew that however hard she tried, she'd soon be in some reluctant relative's way, a nuisance to someone or other.

And it always turned out to be a mustn't-go-out-without-your-hat sort of place, mustn't run or scuff your feet, mustn't speak unless you were spoken to. Like being in one of the nastier fairy tales - a child of Hamelin, borne away to some forbidding mountain cave.

That had been the pattern. Until Leonie. Leonie, affection-ate and loving, who'd held her tight, and said; 'Don't look back, my darling, never look back. You're with me now.'

But here, on her way to meet Cooper, she was about to be the fly in someone else's ointment, the stone in his wheel.

You're a grown up, now, she reminded herself. You can do this.

CHAPTER ELEVEN

'If you are set on marriage, emigration may be the answer.
Go to Canada or the Colonies.'
The Daily Chronicle, 1922

Gerry waited for someone to come and collect her. Waited and waited.

She'd been sitting on a velvet settee in the lobby of the Charles Goodnight Hotel, next to a drooping potted palm, for what seemed like hours, fanning herself with a dog-eared two-year old copy of a hunting magazine and trying to avoid the curious glances of the desk clerk.

In vain, it seemed.

'Parn me, ma'am.' His voice had the southern roll that she was beginning to expect, sliding and twanging like a banjo string. 'Can I git you anythin'? Cold drink, cup of hot coffee, maybe? You look real peaked.'

'Oh no, thank you. I'm hoping someone will be here for me quite soon.'

'Doggone!' The man's mouth fell open. Hair was sleekeddown, bow-tie askew. 'You English, ma'am?'

'Why, yes. Yes, I am.'

'Well I'll be! And us just a little old cow town. How did y'all wind up here?'

'Oh well, you know. Just visiting.' She paused. 'I was expecting someone to meet me here.'

'No kidding. Sure y'all got the day right?'

As a fan looped lazily overhead, Gerry swatted flies away and started to wonder. *Had* she? Had the person collecting her got it right? Was she in the right place?

If not, was it her fault? Oh, bound to be.

She'd stepped down onto the box-step the conductor had put in place at Jericho Wells, hoping to see Cooper. In fact, the only other person the entire length of that dusty platform had been a solitary porter, whom she'd assumed had been unloading her baggage.

That assumption had been wrong. Somewhere between the last few godforsaken stops, most of her precious luggage had mysteriously disappeared. Missing! Almost every stitch she'd ever owned; the entire treasure trove of clothes that had probably cost Leonie two arms and three legs.

'It'll more'n likely turn up, ma'am,' the porter had announced airily. 'Sooner or later.'

She'd stood, alone and stranded, her morocco dressing-case and one travelling bag at her feet, while the Missouri-Pacific Railroad's Sunshine Special clanged and clanked away into the distance. One last, long mournful hoot of the locomotive horn.

Then, silence. A vast, silent emptiness.

WELCOME TO JERICHO WELLS said the huge sign. *Population 509.*

Not a single one of those five hundred and nine, however, had been there to welcome Gerry. Nor apparently, anyone else. Even though she'd telegraphed well ahead.

Now, the strain had started to tell. Her great romantic adventure was beginning to lose its charm.

Luckily, she'd brushed her hair and dabbed wrists and temples with eau de cologne before getting off of the train, because now she was reluctant to leave the lobby. Really! Wasn't it insulting to keep a person waiting this long?

Another half hour, with patience wearing thin, she abandoned an ancient copy of *The Cattleman's Gazette* and approached the desk, with a wall of pigeon holes behind.

'Excuse me?' She cleared her throat.

The clerk looked up from thumbing through a ledger.

'Was a message left for me, by chance? Miss Gerardina Chiledexter?'

'Don't rightly recall one, ma'am.' Shaking his head, he fingered his watch chain. 'Uh-huh. Ah would've remembered a name like that.'

'Well, are you familiar with the Circle-O ranch? Could I get there by myself?'

'Hmn. It's quite a piece from here. On horseback, maybe a day's ride. But travelling alone, with that there.' He pointed to Gerry's travelling bag. 'You prolly be needing horse an' buggy.

Now, someone from Circle-O comes into town pretty reg'lar Thursdays, for supplies.'

She peered at the calendar on the wall, next to a dusty sepia picture; *The Coming Of The Railway To Jericho Wells.* 'But, today's Monday. Isn't it?'

'Sure as beans is, ma'am! And we got plenty of rooms right here, if y'all be needing one. Yessir! You could cast your eye over right now and take your pick.'

Gerry started to feel foolish. Well, thank you, Mister Cooper or Cooper-just-Cooper or whatever his name was. She hadn't expected cheers and a brass band. She hadn't bargained on this, either, high, dry and humiliated.

And she didn't know a *soul* here, not even anyone who knew anyone.

'Do you happen to know the owner of the Circle-O?' she asked the clerk.

'Coop! Sure thing, ma'am. Circle-O's prolly the biggest ranch in the entire territory. Along with the Kittrell spread, o' course. Why, every man and his dog in a hundred miles knows Coop!' He paused. 'Just visitin', huh? Would that be business then, ma'am? Or pleasure?'

'I'm not sure, not yet.'

Still light-headed from days on the train, Gerry wandered out onto the front verandah, with its peeling paint and row of rockers. A blast of white-hot sun sucked the breath from her lungs - as if a sack had been flung over her head.

Shielding her eyes, she squinted both ways. Bank. Barber's shop, boarding house. A few empty buildings in a blur of heat, waving single-starred Texan flags.

Not another living soul in sight, no car, cart, nor any other person. The rest of the town appeared to be dozing. A dog, asleep on its paws, opened one eye and yawned at her.

Was this it? The wild, wild West? The untamed wilderness that still drew the adventurous, reckless and daring?

Hot, gritty wind rushed along the dusty main street, to the spot where she stood in the chic travelling suit that had seemed such a sensible choice thirty-six hours ago. Now, it clung and choked and itched and was uncomfortably warm.

She pulled at her pink straw cloche, with its appliqué trim, trying to shade her eyes. The small brim offered no protection at all from sun or wind. Retreating back into shade, she wiped squashed insects from one of the cane chairs and lowered herself gingerly into it. *Ouch!* Burning hot.

'Mizz ... Gelatina?'

Gerry jumped as the slow-talking clerk poked his head round the door. 'Ah! Has someone ... ?'

'No-one partic'lar, ma'am. Not yet.'

'Oh. Is it always this quiet?'

'Sometimes is, sometimes ain't. Saturdays there's plenty whoopin' and hollerin'. Lookit, how about that cup of coffee? Helps you to face the day, I always say.'

'Thank you,' Gerry said, and as he turned to go, 'um, the Circle-O? It's big, you say?'

His forehead puckered. 'About million an' half? Two million? Maybe more.'

'Cows!'

'Acres, ma'am.'

Gerry's mouth fell open. Fanning her face with a linen and lace handkerchief, she sank back on the squeaky rocker.

The light was too bright here, the landscape too brown; she already had a headache. All excitement had gone, that quickening of the heart she'd felt on arriving. Worse, all this waiting around was shaking loose old childhood memories.

Here she was again. Another piece of lost luggage.

She'd already arranged and rearranged herself and her expression at least a dozen times - imagining meeting Cooper, all smart and composed in her dear little hold-your-breath jacket, hat at a perfect angle.

Not like this, wringing hands and peering left to right.

Fingering her lapel pin, she recalled the furious expression on his face after their last skirmish. The way he'd glowered down at her, his teeth-baring hostility. He'd given her a really nasty five minutes.

Well, he was making his point well enough now, wasn't he? Oh, yes. He hadn't wanted her here, had begged her not to come. She'd been warned.

Taking off her gloves to inspect chewed fingernails, she started to compose the telegraph home. *Help! Stupid mistake, send money!* But then, the desk clerk brought thick hot coffee and after a few mouthfuls, she felt stronger.

Oh, *come* on. Where was that stout British pluck? Leonie had bivouacked on the mountains of Turkestan, hadn't she? All alone. Well ... all alone, except for Chinese servants, native bearers and her current beau, of course, plus his considerable personal army.

'Miss … Charlie - dex?'

Gerry's head jerked up to meet the fierce scrutiny of a boy astride a pony the other side of the porch rail. Skinny, bare-legged, wearing a sun-bleached shirt with the tail hanging out.

A small brindle-coloured dog ran in and out of the pony's legs, yapping and making it fidgety.

'Well, *are* you?' The boy sucked on a piece of straw, eyes travelling slowly from the top of her fashionable cloche to the tip of her pointy-toed shoes - a look of horrified fascination.

A scrape of her chair and she was on her feet. 'Yes, I'm Gerardina Chiledexter.'

'Thought as much. Coop said you'd likely be wearing somethin' fancy.' Tipping his own hat back, he shook hair out of striking blue eyes and tried to hide a snigger. 'You're bulling, ain't you, lady, wearing that hat out here!'

Gerry returned his stare.

The boy was soft-faced, with splattering of freckles. A strange streak of yellow paint on his face stretched from ear to ear, and strings of coloured beads were wrapped tight around his wrist and neck. It was hard to tell his age.

'And, you are?' She flapped a huge horsefly away.

'Scoot. Me an' Wolf come to take you back to the Circle-O.' He didn't sound too pleased about it, either.

'Wolf!'

The boy jerked his head. 'Loadin' supplies back there.'

'Ah, so … Mr Cooper?'

'Coop? Hellfire, lady. Coop's real busy!'

Oh. Of *course* he was.

As he slid from his pony, a yappy blur of brown and white fur rushed the porch steps and started nipping at Gerry's heels, snarling and snapping.

'Indian dawg,' the boy said, tucking thumbs into his belt, 'he don't like females.' He allowed several minutes to pass before yelling, 'Lobo! Git back here!'

At that, a light buggy, drawn by two horses, careered round the corner and came to a sharp halt in front of the hotel. Quaintly old-fashioned and unlike any horse-drawn hack that Gerry had ever seen, it had two upholstered seats at the front and a fringed canopy to keep the sun off, on top.

She wasn't sure what she'd been expecting, but it wasn't this. Perhaps, in spite of his million or so acres, Cooper was poor. Perhaps he really *did* need her to sign over her share of the ranch, straight away.

'She's here, Wolf,' the boy sighed. 'I done got her.'

The driver, his face like the scuffed heel of an old boot, a beaten-up Stetson on the back of his head, studied Gerry through half-closed eyes.

Never had she felt so pink, so Anglo-Saxon. As sweat trickled down the back of her neck, she wiped her face with her sleeve and tried a smile. 'Pleased to meet you, Mister ... erm, Wolf.'

No smile came back, no paw raised in greeting. Chewing on a plug of tobacco, the man put one finger to the sweat-stained brim of his hat and spat on the ground.

Like a camel, Gerry thought, with a moustache.

The camel jerked its head and a growled 'Yrrp' was racked out of him. Scoot snapped back, starting an exchange of choppy gestures, mangled consonants.

Spanish? Gerry wasn't sure. 'I beg your pardon?'

'Wolf don't speak much English.'

'But, what did he say?'

'What's it to you?'

'He was looking at me, when he said it.'

Scoot leaned over to hook a weather-worn straw with broad brim from the back of the carriage. 'Says he's *so* pleased *you're* pleased, and better take off that dumb hat that ain't a lick of use to anyone, and put this on quick, before you fry.'

When her lavishly preserved travelling bag was brought out from the hotel, leather straps bulging, there was another sideways look. 'This all you got, lady? You ain't planning on staying long, then?'

And ignoring Gerry's cry of - 'Wait! Please be careful with that, it's -' her precious luggage was flung into the back of the carriage, to land upside down on a pile of sagging, smelly vegetable sacks. 'Vuitton.'

For goodness sake! It may have looked old and battered, but that bag had criss-crossed the globe with Leonie, several times. It was almost an heirloom! Did these people care? Gerry caught the look that passed between them. Did they heck. This was the sort of place where they rolled down rocks on strangers.

She was left to haul herself up, with an undignified

heave-ho, to a red-hot seat beside Wolf, with his rhythmically chewing jaw and the meanest face she'd ever seen. Baring his teeth, he gave another 'Yrrp, yrrp' of greeting.

Confused, she turned to Scoot for translation.

'Believe me, Mizz whatever-your-name.' Jamming his own hat back on, he whistled to the dog. 'You jest don't want to know.'

When the dog suddenly leapt up behind, Gerry jumped like a frightened rabbit. All of them were baring their teeth at her. Which one would bite first?

CHAPTER TWELVE

'Avoid talking too much. Men love a good listener.'
Advice to Miss-All-Alone, 1924

They started off, sedately enough.

Down the wide main street, past the Ranchers and Drovers Bank, dry-goods store and dust-bitten shed with its splintered door that sold gasoline. Dogs rushed out beside them, in a noisy pack.

They passed buildings with weathered picket fences, Southern Confederacy or Lone Star flags whipping round their flagpoles. One or two sunburned idlers on dusty front-porch rockers eyed them curiously as they rumbled by.

The town soon petered out.

For a while, the road ran alongside the railroad. When they veered off to a dirt track, stretching out over a wide burst of country, Wolf slapped the reins and they picked up the pace, bouncing over bumps and ruts. Rattle! Skip, shake!

Boy and pony thudded alongside, hair, tail and mane streaming. With dust cloud drifting up behind, the gap soon widened between themselves and Jericho Wells.

The driver kept up his silence; there was no conversation. Nothing except the creak of the carriage, the beat of horses' hooves and hot, booming wind flapping the fringes of the canopy.

Lolling back on the hot plush seat, Gerry retreated to a quiet place inside herself, and with the sun on her back, doubts and insecurities started to fade.

Because, oh my goodness.

The enormity of the landscape stretching out around them; a sea of shimmering grassland meeting wide blue sky. No sign of life - no trees, buildings, fences - just silence. For someone newly arrived from the wintry winds and gloomy skies of cramped England, it was like a dream.

Had Leonie felt like this? What had happened to her here?

Relaxing into the bump and sway of the carriage, Gerry started taking slower breaths. A huge bird flapped up from one side of the track - up, up, on warm draughts of air, wings outstretched, until it was just a speck in the sky.

Texas, she thought. *I am here; I'm in Texas.*

It was some time before concerns about Cooper raised their ugly heads again. How would he behave when he saw her? Would he even try to make her welcome?

She reminded herself why she had come. Because of Leonie and a voice that kept nag-nagging? Some strange impulse that she didn't understand? Hardly a sensible basis for a journey of a thousand or so miles, was it?

Yet somehow, she still believed it. She was meant to be here.

Moments later, scanning the horizon, Gerry saw a flicker of movement. Two black flecks, dots against the glare, coming down from foothills, west of the town.

Drawing closer, they took on bigger, blurry shapes. Riders? She squinted into the sun's glare. Yes, two of them, in shimmering waves of heat.

'Someone's coming!' She turned to Wolf, expecting him to pull back on the reins. Instead, he leaned forward, spurring the horses on to frightening speed, faster, faster, yellow dust billowing up all around.

With the two riders starting to give chase, the boy galloped alongside the wildly speeding wagon, whooping and kicking his pony and yelling approval. 'Darn it, Wolfie! Whip them horses on!'

Careering along, the wagon bouncing, bolts and springs rattling - Gerry was thrown forward. Dust in her face, internal organs getting a good shaking, she gripped the side. A terrified look at her companions. They seemed to be *enjoying* themselves.

'Faster, faster! They nearly on us!'

Eventually, the two riders came alongside. Racing ahead, the front one managed to lean over, grab the reins and bring the sweat-streaked horses to shuddering, grinding halt.

Wheels gouged into the road, sending up a thick dust cloud, and for a few moments, silence. Just dry wind rippling the grass and two mewling buzzards overhead.

Gerry coughed and straightened the cracked straw, now hanging over one wild eye. Puffing wisps of hair away from her face, she turned to the new arrivals.

One, a young woman, tall and slender in the saddle, with creamy Southern drawl. 'Why, Scoot. Ah declare! Anyone'd think you were racing.'

Scoot stared fixedly at his horse's back.

'Why in the world you driving this old buggy, anyway?'

'Coop said so.' Gerry saw colour rise in the boy's cheeks.

'Huh, always making mischief, aren't you. Better start being good, you hear, and … don't *dare* look away at that horse! I *said*, y'hear?'

'Yes, ma'am.'

Nudging her horse, the young woman came round to Gerry's side of the carriage, causing the little dog to grumble in its throat. 'Well, how do, Miss Chiledon. I'm Hallie-Lee Kittrell, a real good friend of Coop's and I just couldn't wait to make your acquaintance.'

'Nice to meet you, too,' murmured Gerry. *Chic*, she thought, shading her eyes. Not a single hair out of place and even from this distance, Miss Kittrell smelled sweet and fresh with no hint of horse.

A man's woman? The sort to draw everyone's eye, anyway. Not exactly how she'd pictured the women here. Where was the buckskin and fringing and hair all in braids? She tried and failed to rise above her own dishevelled appearance - a farmyard animal brought in by the turnip truck?

'Coop was real disappointed to pass up meeting you

himself, but I'm sure he'll get back soon as he can.'

Gerry imagined that Cooper would be more likely to think a bad penny had turned up. Not that it mattered. Being this travel-sore and short of sleep didn't put a person in any mood for social graces.

The only thing she wanted now was to lie on a bed that didn't bump and sway, and sleep for weeks. She wouldn't care if she didn't meet anyone else, ever again.

'My,' Miss Kittrell said, with that sky-blue stare, 'you must be broiled in that suit. I guess you aren't used to this Texas sun? Coop said that in England, it never ever stops raining.'

Adjusting her hat, she added quickly, 'Now, I just know he'll give you a mighty fine welcome later. We Texans are known for our hospitality. Anyway, you take care, y'hear?' She wheeled her horse away.

As the couple trotted off, Scoot muttered to no-one in particular. 'That woman. You can't spit without she knows it. If she and Coop git together, man, we're in trouble!'

And they were off again. The carriage jolting, bumping. Miles and miles more mesquite and low brush and burning hot prairie. High grass rippling away to nowhere.

It was late afternoon before they passed beneath the sign, a huge looping circle woven in rawhide topped by a pair of cow horns, and Gerry squinted hopefully towards the horizon. Still no buildings, no signs of life.

Hot, sleepy, headachey, she turned to Scoot. 'Are we nearly there?'

'Yip. Say, couple more hours. Be there before sunset.'

Woken by a frenzy of barking dogs, Gerry heard, 'Hey there!' and sat up in the buggy, blinking. A tall two-storey building loomed up against darkening sky.

The ranch house? Surely not. She'd imagined some sort of primitive log cabin, barely more than a shack, with few facilities. Washing in a stream, perhaps, cleaning her teeth with twigs.

This gracious sprawl - long and wide with verandah wrapped round - had been planned on a grand scale. A huge, two-storeyed mansion disguised as a ranch, and her home for the next few months. Simple folk? Ha!

Helped down from the carriage, she staggered up broad steps to the wide verandah. Two more lean dogs sprawled; a huge door was flung open, a pale rectangle of light.

As tired eyes accustomed to the dimness inside, she stared up at trophy walls lined with stuffed and mounted heads of dead animals. Huge horns, unforgiving eyes. As if they'd charged the walls and got stuck half-way through.

She was too light-headed to take in much else. Just soaring space, blessed coolness and a dry, sharp smell of wood.

Then, voices from the verandah and shadowy shapes, dark and silent, slipping in, out. Bearing bags and boxes, carrying trays, offering refreshment.

'Sorry,' someone said, but Coop was still away. Sorry? Oh, she was in no rush to renew that acquaintance. Too much smoke still hung over her and Coop's battlefield.

What she needed now, was rest. Yes, a few tranquil days to recover from those gruelling weeks, months of travelling. After that, she might *just* feel strong enough to cope with Mister Poker-Face Cooper and his I-dare-you-to-smile-at-me stare.

After all, this was what she'd been looking forward to, wasn't it? Restful naps in the afternoon. Gentle walks exploring the ranch. Long conversations, trying to find out what had lured Leonie here.

Eating, sleeping, pottering. Yes, that was the plan.

'Mees. Please, this way.'

Someone came to guide her across the tiled floor, up the wide staircase, to a huge high-ceilinged room with lots of windows. Her travelling bag was already there, but no steamer trunk. Her vain hope that it would somehow have miraculously found its own way and arrived ahead, was quashed.

Bother.

Coffee on a tray, black and hot. Nods, smiles. Then, the door quietly closing. Silence. Relieved to be alone, Gerry sank into a chair next to the big bed and looked round.

Well-made furniture, burnished with age. Mexican rugs on dark-stained floorboards. A door leading off and beyond, a glimpse of a huge bathtub - deep and long, the biggest she'd ever seen. For giants, obviously. A whole house, built just for them.

Exhaustion hit her then, like a hammer blow. Her poor body, stiff from travelling, felt as if it belonged to someone else; teeth were like flannel. She was too tired to wash off caked dust, brush hair or even take off her crumpled clothes.

What next?

Looking longingly at the mighty feather bed with its carved mahogany bed-head, she stroked the quilt. It was like something out of *The Princess and the Pea*. All she really wanted, was to lie down on it and stay there for a very long time.

For a while, she sat staring into space. Then ignoring good manners and her unpacked bag, she threw herself across the bed's creaking springs, to sleep, sleep, sleep.

Drowning in feathers, she dreamed of Leonie.

CHAPTER THIRTEEN

'Never express strong opinions. Keep them to yourself.'
A Woman's Way, 1923

Gerry woke with a start, to wind bang-banging the shutters at the window.

The first light of dawn just filtering through, and she could dimly hear the thud of horses' hoofs, a barking dog and people shouting outside.

Where in the world was she? Bedsprings whined as she rolled over, rubbing her eyes. The enormous bare room, was still dark and shadowy. Armoire, chest, chair. And no idea at all, of the time.

Bang! Bang! That banging again. Why so loud? Not *shutters,* the door! Hard fists and knuckles.

'Wait! One moment. Coming, coming!' Sliding off the big bed, knees sagging, Gerry staggered towards the door.

'Mizz Chiledexter. You about ready?'

Cooper. Already jacketed, booted, and holding one of those huge Stetson hats they all wore. Taller, broader and fiercer than she remembered, too. Something she *did* remember, was that look. The one that said something was coming.

Ready! For what? Blurry with sleep, she blinked. 'Is it *very* late?'

Too late to do anything about her appearance, that was for sure. Unwashed and dishevelled, she was still wearing the creased and gritty travelling suit from the day before. So confident then too, that she'd looked her very best in it.

A hand went to her hair, which seemed to have taken on a life of its own and was sticking out, in unexpected places. 'How long have I been sleeping?'

'It's five o'clock.'

'In the morning!' A yelp of shock. Something terrible must have happened. Some awful tragedy, bad news from home! 'Whatever's wrong?' Her hand went to her throat. 'What's happened?'

'Nothing's *happened*. We need to get a head's start, that's all. This is a working ranch. We start before daybreak.'

No smile of encouragement, not one single word of welcome.

Wild-eyed, Gerry stared. 'Not me, Mister Cooper, not *today*. I've been travelling, you know, for weeks and weeks.' What did he want from her? 'When I've had time to recover, I'll be glad to come and have a look round. I wouldn't want to get in the way. Not today, not when you're busy.'

'Are you for real? You think no-one's got anything better to do than show you around? You're a partner in this now, lady, not some mollycoddled visitor. I'm still trying to catch up from being away and it's spring roundup.' He paused. 'You know what roundup is, don't you?'

As if he was talking to an exceptionally slow child. 'Mister Cooper ...'

'Don't start mistering me, it's Coop!'

'Well, look, Mist ... look ... um, as I just said, as soon as I'm fully rested, I'll be more than happy to do my fair share of the ... ' *What* was it? *Rounding*! 'But not on my first day, not at this ungodly hour. Anyway ... isn't today Sunday?'

'There are no Sundays, west of Alabama.'

'I'm far too tired.'

'I couldn't care less.'

Gerry stared, speechless.

'Look, lady.' He laid down his ace card with a flourish. 'It wasn't my idea you come here, was it? You're the one who wanted to travel hundreds of miles to have a *look* - as you put it - rather than sell to me.'

'I couldn't sell. My aunt didn't want me to.'

'There were ways round.'

Oh, that's right, Gerry thought, *there were.* There'd been absolutely no need for her to come here, none at all. Everyone had been against it. No, it had been her own pig-headed decision, some wild idea, that it was what Leonie had wanted. Leonie, yes! Dead for almost a year!

And a frustrated Cooper had woken her at dawn, just to make that point. This was cave-man stuff. Well, you bully, she thought. You ... you cad. 'I have a perfect right to be here.'

'You've a right to stay out of my hair, that's what you've got a right to! Did you think you'd just be sitting around, sewing and reading and such?'

No, but she hadn't expected it to be like the army, either. She was tired and dirty; she wanted tea and sympathy. What she didn't have, of course, was a leg to stand on, and they both knew it.

As ye sow, she reminded herself wearily, so shall ye reap, or whatever that discouraging little proverb said. 'Is there any chance that you could leave me alone today, and start shouting at me tomorrow?'

'You wanted to be a rancher. Get used to it.' He was like granite.

Perhaps this was how he trained his animals, those cows and the horses. Treat them rough and they soon came to heel.

'All right.' To her horror, she felt her eyes smart. *Oh, don't you dare! Don't dare cry in front of him!* Because once she started, she knew she wouldn't be able to stop.

'What's that?'

She passed a hand over her face. He'd made his point. Resisting or complaining would only add to it. 'You're ... yes. I'll get ready.'

Leaning against the doorway, he gave her a slow appraising stare. 'What the hell happened to your hair?'

'I cut it.'

Silence.

'It's called a shingle.'

Pause.

'It's all the mode now, at home.'

The expression on his face said it all.

'Well, I have to tell you now,' he said, frowning at her pink appliquéd cloche on the back of the chair. 'The kind of doodads you're used to wearing back home are way too hot and fancy for a small town.'

Gerry tried to blot out thoughts of her Tagel straw, trimmed with faded roses, hopefully soon to arrive, in its own dear little hat box. Along with her cabin trunk, stuffed with absurdly chic clothes - tea dresses, chiffon, silks and lace. And feathers, sourced by Leonie from the best French plumassiers, and gloves and bags. All the latest conceits in accessories.

Stupid! What had she been thinking?

Smoothing her rumpled jacket, she pictured Hallie Kittrell's immaculate riding outfit. Not all the women here wore prairie cottons and braided their hair, did they? Even if they did, she'd no intention of joining them.

'This,' she said, feeling a faint flush of colour, 'is my travelling suit.'

'Uh-huh.'

'Just give me fifteen minutes to bathe and change.' A pause. Then, 'Will we walk?'

'Walk! There's no ranch worth a spit here you can *walk* around.'

'Well, I haven't ridden for years.'

'You'll soon get the knack,' he said, sourly. 'Once you've taken a toss or two. Have you *got* clothes for riding?'

'I've barely any clothes with me. My trunk and portmanteau ...' she waved a despairing hand, '... got lost, on the way here.'

What *did* she have in her travelling bag? Underwear, silk stockings. Small framed photograph of Leonie, plus a few meagre accessories - evening gloves, a red taffeta bow. All utterly useless, all things he'd be sure to sneer at.

'Well, we can't leave you wrapped in a blanket.' He eyed her narrowly. 'I guess Alba can find you something. It'll be rough and noisy and hot as hell out there.'

'Can't I choose which clothes to wear?'

He shrugged. 'The chaps are optional.'

'Chaps?'

'To stop your thighs chafing.'

She stared. 'So, what will I be doing at the ... out there? Working with the animals?'

'I wouldn't trust you anywhere near my animals. You will be looking. That's what you're here for, isn't it? You will be learning.'

Gerry felt some small measure of relief.

'Let's get one thing straight right away, shall we? Whatever that damn will or any bossy woman says, I run the Circle-O. Everything in it and on it. Understand?'

'Rather like us British? Ruling our Empire.'

'Yes, but we don't wear bucket hats and long, woollen underwear to do it. Best eat something first,' he flung over his shoulder, turning away. 'The north range is a fair piece from here. Scoot can wait and ride out with you. Just don't keep anyone hanging around too long.'

Gerry closed the door and leaned against it, listening.

The clatter of boots on stairs and tiled floor, a slammed door. Outside, the creak of leather, and voices raised in a shout, as riders mounted up. After that, nothing. Silence.

Day one. Round one.

She went to the mirror and stared at herself, red-eyed. Oh, Lord.

CHAPTER FOURTEEN

'Never throw yourself at a man. Let him come to you.'
The Bachelor Girl's Handbook, 1924

While Gerry bathed - even the towels were huge and rough - she heard the door open, close. A pile of things was left on a chair.

Canvas pants, too stiff to pull on, with hard seams and rivets. One of those wide-brimmed hats and crumpled shirt with a big brown stain, that made her wrinkle her nose. Boots with heels. Everything huge, everything baggy, everything drowning her.

Dressing, she pulled another face at the mirror. Ugh, she'd aged at least ten years in the night. Well, thank you, Cooper. Hopping around, she tried to pull on the boots. Hurry, hurry! Folding back sleeves, hoisting trailing pants high, she tripped down the staircase to the huge hall below.

Floor to ceiling wood gave it a warm and welcoming look in daylight, except for all those dead animal heads on the walls.

Gerry stopped to peer up. The deer, the coyote and mountain

lion, with their deathly snarls, goggled glassily back.

Beneath the stuffed heads, a line of sepia photographs, of uniformed men and moody-looking bulls with huge horns. And paintings. Men in buckskin, men in battle, men with flags, attacking something or other. Glorious moments on the battlefield. Pioneer days?

Only one prim daguerreotype was of a woman, and she was hatchet-faced with thin lips, wearing a black alpaca dress and poke bonnet, and staring back at Gerry with as much disdain as those stuffed animals.

A house for warriors and hunters? Oh yes, with their loot all round the walls. It even *smelled* male, didn't it? Of leather and dogs, brandy, cigars.

That wide staircase appeared to divide the house into two parts, huge doors to left and right, everywhere silent, everywhere empty.

Gerry hesitated, one ear cocked for footsteps. Nothing. No murmur of voices, no sign of Scoot or anyone else.

Buffalo eyes glowered beadily down and watched her dithering. Coyote ears listened to her sighs. Texas, she thought, probably hated ditherers. Was this what Cooper wanted? For her to feel in the way, so she'd sign his wretched papers and scuttle back home.

But then, a delicious smell. Coffee? Her nose leading the way, she click-clacked through double doors to a room of dark polished furniture, a table that could have seated at least twenty and that faint, stale fragrance of cigars.

No Scoot here, either. Just jams in huge bowls, baskets of

bread rolls and places set, as if a large party was expected. Not unlike an English country house in the early morning.

Gerry stared up, narrow-eyed, at the gilt-framed portrait dominating the far wall. Another man. Hauntingly handsome, blue-eyed, with patrician face. Frank O'Rourke? Must be.

He returned her gaze coldly, without welcome. He didn't want her here, either.

Pulling out a chair, she sat down at the table. What next? She was starting to feel like Alice, dropped down the rabbit-hole.

'Señorita?'

Gerry jumped.

No white rabbit, just a man, all in black, solemn, dignified. 'Buenos días.' He inclined his head.

'Oh, good morning. I'm … Miss Chiledexter. From England?'

'Sí, señorita.' A small bow. 'Bienvenido.' Very formal.

He disappeared, to return with a huge white plate held out for her approval.

Gerry stared at a thick grey slab of meat, of Brobdingnagian proportions, with congealed egg on top. Breakfast? 'Oh … no, thank you. Really, I couldn't.' Even the smell made her queasy.

The plate was set firmly down in front of her.

'Um, gracias … ' she extended a weak hand.

'Cesar, señorita.' He had a fine-boned Spanish face.

'Gracias, Cesar!'

Gerry waited until he'd left the room before trying to saw

up the steak. It was like cutting wood with a pin, and when she finally managed to separate a tiny morsel, she couldn't chew it or swallow, without a gallon of water to wash it down.

Even breakfast here was big and intimidating. Giving up, she buttered a small roll, then helped herself to several cups of sweet black coffee.

So, where *was* Scoot? She would wait. Surely he'd come and find her, when he was ready?

She sat, and waited. Waited and waited.

The table was cleared, the cloth changed. More coffee brought.

'Scoot?' Gerry said finally, to Cesar.

A blank look, and then, 'Scoot go, señorita.' A shrug. 'Go … roundup.'

The boy had gone without her. Was everyone here trying to wear her down? Well, she would *not* get annoyed or let it upset her, not on her first day.

'Cesar?'

'Sí, señorita?'

'Now, I go,' she declared, with far more bravado than she felt. 'I go … roundup?'

Cesar frowned; he looked uneasy. 'Please to wait, señorita. Un minuto.' He hurried out.

Gerry scraped back her chair and went after him, hitching up her pants. Out of the huge front door, onto the verandah, where she stood in the pink light of dawn, gazing around at all the things she'd missed, the night before.

Corrals and barns. A huddle of bunkhouses. Sun-baked

adobes and array of smaller, ramshackle buildings. A vast sprawling estate, almost the size of a small town. Gulp. And she *owned* half of this, half of all of it.

A Mexican boy came hurrying up the wide wooden steps, high-heeled boots tap-tapping. About sixteen years old, she guessed, and already tall and broad-shouldered, with the olde-worlde sort of good manners she was beginning to expect from everyone here. Everyone except Cooper. And Scoot.

He took off his hat.

'Buenos días, Mizz Chiledexter.' Another soft musical voice, a small bow. 'My name … it is Angel.'

'You speak English!'

'Sí, señorita.' He nodded, shyly. 'Better in Spanish, I think, but …'

'I want to ride out to the roundup, Angel.'

A blank look at her over-sized riding clothes.

'Can you find a horse for me?'

'No, no. Cesar say …' He swung round, as if expecting someone else to be there, to accompany her. 'Not alone! You cannot do.'

'Why not?' she said, with forced gaiety. 'Just point the way, and …' a vague wave towards miles and miles of wild Texas plain '… and I will ride. Off I will go.'

His startled eyes followed the direction of her flapping hand.

'Scoot? Scoot was supposed to take me, but he seems to have gone.'

At this, Angel muttered something in Spanish, something

with a stream of rolled r's that sounded disagreeable.

'Is there a gentle sort of horse for me? I'm not very comfortable on horseback.'

Another blank look. 'Con ... for ... ble?'

'I'm used to ... well, just jogging along.'

'Yo no comprendo, señorita.'

A demonstration. 'You see? Jogging?'

Silence hung between them for a few moments more. Dark eyes regarded her, uneasily. Then, 'I take.' He sighed, heavily. 'You come, with me.'

Two horses were brought out and saddled.

Gerry prayed that the huge leggy one, flinging up its head and skittering as they drew near, was for Angel. She eyed the other, hopefully. A stocky, Texas cow pony, which looked as if it should have been put out to pasture, years ago. Old and steady

That was more like it. A clip-clop rather than a gallop. It cocked its ears towards her, as she nervously patted its neck.

The boy insisted she put on the hat and pull the brim well down as they rode away. The sun was now burning off dawn mist, the wind gently stirring.

She'd never been much of a horsewoman, and the uneven ground and high-pommelled Western saddle made riding hard. Both Angel and the little cow pony though, were patient and forgiving, in spite of being forced to stick to her own preferred riding pace - slightly quicker than walking, but slower than bicycling.

They barely spoke, except for Angel to warn of a pothole or

clump of mesquite. The only other sounds were horses' hoofs on hard-baked earth and an occasional disturbed bird, wheeling into flight.

Two miles. Three, four. They seemed to be following no obvious trail, no signposts, tracks or fences. Just that great expanse of sky and prairie stretching for hundreds of miles, in every direction. Distances to make a person dizzy.

The boy kept stopping, waiting patiently for her to catch up. Once, he offered water from a flask and she swallowed it gratefully. Throat was dry, face hot and the insides of her thighs already rubbed raw.

Why on earth had she turned her nose up at those thingies ... those chaps?

The sun was *beating* down now, the sky a boiling blue. No trees or shade anywhere, just wind making the grass ripple in waves. No-one had mentioned the wind, had they? This scorching southwest blast. Didn't it ever stop?

How much further? she wondered, skirting the corpse of a small dead animal.

They heard their destination before they could see it.

Round-up. Rolling hides, rising dust and the ground shaking as thousands of hooves hammered down on it. Miles and miles of longhorns packed close together, a slow-moving mass stretching as far as the eye could see, buzzards hovering over them.

Nothing like the animals Gerry was used to in England, either, those standing peaceably in pastures, munching grass.

These beasts, eighteen hundredweight or so of prime beef with huge horns, looked as if they'd eat you alive.

When she slid from her horse and Angel leaned down to say something, she could barely hear over the bawling, bellowing cattle.

'Please.' He pointed to an old man with a face like a withered apple, sitting on top of the high fence, heels of his boots hooked firmly round the rail. 'To stay here, just here. Stay with Gomez. Sí?'

Keep out of the way, in other words. Well, she was more than happy to oblige. She was already walking unsteadily, bow-legged.

As Angel turned to ride off, Scoot trotted up on his own horse and Gerry saw the Mexican boy's eyes darken, as he lashed out with a torrent of Spanish.

'Okay, okay,' Scoot said sullenly. 'Don't get your feathers up.'

Another blast of Spanish.

Expecting the younger boy to shrug this off, Gerry was astonished to see Scoot stare at his boots and blush - a scarlet wave starting in his neck and rolling up to the very tips of his ears. Close to tears, apparently, he drew his sleeve across his face as he trotted away.

No chance to dwell on that, or anything else.

Gomez helped Gerry haul herself up to a perch on top of the fence, and she clung on, wide-eyed, as riders swerved into the surging herd, separating animals and roping them. When she started to choke on the dust, he solemnly handed her a handkerchief to cover her nose and mouth.

It looked exciting. Gerry *felt* excited, even though she had no idea why anyone was doing what they were doing. She wasn't likely to get any answers from Gomez, either.

Men on foot ran through the dust cloud, wrestling, bawling, struggling calves to the ground and burning them to make a mark. Did it hurt? It looked so cruel. Still, the shouts, roars, all that broiling passion and muscular power made her pulse race.

Cattle and more cattle - to the north, east and the west of them. More cows than she'd seen in her life, at terrifyingly close quarters, too. Men on horseback, men on foot - the riders, ropers, throwers. A sort of gladiatorial circus, with every man confident of his own part and skill.

Gerry half-expected to see Pharaoh's chariots somewhere out there, in the middle.

An hour or more of this eye-popping spectacle. Roiling, heaving, bellowing cattle and skull-splitting noise.

It must now be high noon, Gerry decided. Sun, fierce and blinding, beat down on them, relentlessly. There was no shade, and in spite of the huge hat, her face was scarlet.

Knees and ankles were sore from hanging onto the fence; head and eyes ached and fatigue seemed to be spreading through her entire body. Even breathing was hard work.

'This heat,' she murmured, feeling strangely lightheaded, 'it's so ...'

'This ain't nothing, ma'am,' someone said, passing by. 'Wait 'til June!'

Feeling herself sway, she clutched the fence and scanned the scene all around her, the smell of sweat and leather. It was starting to look like Dante's missing tenth circle of Hell.

How, she wondered later, had she been able to distinguish Cooper from all the others, amidst the dust and hoofs and horns? She wasn't sure.

Somehow she managed to pick him out of the noisy confusion and hustle - the tall figure, hat low over his eyes, who seemed to be commanding proceedings. That air of control and a certain elegance of riding, at one with his horse, a magnificent palomino.

A stunning mix of authority and showmanship; she couldn't help a grudging admiration.

At one point, she saw him ride headlong into the herd, swinging this way and that to scoop someone up who'd fallen amongst the inferno of choking dust and heaving flesh.

Whistles and shouts erupted all around. 'Close call, Coop! Whoo, nice job.' Gerry wanted to shout, too, but settled for a polite clap. After all, she was British.

Now that she'd spotted Coop though, her eyes kept being drawn back. The still, steady centre that everyone else orbited around. His authority was almost palpable. Like some sort of dazzling warrior leader, on his warhorse. No fear, no brakes.

From the midst of all the yelling, bawling and bellowing, the subject of her scrutiny suddenly galloped up, at whirlwind pace. Reining his horse in abruptly by the fence, sun reflecting in spur and stirrup, he shouted at Gerry.

His words were snatched away by the wind.

'Pardon?'

'I said, how the hell did you get out here?' Face streaked with sweat and dust, he pushed his hat back. 'Scoot said you weren't ready.'

Gerry swatted flies away with her hand. 'Angel brought me.'

'Angel's got no time for nurse-maiding; there's too much work for him at the ranch!'

'It wasn't his fault,' Gerry said, uncomfortably aware that all around, men were listening, with interest.

'I say no do.' Angel shrugged. 'She do.'

'That's right. He's right. I ... insisted.'

Cooper's eyes, flint grey, were level with Gerry's. 'Yeah, you're pretty good at that.'

'You said I should come and ....'

'Help. Well, you're not. Look, if you cause any damage to anything or anyone while you're here, I'm gonna hold you personally responsible.'

'Is that a threat?'

'You bet your ass it is.'

Closing her eyes, Gerry took a deep, dizzying breath. She had never, in her entire life, been as hot as this. Like a chicken, on a spit, being slowly roasted over a roaring fire. 'Mister Cooper?'

Someone sniggered.

'Coop!' Her shirt soaked with sweat, her breath coming fast and shallow. 'Please.' She felt sick. 'Let's not ...'

He sat, tall and remote in the saddle, impossible to reach.

A dark impassive shape blocking out the sun. He Who Must Be Obeyed.

'Don't …' Gerry tried to find the words. She started to move her mouth, but suddenly, the ground tipped up, towards her.

'Hey! You okay?'

Sun sizzled, the sky rolled and she pitched forward off the fence.

A felled tree.

She was flat on her back, white light blinding her.

A dark vision loomed. Stricken faces bent over her.

'What's the matter with her? She jest done and toppled over.'

'Prolly sun-sick.' Someone fanned her with a hat. 'Too damn delicate. Fainted, I reckon.'

'I don't …' Disorientated, Gerry tried to struggle up. 'Faint. I never … '

She was pushed gently back down. 'Stay still. Don't move 'til we've checked you over.'

Cooper.

She lay weakly back, breathing through her mouth to shut out stench of burned flesh and singed cow. She could taste blood.

CHAPTER FIFTEEN

'Always be cheerful and gay and sunny-tempered.'
The Single Girls' Guide to Matrimony, 1923

'Knew she'd be trouble the minute I clapped eyes on her. Skinny as a bird dog, with those fussy duds! Why'd she have to come here?'

Stretched out in the tail of the bouncing wagon, with the bellowing and mooing far behind, Gerry had been asking herself the same question, over and over. This rough, primitive place.

She had no friends here; she couldn't speak the language. Now, she was sick. And that stupid dream of following in her aunt's footsteps?

For goodness sake, what had Leonie found to like here? Hadn't she fallen in love with Texas, the moment she'd arrived? Glamorous, fun-loving Leonie! It made no sense.

'Weak ankles! Ha, jest you wait. She's gonna keep keeling over an' we'll have to lug her back from every which place in a cart.'

Brassy blue sky rolled by overhead. Pitiless sun blazed down. No shade, beyond the brim of her hat. Closing her eyes, she saw darting red spots and felt even more sick now, as well as woozy.

'What does she *want*, fer pity's sake. I mean, nobody asked her to come here, did they?' That shrill voice again, raised against the wind. 'Jest wants to take a look, that's what Coop said. Ain't doing much looking now, is she? An' I don't care what anyone says about having to be pole-ite an' all. I was *told* to be pole-ite to Miss Fancypants Kittrell an' look where that got me.'

'Oh, quit it.' A heavily-accented Spanish growl. 'Quit belly-aching!'

'She don't like me, anymore'n ... ow ouch! That *hurt*!'

With painful effort, Gerry raised her throbbing head a few inches to peer in the direction of the voices. The little dog, riding look-out, rumbled threateningly.

'Hear that? Even Lobo don't like her!'

'Huh! That dog, he just mean to everyone.'

A strong whiff of livestock came from the direction of two sweat-stained shirts, two hats pushed back. Scoot, ducking away and rubbing his shoulder. The other, taller one, trying to ruffle his hair, was Angel.

'Stop that, will ya! Just leave me alone!'

'Why, you nothing but great big bebé!'

Gerry sank back onto the sacking, putting up fingers up to explore her cheekbone. Swollen and painful, it was sticky with blood and she flapped circling flies away with a weak hand.

There'd been talk back there of getting a doctor, but when Cooper had come close to examine her, she'd spat out some grit, given a panicky squeak and said, no really, no need, she was quite alright. Yes, perfectly well.

And she must have sounded convincing, because they'd all looked relieved and said that she'd been lucky. A battered face, bruised arm and knee? Yeah. Very, very lucky.

The trouble was, it had been a lie, hadn't it? One that was proving to be a big mistake.

Because now, in the back of the wagon, sore all over and bracing herself against the thump-thump-thump, as they bounced from pothole to pothole - she was not all right, not right at all. Weak and giddy, and with a really bad pain in one of her legs.

And whenever she tried to move, the pain got stronger and started spreading out, in waves.

'Howdy, ma'am. Pleasure meeting you. I'm Doc Hyde.'

The person taking Gerry's hand in a bone-crushing grip, wasn't anything like any doctor she'd met before. Certainly not Doctor Emmett, from Lower Shepney Market, with his eye-glasses, mutton-chop whiskers and strong whiff of antiseptic.

This one was young and tall, with a conspicuous smell of outdoors and horse and cigars about him. No sign of stetho-scope or black bag.

'You often faint?' he asked, a cool hand on her wrist.

'Never. I've *never* fainted before. The sun was in my eyes, that's all.'

Shaking his head, he held a palm to her forehead. 'Heat's mighty fierce here, y'know. Knocks you right off your feet, you don't give it enough respect. Hmm, not much meat and muscle on these bones, is there?'

Feeling weepy and overwhelmed, Gerry snuffled, 'Usually ... I'm strong as an ox.'

'Now, now, ma'am, don't go upsetting yourself.'

His tone was so warm and friendly, that she gulped back a wail.

'I'm sorry, so sorry, doctor. It's just ... oh ... would you mind ... over there, my handkerchief ... oh, I feel... I ... oh, so *upset*.' She wiped her eyes, those shameful stinging tears.

'Want to tell me about it?'

'Why ever did I come here!' Sniff. 'So stupid. Everyone told me, they *said* it was a mistake. But I just wanted ... you know ... to see for myself, that was all, and ...' Gulp. 'I just ... it's not *right* ... I ... oh, I want to go home!'

'Sure you do. You've had a real bad shock. An itty bitty fever now, too.'

'This p-place ... it's not even on any maps!'

'Yeah, we kinda keep it a secret.'

'Well, I don't like Texas, not one bit. And Mister Cooper's so sneery. He hates me!'

'Coop! Nah, Coop don't hate anyone.'

'He doesn't want me here. Even his horrible dog doesn't like me.'

Doctor Hyde patted Gerry's hand and pulled back the coverlet.

'This stuff takes time, that's all. You'll soon win him over.'

'Who? Mister C-Cooper?'

'No, ma'am. The dog. But I guess same goes for Texas.'

He bound a splint to her leg, smoothed soothing oil on her face. 'My advice? Give it time. You gonna have plenty of that, with your leg up this way. Try to enjoy the place, leastways while you're still here.'

He edged round her travelling bag - spilling its meagre contents of silk, lace and ribbonned underwear - on his way to the door. 'Wow, that the hat I've heard so much about?' Her little cloche still lay on top. 'Sure is a piece. Looks like somethin' you'd wear in town on Saturday night, to start a fight.'

A weak smile from Gerry.

'You just gotta take Texas straight, ma'am, like bourbon.'

He went out to speak to a person pacing up and down outside, leaving Gerry, who'd never tasted bourbon in her life, still sniffing.

What did *he* know, she thought, eyes still smarting. Anyway, who did he think he was? Some sort of Texan philosopher?

A bass murmur of conversation outside the door, then a soft knock before it opened again.

'How're you feeling?' Frowning down at her from the foot of the bed, Coop sucked in his breath. 'Ouch! That's gonna be one hell of a black eye.'

He was still wearing clothes from the roundup, shirt open at the throat, dust-covered pants and boots. A strong whiff of horse and cow came with him into the room.

Silence.

Gerry didn't trust herself to speak. She was tempted to pull the covers up over her head. *Go away.*

'Good news, anyhow.' Fists were pushed deeper into his pockets. 'Doc said you'll feel light-headed for a while, but that fetlock's not broken.'

'Pardon?'

'No real damage. Concussion and the bone's cracked, is all. Keep the splint on, leg raised, it should heal just fine.'

'But what did you ... my *fetlock*?'

'Just repeating what Doc said, I guess. He don't have too many human patients.'

Gerry struggled up, the over-sized shirt slipping off one shoulder. 'What do you mean! Isn't he a proper doctor?'

'Sure is. Animal doctor. Real important feller round here.'

'Not ... a *veterinarian*!' She stared, appalled. 'A person who treats cows and ... and pigs and sheep?'

'Yip. Horses first and foremost, of course, but most anything with four legs. A better man never bled a mule.'

'But that's just *terrible*! Passing himself off as a ... a proper physician. It's probably not even ethical!'

'Count yourself lucky. He shoots horses in your condition.'

Gerry felt like shooting herself. 'I told him ...' Oh, Lord. She pressed a hand to her head. 'I said ...'

What *had* she said? Good grief, and what was that smelly stuff he'd put on her face? Horse liniment? Had he even washed his *hands*? She was shaking.

'But you said, Doc. You called him that, I heard you.'

'That's his name. Short for Dockery ... Dockery Hyde.' A defensive note came into his voice. 'Look, he was in the neighbourhood. It would have taken three, four days to get Doc Kitson here.'

Breathing hard, Gerry slumped back onto tangled sheets and stared at the ceiling. '*Mister* Cooper ...' Lips were stiff, she felt confused and sweaty.

'Coop!'

'Well. I'm not going to be much use to you now, am I? I'm not going to be able to help.' She fingered her swollen cheek and the lump, like a goose egg, on her head, that someone seemed to be hitting, with a brick. 'With that ... the roundup.'

'We could maybe wheel you out to mend a few fences.' Coop's face was blank. 'Here, try this.' He held out a glass. 'Lemonade. Cesar made it fresh.'

Gerry's hand shook as she took a sip, and he sighed. 'You'll need tincture of arnica for that eye. Look, it's my living, that's all. I needed you to understand how it is out here, to see what I'm dealing with.'

Oh, she understood all right. These people - a bunch of bullies, the whole horrible gang of them. 'Did you have to be so unpleasant *quite* so quickly?'

'I find it kinda saves time.'

A slant of sunlight showed dust specks floating gently in the air. No sound except the buzz of crickets and distant, unconcerned voices, outside.

Tears threatened again and Gerry's throat closed up. 'Well,

I just want to say ... to tell you now, that as soon as I'm well enough, I intend to leave.' She lifted her chin 'Yes, I shall go home. To England.'

'Fingers crossed, then,' Coop muttered.

'And I hope you're satisfied.' Her voice trailed away, exhausted

'Well. Not exactly.'

'Pardon?'

'Not unless you're intending to sell back your share of the ranch, before you go.'

'I can't *do* that.'

'You can.'

'Well, I won't.' Gerry's voice was husky. 'My aunt wanted me to wait six months.'

'I don't want to shock your English sensibilities, but your aunt ... is dead.'

Gerry's lips tightened. *It's what Leonie wanted, what she asked me to do.*

'Bad news, then.' Walking to the window, Coop gazed out. 'Doc says it's likely to take at least six weeks for that leg to heal. Unless you're planning on hopping your way home. If you started out now, you'd likely reach Jericho Wells in ... what? Maybe, a fortnight?'

Oh who cared, Gerry thought, what that old horse doctor said? She'd probably be left with a permanent limp from his mistreatment, some awful lopsided gait.

Wait a minute. *Six?* Six *weeks!*

Another huge fly buzzed into the room and started circling

the bed. It seemed attracted to her face. She flapped it away, with a faint self-pitying cough. 'But I don't *want* to wait that long!'

'That,' Coop said, 'would make two of us.'

Limp and exhausted, Gerry sank back on to the pillows. She was losing her hold on things; they were slipping, out of control.

An omen. Another one. Back in England, something had definitely been urging her to come, hadn't it? Almost *leading* her here. She'd felt such a powerful pull.

Now, only two days after stepping off the train in Jericho Wells, something else seemed to be telling her to leave. Oh, why didn't the Fates make up their minds?

Her eyes started swimming again.

'Are you going to carry on with this wailing?' Coop edged towards the door. 'Better buck up, would be my advice. Get the female hysterics over with, real quick. Face it, you're stuck here, and nothing you can do about it.'

He left the room without a backwards glance.

Gerry knew just what he meant. *He* was stuck with *her*. Well with any luck, she would die in the night and save everyone a lot of trouble.

CHAPTER SIXTEEN

'Take up a hobby. Embroidery,
knitting or paper-flower making.'
Heart-to-Heart column, 1922

That early morning quarrel, the ride, the heat, the fall. Then,
a fierce, all-consuming infection. Taken together, they almost
did manage to deal Gerry a deathly blow.

For days, she tossed feverishly in her bed. Sleeping, dreaming, waking. As if she were still on that ship with a heaving sea,
a force nine gale. Up, down, up, up ... *dooown*.

When she woke, she could never remember what the
dreams had been about. Ghosts. Shadowy people she didn't
recognize, telling her things she couldn't understand.

Every so often, gentle taps at the door. 'Mees Chil-exter? I
fetch you something?'

And once, 'Gerardina?' A tall figure in a flapping coat
looming over her.

She shrank back.

'You hungry, thirsty? You must try and eat, keep your
strength up.'

Yes, yes. She was fading, slipping away. Soon, she'd be thin as a pin.

She would never be well enough to leave this place. She would stay, for ever and ever. One day, they'd look round that door and find her, crumbled to dust. R.I.P.

As fever ebbed, there were nightmares. Some took her back to India - to thick brown rivers swollen with monsoon rains, to the ceaseless caw of crows and smell of dung-fires.

When she woke, limp and sweating, heat pressing down, her cheeks were wet. What was she doing here, with these awful people? She lay awake, wide-eyed, anxious. *Why did I come*? she asked the darkness?

The answer always came clearly enough. *'You know.'* And that voice again. *'I want you here, my darling.'*

She felt such a fierce longing for England, for Prim and the bookshop, crackling fires, tea in china cups, that it became an almost physical ache.

It would be spring at home, now, wouldn't it? Verges waist-high with cow parsley, sweet dog-roses in the hedgerows, skylarks floating. All heavenly and hey-nonny-no.

Make the most of being here, that man Hyde had said, that awful *pretend* doctor. The most of what? The sort of place where a man's spit is his handshake? Where it takes a long, long time to say not very much?

Please, let me get home.

But. But. If she left now, how would she ever find out what happened between Leonie and Frank O'Rourke? She just couldn't rid herself of the feeling that it was something she was meant to do.

Every day, at dawn, Gerry woke to a distant cockerel crowing and men's voices outside. Muffled shouts, dogs barking, clatter of hooves.

Then silence settled, like a shroud. While they were away, the house and everything in it seemed suspended, held in a sort of trance until they came back.

She began telling the time by the men's boots. Clack, clack, clack, when they went out; clatter, clatter, at sundown when everyone came back.

But neither the mealtime bell that shattered the silence outside nor the clamour of the gong inside, meant much to Gerry. Barely a morsel had passed her lips in days.

Tea. How she longed for tea.

One day, having asked for a mirror, she stuck out her tongue, and saw that it was green. Face white as a ghost and huge dark circles under her eyes. Like a cave dweller, she thought, or some kind of animal, tucked away in a hole, for hibernation.

Or a cow. Oh, Lord. She was turning into one of those cows!

Days merged into nights. Shutters were kept closed; the light never seemed to change. Once, she came sharply awake and pulling the sheet to her chin, sat bolt upright, heart hammering.

A foot coming down on the boards of the floor!

Someone in her room? A dark shape. Someone standing in the shadows like a thief! Her spine prickled. She could ... yes ... she could hear their breathing!

Drawing in her own breath, not moving a muscle, her eyes slowly accustomed to the dimness.

Coop?

Another shiver of shock. Standing there in eerie half-light, his back against the door, he was staring round, with a sort of wary stillness. Looking. At *what*?

Scent. Colour. Drawers frothing with the few bits of lingerie that had arrived with her, frilly, lacy, ribbonned things? Drifts of silk.

But, what did he *want*, what was he doing in here? Whatever it was, seemed vaguely improper. A surreptitious check, perhaps, for signs of her rigor mortis?

Weak, helpless and unsure what to do or say, she waited. Then, 'What *is* it! Has something happened?'

His shadow detached itself from the wall. He met her eyes, his expression unreadable as ever. It seemed an age before he shook his head. 'I was ... I just never saw so many jars and bottles. Frills and ... things. That's all.'

As her pulse stopped pounding, Gerry tore her own eyes away. She'd taken comfort from arranging her few soft, feminine bits and pieces around the bare room. Coop's towering booted figure now looked completely out of place in it.

Baffled by the sudden glare of his attention and interest

in her things, she couldn't think of a thing to say. A few moments, and she cleared her throat, 'Did you ... you never had a sister?'

'Nope.'

'What about your mother? Wasn't her room something like this?'

'No idea. Never knew her.'

Gerry waited for an explanation. None came. Another confusing silence. Acutely conscious now, of her fine lawn nightgown sliding over one shoulder, she fixed eyes on Coop's belt, its steer head buckle gleaming in the half-light.

Then, when he moved to open the shutters, she saw that it was still only late evening, not the middle of the night. Heat was stifling. A sweet heady scent drifted in on dry wind, and the faint sound of someone somewhere, plucking a guitar.

'Here,' he said, carelessly casting books onto the bed. 'I brought you something to read.'

With unsteady hands, she spread them out. *Sense and Sensibility.* A copy of Shakespeare's sonnets. 'Are these yours?'

'When I have time. Frank was the real reader.'

'Mr O'Rourke? Really?'

'Yip. There's a whole library downstairs. While you're here, you should make use of it.'

She held a book up. 'Who's this?' Some pages had been marked with small feathers

'Walt Whitman? American poet, one of Frank's favourites. Mine, too.'

He turned to go, closing the door quietly behind him and

leaving Gerry at a loss. What was that all about? What had just happened?

She looked uneasily round at the few things she had with her, seeing what he'd seen. A few pots of cold cream. Scent bottle, her powder jar with its swansdown puff. The small, silver-framed photograph of her aunt.

Did this strange behaviour mean there'd been a shift in his attitude towards her, then? Was he feeling guilty?

The book she'd been holding fell open. *'Enough to merely be! Enough to breathe! Joy! Joy! All over joy!'* The phrase had been underlined, in pencil.

She thought about it longer than she'd meant to and felt a slight easing of tension. Still, it took some time before she was able to settle down again.

As she started to feel better, Gerry longed for conversation. With someone, anyone. Her only company came with the Mexican mother and daughter, padding in and out with food, cold drinks and little comforts, and helping her to bathe.

They were polite, but withdrawn, tending to her needs with shy nods, murmurs. Eyes were friendly, but they spoke little or no English. Communication was limited to baffled exchanges, mime and blank looks, like some strange game of charades.

It was only when they'd left the room that she heard them chatting. She tried to catch their words and remember them - all those short *a* sounds. After a week, she had at least managed to learn their names - Alba, the mother, and her pretty, flower-like daughter, Elena.

Why, Gerry wondered, had she never bothered to learn a foreign language? Leonie had set her usual example, of course, travelling the world with little more than a smile, a wave and gracious thanks for favours bestowed, in English.

Although she had managed to say, 'Yes, yes, I love it! I must have it!' in at least five different languages.

After so long in that room, dragging herself about like a dying fly, Gerry insisted that she was quite well enough now to be up and about.

A lie, of course. She was still weak, and wobbly as water. Several times when she'd tried to stand, she'd sagged against furniture and fallen over.

No matter. Her first glorious day of freedom, she hobbled through the enormous house in trailing over-sized pants, opening doors, peering inside. Except for servants, acknowledging her with respectful nods and then retreating, everywhere was silent, every room empty.

Parlour, morning room, dining room. No-one in any of them, just huge dark furniture, cowhide chairs. A men's den, full of hunting prints and yellowed maps, papers piled onto a desk. *Music* room? Yes, a grand piano standing proudly in the centre of it.

Running her hand over yellowing keys, Gerry tapped out a few notes. As an out-of-tune jangle echoed round the walls, she quickly replaced the lid.

Upstairs? To the galleried landing and all those rooms leading off - not so much bedrooms, as chambers - each with a picture on the wall of some hairy horned beast glaring out of bleak landscape.

What was she looking for? Clues, Gerry told herself. What were these people like? How did they live? A pity she couldn't do this sort of thing with Coop. Peer into his head to see what he was thinking. She'd give anything to know what was going on in his mind.

Only one massive door, at the end of the gallery, resisted when she pushed it. Locked, no sign of a key. Next to it, Coop's room. Poking her head round that door, seeing his things, she shrank quickly back and paused to catch her breath.

Had there *ever* been any female occupation in this house? A mother, wife? She'd looked in vain, for some small sign. A dropped earring or handkerchief, dusting of face-powder? Nothing, not even one single button or trailing thread.

It was as far removed from her world with Leonie, all scented warmth and flowers, as a monk's cell from a Parisian hat shop.

So, where had Leonie slept when she was here? What kind of clothes had she worn? Not canvas overalls, that was for sure, nor any old cotton wash dresses. She'd always insisted on dressing lavishly, whatever the time, place or occasion.

So far then, Gerry thought, she'd learned absolutely nothing. Nothing that answered any of her questions, anyway.

What's more, that ghost voice - if that's what it was - her aunt's voice in her head, had been silent for some time. Even though she'd listened and listened for it, willing it now, wanting it to come.

Where had it gone? For some inexplicable reason, a picture of that locked door, floated into her mind.

One locked door.

Flopping into a chair, a wave of fatigue washing over her, she stared out of the window. Dust, fierce sun, glaring blue sky. Another blazing Texas morning.

A distant clock chimed the half hour.

'One locked door. Just one?'

She let her head drop back. All that space outside, and her own horizons, horribly shrunk again. Confined to the house, like prison.

No neighbours. No friendly callers or cosy gossip. No shady garden full of flowers and bees. Nothing to do, except stare into space and watch time pass. Not a crumb of comfort anywhere.

Earlier, she'd found herself talking to those animal heads on the wall. Some looked fierce, some frightened, but none of them were any good at conversation.

That familiar childhood feeling settled on her again, of dislocation. The weight of not belonging, being an outsider. What am I doing here? she asked herself, pointlessly.

Once more, she tried to consult her aunt, via the voice in her head. No reply, still silent. Gone for good? The thought left her feeling bereft.

'One. Locked. Door.'

She hadn't seen Coop for days. He'd probably forgotten she existed. Why *was* it taking her so long for her to recover from a fall from a fence? Leonie wouldn't have slumped like this. She would have turned everything happening here on its head.

'One ... locked ... door!'

By now, she would have been wearing her most audacious dress and demanding that someone mix her a cocktail. One of her favourites, a White Lady. If no-one had known how to do it, she would have demonstrated –*'equal parts of this and that and lemon juice, sweetie. And shake, shake, shake, very cold.'*

Charming everyone, delighting them all.

Well, I'm here, Leonie. This is what you wanted, isn't it? Now what?

'Don't hunch, my darling.' The voice in her head, clear and loud this time. *'Lift your head. It makes you look confident, even if you don't feel it.'*

Then, a discovery.

Like a thirsty camel reaching the oasis, Gerry found the library.

When Coop had mentioned it, she'd pictured ... what? A few rickety bookcases, with tattered dictionaries and an old almanac? A pile of cattlemen's periodicals, thumbed copies of the *Breeder's Gazette*.

Not this - a room full of leather-backed books with gold titled spines, most looking as if they'd never been read. Macauley, Milton and a Complete Shakespeare. The Greek poets and brothers Grimm. Austen, Brontë.

Who had collected all these?

Frank O'Rourke. That's what Coop had said, hadn't he? This was Frank's library. *'Frank was the real reader.'*

The air smelled dead and full of dust. Flinging back the shutters, Gerry let sunshine stream in. Then, falling back into a worn leather chair, her favourites in her lap, she read and read, losing all sense of time.

Leafing through tissue-thin pages of Walt Whitman's *Song of Myself*, thoughts drifted back to Frank O'Rourke. What sort of character was he? And how on earth had he managed to make such an impression on Leonie?

Had they been lovers? That must have been what all this was about. One book slid to the floor. Picking it up where it had fallen open, she smoothed the gold-edged page. It had been marked with a pressed flower and a lock of hair, tied with twisted ribbon.

'O Love, what hours were thine and mine,
In lands of palm and southern pine'

Leonie's hair? Definitely her colour, and only slightly faded. Who'd marked that page and what did it mean? Sighing, she shut the book on her finger. How would she *ever* be able to make sense of this? No clues. Just secrets, lost codes.

Few of her aunt's beaux ever seemed to have brains. They had plenty of other attractions, of course. Vast estates, money, motor-cars. Magnetic eyes. Some even had wives.

All those hostages to fortune. Dancers, painters.

That Indian prince, whom the schoolgirl Gerry had watched in fish-eyed wonder, standing on his head in the parlour. The White Russian émigré. The Italian tenor, on one knee amid scutch-grass in the garden, singing an aria from Puccini, molto forte.

Unfortunately, his rows with Leonie had been equally operatic.

What about Frank O'Rourke? Had he ever had a wife? Leonie, of course, had never married. 'Married men always fall in love with other people, my darling,' she'd said. 'I should know.'

Dear Leonie. Her love life had been intense, dramatic and often, inappropriate. She'd gone wherever her heart had led, sometimes trailing clouds of controversy and the wreckage of her passions across several continents.

Mulling this over made Gerry's head heavy. As sun baked the books, and dust motes danced in the air, eyelids drooped and her head lolled to one side.

Jerked awake, a shadow at the door made her sit up with a start. A flickering figure that held out an arm and swung two fingers in her direction. 'Bang,' it said.

Gunslinger's draw.

'Oh. Hello, Scoot.'

No reply. The boy's expression was sullen, fine hair all over his face. His annoying little dog panted at his heels.

Gerry rubbed her eyes. 'Not riding out, this morning?'

'Can't, can I? Coop won't let me.'

'Why's that?'

'Huh?'

'Why won't Coop let you help? Are you ill?'

'You funning me?' He glared. 'He says it's 'cos of me you hurt yourself.'

She stared. 'Why would he think that?'

'Didn't wait for you, did I? I *told* him you weren't ready 'cos you hadn't done prettying yourself up an' all. Didn't believe me.'

'Oh. That's rather unfair of him.'

'Huh?' Scoot's turn to stare. 'Why you *talking* like that?'

'Because … it's how I talk. Look, you didn't make me fall off the fence. It was my own stupid fault.'

A snort of contempt. 'You want to try telling him that?'

'All right. Yes. I will.'

A long pause, a pale, glassy stare. 'Look, lady, don't bother doing me no favours. Won't make a bitty difference to how I feel.'

'About what?'

''Bout you.'

'How *old* are you, Scoot?'

'Old enough. How'd y'all weasel your way in here, anyways? Why you have to come mess with everythin'? Things were just fine as they were.' Another pause. 'Anyhoo … talking to Coop won't do no good. He *never* changes his mind, nossir. About *anythin'.*

Gerry pulled a face. What a perfectly frightful habit.

CHAPTER SEVENTEEN

'Never wear extreme fashions.
Men prefer a quieter mode of dress.'
Modern Girl's Guide to Love, 1922

One afternoon, an unexpected visitor.

In the shade of the vine-covered verandah - sunlight flickering through the canopy, cicadas buzzing drowsily - Gerry was playing with one of the Mexican toddlers.

The baby, a piece of bread in one hand, doll in the other, sat quietly. Scoot's mangy, low-slung dog sprawled there, too.

For some reason, he'd started to attach himself, limpet-like, to Gerry and was constantly under her feet. Every so often, he'd lift his scarred nose and eye her thoughtfully, as if planning to rush over and chew one of her limbs.

Scoot, off sulking somewhere, was nowhere to be seen.

The air was hot, hot and sticky, and made Gerry listless. Everything burned, everything still. From midday, people, plants, animals and every other living thing seemed to seek out shadow and stop moving.

But now, turning her face to the sun, she stretched like a cat and felt almost content. There must be worse ways to spend a Tuesday afternoon. Or, was it Thursday? She'd lost track. Days, weeks.

Staring out at the endless haze of prairie and sky, she felt the tug of the landscape. Rippling grass stretching away like the sea, big brilliant sky. These things were seeping in, through her senses. She was even getting used to that liquid Texan twang, the rhythm and muscularity of the men's voices.

Somewhere out there, on the wild Texas plain, were cows and noise and heat and dust, and all those other awful things. Here, the world was drifting in slow motion, a strange, dream-like sensation.

Lazily, she lifted her head.

Something coming, coming fast! A storm of motion in the distance, raising up a dust cloud. Visitors? Shielding her eyes, Gerry squinted into white hot glare.

The shimmering dot grew bigger and bigger as it rushed towards the ranch, bumping and leaping over uneven ground. As it came closer, she made out the shape of a low, roadster motor car.

Behind the tilted wind-shield, a figure in goggles and driving gauntlets gripped the wheel. And beside the driver, her thick mane of hair tossed this way and that by wind, was a woman.

It looked very much like ... yes, Miss Hallie-Lee Kittrell.

A big horn sounded rudely, '*whanh, whanh,*' as they drew closer.

At home, Gerry thought, peeling herself from the scorching deck, you'd have to be swathed in hats, wraps and veils for that sort of travel.

Another blare from the horn.

Oh, dear. It was hard to feel poised and welcoming in pants three sizes too big, with a habit of slowly slipping past your hips. Feet were bare too, (they'd celebrated their freedom by swelling) and she could feel her hair, damp with sweat, curling into her neck.

But, nowhere to hide.

'Poise, my darling – a perfect balance between mind and body. Elegant dress, perfect grooming.'

With a grinding of brakes, the green car swerved to a stop in front of the verandah. Smoke rose from the bonnet; there was a strong smell of fuel.

A smartly-shod foot appeared on the running board, and a golden girl, the very picture of good health, good living and probably good luck, eased herself out.

Lobo responded with a menacing growl.

'Well howdy, Miss Childboxer.'

Pausing only to kick out at the blur of rough fur that launched itself at her in a fury of barking, Miss Kittrell approached the verandah.

As Lobo retreated under Gerry's chair, his hot breath on her legs, she knew just how he felt. 'Hello!' she said. 'Um actually, it's Chile-'

'Well, I was so sick to hear about your accident.' Hallie-Lee Kittrell click-clacked up the steps and cast herself into a long slipper chair. 'I just had to stop by.'

Wide smile, cold eyes, Gerry thought, automatically assessing the other girl's clothes. Not the height of fashion, but flattering, even so. An afternoon frock that rustled when she sat down. Lovely shoes. All in ninety degree heat, too.

'Coop said you'd surely welcome some company.'

As the car swung sharply round in a spiral of dust to snort off somewhere behind the corral, Miss Kittrell lolled back in the chair, fanning herself with a tiny palmetto fan.

The baby was ignored.

'Oh, my!' Eyes widened at Gerry's oversized pants and shirt. 'I was expecting scratchy tweed and hairy woollies, or whatever your English country style is, but ... gosh sakes, what *are* you wearing?'

'I'm a sight, aren't I?' Telling the tale of the lost luggage, Gerry was somehow aware, that with just one blink of those sky blue eyes, she had been utterly dismissed. One swift up-and-down appraisal and this golden girl had decided that Gerry was neither threat, nor rival.

'Well, really! Coop didn't say a thing! If I'd known, I could have brought some things right over.'

Coop, Gerry thought, would probably prefer to keep her in sackcloth and ashes, throat to hem. As befitted her status.

The visitor was still staring. 'I've just lately been reading about the fashion for shorter hair out East. What d'you call that ... a bob?'

'Um, in England, we ...'

The baby fell sideways and began to cry.

'Goodness sakes!' Hallie-Lee shrilled. 'Whose child *is* that? Cesar? *Cesar!*'

' ... a shingle. Actually.'

'Sí, sí, señorita! Perdóneme.'

'Take it away! And stop it screaming like a banshee.'

The dribbly infant, naked under its hat, was promptly scooped up and whisked away, still wailing.

Hallie-Lee wagged her head, knowingly. 'Don't let folks here take advantage of you, honey. Sets a real bad example.'

'His mother and some of the others are ill. I just ...'

'More'n likely just fakin'. You'll learn. I grew up around these people.' Stretching out a hand, Hallie-Lee turned it this way and that to admire her nails. 'Most are real lazy. They'd squat on their haunches all day if we'd let 'em.'

Gerry opened her mouth to protest, but thought better of it. *Careful*, she reminded herself, you don't know this country, do you? Or the people. Or their customs.

'Best not go near their shacks, either. With their chickens, their dogs, their babies! A mess of disease and everything. You'd likely catch something.' She turned to clap her hands, bringing Cesar scurrying out again from the house. 'So, honey. What's the difference?'

'I beg your pardon?' Gerry was reminded of a particularly bossy head-girl at her old school, with that same ability to make you feel small and swattable as a gnat.

'Between a bob, and a shingle! Ah really can't see one myself. Drinks,' she called over her shoulder, to Cesar, 'cold drinks.'

And lo, cold drinks were swiftly produced.

'Of course, us Texas girls are real fashionable, too, y'know.' Cesar was dismissed with a regal flick of her hand. 'Jericho Wells is the most nowhere place, but we've got smart stores now, all around. Up-to-date ones. In Dallas and Houston, that is.'

Gerry nodded. 'East Coast America's setting all the trends now, isn't it? Amelia Earhart, the Charles-'

'Mmmn. So, tell me. Why d'you say that's a shingle, Mizz Uh, when to me it looks jest like an itty bob?'

'Please,' Gerry said. 'I'm called Gerry. And a shingle has a sort of undulation. See?' She arranged a wave, on a slant, over one cheek.

Actually, she'd started to have a few doubts herself, about the bob or shingle or whatever it was. Keeping the parting neat. That feeling of nakedness at the curve of her neck. Not that she would admit that out loud.

'It's real boyish, isn't it?' Hallie-Lee tossed back the full weight of her own hair. Caught in a clip, it fell in sleek, shiny ripples over one shoulder. 'Somehow, ah can't see that particular fashion catching on here. Now, soon as I get home, I'll send some day dresses over for you. They're too good for playing with that smelly child, though, honey.'

Gerry responded with a brilliant smile.

Hallie-Lee Kittrell had that complacent look about her. The sort born of spending her whole life as the centre of attention. The sort that said - *look at this, this is me, and aren't I just wonderful?*

'Tell me about England,' the girl said, suddenly. 'Is it true what they say? That y'all eat mutton and drink tea all the time, and have bad teeth?'

While Gerry tried to think of a polite response, the driver of the motor car loped round the corner, took the verandah steps two at a time, and set Lobo off to another frenzy of barking.

Another tall Texan. Another sun-bronzed face under a huge hat.

'Hey there! I'm Red.'

'My baby brother.' Hallie-Lee waved a lazy hand. 'Ross Elwood Kittrell - Red for short. Watch out for him, Miss ...'

'Chiledexter.'

'He's a real ladies' man.'

'Only with the pretty ones.' Taking off his hat to reveal a shock of red hair, Red Kittrell bent over Gerry's hand. 'How's old Coop treating you then, ma'am? Guess he hasn't been around much, huh? With all that dry-drilling he's been trying to sniff out, an' all.'

'Dry what?'

'Looking for oil. Black gold! What everyone hereabouts is busy doing nowadays, if they've any sense. The means to untold riches and a long easy life. Yessir.' He stretched long legs out in front of him. 'Ever heard of wild-catting?'

'Oh, hush-up, Red. Don't be boring Miss Chiledexter with all that. So, what have you been doing with yourself, honey?'

'Well .... I've spent a lot of time in the library. You know, reading.'

'Why, you poor thing.' Hallie-Lee looked shocked. 'Isn't

every dull book ever written in there?'

'My sister,' Red said, 'only reads fashion catalogues. Say, Miss Chiledexter, p'raps I could show you around, when your leg's mended? I'd just purely love to do that. Interesting strangers don't often turn up in Jericho Wells.'

'Now, Red. Miss Chiledexter's not real strong. We can't have her fainting all over the place, can we? It takes time to get accustomed to the climate hereabouts.'

Gerry wrinkled her nose. 'How long does it take? You know, to ... get accustomed?'

'About twenty-five years.' Red's drawl was dry.

'And you only here a few months,' Hallie-Lee said, through a flicker of long lashes. 'Such a shame. You'll likely miss the wedding.'

'Wedding?'

'Mine and Coop's. It's been planned since ... oh, rightly since I made my début.'

Well, that made sense, Gerry thought. They would suit each other.

'My poor Mama and my Daddy ... well, they just loved Coop. Our ranches are right next to each other. He hasn't told you?'

'That's because,' Red drawled, 'he hasn't agreed to getting married yet, sister dear. Men like Coop won't always do what's expected, no matter what the story books say. See, this is what us old ranching families do here, Miss Chiledexter. Join two cattle dynasties together. Practically in-breeding, if you ask me.'

'We didn't.' Hallie-Lee pouted her disapproval. She had a rather petulant lower lip.

'Look at the mouth, darling! It tells you more about a person than anything else. The window to the soul.'

'Well,' Red pulled a face. 'I'm looking to avoid the habit myself.'

'Avoid any responsibility, you mean.'

'Ain't that the truth! Leaving it all to you, sis.'

Gerry pushed back the sleeves of the huge shirt. This was starting to sound like a plot in some Victorian melodrama.

'Anyway,' the other girl went on. 'I reckon what you need now, is some femi-nine conversation. The girls are just dying to get over here and welcome you. I can't wait for them to visit and shake up this boring old male stronghold.'

'Girls?' Gerry fanned her flushed face.

'Friends. You know, neighbours. They'll be right along.'

'Well, that would be lovely.' Gripping her glass, Gerry murmured, 'Perhaps, next week?'

'This afternoon, honey! Couldn't hold them back a minute longer.'

Gerry choked on her drink. 'Oh ... I must change; I must tell Cesar.'

'No time, darlin',' Red said, squinting into the distance. 'Here they come now.'

Another billowing dust cloud, another cluster of dots, as a procession of cars raced over the horizon towards them.

'But, I look a fright!'

'Well now,' Hallie-Lee cocked her head with a sphinx-like

smile, 'don't you fret one bit, Jessie. I doubt the girls will even notice.'

So Gerry was stuck - dusty feet, damp patches under the arms - and not a thing that she could do about it.

'*Style, darling!*' She jumped at the hiss in her ear. '*Lift your head. Charm, manners matter more than looks.*'

Then, as Lobo raced back and forth barking - a wave of cherry lips and tossing hair and stylish dresses. Flounces, bibs and bows. And voices everywhere, that syrupy southern talk, like an aviary of honeyed birds, in the house and on the verandah.

Hallie-Lee moved forward to make introductions.

'Mary Lou Adams ... Yolanda Opper ... Cissie Connor ...' more and more names, more eager faces. ' ... and this, girls, is Mizz Chiledexter. All the way from England.'

'Please. Call me Gerry!'

'Isn't thait a boy's name?'

'Well, it's Gerardina really ...'

The girls gathered round and Gerry found herself surrounded by eager chatter, pretty manners and much more style than she would ever have expected, in the middle of this godforsaken prairie.

My word, these girls looked smart. Nothing too long or too short or too tight, nothing homely or plain-folksy about any of them.

Every one had that golden glow. Again, Gerry felt like an alien species - some strange, pale, freckled thing blown off-course from a distant continent.

'You all look wonderful,' she said. 'And I'm such a *mess!*'

And these southern belles looked at her and looked at each other and laughed indulgently, as drinks were passed round and platters of food brought out by the servants.

Gerry laughed, too. Smiling and nodding and behaving as if she was wearing some cream-of-the-county ensemble, rather than these raggedy pants, she listened to the chatter and tried to decide just who, among all the Miss Someone of Something and the Somebody of Somewhere Else, she would like to know better.

Quite a lot of them, as it happened. Warm and friendly, stylish and funny, they were as shopping-obsessed and fond of fashion and spending money, as Leonie ever was.

'Did you ever actually *meet* Chanel?' someone asked.

'No. But my aunt did, several times, in Deauville.'

'Oh, my! And what d'yall think about that Josephine Baker and her cheetah? In Paris!'

Meanwhile Red, with his charming drawl, filled her in with the more interesting bits of information, such as who rated and who didn't in Texan society, who was Texas-bred and who wasn't, who was married to whom, plus a few wicked asides of his own.

'See the angelic-looking one next to Hallie-Lee? That's Baby Gale. Married one of the Memphis Gales, and wow, that gal made one giant leap up the social ladder.'

'Why, say!' someone said, suddenly. 'Look who's here!' and heads turned towards the dusty god in the wide hat and whip-stitched leathers, loping towards them from the corral.

Ah, Coop. The mighty male. Taking off his hat, running a hand through his hair, attentive to everyone. He seemed able to effortlessly charm and control everything, Gerry observed, resentfully. Men, dogs, horses, cows. Women? Oh, yes. That went without saying. A prize catch.

She imagined a trail of broken hearts throughout the territory. Was he even aware of the effect he was having on the girls?

Hallie-Lee certainly was. Arranging herself at his side, lifting wide eyes, she engaged him in a private hum of conversation. Staking her claim? You could just catch that sultry whisper, husky, teasing. Almost a purr.

Watching Coop's indulgent look, Gerry caught her breath. There was an obvious attraction. So, did he love this woman? As much as he loved his cows? Now they were laughing together. Ha, ha. Ho, ho.

Standing absolutely still, she felt a small surprising stab of something. Envy? Oh, yes. Of their intimacy, the sort that shut everyone else out.

'Make quite a picture, don't they?' Red Kittrell's voice, close to her ear. 'Yip. No doubt about it. Women like to be around something dangerous, once in a while.'

Was Coop dangerous? Archie had said so. Prim thought it, too. Was that the attraction he had for women?

Gerry hadn't forgotten, of course, how it felt to be held by him, held against him. Pathetic really, like some stupid, schoolgirl crush. And it had happened once, that was all. Once only.

Ah well. When she was a very, very old lady, all lace-capped and withered and living on boiled rice and brandy, she could try to remember that, couldn't she? Something to keep her warm on cold nights.

Poor Miss Chiledexter, people would say. Dear Miss Chiledexter.

'Tsk. Stop that!'

Yes, *stop* it. Dragging her eyes away, she stared down at her grimy toes and squashed all those thoughts, before they went any further.

CHAPTER EIGHTEEN

'A woman should be precious, alluring.
Like a delicate piece of porcelain.'
How to Attract a Man, 1923

'What the hell's this?'

The first thing said, when he came into the room.

The offending article, a tissue-thin wisp of silk and ecru lace threaded with ribbon and held between thumb and forefinger, was waved under Gerry's nose.

'And, this!'

One solitary chiffon stocking.

'Ah.' She felt herself flush. 'Where did you find those?'

'Blew off a bush out there.'

'Did they frighten the horses?'

'No,' Coop snapped, 'just scared the hell out of the men.'

Edgy, belligerent, he'd clinked in, still booted and spurred, in the wide-brimmed hat and dust-coloured clothes they all seemed to wear, all of the time.

'Well, I've barely a thing to put on. Night wear, daywear ...'

'*What*-wear?'

' ... you know, underthingies. I have to wash them all out, every day.'

'We've a score of servants for that. Give those ... bits to the girls, give them to Alba. I don't want them displayed outside.'

Like a Victorian uncle, Gerry thought, in a Stetson. He didn't say please or thank you. He kept his hat on indoors and was probably used to treating all women like cows, to be roped and corralled and waved at with a big stick.

'It's kinda unsettling. We're not used to females round the place.'

Except for Hallie-Lee Kittrell, of course. And would he talk to her like this, do-this, do-that?

There was a longish pause.

Taking off his hat, he crossed arms and stared at her, narrow-eyed. 'By the way, don't try to make a pet out of that dog.'

Gerry bent down to peer at the malodorous matted heap of whiskery fur under her chair. '*This* dog?' Lobo rumbled, foul-breathed and threatening.

'This dog hates me. He's trying to unnerve me, that's all.' Like everyone else here, she thought, man and beast. 'He won't do anything he's told, either.'

'Like a few other people round here,' Coop muttered. 'Don't go walking too far from the house either, like you have been doing.'

'Why not?'

'Snakes.'

Gerry stared. This was ridiculous. She couldn't wash, shouldn't walk, mustn't pet the wretched dog. What *was* she allowed to do? 'Oh, I'm not afraid of snakes, we've plenty of those at home.'

He didn't have anything to say about that, he just stood there, frowning.

She coughed. 'Um, there's no sign of my trunk yet, I suppose? My portmanteau? It's initialled, you know, did I mention that? Quite unmistakeable.'

Still no response.

'Nothing's arrived yet, then? In Jericho Wells?'

'Don't reckon anyone's checked, not lately'

'But, why not?'

'Why not what?'

'Why hasn't anyone been to the railroad, to see if it's there?'

An off-hand shrug. 'No-one's got time to go chasing off after a heap of lost clothes.'

Gerry frowned. Didn't he realize? This was serious. 'So, when was the last time? You know, that somebody went back to look?'

'It was a Saturday, as I recall.'

Deep breath. 'Look Mister Cooper, I appreciate that wearing a sack wouldn't matter much to some people, but after *weeks* ...'

'There's a pile of pants and shirts here, all good duds. What more do you want?'

' ... with barely a *stitch* of my own to put on, this is important. Some of the clothes in that trunk were from Paris. They're ... irreplaceable!'

'Yeah well, no point dressing like a duchess here. You're not in England now.'

No. Bending over, she pulled up one of the hairy man-sized socks. She certainly wasn't. In fact, she was just beginning to appreciate the joy of leaving behind those vests and scarves and double-knit woollies and everything else a person needed to stay warm and keep the rain off at home. Coats pulled tight against the wind. Hats, umbrellas, boots.

'I'm tired of looking as if I'm about to go out to shoot rabbits every day, that's all. Your clothes,' she pushed one scratchy sleeve back from her wrist, 'are all rejecting me.' Like everything and everyone else here.

Who would choose to look like this on purpose? It was worse than boarding school, with four pairs of elasticated knickers, one box-pleat tunic with girdle, one house tie. She needed her own things. Couldn't he see? Clothes to put her back in control, to take on the world. Now, more than ever.

It was a feminine thing. Deep-rooted.

He looked her up and down. With the critical beady eye, Gerry thought, of the experienced horse trader.

She stared right back. The ruggedly masculine figure in front of her was well-shouldered, slim hipped, strong wristed. A person of seemingly perfect proportions and utterly comfortable, apparently, in *his* own clothes.

Unlike herself, who after an humiliating afternoon with the fashionable Miss Kittrell and friends, had started to feel like something that had crawled out from under a stone.

Skin was desert dry, cracked as a lizard-skin handbag; her face looked washed, but not ironed. She was in urgent need of creams – yes, unguents.

Coop's eyebrows went up. 'Vanity of vanities, sayeth the preacher, all is vanity. You sure don't have the makings of a pioneer. By the way, those pants are falling down.'

Yanking them up to her armpits, Gerry felt like biffing him on the nose. He considered her flighty, didn't he? Someone solely concerned with frills and unnecessary fripperies. As if dressing dowdily somehow made you a better sort of person.

The only requirement of *his* clothes, of course, would be to keep him dust and fly-free, and decent.

Vanity? Ho! Where was Leonie when you wanted her? Why couldn't she be summoned up, to wag a finger at this philistine?

But, he'd already turned away.

'Is that a parable?' She raised her voice to his retreating back. 'Perhaps you'd like me to stitch it onto a sampler before I leave. I'll have plenty of time, because I couldn't even *consider* going home, until I get my trunk back.'

A backwards glance. Did his mouth twitch for the briefest of seconds? She must have imagined it. But barely a minute after he'd left the room, Alba padded in.

'Coop says I mustn't wash these myself.' Gerry waved the froth of fragile silk and gossamer lace. 'But I've barely anything of my own and these man's things are so huge and shapeless.' She snatched at the shirt slipping off one shoulder. 'Look! I may as well wear a ... serge sack.'

Alba looked puzzled. As well she might. Didn't *she* have to wear a uniform every single day here, all plain and black, like the rest of the worker bees? In spite of that, Gerry had begun to realize that whatever went on in this house, the Mexican servants would know about it.

Dark eyes appraised her head to toe. A slow nod of understanding, then 'Momento.' The woman went out.

Minutes later, she was back, swinging a small key on a purple velvet ribbon. When she beckoned, Gerry rose obediently, almost tripping over Lobo, who'd got up to dog her heels.

'Stay!' she said, firmly. He ignored her, as usual.

Into the hall and up the stairs, the rest of the house all still and quiet. No sound from anywhere, no voices or footsteps except their own. Arriving at that one locked door, at the far end of the galleried landing, Alba stopped and held out the key.

'In here?'

'Sí, sí. Entre.'

Gerry put key into lock. One gentle push and the door creaked open.

On the threshold, she hesitated. All of a sudden, this felt underhand, like some sort of conspiracy. She turned, but Alba had gone, melted silently away. Giving an odd sort of yelp, Lobo skittered away, too

The room was in shadow, the air stale, as if it hadn't been disturbed for some time. But bed neatly made? Spotty gilt-edged mirror and scrap of lace on the dressing table? A lamp with silk and bead fringing.

Nothing else, just emptiness, silence. An almost unnatural silence. None of the usual clatter from the kitchen, or hooves clomping about outside. Yet, Gerry had the strangest feeling that somewhere here, ears were listening, eyes looking.

A pause.

She'd grown used to rooms being cool, compared to white-hot heat outside. Something to do with the thick walls and shutters closed against the sun. This though, was different - a shivery sort of chill.

And then, it happened.

Moving to the window to let in some light, she caught a floating whiff of something - a haunting, familiar scent, with strong notes of peach and lilac blossom. Something that stopped her dead in her tracks and made the breath catch in her throat.

Mitsouko. One of Leonie's favourites. Unmistakeable, unforgettable. She breathed it in, almost intoxicated. Suddenly, vividly, it brought her aunt right back to her, in the room.

It was ... this was ... extraordinary.

Rooted to the spot, Gerry half-expected a laughing Leonie to materialize, cocktail in one hand, smouldering cigarette holder in the other. For a few agonizing seconds, she closed her eyes and stood, absolutely rapt, willing it to happen.

Turn round. Look! Yes. Look now!

Nothing.

Quickly, she moved to open the shutters and stood blinking as sunlight filtered in. The silvery mirror sparkled. What *was* this? Communing with ghosts? Was she losing her mind?

At home, these sorts of things had been happening so often that she'd given up trying to make sense of them. She had stopped telling anyone else about them, too. No point. No-one had believed her, had they? They'd probably *all* thought her mind was disturbed.

And to begin with, perhaps it had been, just a little. Those voices and strange vibrations in the air, had unsettled her, made her nervous. But now, with no doubt about their links to Leonie, they'd started to stir Gerry's blood as much as chill it.

This was no mere voice - it was, quite definitely, a presence. One filling the room.

Desperately trying to catch or connect with whatever was going on, she stood still for several more minutes. Then, drawn like a moth to the huge wardrobe, she looked hard at the heavy door, before daring to open it.

Inside, the same extravagant scent, curling in the air like smoke - and three garments, swaddled in reams of tissue paper. Gerry felt a rush of blood to her head and wanted to cry.

Moving aside layers of tissue, she let out a long breath. A shimmer of silk plisse - an exquisite sliver of a dress, light as a bird's wing, with dropped waist and just-past-the-knee beaded hem. Stroking the silk, pressing it to her face, released a flash of memory - Leonie, delectable in this dress and twirling, a single gardenia in her hair.

Wasn't that the night her aunt had sent her latest suitor

away? In his silk smoking jacket, a flea in his ear. *('We're quite incompatible, darling! He can't dance!')*

Hands still trembling, Gerry plucked out a blue Poiret pyjama ensemble, hand-painted with Chinese motifs. Fingering it, smelling the sweet scent, rocking back and forth, her mind stretched back again. *('Shall you sleep in those, Leonie?' 'No, dear heart, I shall lounge. Vogue says this is new boudoir dressing, for masquerades ... and lounging.')*

Lastly, under the most perfect velvet-collared riding jacket, tight whipcord trousers. Leaning her cheek against the jacket collar, Gerry traced the clever stitches on the seam with her finger.

These things spoke to her, as if they were friends. Each had cost a small fortune, a story in every one.

Underneath the clothes, a row of black lacquered boxes stood sentry. Nestling inside, one gold tasselled clutch bag, a pair of the most beautiful evening slippers she'd ever seen and some buckled calf-skin riding boots, shiny as conkers.

All ready to wear, all enveloped in a delectable cloud of *Mitsouko. We're here for you*, the clothes whispered to Gerry, peacocking on the rail. *Take us out. We need lights! Admiring eyes!*

Like a dream, and at last, the sort of sign that she'd been looking for. She felt like an archaeologist discovering an ancient arrowhead or fragment of brooch. This wardrobe bore witness to Leonie having been here. In this place, wearing these clothes.

Why hadn't Coop *told* her about this?

Voices on the stairs! Moving quickly to the door, she leaned against it, holding her breath, and waited. When someone padded past, she exhaled, dizzy with relief.

Why did she feel as if she shouldn't be in here? What was there to feel guilty about?

Because this changed everything, didn't it? She no longer wanted to run away, tail between her legs. This was what Leonie had wanted, Gerry was sure of it. She was exactly where she was supposed to be. It was her destiny, to be here.

She fingered the key on its velvet ribbon. How could she leave now? She wouldn't, couldn't do it.

CHAPTER NINETEEN

'Most bachelors look for a nice modest girl.'
The Single Girls' Guide to Matrimony, 1923

The next night, for the very first time, they ate together.

They were eight in all. Coop, Scoot and herself, grouped around one end of that huge dining table, with four of the men, and Doc Hyde - the veterinarian.

It was the longest meal of Gerry's life.

When she sailed into the room sheathed in Leonie's oyster-coloured silk, she cut the conversation stone dead. Jaws dropped as the men stood up, and there were slow top-to-toe stares - from Gerry's shiny buttoned shoes to the long loop of pearls and tiny headband sewn with feathers - as Coop made the introductions.

'Boys, don't reckon you've been properly introduced. This is Mizz Chiledexter, from England.'

Gerry heard the shuffling of booted feet.

'Mizz *who?*' someone muttered. 'From *where?*'

Another man blushed scarlet.

'Nate, Bud, Lefty ...' Coop waved a hand, 'and right here's

Bren Ryan, my top hand.' They were all big and brown. 'Of course, you know Doc, don't you?'

Oh, yes. Gerry certainly did. She smiled her humble smile.

Having busied himself with introductions, Coop now turned his flinty grey gaze on her. A long, considering look.

As his eyes slowly followed the line of her body under the dress, she tugged at the hemline - uncomfortably aware of just how much the fabric revealed of the shape underneath.

The fall of silk plisse was almost transparent in places, but - oh, well - she'd decided she just didn't care. It was the first dress she'd worn for weeks, and such a relief.

This shimmering slip of a thing with its magic cut and beautiful seaming had given back her self-confidence. Caterpillar into butterfly. At last she looked like herself again, not some sort of imposter.

Why hadn't Coop mentioned Leonie's clothes? Hadn't he known about them? Well, whether he had or hadn't, Gerry was thankful not to be wearing those old canvas pants for her first proper dinner here.

Not something that bothered the men, apparently. Surrounded by long hair, beards and stubble, she felt like some exotic foreign bird, amongst plainer, browner native species. Brown food, brown clothes, brown everything here.

The heat of the day had gone, and goodness, that room felt cold. Rubbing her arms, she soon started to shiver. Well, if the atmosphere was cold and strained, the food was worse.

Mexican girls padded silently in and out bearing huge

platters - giant indigestible slabs of cow, with a few vegetables cowering alongside. This, Gerry was beginning to learn, was a land of carnivores, red meat country. Nothing green was ever shown much respect. Everyone worked the cows, lived with cows, ate the cows.

While the men tucked in with gusto, she tried to banish all thoughts of tender roast chickens, brown farm eggs and garden vegetables from her mind.

Her own teeth now cringed at the sight of steak. She felt like a bear fattening itself up for hibernation. As she struggled to finish the rubbery lump on her plate, counting bites as she chewed, Doc Hyde said, 'You don't care for our Texas steak, Mizz Chiledexter?'

'Oh ...' she choked on the almost raw piece of meat in her mouth. Had she turned green? 'I'm just not very hungry.'

'Guess it's not what you're used to, huh?'

'They don't eat much red meat in England,' Coop said, 'just hares and rabbits.'

Joke? Gerry smiled, wanly. As she swallowed the steak, her stomach rumbled in alarm. Putting down her fork, she said, 'Yes, we usually just have thin gruel for supper, with a few dry crusts.'

And very appealing it sounded, too, at that moment.

'And once a year,' she went on, recklessly, 'a Christmas goose.'

Coop flashed her a look, which she ignored.

There was conversation. About people she hadn't met and things she knew nothing about. Cows, mostly. Or horses. And a few vague hints about something else. Luck? Yes, that was it. Someone's run of luck and a gusher coming in.

She might have found that interesting if anyone had bothered to explain it, but of course, they didn't. Scoot spoke barely a word to anyone.

She cast about for other topics, but when she did venture to speak, the men all turned, as if surprised to still see her there. Only the impeccably mannered Doc Hyde addressed any remarks directly to her.

Each of her own efforts was greeted with polite attention by the other men, as if they were encouraging an extremely shy child. Their tone changed and they spoke loudly and slowly, like the English when addressing foreigners.

'How do y'all spend your time at home then, ma'am?'

'Oh, I have a bookshop. I ... sell books.'

They all stared, and she was left with the impression that if she'd said she charmed snakes or tamed tigers, it would have sounded far less exotic.

Weren't women here supposed to express opinions? Perhaps they'd rather she'd brought a book to the table; she wished she *had* brought one. Her face ached with the effort of nodding politely.

She fingered the long loop of pearls. That feathered headband? Huge mistake. She should've known, should have stuck to those cowboy cast-offs.

Her eyes kept being drawn back to the huge picture on the wall. The handsome, strong-featured man in the portrait stared straight back. Except for the startling flash of blue eyes, there was no colour, not even here. Just dull browns, sepias.

She turned to Doc Hyde. 'Is that Mr O' Rourke?'

'Sure is. Still keeping an eye on us, I reckon.'

Another silence. Just the chink-chink of cutlery.

Gerry glanced round the table. Everyone seemed downcast, a general air of gloom all round. She caught Coop's eye. Oh, dear. It was hard to put a name to that look.

Well, it was becoming clearer and clearer, wasn't it? None of these people welcomed her here. She wasn't wife, relative, or servant. She wasn't anything. Just an irritating female interloper, in this closed order, this ... overwhelmingly male set-up.

Well, she thought, you can't scare me, not anymore. *Leonie* wants me here.

Even so, the atmosphere in the room soon started to wear her out. Could she plead a headache? Stifling a yawn, she began counting the minutes until it would all be over and she could slink off to bed.

When at last the meal was over and coffee served, the four men got up from the table, bade everyone a polite goodnight and went out.

Gerry prepared to follow.

But Scoot moved first, scraping back his chair and slinking out like a whipped dog. He was almost out of earshot when Gerry heard him yelp, to the air, 'Huh! Not fair!' Or something like it.

There was a pause, a thudding of hooves and the sound of a horse being ridden away, hard. Setting her coffee cup carefully back down, she cleared her throat. 'Scoot's a very good rider.'

Her eyes met Coop's.

'Yip. Comes with the territory.'

'Can I ... talk to you, Mist ... Cooper?'

'We *are* talking, aren't we?'

'About Scoot.'

His face was blank.

'He says that you're blaming him for my accident.' There seemed no way of edging politely up to the subject.

Another long, frowning pause. Coop put his own cup down. 'Say again?'

'Scoot says he's being punished because of me, because of what happened to me. And you know, that's really not fair, because ... '

Coop's mouth was twitching; he seemed to be holding back a smile.

'Is there something funny about that?'

'No,' he said. 'Sorry. It's ... yeah, nothing. Carry on.'

'Anyway ... everyone knows it was my own fault that I got hurt. It isn't fair to make him take the blame.'

'I'll bear that in mind,' he said, solemnly.

'So, you'll let him go out again, with the rest of the men?'

'I'll think about it. But, Mizz Chiledexter ... ?'

'Gerry. My name is Gerry.'

'And mine's Coop, okay? *Mister Cooper* gets me looking over my shoulder for someone in city duds, with an attaché case. Anyway, *Gerry* ... just tell me, what's the real issue here?'

She stared. 'There is no *issue*.'

'Then why raise it now?'

'Because Scoot is being blamed for something he didn't do.'

'See, here's the thing. You don't know anything about it, do you? About me, about Scoot, or how we work things out here. Why butt in, why interfere?'

'I told you,' she said, resenting his tone, 'because, it isn't fair.'

'Life's not fair. If it was, you wouldn't own half of my ranch.'

'For the *hundredth* time, that wasn't my fault, was it? In a few months' time, I'll be gone and you'll have the whole place back to yourself.'

A long, utterly unnerving silence.

Gerry felt frustrated. She still hadn't been able to ask any of the questions that she'd wanted to raise when she'd arrived. About Leonie, about Frank O'Rourke. All energy and curiosity had been sapped by her stupid accident.

Pushing back her chair, she got up.

Coop stood up to face her, with another long, up and down stare. That unblinking grey gaze had been one of the first things she'd noticed about him. Like a hunting bird, kestrel or hawk, having spotted its prey.

Sorely tempted to stick out her tongue, she braced herself. For comments, questions. None came, not a single one. Unsettled, she smoothed the skirt of her dress. Surely he was going to say something about it? Did he think that her trunk had finally arrived?

'Just remind me again,' he said, at last. 'Why exactly, are you here?'

Gerry guessed there could be no right answers to this question. Only wrong ones.

'You *know* why.'

'Let's pretend I don't.'

'Because of my *aunt*. Because, I believe this is what Leonie always wanted me to do.' *And since this afternoon*, she thought, *I don't just think, I know.*

Another long pause.

'Regular little idealist, aren't you?'

Gerry assumed it wasn't meant as a compliment.

CHAPTER TWENTY

'Cheer up, dears. Cupid's bow
and arrow can't be for everyone.'
A Woman's Way, 1923

From her first waking moments the next day, Gerry couldn't wait to get back to that room. To touch those clothes again, to breathe their sweet, thrilling scent. To recapture that mysterious sense of Leonie.

She still had the key on its velvet ribbon, but finding the right time to use it was a problem. People, voices everywhere. So frustrating. And her thoughts still chasing each other round and round.

Had Coop known about those clothes? She recalled his expression on first seeing her in the dress. Surely, she'd had every right to wear it?

It wasn't until late morning that she was finally able to slip into the shadowed room. Leaning against the door, Leonie's dress over her arm, she felt almost euphoric.

The distant clock in the downstairs hall struck eleven.

For a few moments, Gerry stood absolutely still. The same stripes of yellow light slanting through the shutters, that same empty silence. Just her own fast breathing and a trapped fly buzzing at the window.

But, something missing? The scent wasn't hanging as richly and heavily as before, barely a trace left. The whole atmosphere seemed lighter, less charged. Pulling at the huge wardrobe door, the merest breath of *Mitsouko* drifted out as she hung up the dress. Last time a cloud of it had risen up, to cling to her.

Resting her cheek against the soft silk, she felt a surge of disappointment.

Everything seemed different, everything changed. *Where are you, Leonie?* What *had* happened the day before? Had she imagined it?

As she agonized - dull, distant sounds from outside. A door slammed, and moments later, the measured tread of heeled boots on the landing. Closer, closer!

Panicked, Gerry scrambled into the wardrobe, pulling the door behind her.

Silence. The small space was stifling, the perfume now a suffocating mist. Feeling as if a fur coat had been thrown over her head, she fought for breath.

Then, in absolute darkness, she was ambushed by memory. Herself as a terrified child, being dragged to similar small spaces - cellar, cupboard - and locked in, after some imagined misdemeanour. She felt a prickle of fear.

Minutes ticked by. Floorboards creaked. Someone else in the room? She pressed an ear to the grain of wood. Or just wood swelling? As dust settled in her throat, she had to pinch her nose to stop herself sneezing.

Spotting the edge of her sleeve poking out through the hinged side of the wooden door, she eased it carefully back. A few minutes more - and now almost unconscious from the fumes - she pressed her face against knots and whorls of wood, trying to see through the gaps.

Then, a chill of panic! A terrible glittering eye met hers and held her there, like something from *The Ancient Mariner*. A hard-breathing ghost.

'Boo,' a voice said, and the wardrobe door swung slowly open, the light blinding.

A moment's silence.

'Well, are you going to tell me?' Coop's languid drawl. 'Or shall I guess?' He sounded bored.

'How did you find me?'

'Why? Are you in hiding?'

'No. I ...'

'You left a pretty clear trail of breadcrumbs out there, Gretel.'

She stepped out, blinking. As her eyes adjusted to the light, they regarded each other, in silence.

'Did I?'

'No. Lobo's sitting on guard outside the door.'

More minutes dragged themselves by. As Coop tapped the toe of one of his fancy boots, Gerry stared down, distracted.

Ho. So much for all the men's clothes here being plain and workmanlike. His boots, stitched and scrolled and fitting like a glove, were as fancy and elaborate as anything in Gerry's lost trunk. Belts, saddles and bridles, too.

He sighed. 'I'm getting older here.'

'It's just … ' she flapped a hand. 'Well. Those are Leonie's clothes.'

No response.

'I wasn't sure I was supposed to find them, that's all, let alone start wearing them. I didn't know if you'd approve.'

'Who do you think gave Alba the key?'

She stared. 'Then, why was the room kept locked?'

'Frank wanted it that way, I guess.'

She waited for him to enlarge on this tantalizing snippet. He didn't, and peering up at his face, she started to wilt. What was the point of all these secrets? About Leonie, Frank O'Rourke, the truth of their relationship?

'So, all this time,' she hoisted up trousers slipping slowly past her hips, 'you knew? You *knew* my aunt's clothes were in here?'

He didn't confirm or deny it. Oh, he was expert at this, wasn't he? A master of the laconic and keeping her at arm's length. 'I've been here for weeks!' Her voice rose. '*Why* didn't you tell me?'

He considered a moment, then shrugged. 'The truth? Same reason we hadn't fetched your trunk. Guess I thought a woman with no clothes wouldn't want to stick around too long.'

Taking a key from his pocket, he went over to the dressing table, unlocked one of the small drawers and picking something out, offered it to her.

A picture in morocco-leather frame.

It was a sepia photograph, formal studio setting. Leonie, on a small gilt chair in front of a painted screen and potted palm. Behind, one hand clasping her shoulder in proprietary fashion, the tall, rugged man with the inscrutable gaze, from the dining-room portrait. Frank O' Rourke.

Gerry collapsed into a chair, attention fixed on the picture.

Again, that voice, whispering inside her head *'Look at us! Look at our faces!'*

Leonie, all sculpted eyebrows and painted cupid lips smiled directly out at her. Too, too beautiful. Radiant, in her black pearls, an almost luminous glow about her. At that time, in that place, everything must have been absolutely right in her world.

'Again, again! Look at Frank.'

'By the way,' Coop loomed over her, 'we've got your things.'

Gerry glanced up, barely registering, then turned her attention back to Frank O'Rourke. Strong chin, thick hair. Wonderful eyes, too, the sort that wouldn't miss a thing, looking out at the camera in that proud and private way.

'Yeah, your trunk's out there, in the hall. We fetched it from Jericho Wells, first thing this morning.'

Her *trunk*? Oh, who cared about that? This photograph was all that she was bothered about now; all other concerns had fallen away. She continued her search for clues.

'So perhaps now, you'll be able to think about going

home?'

Gerry didn't look up and didn't bother answering, either. Go home? Didn't he realize! Everything had changed. 'What do you know about this?' Her eyes were still devouring the picture. 'Where was it taken?'

'No idea.'

'But, when did you find it?' She drew in her breath. 'I mean, what's the story here?'

'Haven't a clue. After Frank died, I found the picture and clothes. That's it, that's all there is. '

Gerry looked up, appalled. Clearly, he had no plans to expand on that statement. Was it really all he'd bothered to find out? She had a hundred and one questions herself.

'Didn't you *want* to know anything else?'

'I've been kinda busy looking after a ranch and a few hundred thousand head of cattle.'

'Because, well ... I do.'

'Yeah.' He sighed. 'I had a hunch.'

'It's why I'm here, why I came in the first place.'

'You already told me. See, the thing is ...' he paused. 'I never figured you'd do it, not in a million years. Come all this way, on the whim of some dead relative?' He nodded at the picture. 'Wasn't she just one of those odd English eccentrics?'

'What! Who said that?'

'Miss what's-her-name with the short skirt, that girl at the party. Kitty?'

'Kitty *Dudley*!' Gerry wished that she'd battered Kitty with a candlestick when she'd had the chance. 'Leonie wasn't *odd*.'

She held up the photograph. 'Look at this, just look at her. She was bold and beautiful. She took in the family stray and gave me love and security. I owe her everything.'

Gnawing her lip, she went on, 'Surely *you,* of all people, can understand that. Don't you feel much the same way about Mister O'Rourke?'

Coop shrugged.

'I mean,' Gerry persisted, unwilling now to let it go, 'isn't yours a similar story?'

Silence.

His expression became so dark and antagonistic that she was taken aback. Weariness swept her then, along with distaste for this whole silly game that he seemed to keep playing.

Was he ever going to give satisfactory answers to any of her questions? Would she ever be able to find out what she wanted to know? The more he retreated, the more it added to the mystery. The more he resisted explanation, the more she was desperate to find out.

'Look, Mister Cooper,' she said, with a sudden rush of emotion, 'how long do you intend to carry on like this?'

'Like what? And drop the damn mister.'

'Miss and Mister feels perfectly appropriate, in the circumstances. How long are you going to punish me for being here, is what I'm asking?'

'No idea. You came to take a look round, didn't you? Not complain about my disposition.'

And that, apparently, was an end to it.

CHAPTER TWENTY ONE

'Beware of Mr Wrong: the mean man, the know-all,
the flirt and the gambler.'
The Bachelor Girl's Handbook, 1924

When Gerry returned to her room, it was all there, that formidable array of lost luggage. Huge cabin trunk and her talisman, the shiny leather portmanteau, with its fusty, oxblood insides. Chic dressing case and hat boxes, one, two, three.

Elena and Alba were busily sorting through her precious clothes and for once, Gerry and the Mexican women had absolutely no problem understanding one another.

As mother and daughter shook out silks and frills and lace, their coos, oohs, aahs of delight breached all barriers, a language common to all women.

The inadequate wardrobe was soon full to bursting with chiffon and crêpe de-chine, a line of shoes and satin slippers. Hats, gloves and a huge red taffeta bow, trimmed with black net.

Gerry suspected that she'd lost weight. The arrival of her trunk confirmed it.

Luckily, she loved to sew - tucking, hemming, making alterations with invisible stitches. Another skill owed to the Saved Mary Magdalens in India, along with knitting oddly shaped garments for orphans at Christmas, with hairy twine and old corset strings.

Useful too, for living with Leonie, with all her hand-sewn, one-of-a-kind pieces of clothing, who'd never knotted a thread or sewn on a button in her entire life.

First, she needed to raid Alba's workbox, for scissors, needles, thread.

'No!' The horrified woman clung to the casket. 'I sew. I sew for you.'

'Yes, Alba. Thank you so much, but I *like* to do it. Really, I want to do this myself.'

Then she came across Elena in her room, fingering the lace on a dress, holding it up against herself and turning this way and that in front of the mirror.

'Oh! Por favor ... pardóneme!'

'No, no, don't move. Stay there!'

With the Mexican girl still stuttering excuses, Gerry snatched up a pincushion and draped the dress round. A tuck here, dart there, and having pulled up the shoulder seam to emphasize the girl's slender shape, she bent to pin the hem.

'There!' She made Elena lifted her arms and turn slowly around. 'See, perfect with your hair.' And later, having followed the lines of pins with tiny stitches, Gerry presented her with the dress.

A startled look, a vigorous shake of the head. 'No! I cannot ...'

'Yes, yes! I *want* you to have it.' Gerry said, and then forgot all about it. But, before you could say slipstitch, that gift came back to hit her sharply in the nose.

Scoot and Hallie-Lee had started turning on Gerry like curs in a dog fight, and she was the one always ending up with torn ears. Hearing about the dress, both made a beeline for her, round-eyed with disapproval.

Scoot first, hands pushed in pockets, patched pants bagging at the knees: 'Isn't it about time you headed off home, now? Yeah, and take all those fancy duds with you. They don't fit in here. And I'm a-telling you, lady, you don't fit in here, neither.'

'Lookit, Gerry, it's not rightly your fault.' Hallie-Lee next, trailing clouds of queenly condescension. 'You're not acquainted with our ways here, but we never, ever make that kind of fuss of the servants. I mean, what does a Mexican girl know about those fancy clothes? It's *couture*, isn't it! Where did you think she'd wear it?'

Gerry had no answers. Would she ever get anything right? Probably not. These whiners and nay-sayers were campaigning to get rid of her.

She was beginning to realize that, in spite of having a voice that dripped honey, Hallie-Lee Kittrell was not a person to cross. Her visits were becoming more and more regular, too; she slithered in and out like a sulky python.

Of course, the other girl wasted no time repeating the whole sorry saga to Coop. Gerry could only imagine the huffing, puffing and eye-rolling that had gone into the telling of that tale - the dress, the gift, the error of Gerry's strange English ways.

Finding her busily altering another garment, he said, 'You sure like to stir things up, don't you?'

'Elena liked it; she thought it was pretty.' She stabbed the needle fiercely into a seam. 'What's wrong with me giving it away?'

'Because it's not how we do things here. It won't do, you know. You don't understand these people.'

No. She didn't know anything, didn't understand anything. In the opinion of almost everyone here, she was a meddlesome brat.

'It was just an old dress.' She waved a weary hand. 'A copy.'

'Y'know, it's not fitting -'

'All women deserve pretty clothes.'

' - to try and turn Elena into some prim English miss.'

She frowned, biting off the thread with her teeth. Was *that* what he thought of her?

'Would you pass personal things on to a servant back home?'

'I don't have domestic staff at home, not anymore.' She paused. 'But, if I did ... yes, I would. Of course, I would.

They're human beings, aren't they, just like us.'

He rolled his eyes. 'Well, God Save the King.'

Letters flew back and forth between Gerry and Prim every few weeks.

In her small, precise handwriting, Prim detailed bookshop business, *(bad to worse)*, news of Igor, *(disappeared again)*, and all the Lower Shepney Market gossip.

She wanted to know every single thing that had been happening to Gerry. Was she enjoying herself, had she found out all that she wanted to know, would she soon be coming home? Money from the sale of Gerry's share of the ranch was now sorely needed.

In response, Gerry described the ranch and how she longed to introduce more comfort to this austere household. It was a dwelling, not a home. Beautifully built, no expense spared, but spartan furnishings. No colour, style, no arrangement of lilies in cut-glass bowls.

Of course, she wouldn't dare touch a thing. It was nothing to do with her, was it? Except, of course, that she owned half of everything. That was something to think about. The thing was, when she went home, she would be giving up all rights to the place.

On the porch, she stopped writing and stared into the distance. *Give it time*, Doc Hyde had said. What had he meant, what had he been talking about? Her leg, the dog? Or Texas?

A breeze took the top pages of her letter and sent them fluttering to the ground. Sighing, she collected them up, spread them out again.

Would she ever get the hang of Texas?

Every night, every single night now, she dreamed of Leonie - dancing, twirling, singing. What was *that* all about?

CHAPTER TWENTY TWO

'Try not to have 'opinions'.
Rather, learn to cook a decent dinner.'
How to Attract a Man, 1923

Silence in the house.

Something wrong? No murmur of conversation, footfall of servants, none of the usual breakfast clatter. When Gerry woke, no-one else seemed to be stirring.

Downstairs the table wasn't laid and Cesar, nowhere to be seen. Then, from the kitchen wing, a crash of china and Spanish voices, rising to a high C screech.

Following the sound of this pandemonium, Gerry poked her head round the kitchen door. Two red-faced girls, Elena and one other, were wrestling with spitting pans on a huge black range, while the hot kitchen appeared to have exploded around them.

'Cesar?' Gerry raised her eyebrows.

The girls, in dark dresses and huge white aprons, stopped in their tracks. Blue smoke drifted up; there was a strong smell of burning. A flurry of Spanish, and then, 'Seek, seek.' Elena mimed someone's head pillowed in hands.

'He's ... ill?'

'Sí, sí, enfermo. Fiebre. A fever. And Vicente y Juan y ...' a long list of other names, including the cook.

'All of them?' Gerry looked round at the mess. Had *that* been breakfast? 'Well, can I help?'

Wiping hands on her apron, Elena shook her head nervously, then offered Gerry a cup of coffee that tasted of feet.

'So ...um, esta noche? What about dinner?'

A high-pitched stream of Spanish, more shrugging and wringing of hands. Exchanging glances, the girls seemed close to tears. Eight men were out with Coop, apparently, four more at the ranch, and there might be another two around, somewhere. Dinner for fourteen? It couldn't be done. No, no, no.

'Don't worry.' Gerry reached for an apron. 'I can help.'

'No!'

'Really, it will be all right. We'll manage.'

But, will we? she asked herself, feeling the first stirrings of panic. *Where should I start?*

'Hey, wha'd'ya take me for?' Scoot held up his hands. 'I don't cook!'

'Well, if you want to eat, you'll have to help.'

What was in the larder? Beef. Gerry's heart sank. Of *course*, beef. Enough to withstand a siege. Great hanging haunches of cow, slippery slabs of cow organs. The Sweeney Todd school of cookery.

Was there *any* food in this house that hadn't come from that animal? If so, Coop would doubtless have got rid of it. As for herself, she was tired of picking pieces of cow out of her teeth.

At home there'd be local game and fish. But, here? Prairie hens? Jackrabbits?

Chickens. Of course! Plenty of those scratching round. Nothing controversial about a chicken.

Could Scoot get some for her? They had to be big, she told him. Small ones weren't worth the aggravation. Eight? Or, maybe ten?

He looked at Gerry as if she were mad. 'We *only* eat beef.'

'Who says?'

'Coop. And round here,' he squared slim shoulders, 'we do what Coop says.'

'Well, he's not here, is he? And when he gets back, he'll be too hungry to mind.'

'Well, hey! Don't go mixing me up any of in this. We do things different here, yessir. And don't try being no do-gooder, neither; you'll make even more of a horse's behind out of yourself.'

He stamped off, and she stuck out her tongue at his retreating back.

Gerry had plucked and drawn many chickens, many times, but never ever had she caught a live bird and wrung its neck.

These birds weren't clucking around peaceably in any old coop, either, like the ones at home, with their vacant expressions. These were strutting free, wherever they pleased, and seemed to spend a lot of time fighting each other.

What's more, much the same as everyone else here, they didn't seem to like the look of her, not one bit, squawking fiercely whenever she came near.

How *could* birds be so difficult to catch?

With the air full of high-pitched squawking, feathers and chickens flapping and flying up in every direction, a man appeared. 'Missie! What you do?'

Fair question. Blood-stained up to her elbows and shifty as a fox in a chicken coop - Gerry pushed hair back from her eyes and tried to explain.

Hadn't she always been used to mass catering? Filleting fish and preparing pheasants, snipe and woodcock for a never-ending stream of Leonie's house guests - actors, artists and adventurers - a dozen or more at a time.

Leonie, of course, had found slicing the top off her own egg too demanding. So guests, often straight from the pages of *Tatler,* were always most appreciative.

'Dulling, she just chopped up those little green herb thingies and flung them in, and it tastes dee-vine!'

Here, things were different. None of the ingredients Gerry wanted were to hand, and no butcher or greengrocer in sight. The girls were still wailing, and Scoot - forced to help - bitterly complaining.

One thing was clear. In just a few hours, a large number of tired hungry men would come piling through that door demanding food. And there'd be hell to pay if it wasn't ready, and probably hell to pay if they didn't like it.

In spite of some panic, difficulties in comprehension and bouts of tripping over the dog, Gerry soon got into her stride. One meal, without barely-cooked slabs of red meat! Hurray!

And when the Mexican girls saw that she knew what she was doing, they started to trust her and gain confidence themselves.

'Are there spices?' she asked.

A firm shake of the head. 'Coop - he no like.'

'Well, let's just try a little, shall we?'

'She's going to *poison* us,' Scoot muttered, darkly.

After a day of plucking, chopping, braising and basting, there was an air of sunny optimism inside the kitchen and a delicious aroma wafting out of it.

And after a long spell of, 'What's this?' and, 'What the heck's that?' even Scoot went to work with a will. Gerry felt almost light-headed.

Hallelujah! At last, a place in this house where she fitted in.

Busily tending a huge pot, large enough to cook a small missionary in, Gerry barely noticed clattering hooves and the tap of heeled boots.

'They're back, the men are back!'

A hush descended on the hot kitchen.

Then, a voice like the wrath of God from the doorway. 'What the hell's going on? Cesar! Where's Cesar?'

Coop. Who else? The Faultfinder General. A man, Gerry thought, who seemed to spend much of his life in a towering temper.

'Sick.' Still wearing her bloodstained apron and counting out joints of chicken, she avoided eye contact. 'Like the rest of his family and quite a few of the others, apparently.'

'So, what are you doing in here?'

'Cooking.'

'Say again?' He looked taken aback. 'Cooking what?'

'Dinner. These girls were the only ones left standing and they'd exhausted themselves getting breakfast ready.'

Lifting the lid from a pot, Coop sniffed the cloud of scented steam. Idly sticking in one finger, he licked it. 'What's in here?'

'Chicken. Please, don't do that.'

'This is Texas. We always have beef.'

'Sometimes it's good to have a change.'

'Not if I have anything to do with it.'

'Well, you didn't.' Gerry sighed, while everyone else seemed to be holding their breath. 'So unless you can get cow on the table in five minutes, this is what we're going to eat. It's an Olde Englishe meal.'

'Look, I'm not ungrateful, but these are hard-working men, used to eating hearty. They won't want fancy, like those green things, whatever they are.'

'Those would be vegetables. Please! Don't *do* that!'

'I'm not wild about those, either.'

'They're good for you, keep you healthy.'

'Who are you? The food sheriff?'

Hold me back, Gerry thought, *before I throttle him with his own neckerchief.*

Had he, she asked, got any other ideas about getting everyone fed in the next few minutes? Apparently, he hadn't. She waited for that fact to sink in, then turned back to the pot.

Coop didn't move, but seemed to have stopped pawing the ground. Acutely aware of him leaning against a cupboard and watching every move, she tripped backwards and forwards, from cupboard to range to table, cloth in one hand, spoon in the other.

'Look, I'm going to serve this up now. So please go and do ... whatever it is that you usually do ... and let me get on with it.'

'Guess I just never saw you as the domestic type.'

'How did you see me? The useless type?' Tempted to reach for the boning knife, she turned to face him. 'I'm domesticated, because my aunt wasn't. I'm no beginner, either. My ayah in India taught me to cook.'

And to sew and to play mah-jong and ring her eyes with kohl, but she didn't bring that up. 'We used to make huge cauldrons of rice and fish curry for the beggars at our gate. Three or four times this amount.'

'Rice and fish?' He looked only slightly penitent. 'Is that what we're having? I only ask because we had a Chinese cook once. Had to fire him.'

'Please, go away. And tell the men, it's ready.'

When Gerry carried in food, she ran the gauntlet of suspicious faces round the table. Luckily, the meal turned out to be something of a sensation.

'Well, say! What's happening here, Coop?'

Succulent chickens with oomph and flavour ... 'wait, this is fine, real fine!' ... neat mounds of buttery vegetables ... 'wow! 'Scuse me licking mah fingers, ma'am,' and enough of everything to feed a regiment.

Gerry helped the girls with the kitchen-to-table sequence, and the men fell on the food with rollicking enthusiasm and pleasure.

Coop's look of disbelief after his first few mouthfuls, almost made Gerry laugh out loud. Hopefully, he would soon be eating his words, along with the chicken.

When only bones picked clean of meat were left, she staggered out of the kitchen again with a heavy tray. As Bren Ryan stood up to hold open the door, Coop pushed back his chair. 'What now? Where you going with that?'

'It's food for the sick. Those people -'

'Nope.' He blocked her path.

'But we cooked extra, we - '

'No.'

'Why not?'

'Because I say so. Stay away. You'll end up sick again too, if you're not careful.'

'I'm perfectly well now,' she said. Actually, her head ached. 'I've the constitution of an ox. Those people ...'

'Not your problem. Be told.'

'Well, that's just *silly*; they haven't had anything to eat for days!'

A dark look. 'My say, my ranch.'

'As far as I'm aware,' Gerry sniffed, 'at this moment, it's still *our* ranch, isn't it?'

There was an acute silence in the room, a snapping to attention all round. Someone sucked in a breath and they all looked elsewhere. Red rags and bulls came to mind, and at her side, Bren Ryan shifted, uncomfortably.

At that point, with Coop still barring her way, Gerry's knees sagged. 'Look,' she said. 'What do you *want* from me? I'm tired of being the butt of your temper all the time; it's so … draining!'

'Whoa!' Coop took the tray out of her hands. 'What's put the burr under your saddle today? Calm down.'

No, she said, she would not calm down. Yes, she did think this was a life-and-death matter! And yes, she thought it perfectly reasonable to mention ownership of the ranch in front of all the men.

'Well then, do you want to, maybe … step outside the door?'

As they went out of the dining room, he moved to nudge the door shut with the toe of his boot and Gerry heard the snort of someone trying not to laugh.

She didn't falter.

'All right, I'm an English interloper meddling in your affairs, but I'm stuck here, aren't I? How long must I keep apologizing for that? Because believe me, I don't like it, any more than you do!'

Coop stayed silent.

'From my first day here,' she said, building up to a rolling boil, 'when you hammered on my bedroom door, you've been horrible to me. Smug and critical and ... and ...'

'Mean! I've been *mean* to you?'

'Taunted me, humiliated me. You even tried to frighten me! Do you *like* torturing people?'

He shrugged. 'It's one of the perks of your being here, yes.'

'Because where I come from, we don't behave like that!'

'Ah,' he said, with a wry drawl, 'I take it you're not impressed then, by my folksy Texan charm?'

'As for today, goodness knows I had the best of intentions. Those girls were at their wits' end and I was trying to help, that's all. Did you have to belittle me?'

'*Be-little*! What the heck does that mean? Where *I* come from we don't use language like that.'

'No, you wouldn't. It comes with education and good breeding.'

Her words hung there, in the silence.

Coop's eyebrows arched. 'Well just for the tally books, lady, you could've been nicer to me, too. Oh, yeah. Back there in Olde England. When you were showing off?'

'What do you mean?'

'Talking like a dictionary. All that stuff about Dickens, thinking I wouldn't know? Trying to be *smart*.'

Gerry felt herself flush.

'That's right,' he drawled. 'So go pick the bones out of that chicken!'

'Well.' Gerry's face felt stiff. 'You won't have to suffer much longer, because my leg's getting stronger all the time. I'll soon be able to go home and you'll be rid of me. For ever.'

The words 'good riddance' lay unspoken between them.

'Look. I just don't want you to get sick again, that's all.'

'And delay my departure? No, I'm quite sure that you don't.'

'Thing is,' Coop murmured. 'I can be so nice to people when they do what I want.'

'Yes, and everyone just rolls over to keep you happy, don't they? They all go wherever you point. Like ... like King Rameses.'

'Ah, except for you, apparently. Don't you ever do anything you're told?'

'Not when it's unreasonable, no. Not since I was twelve.'

Coop ran a hand through his hair. 'And to think, when we met, I thought you were a nice quiet sort of girl ...'

'You were wrong.' Gerry said.

'... with a kinda strange dress sense, maybe. Wrong? Oh, I sure was.' A deep sigh. 'Okay. Go get the rest of the food. We'll deliver it, me and the men.' He shouted for Bren Ryan. 'And Gerry ...'

'*What!*

'Thanks, I guess. For the meal, the food. Yeah, good job.'

That took the wind out of her sails. It didn't make her feel any better, though. Ho no, most unsatisfactory.

Exasperated by his coldness, his irritability, she'd wanted to force a row. Naturally, she'd made a mess of it. He'd sabotaged her, hadn't he? Laid waste to her defences with sweet reason.

Then, just sauntered off, whistling *Dixie*.

Now, she felt thoroughly deflated. Like a leaky bag of wind. And more touchy and irritable than ever.

In her dream, swimming in the Hall lake, Gerry had become tangled in weeds and couldn't kick herself free. Air, air, struggling for air!

Gasping for breath, she woke at first light.

Again, no early morning clatter, smell of coffee or frying steak. Oh, Lord.

Nothing happening downstairs, either. The dining room bare and empty, except for an unshaven, weary-looking Coop - cup of cold coffee in front of him, map spread out over the table.

'Is Cesar still ill?'

'Yip.'

'And the cook ... Vicente?'

'The girls as well, this morning.'

'Oh, dear.'

She cleared her throat.

All attention now, and tilting back in his chair, he shot her an innocent look. 'It's all right. I forgive you.'

She stared. 'I wasn't apologizing.' Well, perhaps that was what she'd meant to do, but all of a sudden, she couldn't be bothered. She wasn't *that* sorry, and Coop probably knew that she wasn't.

Anyway, he'd started it.

'I thought it went pretty much same as usual, myself,' he said. 'Yeah, I threw my weight around, you were ... uncooperative.'

She felt her colour rise.

'You were out of line,' he went on, straight-faced. 'I was a jackass. Now, I'm not real used to this sort of wrangling with a woman, but I'd say we were about even, wouldn't you? Truce?'

A long pause. Horses clattered outside. A dog started barking.

'So ... is my career as household cook over?'

'Pretty much.' His lips twitched. 'Hallie-Lee says I need to arrange something else.'

Ah. Gerry beat a swift retreat.

CHAPTER
TWENTY THREE

'Always keep a man on tenterhooks.
Never let him know what you are thinking.'
The Bachelor Girl's Handbook, 1924

A library. A music room. In the middle of the prairie? These
were the dusty, neglected places Gerry retreated to when she
couldn't do anything else.

That was the problem. She wasn't allowed to do anything
else, nothing useful, anyway. Not cook, nor sew, nor express
an opinion. Just sit quietly on her hands in a corner and wait
for someone to object to that. Ha! Let them try.

A day or two after the chicken dinner crisis, she went back
to playing the piano. Banging out ragtime suited her mood
perfectly, and the piano trembled under her treatment.

It was some time before she saw Scoot, sulky, lip-drooping,
leaning against the door.

'How long you been able to do that?'

A shrug. 'Since I was knee-high to a grasshopper. In my

family, it was the sort of accomplishment that a young lady must acquire.'

'You sure talk a load of bull.'

'They wouldn't have approved of this, though.' A few jazzy bars, and she threw back her head to trill loudly: '*Olga, Come Back to the Vo...ooo...lga!*'

'You're nuts, you know that?'

'Come, dance with me, Scoot.' Gerry got up from the piano. 'Can you dance? Look, I'll teach you. The Grizzly Bear, the Turkey Trot? Oh, come on!'

As she pranced around, flicking up feet in their elaborately strapped French slippers, Scoot backed away. 'Huh, better sober up, pretty darn quick. Doc Hyde's waiting on you.'

'He wants to see me?'

'S'what I just said, wasn't it?

'Well ... oh, stop that! No need to kick the piano.'

'He's outside, lady! Right this minute.'

Almost noon, it was stiflingly hot and sure to get hotter. Prairie stretched away in a shimmering heat haze. Nothing moved, no-one else around.

Dockery Hyde - Gerry's one and only ally in this place - was sprawled in the shade of the verandah. Luckily, he was a regular visitor.

After the evening meal, he and Coop could usually be found locked in conversation, heads together, voices low. Lately, Gerry had noticed that when anyone else came near, all talk would stop.

'Well, how-do.' Getting up now, he loped towards her, dogs at his heels. 'My! You sure are a sight for sore eyes on a hot, dusty day. Don't reckon this porch has ever seen the like.'

Gerry's day dress was floaty silk organza. A dress meant for meeting people and being introduced at afternoon tea parties, not sitting wild-haired and perspiring in a dusty wind. Well, she had her morale to keep up.

'What did you do to Scoot? Kid streaked past me like a lightning bolt.'

'I asked him to dance.'

'Yeah, that would do it. You like to dance? C'mon then, let's give it a whirl. I can do-si-do with the best of 'em.'

'Too hot!'

'Yep, Texas sure ain't for sissies. Come sit, then ... not that chair, dog just tossed a frog in, take this one. Leg not still bothering you, is it?'

'D'you mean, my fetlock?'

'Just can't forgive me for that, can you?' Dropping down beside her on the verandah, Doc shooed the dogs away. 'None of my other patients ever complain. You still look kinda tuckered out, though. Pale, y'know.'

'I'm always pale.' She fanned herself with her hat. 'White as bacon rind, Scoot says.'

Silence. Just the squeak of the swing, as she pushed it gently back and forth; the breeze flirting with the hem of her dress

Propping himself on his elbows, Doc cleared his throat. 'Can we talk a little, Gerry, you and me? About Coop?'

She stopped swinging.

'He's worried about you.'

'About *me*?'

'Uh-huh.'

'Really?'

'Yip.'

'But he barely talks to me, and when he does, it's to pick fault.' She could hear the peevish tone creep into her voice, almost a bleat. 'He's always cross, he won't answer any of my questions, either. Do you know, since I arrived,' she flapped an arm, 'I haven't once -'

'Questions? What questions?'

'Oh.' As soon as the words were out, she'd regretted them. 'He calls me 'the who and why girl'. Mostly, to do with why I came here.'

'What d'you want to know?'

Gerry bent to fiddle with her shoe. How much had Doc been told? Did he know about her aunt, about the will?

'Has Coop talked about his own background?' As if he'd read her mind. 'I mean, how he ended up here, where he came from?'

A slow shake of her head.

'Well, ask him, will you? Will you do that?'

She tensed. 'He won't answer. He shies away from personal questions, discussions of any kind - at least, with me.'

'Yeah, he's private, all right. Want to know what he's thinking? Me, too. I've known him since he was ten years old, and any time, any day, I've no real idea.'

'Can't you tell me, then? About his background?'

'Reckon it's up to him. As for the rest ...' he leaned forward. 'Let it go, will you, Gerry?'

'I ... beg pardon?'

'He's not picking on you, he's just doing his job. Running the ranch and cattle, keeping everything going. It takes all his time, anythin' else has to be second place.'

She stared out at the plateau of prairie. 'What about women friends?'

'He's done his fair share of tomcatting.'

Oh, yes, Gerry thought. *I'll just bet that he has.*

'Hallie-Lee?' She couldn't help herself.

'Now, that's a whole other story.'

Silence. Just breeze riffling overhead vine leaves; a light laugh from the kitchen. 'When he looks at me,' she said, 'I think he sees a heifer who won't do as it's told.'

'Yeah. Well, he knows cows. He trusts cows.'

'They don't answer back, do they? Do you know what I *really* think?' Fixing her gaze on a bloated black beetle-thing close to her foot, she said, 'I think he's punishing me, I do. For being here.'

'Pardon me, ma'am, but that's a load of horse manure. Sure, he was worried about you coming, sure he was. He knew there'd be consequences.'

'He doesn't like anything about me. I should never have come. I ... um, what sort of consequences?'

'The money sort.'

'So his problems are my fault? Because I, well ...'

'Because you own half the ranch? That's part of it, sure

nuff.'

Gerry stared. 'Does *everyone* here know about that?'

'Oh, sure.'

'Lord.' She bit her lip. 'And I suppose they all think I've stolen his inheritance.'

'Lookit, there's a hell of a lot going on in Coop's mind right now, is all I'm sayin'. He's having a hard time and it's making him punchy.'

Gerry let out a heavy Ophelia-like sigh. 'I see.'

'No, you don't,' Doc said, gently, 'you'd have to be born here for that. But let him off the hook, anyway, will you? Start by asking what's on his mind and get to know him a little better.'

Another sigh. 'He's got friends for that, hasn't he?'

Doc met her eyes. 'Not at the moment, he hasn't, no.'

A long pause.

'And, Gerry ... while you're at it, ask him about Scoot.'

Scoot?

Ask Coop what was on his mind? Gerry stayed on the swing seat for some time, mulling things over. Well, she'd tried, hadn't she? Was it worth trying again? Trying harder?

That insect - or another just like it, there were probably hundreds of the wretched things - came back. Fat and black with proboscis and huge wings, it seemed to be deliberately sauntering close to her feet, daring her to jump. The biggest bug she'd ever seen. Well. If she managed to avoid being trampled to death here, she'd probably end up being eaten alive.

No-one realised, did they? In coming here, she'd left so much behind. First, her dignity. Then, all sense of being in control of her life. Did anyone appreciate that? Did Coop?

As she brooded, raised voices floated out from behind the barn. One of the ranch hands? And ... yes, Bren Ryan.

'Someone's gonna have to tell him, Bren. What's hanging off his tail? He's been mean as all hell for weeks now, drivin' us way too hard.'

'I know it. Reckon it's high time he got married. Hallie-Lee's been chafing at that bit for too long. They'll be no crawling out of it this time.'

'Is he still thinking about it?'

'Maybe he's thinking too much about it, that's why he ain't doing it.'

Hidden from view, Gerry shifted, uneasily. She shouldn't be listening; it was none of her business.

She recalled Hallie-Lee's own comments about a wedding. It would be a big affair, wouldn't it? Yes, a perfect match. Two dynasties joined, that's what Red Kittrell had said. Did they exchange cattle or something? Coop, all granite jawed and rugged masculinity; Hallie-Lee, the most sought-after beauty in the state.

'What about the other one?'

'Who you yakkin' about now?'

'Miss English, who owns half the place. She's shaking his tail too, ain't she?'

Gerry froze. Did everyone here know everybody's business?

'She's sure nuff ain't helping none.'

A long pause, and just when she'd thought it was safe enough to sidle away, 'And them Kittrells. Mad for that oil, and still pushing on about wild-catting!'

'They can push all they like. Nobody tells Coop when and where to head in. That's somethin' else the boy's holding out on.'

Gerry frowned. What did she know about oil? Nothing, nothing at all. Or wild-catting, whatever that was. Interesting, though. The only other person she'd ever heard mention it, had been Red Kittrell.

CHAPTER
TWENTYFOUR

'Be womanly. Always show decorum.'
A Woman's Way, 1923

Gerry had been working her way round the library shelves, peering at titles, picking out books. Day-dreaming? Looking for ... well, for Frank O'Rourke.

Because he was here, all right. She could sense it. Like Leonie and the wardrobe of clothes, this was his room. Any clues to his character would be here somewhere, she was sure of it.

Something that had started to surprise her, was Scoot's appearances. Several times, as she'd pretended to read, he'd hovered in the doorway, scuffing his feet.

'Lady,' he said one day, leaning against the shelves, 'you *read* too much.' He moved to sprawl in a chair, chin cupped moodily in his hands. 'Anyhow, what's so interesting in them books?'

'Do you read, Scoot?'

'Not if I can help it. Y'all have to sit still and quiet fer reading.'

Gerry sighed. 'Is Coop still not letting you ride out?'

'Says I spend too much time with the men.' He pulled a face. 'Thinks I should stay here an' help around the ranch. Huh! Wimmen's stuff. '

The boy hooked hair behind his ears, setting Gerry to wonder about his age again. Twelve? Thirteen? In some ways he seemed older. Features, though, were very soft.

'Couldn't you help Angel? He's always busy and you're so good with those horses.'

'Busy! He *sure* is. Busy hanging round that Elena.'

'Alba's daughter! Well, she is very pretty.'

'Oh yeah, thinks she's so all-fired cute in that dress you gave her.'

Ah. 'Pity to let a girl come between you and Angel, though, isn't it? To ... you know, spoil your friendship?'

'Huh!'

A long silence. The room was bright with sunlight, dust motes drifting idly in the air.

'Anyhow,' Scoot sniffed, 'I won't be staying round here much longer if *she* has anythin' to do with it.'

'Who's she?'

'Miz sour-as-a-pickle Kittrell. She wants me outta here, sure nuff. Thinks I should go away to school. I'm un-con-troll-able, she says, an' need a firm hand an' all. Keeps on an' on to Coop about it.'

'Perhaps you've misunderstood.'

Scoot looked scornful. 'I may be dumb, lady, I ain't *that* dumb.'

'Coop wouldn't make you go away if you didn't want to.'

'Ain't so sure about that.' Scoot's eyes slid out of focus, and he looked away, chewing his finger. 'Ain't sure about anything, anymore.'

Gerry remembered that feeling. She felt sorry for the boy. 'You ride really well, Scoot.'

Careless shrug. 'Person has two legs, he can ride. Round here, folks git put on a horse before they can walk. Hell, we do more riding than walking.'

'Well, I envy you.'

Times now, she'd watched in admiration as Scoot - all loose and long-limbed, like a string bean - somersaulted in and out of the saddle, while his horse stood perfectly still.

Lately, in this land of tough men and fierce animals, she'd felt an urge to do the same - to throw off English timidity and gallop into the sun. Heatstroke! Or because she'd been restricted for so long?

'I'd dearly love to sit on a full-sized horse and ride really fast,' she said, 'like you do. Perhaps even jump over things. I've never learned to do it, properly.'

A scornful sound. 'A person don't need teaching for that! You jest grab a hunk of mane and sink spur.'

'Oh, I like horses well enough from a distance. But close up, those big teeth and flared nostrils and heads lunging up and down.'

'Holy cow!' Scoot hooted. 'You ain't scared? Of a *horse*?'

Oh, yes, Gerry thought. She'd never quite lost her dread of them.

At three, she'd been set on an Arab stallion by her father. A gift from some maharajah or other, after his investment. When she'd screamed in fear and struggled to get off, her father had seen that as a sign. Not only was his child without charm and curls, she also lacked courage. A perfect horseman himself, he'd threatened to tie his cowardly offspring onto the animal. He would have done it, too. And that, had been the start.

'That child,' Gerry remembered hearing him say one day, to her mother, 'is my greatest disappointment.' A hidden sore. She'd never, ever managed to please him.

'That's the British for you,' Leonie had commented, when she'd heard the tale. 'Only show affection to horses and dogs.

'So how d'you git around places at home?'

'Walk. Or bicycle.'

'Jeez!'

Some time later.

'Ah been thinkin',' Scoot said, carelessly. 'Maybe I could teach you. Yeah. Nothing much else to do 'til Coop lets me ride out again.' He clicked his fingers. 'Jest need to find me the right horse.'

'Really? How kind.'

And snap, Gerry was to remind herself later. The trap had been set and she'd marched straight into it, hadn't she, eyes shining and not smelling even the faintest whiff of rat.

Scoot was a good boy, really. Misunderstood, that was all.

People were so mistrustful, weren't they? Poor boy just needed to be given a fair chance.

'Found a nice little filly.' Scoot again, with his best butter-wouldn't-melt-in-his-mouth expression. 'Jest right for you, reckon. Yip, real good ride. No ounce of bad blood in her.'

With his hat set at a particularly jaunty angle and Lobo at his heels, he was unusually chatty as they walked towards the corral. *My, a beautiful day, wasn't it? Yessir. A real fine day for a ride.*

Not even then, Gerry recalled afterwards, had she considered his behaviour at all odd. Idiot. Dolt!

A dozen or so horses were already standing out and she eyed them, thoughtfully. Every last one looked huge - the grey that Scoot had picked out, one of the biggest. It started to roll its eyeballs and skitter sideways as they drew near.

'*This* one?' She stepped back, stomach turning. It already looked as if it had some sort of grudge against them and wanted to get even. 'Are you sure it's not too frisky?'

'Nah,' Scoot said, as the flighty-looking horse flattened its ears and plunged its head up and down. 'That's jest the flies. She'll settle down; she's gentle as a lamb. Not still scared, are ya?'

Standing next to the horse's great, gleaming flank, Gerry gulped, and had to screw up every ounce of courage before putting one foot in the stirrup, and allowing Scoot to heave her onto the animal's back.

'Ready?'

A moment's frozen silence. Bolt upright, tense with fright, she sat in the saddle.

Then a yell from Scoot, as he slapped hard on the horse's rump, and - *whap! whap!* - all hell was let loose. The wild-eyed filly was off, leaping, bucking, desperate to unseat its rider - forwards, sideways, backwards - Gerry's head nodding violently in time with each jolt.

She held the reins so tightly that they burned her sweaty hands, but still lost all control, as the horse plunged sideways, taking off round the corral like a lightning bolt. The muscles in its neck stood out; there was no stopping it.

From somewhere, 'Yee-haw! Ride him, cowboy!' and a high-pitched whinny of a laugh.

Then, shouts in Spanish, and someone else's angry bellow. 'What the hell! *Gerry* ... no!'

With a white-knuckled Gerry clinging on for dear life, they raced wildly for the fence. Before the sweating horse, flecks of foam round its mouth, could take a jump, Gerry gave a squawk of terror, and slid sideways off the monster's back.

The world turned upside down, birds rising up in noisy protest as she landed, a crumpled heap on hard baked earth. A limp rag doll.

A bone-shuddering eight or nine seconds was all it had taken for the unforgiving animal to unseat her. On the tenth, Coop had vaulted the fence and crouched beside her, his expression an unsettling mix of cold fury and concern.

'What the *hell* did you think you were doing?'

She squinted up, coughing through the dust. 'I'm all right.'

'The hell you are. Don't talk. It'll hurt!'

Muttering under his breath, he slid one arm around her shoulders, and scooping up her limp form, carried her back to the house.

Over his shoulder, a trembling Gerry saw Scoot, legs pumping, going hell-for-leather in the opposite direction.

'Are you dead set on killing yourself while you're here?'

Gerry blinked, with what must surely be bloodshot eyes. What could she say?

That she'd thought Scoot had been waving a white flag, not another red rag? That she'd wanted to gallop off with the wind in her hair and soar over fences, like Hallie-Lee Kittrell and every other person here? That she was an idiot?

'I'm an idiot.'

'No kidding. Who put you on that crazy filly? She's hot as a pistol and barely green broke.'

Gerry swallowed, tasting grit.

'Did Scoot devil you into this?' Coop gave her a hard look. 'Listen, some shenanigans, that kid can just be spanked for. This is different.'

'I don't think he wanted to hurt me.' Gerry flexed sore fingers carefully. 'Not really. It was probably a *that'll-teach-you* sort of thing, to make me look silly.'

'And nearly kill you in the process? Jackass!'

'Oh, don't worry about me. I've been humiliated by experts. See, I'm all right.' She got gingerly to her feet, but sank quickly back down again. 'He's got some sort of grudge against me, that's all.'

'Scoot's got a grudge against the world and needs to learn how to behave. Here. Drink this.' He held out a glass. Something brown swirled round inside it.

'What is it?'

'Medicine.'

She choked as fiery liquid reached her throat. 'It's whisky!'

'Southern cure. For the shock.' Unlacing her boot, Coop eased it off. As he probed her ankle with deft precision, she could feel the calluses on his hand. 'That hurt?'

She shook her head, hiccupped. 'Oh ... pardon!'

'Granted. You could've broken your neck.' Leaning forward, he touched her lips gently with his thumb. 'Your mouth's swelling up. Listen, there's something I need to tell you about Scoot. Yeah. But now's not the time. Let's get a cold compress for that head.'

When he left her, she was still shaking.

Early next day, a commotion outside.

Easing herself out of bed - every muscle aching, every bone feeling bruised - Gerry hobbled to the window.

In dim, cool light, she could just make out Scoot's figure in the corral. He was saddling a horse - grey, long-legged, with a muscular neck and satin coat - Gerry's nemesis of the day before.

Someone shouted. 'No, no! Bad horse!'

Ignoring all warnings, Scoot leapt into the saddle and galloped wildly away.

'How is it? Let me look.' Cupping her chin, Coop turned her face one side, then the other and let out a long, slow sigh. 'Don't you ever do anything stupid as that again. Looks like you've been in a fight.'

Trying not to flinch, Gerry mumbled that really, she was quite all right. Not the whole truth. She hurt all over and first glimpse in the mirror had shown a stricken white face, with yellow spreading bruise and a big fat lip.

'Yeah, only just.' Moving his thumb softly across her cheek, he traced the outline of her swollen mouth and sighed again. 'I'm real sorry, Gerry.' His own mouth seemed to soften.

For what, she wondered vaguely. Absolutely still, acutely aware of the line of his jaw and blood whoosh-whooshing in her ears, she felt a sudden urge to bury her face in his neck.

Her throat closed. Enough! Every one of her nerve ends seemed to be tingling, and she hated herself for it.

'Some men,' Leonie used to say, 'just have that thing, darling. A certain *je ne sais quoi.* You'll know it when you feel it.'

'And now you know just what I meant, don't you, my darling!'

When she was able to breathe out, she took a shaky step back, tripping over Lobo at her heels.

'Next time you decide you to get back on a horse,' he said, 'come and find me.'

'Don't they say to do that straight away?' Why on God's earth had she said that!

Coop just stared hard at her, a question behind his eyes. He seemed as taken aback as she was.

CHAPTER
TWENTYFIVE

'Bachelor girls sometimes fall into free and easy ways.
This is a mistake and may lead to serious trouble.'
The Bachelor Girl's Handbook, 1924

Coop seemed to be driving himself harder than ever. Out all day and shut in the den for hours afterwards. Several times, he didn't even turn up for the evening meal.

On one of those dark, fragrant Texan nights, with the air still and hot and every insect whirr, night bird call, loud in the silence - Gerry found him asleep on the dark verandah. Sprawled in a chair, half-empty glass hanging from nerveless fingers.

When she gently removed it, he barely stirred.

The cattle? Or something else, some private struggle? She'd no idea. He wasn't about to confide in her, either. She wasn't privy to any of his movements.

Later though, desperate for an opportunity to talk, she forced herself to go back and seek him out.

Under that purple sky filled with brilliant southern stars - still unshaven, dust-stained - he was now staring out at his sacred land, dogs sprawled panting at his side.

Gerry cleared her throat to get his attention. The dogs lifted their heads, tongues lolling, but the man didn't move or even look round.

'Coop?'

A half-turn, a puzzled stare, as if he could barely remember who she was, and still, that air of exhaustion. She felt a sudden impulse to reach up and press her hand against his cheek. 'Is anything wrong?'

'Nothing to bother you.' Eyes narrowed, as he looked her slowly up and down. 'I sure hope there was someone around at dinner to appreciate that dress.'

She fidgeted with the clasp of her pearl choker. The dress, in soft, beaded silk, had been rather a reckless choice, but she'd always loved it, adored wearing it. The way it dipped away from her neck, the sensation on her skin and swish-swoosh of it when she turned, walked.

Well, the men at the dinner table might have appreciated it, but Scoot certainly hadn't.

'Why y'all rigged up like a birthday cake again?' he'd muttered. 'That stuff's too fussy even fer a dance, if you ask me.'

Bren Ryan had said sharply that no-one had, and wasn't he in enough trouble already, and to hush right up.

'Another of Leonie's,' Gerry said now, trying to pull the skirt down a little. 'Rather out of place here, I suppose.'

'Oh, I wouldn't say that.'

Leaves of the vine shivered, the breeze bore a faint, dusty scent. As silver moths fluttered overhead, moonlight on her dress made Gerry feel pale and moth-like, too

The mad impulse to touch Coop had thankfully left her, but she still felt disorientated, confused by his closeness. As fluttery one of those moths.

She bent to scratch the belly of one of the dogs.

What *was* it, this feeling? Sultry weather, mercury rising? Or just this man's overwhelming physical presence? Would she ever get used to it? The heat it generated in her body, the way it made her want to respond.

Better watch out. Remember Prim's relative? Poor Marjorie carted off to that asylum? Yes, clamp down on these feelings, before they get a hold.

Then, when the silence seemed to have gone on for far too long, Coop said, 'Did you want something?'

'Well.' She dragged her mind back. 'It's - '

'Please don't ask me about Scoot.'

' - about Scoot. I feel responsible!'

'Well, you're not. Look.' A frown between his eyes. 'You're entitled to feel upset, but I haven't got time for this, not now. Whatever it is, leave it to me, will you? Scoot's my concern, not yours.'

He turned back to the stars and Gerry felt herself dismissed again. Then, 'Y'know, Frank could name every constellation in the night sky.'

'Mister O'Rourke? Really?'

'Yep, planets, stars. When I was a boy, he'd point them out

and tell me the stories about ... you know, Pegasus, Cygnus the swan, Cassiopeia.'

Gerry gazed up, too - for a moment, charmed and distracted. The stars were so bright, she felt almost disorientated. Then, 'Scoot says you still won't let him go out with the men.'

'That's right.'

'Because of me? So, you *do* think it was his fault.'

'Damn straight!'

'The horse, yes - but not my leg.'

He rocked back on his heels. 'Now, just hold on. One thing needs straightening out here.'

'It really isn't fair, you know. And I have to say - '

'Listen to me, just listen, will you? Scoot, well ... *Scoot* is a girl.'

A stunned silence.

'A girl, not a boy. Understand? And I'm responsible for her. God knows, it's hard enough. Fifteen years old, always wearing pants and out with the men. Never had a bridle on her. She needs, hell ... pardon me ... I don't know what she needs, but something more than the company of hard-riding, bad-mouthing men every day, that's for sure. She's running hog wild, turning into some sort of tomcat.'

As his words started to sink in, Gerry cast her mind back. How had she managed to get this so wrong? A *girl!* 'I had no idea.'

'Of course you didn't. Talks and acts like a boy, even thinks like one, most of the time.'

'But, her ... family, her parents?'

He passed a hand over his eyes. 'She hasn't any. None that she's known, anyway. Frank adopted her, like he did me. Scoot's not even her real name. It's what everyone used to yell at her, before Frank came along.'

'Scoot!'

'Yeah. Go away. She was five years old and stealing scraps.'

Another silence, as Gerry struggled to adjust all previous ideas and misconceptions. 'But, she's jealous. Of Angel.'

'She's jealous all right. Of another girl, of Elena. It's Angel she's sweet on.'

'Oh *dear!*'

'Oh dear's right.' He sighed. 'Bound to happen. Raised in an all-male household, no mother or sister to advise. The only women around here are the servants.'

Hallie-Lee? wondered Gerry. But then, she was hardly the maiden-aunt type. She said, 'That's why she was so cross about the dress I gave to Elena. She's confused, isn't she, all mixed-up.' A pause. 'Is this what you've been worrying about?'

'Who says I've been worried?'

'Ever since I got here, you seem to have had something on your mind.'

'Lots of things are on my mind. Only one of them's Scoot.'

'Well, I wish I'd known this before; I wish you'd *told* me.'

'Yeah, yeah. I should've.'

A long pause. Fireflies winked and drifted beyond the verandah. Shadowy horses moved in the corral.

'So,' she said, carefully, 'Mr O'Rourke ... Frank. He took

you in first?'

Brief nod.

'How did that happen?'

Silence.

'Long story,' came the cool response. 'Not interesting.'

'But, he never married himself?'

'What is this? A whole damn night of nosy questions?' His face closed, like a door, and he turned away.

A bird, disturbed from its roost, hooted somewhere off in the distance, and Gerry bit her lip. *Ask him about his background*, Doc Hyde had said. Well, she'd tried, hadn't she?

She didn't like his spats of temper, but could guess the cause. They probably covered deep hurts. He looked exhausted, too, at the moment, utterly worn out. Whatever his problems, they must be big ones.

'I'm trying to understand,' she murmured, 'that's all.'

He turned back, the guarded expression still on his face. 'Look, don't ask me to do this. Where, what, why? Picking over relationships. I can't handle that stuff.'

Then, when Gerry had given up hope of anything else, he said, 'Frank's wife and baby son died, in childbirth.' Grim-faced, he waved a hand. 'Two gravestones sit under a tree out back. After that, he couldn't settle, started to travel again. At heart, he'd always been an adventurer. Yeah, met a lot of people, saw things, a lot of suffering.'

'It made him bitter.'

'Not bitter, no. He was too big a man for that. Tough. I was eight years old when he picked me up. Scoot ... came later.

Frank didn't do anything by halves.'

Gerry's thoughts drifted. It was the first time she'd been able to build a proper picture of Frank O'Rourke. Or Coop, for that matter.

'You said ... you told me you never met Leonie?'

A shake of his head. 'There were plenty of women, but he kept them away from us, away from the ranch, at least when we were here.' A slow nod. 'With your aunt, it was different. I knew something had knocked him off his feet. He'd got his old appetite for life back.'

He looked back up at the sky.

'Before he could tell me about it, he was away again and then ... well, all of a sudden, he started to let things slide. Too much money got taken out and ...' He paused. 'I need to put it all back.'

At the mention of money, Gerry stiffened.

'Look, it's late. I'm beat, got to make a real early start again in the morning.'

A long breath. This wasn't enough, she wanted more. When and where had Frank O'Rourke and Leonie met; how had they felt about each other? Trouble was, Coop didn't seem to know much more than she did. Just the barest of facts. And every one needing to be wrung out of him.

Suddenly, 'What was she like? Your aunt.'

'Oh. Glamorous, flamboyant. Funny! Heads always turned when she walked into a room and straight away, you could see the effect she was having. Whispers going round, the men changing their behaviour. She was irresistible.' Sigh.

'You know, I'm just beginning to understand the attraction. Between her and your -'

'Frank? Hell, wish that I did.'

'Don't you think it's odd, though,' Gerry said, 'that neither of us knew about their relationship?'

A shrug. 'Guess they didn't want us to.'

'But, why not?'

'We'll never know, will we?'

Trouble is, Gerry thought, I can't bear it, this muddle of unknowing. Just coming here, hasn't been enough. Before I go home, I *have* to find out everything. I think Leonie wants me to.

They stood for a while, occupied with their own thoughts.

Then, 'You want to see the ranch?'

'Yes! Yes, I really, really do.'

'The two-bit tour or the ten-dollar one?'

'Oh, all of it! I want to see everything.' She hesitated. 'Would it have to involve riding a horse?'

His mouth twitched. ''Fraid so. You could ride out with me tomorrow, if you think you'd be up to it.'

'I am, yes. I would be!'

'It'll be tough going and a real early start before it gets too hot. On horseback all day?'

Crossing fingers tightly behind her back, she nodded again.

CHAPTER
TWENTY SIX

'Don't be too bold, dashing or knowing.'
How to Attract a Man, 1923

Dressed for riding in Leonie's whipcord britches, a high-necked shirt and huge hat, Gerry went out into starlit dawn.

Coop was already outside, throwing a heavy saddle, coiled with the Circle-O brand and stamped with his initials, over his own horse. The other animal already saddled, a leggy brown mare with rippling muscles, sidled and fidgeted as Gerry drew near.

'Thought you might've got cold feet.' Coop touched the brim of his hat. 'Sure you're up for this?'

Quick nod. 'That's a beautiful horse.' She stopped at least a foot away from it.

'Hold out your hand. Let her get used to the smell of you.'

As the horse snuffled into her outstretched palm, Gerry stiffened and Coop gave her a sharp look, his eyes that dark flint colour.

He showed her how to hold a handful of mane, put a foot in the stirrup and jump up. Whey-faced, Gerry held her breath, but the horse stayed steady and she landed safely in the broad saddle.

'Okay?'

With dawn air moist and cool, and the moon still up there in the sky, they set off sedately enough, side by side. Just the thud of hooves on dry earth, creak of leather and Gerry, straight-backed in the saddle.

'Why, Miss Chiledexter,' he said, solemnly. 'You ride just like a Yankee.'

Then an easy lope and they broke into a gallop. As dust flew around, Gerry felt the hard strength of the mare, and fear made her stiffen again.

'Sway your body with the horse,' Coop yelled, 'and she'll turn with you.'

As for himself, he might have been born in the saddle - his strength and ease of movement so much at one with the big quarter horse, that you could barely separate them.

The sun came up but wind was still gentle, lifting the animals' manes and fluttering them like feathers. Slowly, Gerry felt herself start to relax. But this was tough riding. The saddle was hard; the ground dotted with dust-covered mesquite clumps and gopher holes, waiting to trip up the unwary rider.

The only words between them, were when she asked Coop to name a plant or bird. Even so, that wild Texas plain stretching out ahead of them, the big sky and fresh early morning scent was so exhilarating, that Gerry started to hum under her breath.

Immediately, her horse stopped dead.

'What's happened, what have I done?'

'Nothing, she's a cow pony. When the cattle are restless, we stop and sing, to quiet them.'

'Really?' As they kicked on again to a sedate walk, she said, 'It's all wonderful, isn't it? Wonderful, but ... scary.'

'Scary?'

'I'm used to land being parcelled up into manageable pieces, by fences and hedges. Not this.' Her arm swept the horizon. 'Stretching so far that you can't see the edges.'

'Yeah, guess it is pretty wonderful.'

'I wanted to see all this so much.' To look at what she now owned, to feel part of it, part of what had been left to her.

'And I wanted to show it to you.' A long pause. 'So, you'd understand.'

They walked on, in silence. As the sun climbed in the sky, it grew hotter; the throb of insect life, louder.

'Gerry?' He hesitated. 'What is it, with you and horses? What happened?'

She turned her head away, warm wind blowing hair over her face.

'It's okay. I shouldn't have asked.'

Taking a breath, she told him about that first incident with her father, and the many others that had followed, and watched his face change.

'He really was a piece of work, wasn't he?' he said. 'Pretty much like my own old man, as it happened.'

Who was he talking about? Watching his fierce expression, Gerry decided not to ask. 'The land looks so parched and dry here.' She steered the subject away.

'Oh, we're lucky. There's water on the Circle-O, tributaries of the big rivers. A tad sluggish maybe, but vital for cattle raising.'

'You told me once that Texas has everything, every type of terrain, every sort of climate.'

Reining in his horse, he looked hard at her.

'Mountains and deserts, heat and cold,' she said. 'The greatest state in the entire country, you told me. Remember? The party at the Hall?'

'That hell of an evening.' His voice was dry. 'How could I forget? I felt like a bull elephant in a china shop.'

'You barely spoke, and were so steely and unforgiving. I had to drag the conversation out of you.'

'You didn't act real friendly yourself, Missy, with that superior air and all the talk about books.'

'Yes,' she said. 'I thought you needed putting in your place.'

'You did that all right.'

'Well ... I was a little bit tipsy.'

'Tipsy! You were tight as a tick.'

Their horses were side by side now. Leaning in to offer water from a flask, his knee nudged her leg and their heads came close. Gerry was intensely aware of the places where they touched, and the smell of him - that mix of raw leather, warm skin, dust. Neither of them moved away.

A rare moment of sweetness, free and wild, and a sense of something between them? Half-glimpsed, fragile.

'You looked like some sort of sprite in that dress,' he said. 'If you hadn't been such a pain in the tail, I'd have been in quite a trance.'

Gerry shot him a look. With the hat low over his eyes and face in shadow, it was hard to make out his expression. Taking a quick gulp of water, recalling her own reaction to him at that party, she passed the flask quickly back. Change subject?

'Does Scoot wear those same patched clothes every day?'

'Guess so. Pants and shirts all look pretty much the same to me.'

'Has she got any girl's clothes? Are there any in the house?'

He shrugged, looking slightly shame-faced. 'I've never thought about it.'

'Has *anyone* thought about it?' A pause. 'She did have paint on her face when we first met. And she keeps her hair long.'

'Puts oil on it too, and keeps it off her face with a rag headband. Know why? To look like some renegade Apache.'

'She spoke to me about being sent away to school?'

'Yeah, just an idea. A girl's boarding school. Hallie-Lee reckons it might solve some problems.'

'I was sent away to school,' Gerry said. 'It created more problems than it solved.' A moment later. 'Well, would you like me to do something about her clothes? Or would that be interfering?'

'How much do you know about ornery, confused fifteen-year-olds?'

'I was one myself. Does that count?'

His mouth twitched. 'Do you really think you could get her out of those pants?'

'I could make some suggestions. But there's nothing wrong with being a tomboy, is there? She needs to make up her own mind, about who she wants to be and what to wear. She should be allowed to be herself.'

Conscious of his scrutiny, she took another gulp from the flask.

'Well, good luck with that,' he said, 'is all I can say. Just give me some warning, though, will you? Before you tackle her.'

She wiped her mouth. 'You're saying, I can get on with it?'

'You can try. As long as I don't have to deal with the hooting and hollering. I've got bigger battles. Just don't ...'

She waited.

' ... don't get your hopes up too high.'

As they jogged along, kicking up puffs of dust, Gerry's throat felt dry again. She licked her lips. 'What if a ranch doesn't have water?'

'Hard luck. Basically, it's the pirate's way. If it's on your property, it's yours and yours alone.'

Loosening her hat, she looked around. Millions and millions of acres, dozing in the sun, all belonging to the Circle-O.

And this Englishwoman, ignorant of cows and horses and everything else here, had been left half of it.

Of course Coop had resented her, of *course* he had.

Sighing, she stared into aching space. The only other moving thing between themselves and distant mountains to the north, were whirling columns of dust. Dust devils, they called them, didn't they?

She and Coop could be the only two people in the entire world, sun beating down on their backs and no shade for miles and miles. Just sky and sky and sky.

A mewling buzzard drifted overhead, and she thought - a person could wither and die here. Just dry up and blow away. 'Doesn't anyone ever get lost?'

He shrugged. 'If they do, it's a death sentence. No-one short-cuts across the Circle-O.'

But then, squinting into the sun's glare, Gerry saw movement. A blur of dark figures, way off, close to the mirage-quivering horizon. 'Coop?' Shielding her eyes, she pointed. 'What's happening over there?'

He swung his gaze round.

'Those people ... the trucks. Are they ranch hands?'

She saw his jaw tighten, but was distracted by another huge bird of prey, swooping down on a snake, just a few feet away!

'Oh, goodness, look. A snake ... a huge snake!'

He wasn't listening. Hands clenched around the reins, hat tilted lower on his forehead, muttering something. About ... dry-drilling?

'Coop! That ...'

'Rattler, most likely.'

'Oh, *goodness*!'

Gerry shifted uneasily in the saddle. Coop's whole attention was now fixed on the horizon. Following his gaze, she said, 'Anyway, what is this *dry drilling*?'

'Not for you to get into.'

'You said you wanted me to understand.'

He swivelled round. 'It's taking core samples from the ground to see if there's a chance of oil. Frank was dead against it; he didn't want holes punched in his land while he was still alive.'

'*Is* there oil?'

'There's a chance.'

'Have you said they can look for it?'

'No, I haven't, and they damn well know I haven't. They're pulling one way, me the other. They want the money. I want to do the right thing by Frank.'

She stared at the distant figures. 'What are you going to do?'

'I know what I'd like to do, but there's a law against it. Wait here.'

'With snakes wriggling round? No, thank you.'

'Not afraid of snakes, huh?'

'Why didn't Mister O'Rourke want anyone to drill for oil?' she said, as they wheeled their horses round.

'Apart from not wanting the landscape carved up? Don't rightly know.' A pulse beat in his cheek. 'Problem is, I stopped knowing what he thought about anything a long time ago.

Look, if you're dead set on coming, better hold onto your hat!'

And kicking his horse hard with his heels, he streaked off, full-pelt towards the horizon.

Gerry started to follow, but that sort of pace and locomotion took a great deal out of a person. Insides soon felt as shaken up as one of Leonie's cocktails.

As Coop disappeared into a dust cloud, she slowed right down. Things were beginning to hurt - muscles complaining, thighs aching - and with the sun growing hotter and hotter, she trailed on behind.

Coop didn't look back.

Drawing closer to all the activity, she was in time to see him ride right into the crowd of men, who parted in front of him, like the Red Sea.

Then, shouting, a clamour of voices, and moments later, two figures a few paces apart, setting up against each other. Coop? Yes, he was one of them. Others ranged round in a ring, watching.

Still a short way off, Gerry pulled up her horse and slid to the ground, trying not to draw attention to herself.

All of a sudden, 'You dirty, lying ...' and tension erupted into violence. Everyone pushing and grappling, and as Gerry watched, Coop swung back his arm and hit somebody, biff-bang, with a hard upper-cut to that person's jaw. As the man's body twisted, doubled up, sagged, all shouting stopped.

Leaping back into the saddle, Coop kicked his horse and streaked back towards Gerry, yelling at her to follow.

CHAPTER
TWENTY SEVEN

'Always be light, amiable and wonderfully feminine.'
How to Attract a Man, 1923

Some distance away from the scene of the fight, Coop slowed to a trot.

'You okay?' he said, sounding almost nonchalant.

No, Gerry thought, *I'm not.* 'What were they doing, those men?'

'Like I said, looking for oil. Sneaking in drilling tools and timbers to build derricks. Crawling over my land, like flies over flypaper, and thinking they could get away with it.'

'But, you ... *hit* him! You hit that man, I saw you.'

'He took a swing, I got in first,' he said, in a tone that didn't brook any argument.

'Then you hit him again.'

A shrug. 'That's how you keep the peace in Dodge City. Stakes are high here, and that gang draws trouble. Plotters, land grabbers. Oil's turning everyone's head.'

'Couldn't you have talked it over, reasoned with them?'

'Well, that's a mighty interesting notion, but waste of wind. We don't talk the same language. What you saw? That's Texas talk.'

Texas talk. Texas rules. 'But -'

'You planning to tell me what to do now? I don't believe this. What do you know about it?'

'Not much. Well ... nothing.'

'Dead right.'

'But, if the Circle-O needs money ... would finding oil be such a bad thing? Perhaps it's the right time?'

'Can't help being contrary, can you? I run this ranch. It's how I make my living. And Frank ... he hated their stinking oil wells.'

Avoiding his fierce stare, Gerry turned away. Then, 'How did you learn to fight like that?'

'Practice.'

Oh dear. And it had all been going so well, hadn't it? A more intimate conversation, a closer understanding. Now any spark between them had been snuffed out. And that flickering thing, that butterfly moment - completely lost.

In shimmering heat, with wind booming around them, they went on in stony silence.

Miles later, squinting into a merciless sky of hard, lonely blue, she watched two buzzards idle round in careful circles, floating up, up, on thermals of hot air. 'What are those birds doing? I saw them before, swooping over the herd.'

'Buzzards? They keep the country clean. Clear up after the dead and dying.'

'Clear up?'

'Pick over the remains.'

When she shuddered, he said, 'This is no place for sentiment, nor any other stupid romantic notions about nature. It's natural law, it's what they do.' A pause. 'We're not in the English shires, now.'

The steel edge was back in his voice; he sounded as hard, angry and unforgiving as ever.

Gerry stopped talking.

Once again, they rode in silence.

Some way on, Coop reined in his horse and Gerry gazed round at open range. 'Why have we stopped?'

'Never mind. Get off.' His boots hit the ground and he came over, holding out his hand. 'C'mon.' His jaw was tight, eyes very grey, very cold. 'Get down.'

A wary look. She'd learned to trust this man, to admire his gritty authority, his instincts. But he had a short fuse and could get red-raw, very quickly. More than once, she'd been on the receiving end of that temper.

And they were a long, long way from anywhere.

Sliding from the horse's back into his arms, she was firmly set down. Then holding her shoulders, he guided her to a spot a short way off and turned her in the direction of blurry, distant hills.

'Look out there,' he said, standing behind her. 'What d'you see?'

Pushing hair from her eyes, Gerry looked. Miles and miles of flat plain, shimmering in the heat, as far as she could see. Wide bowl of blue sky. No moving thing.

'Well?'

'Just the range. Open, empty land.'

'That's right. Beautiful, isn't it?'

'Yes. I suppose it is.'

'What can you hear?'

'I ... pardon?' She turned to look at him.

'Listen. Open your ears and just listen.'

Texas sounds? Dry wind - full of energy and carrying a sweet fragrant scent - swirling grass this way and that, like the sea. Gerry took a long breath. Insects throbbing, buzzing and high overhead, the sharp mew of a bird of prey.

'D'you have any idea what you'd hear if they found oil?'

She didn't.

His hard voice in her ear set out to enlighten her. The endless thump-thump of heavy machinery, day and night. Huge wooden derricks like great grass-hoppers rearing up over the landscape.

'And all those fat folks swopping gold-foil cigars and stuffing their pockets with money. There was nothing Frank didn't know about ranching. His granddaddy bought this land, pioneered it. They'd turn in their graves if it were taken over by oil.'

A long pause. Then, 'Are you sure?'

'About which part?

'Wouldn't Mister O'Rourke have understood if you *had* to

let it happen, if you'd no choice?'

'There's always a choice.'

'I know, yes, but after all, that place *is* on your furthest boundary, isn't it? Perhaps, Frank's father and his grandfather were old Texas. And you are ... well, you're new Texas.'

'Only thing that matters, is Frank didn't want any part of it. That's good enough for me.'

In this peaceful setting, with the two horses grazing peacefully nearby, Gerry's mind drifted. The hold that Frank O'Rourke and Leonie still had on herself and Coop, was astonishing. Such big presences, so powerful. In life and in death.

'Ghosts,' she said, quietly.

'What say?'

She waited. Then, 'How did he ... I mean, where did Mister O'Rourke first meet you?' A risk bringing this up, and she knew it. 'What happened?'

'Not that *why-why-why* again.'

'You said, he took you in when you were very young.'

A sharp, sideways look. 'Eight years old, and crying my eyes out in a weed-choked ditch when he found me.'

'What of your own family?'

She saw his jaw muscle tighten.

'D'you know how I got my name? After the coup stick. A sign of bravery for Plains Indians. Story goes that warriors had to get close enough in to their enemies to touch them, with a hand, bow or coup stick, and get away alive. Well, from four years old, that's what my old man got me to do. Get in, get the money and get away.' He paused. 'Yeah. I was his coup stick. I was good at it, too, good at the thieving. He'd boast about me to his friends.'

'But ... your mother?' Gerry couldn't take her eyes from his face.

'Died when I was born.' He spoke slowly, deliberately. 'My daddy and me, we just went from town to town, never knowing where we were headed. He said the quicker I learned about this mean, money-grabbing world and the bums in it, the better.'

Taking off his hat, he wiped a hand over his forehead.

'When I was seven and couldn't stand it anymore, I said I wouldn't steal. So my old man cut a switch off a tree and beat me, 'til I could taste blood and my rotten shirt was in shreds. Never saw him again. Weeks and weeks, I was sniffing round like a wild dog, looking in people's windows and picking up scraps.'

Gerry put out a hand, but knew she couldn't reach him. Broad shoulders were stiff, his head turned away. They just stood, side by side, without speaking.

Then, 'Frank gave me peace, gave me dignity, I guess. Never looked back. *Now* can you see, why it's so important I do right by him?'

A slow nod from Gerry.

'I'll fight them all off, if that's what he'd want. What's killing me, I can't seem to know what that is, anymore.'

A long sigh. 'You could try asking.'

'Asking who?'

'Mister O'Rourke. Frank.'

'Oh, yeah?' He stretched out a drawl. 'And just how do you suggest I go about that?'

'Don't be so sneery. Just ride out to a place on the ranch that he loved, and ask the question.'

Eyebrows slowly raised. 'You're surely not telling me to expect an *answer*?'

'Listen, that's all. Just listen to the wind, as you made me do. Then, see what happens.' Her voice tailed away.

'Sounds plumb crazy.'

'I know. I know that it does.'

'Ah said, drop it! *Holy Moses*!'

'All I said - '

'Stop!' Scoot clapped hands over her ears. She didn't want to hear about dresses or petticoats or slides for her hair. Nor anything, in fact, the least bit feminine. No, no, no. Not *interested!*

'*She* got you into all this, didn't she?'

'Who she?'

Scott tossed hair from her forehead. 'Ole Mizz Texas Queen Kittrell. It was her stupid idea. She hates me. And boy, oh boy, she doan like you too much, either.'

'Oh. I'm *sure* ... um, how do you know that? About me?'

'I got ears. The sooner you go home, the better, she says. When you decide to kiss goodbye to your ... your Texan milch-cow.'

'What!?'

'Then they can git on with their lives. Her and Coop, she means. Then they can git *married*.'

A long pause.

'Are they getting married?'

'Huh, she's real keen. Oh, yeah. Talks about it all the time. Talk, talk, talk. Mornin', noon and night.'

'And, Coop?' She couldn't help herself.

Scoot shrugged.

'Anyway,' Gerry sighed, 'the clothes were my own idea.'

'Well, it stinks, you hear! Y'all leave me alone. Yes, ma'am. Any fool can be fancy. I don't want none of them prissy party manners. Ah'm just fine as I am.'

Gerry turned in the direction of men bringing out the horses. 'Well, good,' she said, fanning herself with her hat, 'that's all that matters, isn't it? It's just that Angel ...'

'Him? Huh! Still moonin' round after that *Elena*, all bug-eyed.'

'Perhaps that's because he knows for sure, that she's a girl.'

CHAPTER TWENTY EIGHT

'Honey-pot looks don't always attract men.'
A Woman's Way, 1923

Startled from sleep, Gerry heard the furious clamour of a bell. Clang! Clang!

Then, 'No! No! Oh, Lord!' Running feet, shouts in Spanish, frenzied dogs barking.

A strange glare at the window, swirling roar outside and looking out, Gerry saw the big barn on fire and already taking hold on the one next to it. Smoke billowed out and up, darkening the sky.

Then she was running, running. Down the stairs, onto the porch where the smoke rose up in front of her, thick and yellow, like a wall.

And all the while the clang, clang, clang and grim-faced men shouting. And frantic hoof-beats, the terrified squeals of maddened horses with wild eyes and tossing manes, erupting from the barn, flames sucking greedily away behind them.

Shadowy shapes ran this way and that with water and beating sticks, but nothing seemed to be quelling that roaring inferno and smoke rippling upward in the wind.

As Gerry inched forward, someone yelled, 'Stay back, stay well back, ma'am!' But as she watched - a flutter of cloth, a hat pulled low and she saw Scoot disappearing into the barn, hand held over her mouth.

'Scoot!' She yelled, pointing. '*Scoot!* Scoot!'

But the shadows running backwards and forwards, didn't see, couldn't hear.

So, Gerry dodged in after the girl, head down through the smoke and the crackle of flames - calling out, edging forward sightless, she shouted out, screamed and shouted Scoot's name, over and over.

The ground red hot under her feet, acrid smoke in eyes, mouth, hair - stinging and choking and filling chest and lungs. And still the roaring, the flames and Scoot, nowhere! *Gone*!

Stumbling over a blackened beam, Gerry's legs buckled and she sprawled, arms over her head. Prone on the smouldering barn floor, everything blurred. Smoke closed over her, senses dulled. In the dark and blasting red heat, a strange, flat blackness settled. Hell on earth.

A shout, 'Over here! She's here.' And strong arms snatched her up and ran, ran out of the furnace, head bent low, arm clamped round like a steel band, holding her hard against chest. The fast, heavy thump, thump, thump of a heart next to her breast calmed her own shaking.

'Scoot,' she rasped, addressing the pocket of a thick shirt.

'All right, it's all right.' A voice in her ear, deep, familiar. Carrying her to the porch, Coop set her gently down. 'Listen, Gerry. Can you stand?'

She gagged and coughed for breath, the air still sizzling and crackling all around them.

Smoothing back hair that had fallen across her face, he grazed the side of her face with his knuckles. 'That was so brave ... but so *stupid*!' His voice was hoarse. 'You could have suffocated, *died* in there.'

'Scoot ...' she mouthed, and tried to say more, but tears welled up to trickle forlornly down her cheeks.

'Come here.' He opened his arms and she cast herself into them, gulping and sobbing, burying herself in the creases of his shirt.

'She went ... right in ...' the words jerked out '... but the smoke ... I couldn't see ... and she ... she didn't hear ... smoke, the flames ... '

'I know, I know. Once that smell hits the back of your throat, you never forget it.'

His arms tightened and he let her cry, cradled against his chest. His shirt smelled of dust and ash and that made her cry even harder. She was inconsolable.

Through her misery, she felt the thump of his heart, more even now, more regular as he shushed her gently.

The weeping died down. Humiliated, and acutely aware of his body hard against her, there was a moment of paralysis. She breathed in the warm, safe smell of him for a minute more, before forcing herself away.

'Listen, Gerry. Doc got her, Doc got Scoot.'

Wide-eyed, cheeks wet, she was perfectly still. 'She's ... all right?'

'She went in after her horse, but he dragged her free. Everyone's safe, thank God. Animals, too.'

Her limbs heavy, Gerry sagged against him.

Outside the next morning, a war zone. Dead and desolate.

Ash still floating, scorched earth all around. Smoke - acrid and heavy, hung like a pall over everything; the blackened shell of the big barn stood out against the sky, broken limbs and stumps still smoking. Nearby buildings were scorched, too.

A knock, sharp and loud, at the door. 'Mees ... you awake?'

'Noo...oo!' Gerry's voice wheezed and croaked like an old harmonium. Lying back, she closed her eyes. 'I don't want to see anybody.'

The door flew back and Coop stared down at her. Unshaven, eyes heavily lidded, exhausted. 'Was it the smoke, d' you feel ill?'

'No.' She put an investigating hand up to her head - ouch! 'Just tired.'

'Well, someone out here's pretty keen to talk to you.'

'I'm soo sorry, Gerry.' A small voice from the door and Scoot sidled in, still in filthy clothes, smears of ash over her cheeks. It was everywhere, on everyone, that awful smell of smoke.

Lobo skittered in, short legs flying, and leapt onto the bed.

He was swiftly shooed out.

'Coop says ... he says ... you went into the barn just to get me out.' Scoot traced a shape on the floor with her boot. 'Nearly had yourself burned to death, trying to save me, he says. An' that's three times now you've been hurt bad 'cause of me.'

'Oh, I don't -'

'Coop says that's how it is, an' I know it, too. Jeez, Gerry, I'm sorry. For being so mean, for thinking you were here to ... to ... y'know, make trouble an' all, for me and Coop. I thought ... heck, don't rightly know what I was thinking; I've been real mixed up.' A tear rolled from her eye. 'Can you forgive me?'

'There's still soot on your nose.' Coop watched while Gerry wiped her face. His own was still streaked with ash, eyes red-rimmed and bloodshot.

Her mind kept straying. Nightmare flashes to fearful heat, screaming, shouting. How it had felt sprawled on hot earth. How she'd almost given herself up to it.

'Did you see me?' A croak. 'When I went into the barn?'

A fly buzzed round. Flapping it away, Coop shook his head.

'How did you know I was there?'

It took a while for him to answer. 'I was back of the big barn, driving horses out, when I felt ...' he stopped, shook his head, '... not sure what I felt, just some kind of weird feeling making me fight my way to ... wherever you were, I guess.'

'A feeling?'

'Sounds stupid, doesn't it. That's the only way to describe it, a sort of dread.' He stopped, suddenly.

'What? What else?'

'Well, here's the thing. A scent?' He shrugged. 'Yeah, in all that smoke, out of nowhere. A really strong perfume. I guess, well ... it led me right to you.' He shrugged. 'Led by my nose.'

Oh, thought Gerry. 'That was Leonie.'

He stared.

'You think I'm deluded, don't you?'

'You're saying, she's *haunting* you?'

'That sounds like guttering candles, ghostly hoots. It's not like that. She just ... well, she's never left me, that's all. Somehow, she drifts in and out of my life, telling me what to do.'

Coop sat down heavily on the bed. 'Are you saying, you *see* her?'

She shook her head. 'Sometimes, it's just lightness around me, a sort of change in the air. Sometimes she's almost shouting in my ear. I catch her scent too, just as you did, last night.' She paused. 'It frightened me to start with. Now ... I'm used to it.'

'I sure wish Frank would start haunting me. Tell me what he wants me to do.'

'I've told you. You need to ask him. Then, just listen.'

He sighed. 'Hmm, maybe.'

Taking her hand, he turned it over. 'What's this?'

'A little burn.' A raw red slash on her palm, black rims

under her nails. 'It doesn't hurt.' And still wheezing, like a concertina.

As he scrutinized her face, Gerry felt the pull of him, like a magnet. What *was* it? This something in the air hanging between them? The something she'd felt when they'd ridden together, that floating, insubstantial thing.

Lifting her palm to his mouth, he brushed it gently with his lips. 'Well, Gerardina. Once again, you're quite the hero.'

'All *right*!' Scoot said. 'Tell me what to do. How can I make Angel look at me, like he looks at her?'

'Well it doesn't work quite like that. But, if you want him to notice you ...'

'Yeah, let's just get one thing straight. I know I've got a lot to thank you for, Gerry, and I'm warming to you right enough, but ah wouldn't be seen dead wearing the sort of sissy things you got on.'

'I thought you were teaching Scoot to be a lady.'

'Was *that* what I was supposed to be doing?'

'I was counting on more ... y'know, gentleness, refinement? Instead, you teach her to play cricket. She's slamming balls all over the place.'

'Well, she's fearless, a demon batter and bowler. But there are strict rules, you know, cricket can be quite ladylike.'

'She hit Bren over the head. With her bat!'

'Ah. So ...'

'I applied the said bat to the seat of her britches. Anyhow, cricket's a man's game, isn't it? How come you know so much about it?'

'Oh.' Sigh. 'Nine of our Lower Shepney Market XI, estate workers, gardeners, Oxford blues, went to war and didn't survive the Armistice. All gone. No-one had much enthusiasm after that. Choice was, disband the side or ... well, take anyone who knew the rules and could hold a bat.'

'That was you, I take it?'

'A few of us ladies were reasonably well co-ordinated. And we turned out quite well, though I say it myself.'

'Why doesn't that surprise me?'

Lower Shepney Market? A pang of nostalgia. How far away the little town seemed now. Saying the name out loud made Gerry realize how long it had been since she'd thought about home and England. About going back.

CHAPTER TWENTY NINE

'Husbands may be scarce, but lovers grow on every tree.'
The Bachelor Girl's Handbook, *1924*

'He's talking about a dance,' Scoot said. 'A dance! Now everyone's well again. Why'd *anyone* want that?'

'Might be fun.'

'Huh! Sissy stuff. All that dressin' up.'

'Oh, leave that to me.'

Gerry spent ages deciding what to wear. An hour, at least, debating the merits of silk versus crepe. Print, pastel, were all flung aside; none of the things she had with her seemed suitable. That one, too ruffled and flouncy. This, too modern, too severe! Sequins? No!

'The pale silk chemise, my darling. Perfect! Now loop my little silk tassel and crystal necklace round and bangles for your arms.'

The rhinestone comb - another mistake. Her hair had lost its battle with the hairbrush. She'd done it three times now, trying to torture a pin curl into that sleek shingle. Two spots of rouge? Horrible, horrible! She pulled faces in the tiny mirror. The pale English wallflower.

Nothing was right – her face, her dress, that little hole in the seam she hadn't managed to mend. All those weeks in oversized man-things, and she'd *so* wanted to make a good impression.

'Stop it, dahling! So verrry tiresome.'

'What'll you be wearing tonight?' Coop had asked, earlier.

What would she ... *what?* She'd stared, bemused. 'At the dance?'

'At the dance, yes.'

'Oh, it's ah ... well, I'm not sure, not yet.' Pause. 'Why are you asking?'

'So I can look forward to seeing it.'

Why then, Gerry wondered, was it taking her so long to come out from the house? Why hang back? That feeling again. Yes, of trembling on the brink of something, of something about to happen.

A large barn had been transformed - masses of fresh greenery, flags and flickering candles all round. Tables piled high with food and drink.

At one end, a group of musicians - three fiddlers, smiling broadly and sawing away for dear life, with banjo and harmonica players alongside.

Nothing like the formal dances at home, those sedate promenades where men with blank faces and noses in the air, held partners at a respectable distance. No dance programmes dangling from white-gloved hands, no wild demonstrations of the Charleston and Turkey Trot, either, à la Leonie.

This looked far jollier. Waltzing, sort of, yes, but not as Gerry knew it. More like bouncing along to rollicking, toe-tapping tunes. Loud voices and laughter, clapping hands, stamping feet. Sheer, undiluted delight, with sweet scents, of cologne, perfume, pomade.

Children were sliding around people's feet and someone danced by, jiggling a baby.

The barn was packed with people that Gerry had never met and didn't know. Almost the entire territory appeared to be there.

Still, she managed to attract some attention. In the middle of flushed women in fancy frocks and swinging skirts, her own dress - a fragile silk tunic with loose waistline in washed pink, a sort ashes-of-roses colour - stood out.

Her eyes travelled round the room.

Hallie-Lee Kittrell, in the middle of an admiring group, in something ruffled. Scoot, oh my - pretty as a picture, surrounded by boys and smelling rather strongly of Gerry's scent. ('Not so much! Just a puff!')

A whirl of brightly coloured dresses around the floor. Music stopped, then started again.

Gerry scanned faces and when he walked into the room, she knew who she'd been looking for. Someone head and shoulders above the rest, working the room. A nod here, a smile and word there.

She wasn't alone in this awareness, either. Ho, no. Coop, the head-turner.

'Honour me, ma'am.' A touch on her shoulder.

'I beg your pardon?'

'Would you like to dance?'

A moment later, over her partner's shoulder, Gerry saw Hallie-Lee and Coop drawn together, heads close.

'That sure is a purty dress, ma'am.'

'Well, thank you!'

'Ain't never seen anythin' like it.'

'Oh. It's um ... well, it's ... from Paris, actually.'

'Well, ah'll be! Paris! Y'don't say!'

Once Gerry had started, that was it, her feet didn't touch the ground. She danced with Doc several times, then took the floor with Bren Ryan in his bear-like embrace. ('How you doing now, ma'am? Liking Texas any better?)

Red Kittrell came to claim her then, with a courteous bow. And when Coop and Hallie-Lee danced by, Gerry murmured that they looked really well together, didn't they?

She'd been half-hoping that Coop would have two left feet.

'Oh, he's a heart-breaker alright. Gits 'em every time, right in the knees. Y'know, I could tell you some things about ole Coop, that'd knock you sideways.' Red leaned closer. 'Yip, some pretty hair-raisin' things.'

'I don't much care for gossip, Mister Kittrell.'

'Then I won't bother passing it on, Mizz Chiledexter.' He rolled his eyes. 'But, y'all more'n likely wish that I had!'

Then, a lawman from north of the territory touched her shoulder, and a cattleman from somewhere else and other partners, whose names she'd never learned or didn't catch or couldn't remember.

And every time the music stopped, Hallie-Lee was there, at Coop's side.

Later, while Gerry stood flushed and breathless, laughing at something that someone had said, Coop was at last in front of her, taking her hand and leading her onto the floor. 'Seems to me, you're getting far too much male attention, Miss Chiledexter!'

Now that he was no longer a comfortable distance away, she was suddenly self-conscious and unsure of herself, all arms and legs, and hating herself for it.

With no space between them and music and talk and laughter all around, she concentrated on clamping down on treacherous feelings that always resulted from his touch. Holding herself stiff against this unsettling intimacy, her eyes came level with the buttons on his shirt.

The trick, she reminded herself, making it sound like some sort of a disease, was to deal with the symptoms straight away.

It didn't work. The clamping down. Something to do with the music, his red-blooded maleness, the warm scent of him? His hand on her back, he pulled her tighter and she felt that breathless flutter, high in her chest.

'Gerry?' His hair on her cheek and she felt the heat coming off him. 'I won't bite. Can't you at least pretend you're enjoying this?'

'I'm just not very good at this sort of thing.' She couldn't remember the steps; her feet wouldn't do what she wanted and kept turning in the wrong direction.

He pulled her even closer. 'I think you may be over-estimating the box-step. Don't think, just move.'

Then, everything seemed to slow down. Music receded and Gerry closed her eyes and followed his lead, no longer aware of anyone, anything else. Twirling round and round, the turns seemed to get tighter.

Lights blurred and spun and suddenly, they were outside, dancing under a brilliant sky. That starry, starry Texas night

All heartbeats and closeness and rhythm, and the shape and smell of him, and just as Gerry was hoping it would go on for ever, there was a shift. A heart-skipping moment when he held her away and she looked into his face, barely breathing.

Under a perfect moon, the world stood still.

Then, 'Real close in there, wasn't it? Thought we could do with some air.' And *pouff*, just like that, the spell was broken.

A deep breath, and he tipped his head back. 'Those stars, the constellations always somehow bring me closer to Frank; he loved the night sky.'

'Yes, you told me.' She followed his gaze. 'Do you know all the names?'

He pointed out some common ones, Orion, The Great Bear. 'See that one,' he said, 'over there, the really bright one.

That's the planet Jupiter.'

'A Roman god, wasn't he?'

'Yeah, and Jupiter up there, carries certain associations, Frank used to say - has done for thousands of years. Health, happiness ... and others I can't ... oh, yeah ... hope. That was another one. Good fortune. *Bon homie.*'

'Millions of miles away.' He sighed. 'Makes everything else seem pretty insignificant, doesn't it? Helps keep problems in perspective.'

'Have you,' Gerry's face was still turned up, 'got problems?'

'Some. Haven't you?'

She shrugged. 'People here just don't seem to like discussing those sorts of things, out in the open.'

'Are you talking about me?'

Avoiding that narrow-eyed gaze, she said, 'It surprised me, that's all. I thought the British were the only ones so buttoned-up and sensitive that they couldn't express their feelings.'

'Is that right?' He came so unsettlingly close that she thought she might go cross-eyed and fall over backwards. 'Well, this is Texas.' His voice was smoky as kippers, 'Let's try doing what Texans do best, shall we?'

'Um, I didn't - '

Locking fingers behind her waist, he pulled her to him, arms tight around and kissed her on the mouth, a kiss warm and full and unbelievably sweet. A simple embrace that suddenly unfolded into something more lingering and sensual - lips achingly tender, but demanding a response.

A pause, when finally he let her go. Then, 'Guess it's time we went back.'

As if nothing had happened? Like a pat on the head! Or as if ... well, he'd changed his mind.

Confused and ridiculously shy, her own heart still thunder-clapping, Gerry twisted her bangles. Had nothing altered for him? Had it meant so little? For her, that kiss had been momentous. That wild surge of delight, the physical ache in her body. The longing for him to do it again and again and again.

A deep breath, and she tried to slow her heartbeat, steady herself.

Had it been an accident? Had she somehow leaned in too far and gravity had taken over and she'd just ... fallen against him? *I fell*, she thought, *yes. I have fallen.*

The air was hot and heavy, the beat of the music still in her ears and her dress sticking damply to her now, in unexpected places. Places where he'd held her, pressed her to him.

One thing. He must never know how he'd made her feel.

Taking her hand, Coop stared back at the sky. 'Real beautiful night, isn't it?' he said, then led her straight back into the crush and the heat and high-pitched conversation of the crowded barn.

He saw her to a chair, then disappeared into the throng to find her a drink, and she quickly lost sight of him.

Was she supposed to just forget what had happened, then, to banish all thoughts? Perhaps, she'd disappointed him. After all, he'd probably kissed every girl in the room, in the *state*.

They weren't just from different worlds; they were different species. Not like chalk and cheese, oil and water. More, a coyote and ... a cloche hat.

In a misery of confusion, she thought, *I have no idea how to love someone.*

CHAPTER THIRTY

'Our aim: Orange blossom and the church door.'
A Modern Girl's Guide to Love, 1922

'Mind if I join you?' Hallie-Lee, in a cloud of seductive scent, her smile as sweet as sarsaparilla. 'Real noisy, isn't it? A person can barely hear themselves think.'

Gerry's head was still full of that kiss. Her eyes strayed over the other girl's shoulder, looking for Coop, wondering if he'd come back.

'How brave of you to wear that dress, Gerry. So ... well, plain.'

'It's French.'

'Hmm, guess that explains it. My, it's hot in here.' Her hand gripped Gerry's arm. 'Let's you and I take a stroll outside, shall we, get us a breath of air.'

And Gerry had no choice, but to be led outside again, under those same bright stars. Moonlight glimmered on her filmy sliver of a dress and on Hallie-Lee's fall of pale hair. *Like two moths*, she thought, luna moths, flickering round each other.

After a few moments discussing the heat (heavy), the sky (starry), and her dress (was it *very* old?), there was silence.

Then, 'I've lately been wondering, Gerry, about your plans. I mean you've been here a good while now, haven't you? Two months?' Hallie-Lee held up fingers. 'Three?'

'Almost.' Gerry turned in the direction of the barn. Music was starting up, she longed to go back.

'Time enough to have a real good look round, I guess, and check out your ... inheritance.' A pause. 'So, when would you be thinking of leaving?'

'I'm ... not sure.' Gerry chose her words carefully. 'I came because of my aunt, you see, to find out why she was here.' Her voice drifted.

'Mmm-hmm. And have you done that?'

Well, had she? She'd learned some things, not nearly as many as she'd wanted, of course. Perhaps certain secrets weren't meant to be uncovered. Perhaps, there were no more left to find.

'So, isn't it about time you went home?'

And there it was. No more circling around.

'See, me and Coop, we were made for each other, just about everyone says so. He's all I've ever wanted. Lord, even when he was running round wild all that time, every woman in the state chasing after him.' Eyebrows went up, lips turned down. 'You know, an itty while back, I thought we were getting closer, but now ... why, he can't even find time for a proper conversation. He's barely said boo to me for weeks.'

Her dark look took Gerry by surprise. Hallie-Lee couldn't

be *jealous,* surely. *Don't be jealous*, she thought. *It's nothing to do with me.*

That fleeting kiss? She felt herself flush. Something to do with loss and loneliness, most probably, a search for meaning. Nothing to worry Hallie-Lee.

'Oh, piffle!' Her aunt's voice, suddenly, unexpectedly. *'You can't fool me, my darling! Forget your mind. What does your body say?'*

Gerry didn't want to think about her body, thank you. That kiss meant nothing to Coop, less than nothing.

Hallie-Lee was ready for marriage. She just wasn't used to not getting what she wanted, that was all. All she had to do now, was ... well, give Coop a little more time.

To love and be loved by him. Gerry felt a little twist around her heart. *Romance,* she thought. *Grabs you, taunts you, teases you. Why didn't anyone ever tell me?*

'He needs pinning down, my daddy says, while I still got some life in my body.' Those soft Texan vowels stretched to a languid drawl, the consonants rolling. 'There's so much to decide about everything, not just about him and me, you know, but about Scoot.'

'Scoot?'

'Well, something's got to be done about the little wretch. It'll take more than cricket to civilize her. Not very womanly, is it?'

Why, Coop! You snitch!

'Then there's the drilling. If Coop doesn't stop wasting time and make up his mind, well ...' shrug, '... he's going to be mighty sorry. My daddy says if the Circle-O don't soon take up its oil, it's going to be in real bad trouble.'

A silver moth fluttered round Gerry's head. She waved it away. 'But, Coop doesn't trust those oil men, does he? He told me -'

'Listen, honey, if you're trying to hold a ranch together, you have to do what it takes. No point feeling sour 'bout it. That's what my daddy says. He reckons oil's a sure thing and that I'm just plumb crazy waiting and waiting around to find out what Coop's thinking.'

Well, good luck with that, Gerry thought.

'One thing me and my daddy are sure nuff about, though.' Sideways glance. 'We reckon Coop'd be far easier in his own mind, if you sold back your share of the ranch, right away. Yes, just settled your business and high-tailed home to that itty bitty island of yours.'

Gerry blinked and Hallie-Lee stared back, blue eyes narrowing, like a Persian cat. She said, 'Jest so we all stop crowding one another out here, y'understand. Y'know, I've seen it time and time again with Coop. Women just can't seem to help themselves around that man. And ... y'see, I *don't* share.'

In spite of maintaining a dignified silence, Gerry was sorely tempted to throttle Hallie-Lee with Leonie's silk tassel and crystal necklace. Fingering it now, she felt all confidence dribble away.

The pin curl she'd arranged over one cheek had drooped, her fringe was a frizz. Her plummy Cupid's bow had probably been smudged by that kiss. She felt uneasy, out-of-place.

Why hadn't she worn a dress that swirled?

'Let's face it, Gerry, you're a greenhorn here. As my daddy says, what kinda person has the all-out gall to try and ruin someone's livelihood? These are big boys' dealings and we jest have to stop all this puss-footing around.'

Daddy this, my daddy that. Gerry hadn't met Mr Kittrell, but already felt an acute animosity towards him. A Big Daddy, surely, with puffed-out chest and red face, like an enraged bull.

In the silence now hanging ominously between them, a night bird cackled. Something else warning off trespassers?

'Well now.' Hallie-Lee put her head on one side. 'Is that a waltz I'm hearing? One for me and Coop, I think, don't you agree, Gerry? Excuse me.'

As the girl, a pale ghost, disappeared into the darkness, Gerry stood in the shadows, going over their conversation in her mind. She couldn't recall every word said, but the hissing had been clear enough.

Go home. That had been the main part. *Go now, and stop wasting everyone's time.* The rest had been flim-flam.

Had she had stayed too long? She forced herself to think about it. So much had been happening lately. This place, the people, had drawn her in.

A commotion in the bushes and the night bird whirred away. *Should I go?* Gerry asked herself. *Is it time?* She thought, *I don't fit in here.*

'Oh, sweetie! Who wants to fit in? Not you - you stand out!'

Returning reluctantly to the dance, she spotted Hallie-Lee and Coop close together. The girl turned to him, and he put his hand on her shoulder in such a fond and gentle way that a feeling of utter loneliness crept over Gerry.

Those two seemed to be in their own private world, didn't they? How could anyone help staring? A golden girl with smooth fall of hair, and caramel skin that would never be spoiled by freckle or spot. A pretty cat who deserved the cream.

And next to her, a perfect specimen of manhood.

Meant to be together? Oh, yes. It had been written in the stars, apparently.

Gerry felt stranded again. In the wrong place, wearing the wrong clothes.

Of *course*, Coop's touch, his kiss had gone straight to her head, of *course* it had. Hadn't she arrived here from a world without men?

One long last look at the golden couple standing together, and she crept away.

Cinderella, leaving the ball.

In the middle of the night, and still wide-eyed, she asked the darkness: *have I seen and done everything that you brought me here for, Leonie?*

Silence.

Why was there never an answer when she needed one?

What *had* she been planning to do? Wait another month before selling her share of the Circle-O back to Coop? Then, stagger off to England with that huge pot of money? Because the original sum he'd mentioned would be more than enough to deal with a debt-ridden bookshop,

Trouble was, she *hadn't* been planning, had she? For quite some time, she'd had no thoughts about home, at all. Country life, cold winds, low skies.

Perhaps it was time.

Her mind drifted back to market day at Lower Shepney Market, with the high street full of sheep. The Hall, that great house where she'd spent so much of her childhood - walled garden, now overgrown, and sundial under a tangle of ivy. Those mournful peacock cries.

And the little temple on the island in the middle of the lake, with its statue of Aphrodite, like something out of a painting by Seurat. An almost unbearably precious place; one that she hadn't been anywhere near since Leonie's funeral.

A clock chimed two o'clock. Three, four.

Middle-of-the-night loneliness, Leonie used to call this.

Sleep just wouldn't come.

If only he hadn't kissed her. If it hadn't been for that, this decision would have been so much easier.

Don't think about it.

'I've made up my mind,' she told Doc Hyde. 'I shall sell my share of the Circle-O back to Coop and go home, straight away. Yes, then he won't need to let those oil men in.'

'Ah, Gerry, Gerry. If only it were that easy. Coop's real pinched for money, don't you know that? There's maybe a million or so in the ranch, but no ready cash. See, that's how it goes here. If he buys you out now, it'll leave him with nothing. Yeah, sucked dry with no resource.'

'But in England, he *said* ... yes, he definitely told me that he could give me a good price for my share.'

'Yeah, that was then. Reckon it's cost him a heifer or two every day since you've been here, trying to sort things out. Oh, he'll find the money to pay you right enough, somehow. Don't worry about that. But it won't help *him*, not anymore. Things have changed.'

'That sounds quite desperate.'

'Yip. And that damn fire put the tin lid on it.'

'What about the oil, then? Hallie-Lee's father seems to think it's a sure thing.'

'Clay Kittrell? Oh yeah, and he'll be planning on getting get a nice fat slice of it, too. Don't go making any bets on that honcho. Like Coop always says, the old fool's short on sense, but real big on ideas. Just like *his* daddy and Grandpappy before him.'

'So, just explain it to me.' Gerry frowned. 'How would finding oil here, on the Circle-O, benefit the Kittrells?'

'Good question. There's the joint boundary, of course. That's the spot the drillers seem most interested in. And if Hallie-Lee and Coop were to, well ...' his words were left to hang.

'Marry? Will they? Are they going to?'

A shrug. 'She's been part of his life a long time. Spoiled as hell, of course. Always gets what she wants.'

'And, she wants Coop?'

'Thinks she does.'

Another silence.

'What about Coop,' Gerry said, 'what does he think about it?'

'All that's on his mind, the whole time, is what Frank would want. That's what's tearing him apart.'

Gerry sighed. 'Hallie-Lee says she's tired of waiting. She thinks I'm in the way and it's time for me to leave.'

'Does she now? And how do you feel about that?'

'That perhaps she's right, perhaps I have stayed too long.'

'And that's it? You're not going to put up a fight, just roll over and let her have what she wants?'

'What are you talking about?'

Another shrug. 'Oh, just something I've been getting a feeling about, that's all.'

'But, Doc ... listen. Are you telling me, that even if I sell back my share to Coop now, it won't help him at all?'

'That's right. Unless he can pay you in cows or grass.'

'What *should* I do then?'

'Nothing. There's not a darn thing you can do for him now, nothing at all.'

'I'm so sorry.'

'Yeah, we all are, Gerry.'

The solution came to her in the early hours, suddenly, unexpectedly. Wide-eyed, bolt upright in bed, she tried to rub the ache out of her head.

Was she mad?

Because there would be consequences. Oh, yes. How would she face them back in England? Slings, arrows and imprecations would rain down on her head from all sides. They'd say she was muddle-headed, that she hadn't known what she was doing.

Did she know what she was doing? Because once the decision was made, there could be no dithering, no going back.

CHAPTER
THIRTY ONE

'Marriage isn't everything in life, dears.'
A Woman's Way, 1923

'All things bright and beautiful, all creatures great and small ...'

The voice floated up from the kitchen. Louder and louder and ...

'*... the rich man in his castle, the beggar at the gate ...*'

In the bedroom under the eaves, Gerry hid her head under the quilt. She wasn't ready for this, not yet. Explanations, apologies. Would she ever be ready?

'Gerry?' Prim called. 'I know you're awake.'

She'd been awake for hours. Listening to the clock chime, four, five.

Her first night for months in a bed that didn't rock or shake, and she'd been woken from uneasy sleep by bitter cold, unfamiliar sounds. Owl's call? Fox's bark?

No clatter of hooves, no shouts, no dogs, just ... darkness. Rain. Drumming on the roof, spattering against the tiny windows of Prim's smoky cottage, sounding spiteful and bitter.

'You're going to have to face me, you know. Sooner or later.'

Her travelling outfit flung over an upright chair, bags and baggage strewn all around. And there, against the wall, her trunk with its yellowing label: MISS G. CHILEDEXTER. IN TRANSIT.

Oh, she was that, all right. Trains clanking, fizzing, wheezing. Great seas heaving. Many suns and many moons risen and set, and here she was again. Her great adventure, over.

How long would it take to get used to everything again? Not just this clammy cold, but the size of things, the scale? Shrinking horizons. Dim rooms crowded with furniture. The changed light.

All her worldly belongings pushed into cupboards or piled against the wall. She'd taken over Prim's cottage like some sort of infestation, a bat in her friend's belfry.

Stretching out a hand, she fumbled for her boots. Bedsprings squeaked, everything smelled damp and it all looked much smaller, shabbier than she remembered. Even Prim, especially Prim.

Yesterday, at her homecoming, they'd thrown arms around each other and Gerry had felt a stab of guilt at how thin the other woman had seemed, how pale. Neat as ever, hair coiled tidily in the nape of her neck - but, oh were those threads of grey?

When she finally got round to giving Prim a full account of

what she'd done, Gerry thought, there'd likely be a few more. Of course, her friend was going to be stricken. Of course, she was.

Security for the two of them? A bright future for Bent's Fine and Rare Books? *All gone,* she thought, *all come to nothing. All my fault.*

Breakfast. Gerry braced herself.

'Perhaps I'd misunderstood.' Prim waved the pearl-handled butter knife in a rather threatening manner. 'You see, I'd thought the whole purpose of that trip, was to realise money from your share of the ranch. To pay bookshop bills, settle our debts.'

Sigh. 'Yes ... that was the plan.'

'You *promised*, Gerry. And I trusted you, I did.'

'I know.'

'I told you, didn't I? Fool's errand. I remember saying it!' A frowning pause. 'You look terrible.'

'I feel terrible.'

Gerry wrapped her cardigan tightly round herself. Was she going to spend the rest of her life like this, hunched and miserable, shivering?

'So, what *happened*? How did it all go wrong?'

'In a nutshell?' As wind drove rain against the window, Gerry sipped the tea, gratefully. 'I just decided ... well, I gave back my half-share of the ranch.'

'*Gave!*' Prim peered over her spectacles. 'You mean, without accepting any payment?'

'Well. Just enough to cover my travel expenses, both ways.'

'And that's it, that's *all*? I don't believe this.'

'I am sorry, Prim.'

'Oh, you will be. There'll be bailiffs winging round our ears like wasps! How d'you think we're going to live?'

'On Sully's stewed rabbit? How is he, by the way?'

'Don't be facetious.'

'It's hysteria.'

'Then, *why* do it? Explain yourself. I still don't understand.'

'Because, Coop was struggling, because the ranch needed capital. After all ... oh, what a sweet cat!' She bent to scratch the ears of the small furry shape, threading through her legs. 'What's happened to Igor?

'Wretched creature disappeared after you left. Now the bookshop's riddled with mice, and Dido's no mouser. Gerry, Gerry! What did Coop say, when you told him?'

'I *didn't* tell him. When I'd decided what to do, Doc Hyde - you know, the vet - arranged everything. He took me to see the lawyer and helped me to leave Jericho Wells, without anyone else knowing.'

She'd spent some time on the journey back to England, of course, trying to picture the scene when Coop eventually heard the news - that cool, grey gaze on the horizon, his dogs at his side.

Would he have felt some glimmer of gratitude for what she'd done? Or just been mightily relieved that she'd gone, so that he could get on with his life.

Did she care? No point pretending that she didn't.

Would he write? He didn't like letters.

Should *she* write?

No, no, no. He might think she wanted something.

'Didn't anyone try to dissuade you?' Prim said. 'What about that animal doctor fellow?'

Gerry's mind flew back to that moment on the verandah when she'd confided in Doc Hyde about her plan. The night had been hot, the crickets loud.

'What do you think?' she'd said.

'Don't do it.'

'I have to, Doc, there's no other way. And I want you to promise that you won't tell anyone else.'

'What about Coop?' Eyes had been fixed on her face.

'Especially not Coop.'

'Whoa! This is plumb crazy, Gerry. How're you going to make out? What will you do?'

'I'll just go back to who and what I was, I suppose, before I came here.' Back to the tame and domesticated, that world without men.

'And just how do you suppose you'll do that?'

'Gerry!' Prim brought her thoughts winging back from over the Atlantic. 'What did he say to you, that person?'

'He told me to get some advice before I made up my mind. But -'

'You didn't listen! You know, you're starting to sound more and more like Leonie. Always an excuse. Always something else, *someone* else. Always taking things too far.'

'But Prim, that ranch, his cattle ... they've been Coop's whole life. He's earned the right to that money. Was it fair for me to benefit from all his hard work, some unknown person from the other side of the world?' She hesitated. 'As I see it, something had been *given* to me. So, I simply ... I just, gave it back.'

Another deafening silence. Minutes ticked by.

Then, a slow, slow shake of Prim's head.

'Oh ... my ... Lord.' She folded her arms across her chest. 'What?'

'You *admire* him, don't you?'

'No! No, not in that sort of ...'

'You do. You've fallen for him.'

Silence.

'Well ...' sigh '... what if I have? Nothing *happened*.' A few lovely moments of closeness and understanding, a frisson of pleasure. Nothing more. 'It's the land that Coop loves, the Circle-O.'

'I knew it. Oh, *Gerry* ...'

Fallen? Gerry was thinking, while Prim continued to voice her frustration. Is that like casting yourself over a cliff? Out of control, tumbling, floating through air? How do you get back, then? Can a person recover?

If only he hadn't kissed her. She could have stayed as she was, a frustrated spinster, in her narrow monk's bed. Like Prim and most other women here. All those slowly breaking hearts, under buttoned-up layers of woolly cardigans.

Must stop thinking about it, must, *must*. Such a bad idea. But thoughts kept running away, out of control. She'd forget, eventually, of course she would.

'Mmm, yes,' she imagined herself saying, eons later, 'of course. I remember it now. There *was* someone once. That man, the man with no last name. Wrong time, wrong person.'

How long would it take to reach that stage, that blessed blur of not remembering? Until then, whenever the urge to think of him came over her - his touch, his mouth, that kiss - she'd have to lie down and wait, until it passed.

Whatever it was, it was over. The end.

Coop would marry Hallie-Lee. Well, good for you, Hallie-Lee.

'Anyway ...' she said brightly, to Prim. 'I'm here now, aren't I. I'm home.'

Home. With rain pecking at the windows and the entire rest of her life stretching out emptily, in front of her.

Never again, she said to herself. *Never again.*

And so, it began. That endless round of interrogations.

Mr Peale listened, and seemed so kind and understanding that Gerry half-expected him to throw her a straw, or bag of money, for clutching purposes. None arrived. No advice, either.

Mr Grewcock? Like bearding a beast in his lair. First, he first turned puce, then levelled horns and charged. Questions were fired, pop, pop, pop. Had she taken leave of her senses? Couldn't she see, hadn't she cared, didn't she think?

What could she say?

Why had she done it? Because a ghost told her to, that's why.

Oh, she had erred, yes. She had stumbled. She'd been foolish and unwise.

Just punish me, then, she thought. *Punish me now. I know I deserve it.*

'Well, as hanging, drawing and quartering are no longer an option, they don't quite know what to do with me,' Gerry reported back to Prim, 'not yet. Mr Peale claims that we can't even try to sell Bent's Books, because of some sort of legal covenant. Besides, the building's in far too bad a state of repair. Mr Grewcock insists we take a full inventory of all stock, immediately. Perhaps he thinks we might find something rare and antiquarian, in the cellar.'

'Yes, antiquarian mice and spiders. Leonie sold off anything of value a long time ago.'

Gerry was quiet for a moment.

'You're entitled to be cross with me, Prim, everyone is. There's only a tiny amount of money left. Barely enough to keep a mouse alive, let alone pay off a mountain of debt. I've no prospects, no plans. So you see, I can't ... I really don't expect ...'

'I know. I know that you don't.'

'So, if you want to ...'

'Oh, I'm not leaving now. Where would I go?

Where are *you,* Leonie? Gerry found herself asking, a lump in her throat. What has all this been for? You wanted me to go to Texas? Well, now I'm back. No money, no prospects. Have I missed something?

Or have you just decided to rest in peace?

CHAPTER THIRTY TWO

'Men shrink from the craze for 'independence'
and 'equal rights'.
*'Heart-to-Heart Column,*1922

Prim opened the bookshop door to a damp, musty smell.

More buckets to catch more drips, floorboards cracking, curling. Venturing to the top floor, they found a hole in the roof, and a thin layer of mould. It was cold as Siberia.

Ye imminent end of Ye Olde Bookshop?

Well, Gerry thought, what had she expected? 'It's infested with mousies! Just the scent of Igor used to keep them away.'

'Didn't I tell you? No sign of Igor since you left.'

Gerry sighed. Lost cat, lost hopes.

They found a few lumps of coal, lit the stove, made some tea.

'Now, come over here.' Prim beckoned, from behind the counter, 'and crouch down so that no-one can see us.'

'Whatever for?'

'Hordes will advance, you'll see. I'll explain later.'

Stretching out her legs, Gerry looked to one side. All those missing titles! The dusty spaces between books looked like gaps in someone's teeth. A bookshop with no books, and no money to buy any, either.

Behind her, on the desk - two piles of paper. That fairly modest heap must be personal. The tilting mountain of fierce red ink, exclamation marks? Bills, yes. Final demands!

'We're not the only ones fallen on hard times, you know,' Prim said, steam rising from her cup.

'Oh?'

'Lord Evelyn? The Hall? Since you left, he seems to have withdrawn from everything. The house, parkland ... all in a state of ruination. Oh-oh!' A finger to her lips. 'Shhh!

Rattling and banging at the door, then a quavery, 'Yoo-hoo! Are you in there, dear?' The bell clanged; the door was flung back.

Struggling to her feet, Gerry's eyes widened at the vision gliding over the threshold. A swirl of voluminous cape, topped by a velvet-lined hat that looked as if poultry was exploding on top of it.

'Oh, Mrs Applegarth, it's you! How *very* nice to see you again. Have you ...?'

'Now, don't bother about me, dearie.' A long cerise evening glove was waved majestically in Gerry's direction. 'Just carry on. No tea, thank you, it disturbs my vibrations. Gin? Well, never mind.'

Dazed, Gerry turned to Prim, who propelled her towards the stock cupboard and pushed her in, hissing, 'That's why we were hiding. Mrs Applegarth comes in here, every ... *single* ... day.'

'For a book?'

'Not books, no! She's almost taken up residence. It started after Mr Applegarth died.'

'Aah. How sad.'

'Yes, one minute she's singing all those Sankey and Moody hymns about *'daring to be Daniel'* or something; the next ... ' she lowered her voice.

Gerry leaned forward. 'What!'

'It's the vibrations, she says. From ... the other side.'

'Other ...?'

'Spirits! In here, apparently. Claims she's psychic and can sense their aura. All hokum, of course, but well, I hadn't had the heart to shoo her away. If it keeps her happy ...'

Gerry chose not to comment. She'd had enough experience of spirits of her own, thank you, unquiet and otherwise. And she remembered, only too well, Prim's scathing response to those.

'She says some distant forbear was a Romany, and she's inherited second sight and the gift of healing.'

'I always thought she was deaf,' Gerry said.

'Mmm. That may have been the strain of living with Mr Applegarth. If you remember, he was a very ... loud sort of person. She did heal his sciatica, though, apparently.'

Out of the blue, Igor came back.

'Hello,' Gerry said, 'remember me?' She enquired as to

where he had been.

He didn't deign to reply.

'Bold as brass,' Prim said. 'No-one's seen hide nor hair of him since you left. Now, he just sits and stares with those polished glass eyes. And have you *seen* Dido? She goes all stiff when she sees him; the fur between her shoulders stands on end!'

A pause.

'Speaking of strangers, I saw Archie this morning.'

'Oh?' Gerry said. 'How is he?'

'Charming as ever. *Still* a bachelor.'

Misery doesn't like company, Leonie used to say.

Six weeks? Gerry had been home for *six weeks*, and still, she was avoiding people. Ducking into doorways to dodge anyone she knew in Lower Shepney Market.

The Dutt-Dixon-Nabbs and Colonel Dudley. The butcher, the baker. Consequently, few people in the little market town had seen sight or sound of her, since her return. Of course, by now, everyone and his horse and dog would know her business. She could imagine the gossip.

'That Miss Chiledexter! Haven't you heard? Home again, tail between her legs. Reduced herself and that poor Primrose Green, to abject poverty. I blame the aunt. Ha, the apple doesn't fall far from the tree!'

All true, of course, all absolutely true.

No voices, either. Not in her head, nor Prim's cottage. No advice, no guidance or encouragement, just silence. Her ghosts had deserted her. Only demons left.

Even Sully had retreated. After poking his head round the door a day or two ago, and being sent away with a flea in his ear, he hadn't been back.

She was on her own, and prone to crying in corners. Boo hoo.

'Oh, for goodness *sake*,' Prim said. 'Stop that sighing, and moping.'

'I'm feeling sorry for myself; I'm *suffering*.'

'Suffer in silence, then.'

'Aren't I entitled to wallow?'

'Not any longer, no. No more snivelling or bouts of the vapours in my company, thank you.

CHAPTER
THIRTY THREE

'Don't age miserably. Try to keep your heart young.'
The Single Girls' Guide to Matrimony, 1923

In spite of Gerry feeling that the world had stopped turning, January and February followed Christmas, both bitter, both unforgiving. That bone-chillingly cold weather suited her mood, perfectly.

Shrove Tuesday, pancakes. Ash Wednesday - penance? Ah yes, sackcloth and ashes and beating yourself with sticks. She couldn't eat, couldn't sleep.

One day, seeing Archie in the distance with his dogs, she turned sharply through the lych-gate into St Cyriacs, setting wood pigeons bursting from the beeches.

It was too wet to lurk around the mossy headstones with their sad verses, so she slipped into the church porch. The gargoyle overhead, spitting rain from its stony mouth, looked down disapprovingly.

But inside, in that heavy silence, where thick walls held the prayers of hundreds of years, she felt a familiar peace. As she slumped in the tall box-pew, peering at memorial tablets of the Evelyn family dating back to the sixteenth century, a watery ray of sun slanted through the stained glass.

'Why, if it isn't the elusive Miss CeeDee.' A slender figure slid in beside her, with a whiff of damp tweed, the voice high and light. 'Are you avoiding me?'

Sigh. 'I'm avoiding everyone, Archie.'

'Well, the dogs are outside. When you've finished praying for guidance, come walk with us.'

When Mrs Pratt-Steed appeared in the organ loft and someone else turned up to polish the pews, Gerry pulled on her gloves. Leaving the organist to bang out *Sheep May Safely Graze*, she slipped quietly away.

Outside, hat over her ears, she called to the dogs. 'Hello, you fellows,' and they pranced excitedly round the clipped yews, tails wagging.

Archie, handsome and elegant as ever, in long herringbone coat with a canary yellow scarf wrapped round, took her arm.

Yellow?

His scarf, she couldn't help noticing, as they went out of the grassy churchyard, past the parsonage, perfectly matched gloves and socks. Was he *ever* untidy, rumpled? Was that tie ever askew? There was certainly something about him that made you look twice. Always clean as a whistle.

How long did it take him to dress in the morning, to put that crisp wave in his hair? Not the sort of thing to ask out loud, of course. Unless you were Leonie. Fragrantly well-mannered, she'd called Archie. It hadn't sounded like a compliment, either.

Why *hadn't* her aunt warmed to him? She'd always greatly admired swagger in anyone else. For some strange reason, Gerry suddenly tripped over her own buttoned boots.

'Steady!' Archie caught hold of her. Then, 'Why did you go into hiding when you came back?'

'Embarrassment? I've made such a mess of everything.'

'Haven't we all, dear heart,' Archie's murmured response.

As the church clock chimed the hour, they walked briskly by the pond and its shivering ducks, past thatched cottages, smoke curling from their chimneys.

English air, Gerry thought, taking deep lungfuls. Wet and fresh.

Then, following the high wall, almost hidden by lichens, mosses and snaking stems of ivy, they came to the tall wrought-iron gates, decorated with Evelyn family arms.

Sections of wall were crumbling, and one of the huge stone griffins guarding the gate was badly chipped. She peered through, past the gatehouse to the great park. How overgrown it all looked, how run down.

'Sad state of affairs,' Archie muttered, as they pushed open the unlocked gates. 'D'you know, he's even sold off his hunters?'

Good grief, Gerry thought.

Wandering through the great avenue of oaks, they saw dead trees amongst the drifts of bluebells. Bushes flanking the steep curve of the drive hadn't been cut back and you could barely glimpse the lake.

'What on earth's happened?' Wrapping her coat tightly round - Leonie's très chic, ankle-skimming velvet, bordered in fur at neck, cuffs and hem - she skirted a fallen branch.

'Most staff have gone. Gardeners, too.'

'What of the Borleys?'

'The who?'

'Oh, Archie, you know. Borley, the butler. His wife.'

'Not sure.' Careless shrug. 'Haven't heard. Most have been let go.'

Coming to a stop between the two magnificent cedars at the end of the lawn, they stared at the house. It had that same forlorn, abandoned air about it. Most of the windows were shuttered, closed against the world.

Still, from somewhere, the mournful cry of a peacock.

'It all seems so sudden,' Gerry said.

'Not really. Pretty predictable, I'd say. Battle shock, once removed. Lord Evelyn? Lost his son, lost hope. Now, his money. Hall's gone to rack and ruin. Almost everything's been auctioned off.'

Turning around, they walked back alongside fields belonging to the estate. No horses peacefully grazing, just a few sad-eyed cows huddled by the fence, coats slick and wet, standing like statues. Rain dripped from ears and tails into deep, sludgy hoof-prints.

How patient and uncomplaining they were, Gerry thought. How unlike their fearsome Texan cousins.

'So,' Archie said, after hemming and hawing a bit, 'I hear

that you're rather in the soup, yourself.'

'What have you heard?'

'That you're back, with no money, just huge debts. Right or wrong?'

Gerry pulled a face.

'Well, then. I may have a solution.'

'Oh, yes?'

'Marry me.'

'Oh, Archie.' She stopped to look up at the sky, flat and puddle-grey and weeping again. Her own mood, exactly. 'We've been through all this ...'

'You could keep the bookshop, pay off those debts.'

'... many, many times. Nothing's changed.'

There were back at St Cyriacs. Casting himself onto the wooden bench outside the churchyard, Archie pulled her down next to him.

'We could have a good life, y'know. It would be so convenient.'

'You want to marry me because it's *convenient?* But, we don't suit, do we? Anyway, you're much too tall for me!'

'I can be shorter.'

'Too ... well-connected.'

'Shackles! I'll cast the dratted relatives off.'

'We don't love each other.'

'What's that to do with anything? These days, everyone has to compromise. We started out as friends, didn't we?'

'But Archie ... you could have your *pick* of girls in the county, suitable ones to fit in with your life. Girls your parents would approve of, for goodness sake. Why me?'

'You know why.'

Well, yes, Gerry thought. *I'm beginning to*. 'Because you want to do what's expected, but ...'

'Yes, it goes against every instinct, every fibre of mind and body to do so.'

'Has there ever been anyone that you'd want to spend your life with?'

A long pause.

'As a matter of fact,' he murmured, staring down and moving one carefully polished shoe in a circle, 'there is. He's been sent off to the Colonies to get me out of his system.' A quick glance to check her reaction. 'Either that, or to get yellow fever and die. His family don't seem to care which.'

'Oh, Archie ...'

'You see, you *do* understand. Marry me, Gerry.'

'But, your parents.' His mother! Her malicious tongue! The Colonel and those exclamation marks. 'They'd be appalled.'

A puff of contempt. 'Not anymore. Truth to tell, they'd be relieved. If you could just see your way to abandoning that alarming dress sense and - '

'What about you, Archie? What would *you* want of me?'

He took her hands. 'To take my name, live in my house.'

'To have your children?'

'Ah.' His nose indicated some distaste. 'Mmm, I ... probably not. Look, will you consider it, Gerry? Promise you will.'

Gerry stared down at her hands. Red and cold, they lay limply in his like a pair of stunned mullet. At his touch, she'd felt nothing, had never felt anything. Did that matter? Would a life together be so awful?

After all, he was kind. He dressed well, he had ... beautiful diction. 'Ouch!'

'What's the matter?'

She rubbed her ear. 'Something bit me.'

And suddenly, treacherously, her mind was back in Texas, with a completely different sort of feeling. The one she'd had when Coop had held her, danced with her, kissed her.

The kiss, that one kiss, it kept coming back to her. When she was clearing cupboards, teasing out disobedient hair. In her dreams. Would it haunt her for ever? No, eventually it would go away. When she died.

'Promise me, Gerry?' He was studying his shoes again.

'All right.' Did he iron those shoelaces, she wondered, distracted? Like the Duke of Westminster, according to Leonie. How had she *known* that? 'I'll consider it, I promise.' A pause. 'Should we ... hug?'

'Mmm, I don't think so.'

No, she didn't think so, either.

He *is* charming, though, she thought, carrying on with her list of attributes, and handsome. He didn't seem to do much, of course, apart from spending hours on his appearance and deciding what to wear.

She cast an admiring eye over his herringbone coat. Marvellous tailoring, the fit, the style, the line, but ... something amiss. She narrowed her eyes. The underarms, yes. They were all wrong.

'Archie? Forgive me, but the sleeves on your coat. They haven't been fitted properly.'

'Oh! Can *you* see it, can you, really? How irritating. It bothers me, too, but my Sackville Street tailor simply won't have it.'

'I know what's wrong, I can do it. Give it to me.'

'Do you know someone who can fix it?'

'Yes, me!'

'Ah, Gerry. Don't you *see*? We're a perfect match!'

'Archie has asked me to marry him.'

Stopped in her tracks, Prim stood absolutely still. 'The brass neck of that man. What was your answer?'

'I said I'd think about it.'

'No, Gerry. Men like Archie … they weren't meant for marriage.'

'I can't help it, I like him, I just do. And he's offering a way out, isn't he? As I see it, all he's suggesting is a kind of business relationship.'

'A lavender marriage, they call it.'

'Well, wouldn't that be better than ending my days knitting in the chimney corner? He'll settle all our debts.'

'And what would he want, in return? Remember what your aunt said about him? Too milk-and-water.'

'Well, I'd have to try and fill a role for him, wouldn't I? To satisfy his parents and everyone else. Where's the harm? Haven't women always had to compromise? Anyway,' she paused, biting her lip. 'There wasn't *any* suggestion … I mean, under no circumstances, would there be ... well ... you know.'

'What?'

'Um ... intimate relations.'

No kisses from Archie. No hugs, either, apparently. Well, that was all right.

'Mmm. And what would the two of you be doing together all alone in the evenings? Having one or two rubbers at whist?'

A long silence.

'What about that American? Have you managed to put *him* out of your mind? Thought not, you've had that look in your eye again.'

Gerry didn't respond. Of course she hadn't forgotten Coop. How could she? She was tired of thinking about him. 'It would never have worked,' she said. Then, almost to herself, 'If only hadn't kissed me.'

'What! He what? He ... *kissed* you! When?'

'Just once.' That was all. The heart-skipping moment when he'd leaned in, closer, closer, fastened his body on hers, and ... oh, she didn't want to talk about it. It was too precious to be picked over by anyone, even Prim.

Surely the memory *would* start to fade, eventually? Bit by bit, until there was only a scrap of it left. Until then, it had to see her through a lot of cold English winters.

'That Dutt-Dixon-Nabb fella,' Sully said.

'Yes?'

'You walking out with him?'

'None of your business.'

'Steer clear, is my advice, if you know what's good for you. He loves dogs and horses, that man. Loves himself. Nought else.'

CHAPTER THIRTY FOUR

'Try putting on a brave face, and jolly well enjoying yourself.'
The Bachelor Girl's Handbook, 1924

Visiting the Borleys.

As Gerry trudged through the avenue of oaks, crows rose up from bare branches and a fine grey mist half hid the choked lake.

How sad.

Ever since childhood, whenever she'd been confused or upset, she'd rowed across the lake to the little island, with its temple and statue of Aphrodite. Her favourite hiding place and refuge, until darling Leonie had been buried there. After that, well ... she could never face going back.

The big house loomed up.

It breathes history, Gerry thought, her breath thickening the mist. It's survived storms and wars, for goodness sake. Are taxes and financial ruin really going to be the end of it?

At the huge door, no scurrying feet, no-one to greet her.

The box of wires and bells to summon the household seemed to be broken. Pushing the door, she wandered into the marble hall, and stood staring at the gracious stairwell.

Footsteps echoed. No sound from anywhere, just stillness, secrets. Old ghosts drifting out into the silence.

Gone all those huge oil paintings of bewigged grandees and swaggering nobility, the tapestries, antiquities. No dogs in the hall, game in the larder. Huge fireplaces swept and empty.

Although the servants' hall looked lifeless, a fire still burned brightly in the Borleys' parlour, with its comfortable faded furniture. Spirits, however, were low.

'It's not just empty,' Gerry told Prim, 'it's a hollow shell. Lord Evelyn's gone away to his other property in County Kildare, apparently. The Borleys are trying to hold everything together, but it's falling apart around them.'

'Here's an idea, Prim.' A pin in her mouth and scissors in her hand, she was folding and snipping at Archie's coat. 'Why don't I take in sewing?'

'Don't be ridiculous.'

'Desperate measures. Mr Grewcock is losing patience. If I'm not careful, I'll end up in the poorhouse, gaps in my teeth and sucking on straw. Anyway, I'm tired of 'poor me' drooping around like this. I want to roll up my sleeves and *do* something.'

'Say again?' Prim cupped a hand to her ear. 'I couldn't quite hear over the angels singing.'

The first primroses. Flashes of snowdrops in the woods. Freewheeling down to the bookshop, warm breeze in her hair, Gerry felt the sap rising.

The best thing about bicycles? They were reliable. Yes, speedy and safe and best of all, they didn't frisk about when you were riding them.

'Good morning, Mrs Applegarth!' Flinging back the book-shop door, she set the bell clang-clanging.

'Don't be exuberant, dear. It disturbs the perturbations.'

At a small table close to the stove, draped in beads and a lor-gnette, Mrs Applegarth didn't look up. A moth-eaten fur hung round her shoulders; a silver cloche fitted closely to her head with fuzz of orange fringe peeping out from underneath.

There was a distinct whiff of old rose leaves around her.

Prim and Gerry had discovered that if they plied her con-stantly with tea - for the leaves, of course - she'd sit happily for most of the day, with her Tarot cards, her palmistry and readings.

Somewhat disconcertingly, people had started coming in to consult her. 'She has the gift, you know,' someone had whispered to Gerry, 'of *seeing.*'

It had seemed churlish to disapprove, especially as the number of people visiting the shop had at first doubled, then tripled. Some of them even bought books. (Mrs Applegarth had advised on the purchase of some relevant titles.)

'I've been thinking, dear,' she said now, to Gerry, 'of setting up a little salon here. For séances and such.'

'Ah.' Gerry eyed her suspiciously. 'Now, I'm not sure about -'

'All in the best possible taste, of course. Under my *professional* name.'

'Oh ... and, what's that?'

'Madame Athena. Athena is my Christian name, you see.'

'Is it, really?'

'Yes, dear. The ancient heroine. Some say, quite the *best* Olympian deity. She was Odysseus's protector in the Odyssey, you know. Gave him pep talks and provided magical disguises.'

Gerry was suitably silenced. 'Well,' she said. 'I'll have to talk to Prim.'

'Oh, I don't think that nice Miss Green will object. She wears such sensible shoes. Not like you, dear. You ... well of course, you are a *Bent* girl!'

'Actually, I'm a Chiledexter now.'

'Oh no, dear, no. Look at you. Nothing dull, nothing ordinary. You'll always be a Bent girl. Like your mother and your dear aunt before you, those bright young people.' Her eyes moistened. 'So beguiling, so determined to enjoy life.'

'I'm afraid I haven't their cheekbones *or* their money, Mrs Applegarth.'

'Well then, dear, that's just where my little gatherings will help. I'll pay you, of course, for use of your premises, oh yes. You see, people will give me some small token for contacting their loved ones. And I will pass it on to you. An excellent arrangement, if I say so myself. I've no need of the money.'

And so, it began.

Handbills were produced and people came, once or sometimes twice a week, to Madame Athena's salon in the bookshop. Candles flickered, voices were hushed and hands joined around the covered table.

The lady herself, her own hands heavy with topaz rings, usually wore an oriental turban for these proceedings, and flowing cloak in bluebottle colours - cobalt blue, purple, violent green.

Were spirits summoned? Was it all trickery? Gerry and Prim didn't know and weren't sure they wanted to, either; they tried to stay out of the way.

Although, after one particularly strenuous session, when Madame's cloak had been singed by a candle, Gerry offered an opulent beaded opera cape of Leonie's, as alternative. 'Oh, my *dear*,' breathed Mrs Applegarth. 'This garment has such an aura.'

Apparently, in her expert opinion, Igor had an aura, too.

'Yes,' Prim hissed at Gerry, 'from all the cods' heads you cook up for him. When I tried to shoo him away tonight, do you know what she said? That we should *treasure* him. She said Egyptians used to shave off their own eyebrows when their beloved cats died!'

One minute, you were all hatted and gloved and buttoned-up. The next, swifts were back, screaming round the church spire, and everything was buzzing and blossoming.

May morning though, dawned grey and misty.

As the sun broke through, Gerry stood amid clumps of wild daffodils on Lower Shepney Market green, watching the maypole dancing. Children holding coloured ribbons skipped in and out to tunes from the accordion player, weaving patterns around the pole to celebrate the first day of summer.

The bookshop was closed. They'd had no choice but to get 'Cyril-and-his-ladders' in, to deal with the drips. How long was it likely to take? How much would it cost? Gerry had no idea.

Such a fine day, though. Why waste spring sunshine worrying? She would walk up to the Hall; she hadn't seen the Borleys for such a long time.

The sky was now soft blue with wisps of cloud, the bleat of new lambs on the air. Wandering along the narrow lane, she stood back to let a pony and trap trot briskly past, and heard a cuckoo call.

How English it all was. She sniffed the breeze. How timeless. The customs, smells. This beautiful ancient landscape. Closing her eyes for a moment, she tried to recall the colours of Texas, that breathtaking scenery. Why, they'd almost faded from her mind.

Well, good. She passed a field speckled with dandelions, a gigantic lop-eared sow of Sully's sprawled in shade, the other side of the hedge. Yes. That was exactly what she'd wanted, wasn't it? To put everything to do with that place, out of her mind.

Cyril and the roof. The roof and Cyril. That was what she should be thinking about now. Even those birds, whatever they were - chaffinches? - seemed to be whirring *how-to-pay, how-to-pay, how-to-pay?*

Arriving at the tall gates, she saw the gatehouse, closed and empty. Except for skylarks twittering feverishly overhead, it was very quiet. No-one else around.

At the curve of that long, sweeping drive though, she heard voices, a murmur of conversation, people calling out to each other. Rounding the bend, Gerry stopped, gaped.

Builders were working on the Hall's rooftop parapet. Men carrying ladders going hither and thither, while carpenters and other craftsmen were absorbed elsewhere. Shielding her eyes, peering up, she recognised some of the older workmen.

In the grounds, too, gardeners were bent over in the herbaceous border and kitchen garden, forking out weeds. The glasshouse was under repair. Hedges of box and yew, all neatly clipped.

What *was* going on?

In the stable yard, as the clock struck the hour, as she crossed the cobbles to peer inside the box stalls, horses whinnied a welcome. There must be grooms to look after them, too. A new owner? A new Lord somebody-or-other for everyone to touch a forelock to?

The Borleys would know. She glanced around, but was reluctant to stray inside the house, and the men all looked too busy to be bothered with questions.

Confused, she turned tail and walked away. When the lake came into view, she was tempted to go and see if that had been cleared, too.

Instead, she hurried off to tell Prim, and found her watching the skipping group of Morris dancers now on the green - in bright tatters and flowery hats, clashing sticks and bells and waving handkerchiefs.

Well, here we are, Gerry thought, *two old maids watching an ancient fertility rite.* At the beat of the drum, the concertina and melodeon, swifts spiralled up into the sky.

At the end of Mayday, still feeling as twittery as those birds, she stood gazing up at the sky. Except for a tawny owl's hoot and the occasional bat twisting low, all was still and silent.

Thoughts drifted to another night staring at stars. This was how Coop continued to haunt her, wasn't it? Unexpectedly, at moments like this. She recalled that evening's heat, the sound of a guitar being quietly played by one of the Mexican hands.

And Coop, telling her about the constellations.

What could she see now? Venus? Bright and luminous in the north-west. Standing for beauty, apparently, pleasure, love. *Ho, not for me*, she thought. No sign of good luck, either.

Because according to Cyril, the bookshop roof was leaking, buckling and rotting. It would soon be down round their ears. That black hole of debt was getting bigger and bigger, and Gerry lay awake at night worrying about soon being in a serious state of destitution.

Living on charity? Yes, and possibly scavenging for potato peelings and acorns, alongside Sully's pigs.

Why had she skipped off to America? What had that trip achieved? Nothing. Actually, less than nothing. Because of her pig-headedness, they were in a worse state than ever.

CHAPTER THIRTY FIVE

'Take up astrology, palmistry and tarot.
Use to intrigue, charm and waylay men.'
How to Attract a Man, 1923

In the weeks that followed, rumours flew round and round Lower Shepney Market.

What was happening? Had Lord Evelyn really sold up and off-ed to Ireland? Why, that estate had *always* been in the family, handed down through impoverished generations. What would it mean for the workers, the tied cottages?

No-one had answers; there was nobody to ask, but a grandeur of sorts was certainly being restored. A new steward seemed to be organising things.

As ever, Sully was privy to a great deal of the gossip. 'Gimson's been let go,' he said, rubbing his hands. 'That new chap's taken over.'

'Who?'

'Scot. Don't know the feller. Red hair, big beard. They say he's a fair sort.'

Mrs Borley, head to toe in black, her ancient hat held in place by a silver pin, brought a letter, from Mr Mactaggart, the new steward. 'He was most particular I deliver it to you in person, Miss Gerry,' she said, importantly.

'Oh.' Gerry sat down, quickly. These days, communications came in two sorts. Polite requests or angry demands. Both concerned money. Tentatively, she opened the envelope. 'It's a list.' She looked up. 'Of books.'

'That's right, Miss. To replace some of those ones missing from the library, Mr Mactaggart said. It's in a real sorry state, you know. Such a shame.'

Gerry pictured the library as she remembered it. Fine panelling, precious calf-bound books with brittle gold-edged pages, rich smell of leather.

'But, who made this up?' She waved the piece of paper. 'Who took the inventory?'

'Now I don't rightly know, Miss. A gentleman came from London, I think. T'was the steward gave it to me, such a nice man. Send the account straight to him, he said.'

Gerry's felt her spirits lift a little. A lifeline? For someone drowning in debt, yes. 'What of the new owner?'

'No sign of him yet, Miss Gerry. Still a mystery. He's been making changes, though. Oh, yes. Me and Borley are still trying to get our heads round them. New plumbing, all modern.' Lowering her voice, she dropped her eyes to black buttoned boots. 'Water closets, bathrooms.'

'Goodness.'

'Even one of them ... telephone machines. All crackles and clicks.'

In spite of that order of books for the Hall, Gerry was still barely managing to keep their heads above water.

There was, of course, a solution.

To marry Archie or not to marry Archie?

Thoughts kept see-sawing. Yes, no, no, yes.

Love? Happiness? They never really came into it. This was a business transaction. A secure future for Prim and the bookshop. A marriage of convenience for Archie. He wanted an answer, and time was running out.

There would be consequences, of course, a price to pay. Gerry would have to change, wouldn't she, that had been made plain enough. She'd have to fit in. A life of stifling conformity.

Oh, well. Wasn't that something she'd had to do her entire life? In India, with her parents. At school, those bad old days. She'd never ever been the person that anyone wanted her to be.

A cat when they'd wanted a mouse; liquid when they'd wanted a solid. Skinny, not rounded. Short, not tall. Only with Leonie, dear, dear Leonie, had it been different. Leonie, with her way of making you feel perfectly fine, just the way you were.

I was full of hope then, she thought. We laughed, we danced! We told jokes! Will I ever be allowed just to be myself, again?

'If we *were* to marry,' Gerry told Prim, 'Archie's says his mother couldn't countenance me working in the bookshop. I love the bookshop!' A pause. 'She thinks I need a more suitable wardrobe, too. She says my clothes are too outrageous for country living.'

Prim just raised an eyebrow.

'What?'

'Well, perhaps geometric patterns are a little ... aggressive for the daytime.'

'I adore this dress. It was one of Leonie's favourites.'

Perhaps, Gerry thought, *I'm trying to summon her up again, too. I need her help!* Strangely enough, for some time, there'd been no sign.

Might all that just have been a figment of her overheated imagination? Voices in her head, that aura of perfume? Some sort of hysteria brought on by mourning? Perhaps she'd been unbalanced by the agony of losing Leonie. P'raps, that's all it ever had been.

What to do, what to do? Gerry became more and more distracted and started losing things. Her purse, her keys. Prim's keys. An ebony and onyx brooch that Archie had given her.

Worse, she'd lost that list, the vital one, detailing books to be supplied to the Hall. Hours had been wasted hopelessly searching for it.

She remembered taking it to the bookshop. Had she forgotten to bring it back? Perhaps it was in her bag? And, where was that? She didn't know.

'Things keep disappearing!' she said, to Prim.

'Oh, I know. Yesterday, Mrs Applegarth lost her teeth in the bookshop.'

After yet another 'would-she, wouldn't-she' conversation with Archie, Gerry was helping Mrs Applegarth - or Madame Athena, as she now insisted on being called - set up her salon in the bookshop. With only a very small hole left in the roof, they'd been able to open the premises up again.

Something else, of course, for Mrs Dutt-Dixon-Nabb, that eternal thrower-about-of-weight, to disapprove of.

'Mother thinks it unwise,' Archie said, 'to let that ghastly Applegarth woman practice sorcery in a respectable bookshop. What would the vicar say?'

'It's hardly witchbane and frogs, Archie. Anyway, some people think she's psychic.'

'Nonsense. The old girl's scatty. Complete fake, an impostor.'

Anyway. The room had been prepared, the stove well stoked. It wasn't yet dusk, but curtains were drawn and, except for a few smoking, dripping candles, everywhere was dark and airless.

Gerry already had a headache. Several times, she'd bumped into chairs, tripped over Igor. Now, arranging seats, she felt herself sway and had to hold onto the table.

'Gerardina! Whatever's wrong?'

'I feel a little faint. It's rather warm in here, isn't it?'

'So *pale,* dear. I sensed you were disturbed. Here, a sandwich, cucumber, good for the nerves. Now sit down and I'll make some restorative China tea.'

When she came back with a tray, Gerry blurted, 'I'm at a crossroads in my life! I don't know which way to turn.'

'Gracious! Have another sandwich, and we'll see what the cards have to say.' Rummaging around, Madame produced an ornate deck of Tarot cards. 'Very powerful, you know.'

'No! No, thank you.'

'Drink up then, and we'll look at the leaves.'

Gerry sighed. She knew the procedure. Leonie had practised it, many times. Dregs tipped out, leaves swirled round, cup handed over for inspection.

'Good news, dear.' Madame turned the cup this way and that. 'I see a tall, dark stranger. Yes, yes. Quite clearly.'

Stifling a laugh, Gerry couldn't wait to tell Prim.

'Sceptical, dear - aren't you? Yes, you are, I can see it. Well, I'm hardly ever wrong, you know. Wait and see.'

Distracted by the arrival of four rather nervous-looking ladies, Madame rose and, with a whisk of velvet cloak, went to welcome them.

When all were seated around the table, she beckoned. 'Why don't you join us, dear?'

Gerry shrank back. Not that she was completely sceptical. Hadn't she been haunted by Leonie for over a year? Anyway, resistance was useless. Another chair was pulled out and she was gently propelled into it.

The room was now hotter than ever; the atmosphere heavy with smoke from the stove. Except for wavery wisps from the last candle blown out, it was completely dark. The shadowy shape next to her gave a nervous cough.

Those present were asked to place their hands lightly on the table, palms down, linking little fingers. As Gerry's finger curled around the quivering digit of her nearest neighbour, she thought, what am I *doing*?

There was definitely something witchy about all this. Might there be gibbering? A protoplasmic materialisation? Eye of newt and toe of toad.

'Quiet everyone, please. *Con-cen-trate!*'

Having instructed them all to empty their minds and neither speak nor move, Madame Athena closed her eyes. 'Is there anyone there?'

Silence.

But. But. At that very moment, in the fug of heat, Gerry caught a strong waft of scent. Not Mrs Applegarth's old rose-leaves either, something else. Something intoxicating, heavy, hypnotic. Something that started a spine-tingling, physical reaction and caused a chill at the back of her neck.

Mitsouko? Yes! Her aunt's perfume.

'Gerardina! Stop fidgeting.'

'Is there anyone out *there* who wishes to speak to someone in *here*?'

Gerry's pulse fluttered. Leonie? Nothing. Just the creak of a chair, fly buzzing round their heads.

'One rap for yes, two for no.'

A quivering pause.

Bang! Bang! Bang!

'*Three* bangs, Madame Athena?'

'*Shhhh*, shhh!'

Another pause.

Bang! Bang-bang! *Bang*! The bookshop door was flung

back and a huge shadowy figure materialised on the threshold. A wavery giant, moving forward through the smoky gloom.

For a few seconds, time seemed suspended. Then ...

'Oh, my word,' someone breathed, 'a ... a phantom, an *apparition*.'

'How perfectly thrilling. Something's been released! You know, I've never quite managed it before.'

Only Gerry knew better. Her mouth fell open; she felt the blood drain from her face. Apparition? It was nothing of the kind.

A great surge of emotion sucked the air from her lungs. It made the world whirl and go dark. Scraping her chair back, she tried to stand, but knees gave way and she slid slowly under the table.

A dead faint.

CHAPTER THIRTY SIX

'Plainer girls often get married before their prettier sisters.'
A Modern Girl's Guide to Love, 1922

Someone was speaking, a low drone in the background.

'She's coming round ...'

Gerry felt arms lifting her up and lowering her gently into the battered leather armchair. Lamps were lit, water offered. There was talk of calling the doctor.

Then some brandy, and she coughed.

'Thank heaven. Colour's coming back.'

Concerned faces peered down, a cloudy blur. Only one stood out. A face carved in stone.

Coop. Was she hallucinating? Had he really just appeared, in a puff of smoke? Might he waft away, in the same fashion?

'You okay?' he said, softly.

She'd almost forgotten that slow, deep drawl. Rich. Rich as treacle.

'Thought I'd just drop by, and ...'

Drop by? Drop ... *by*! He lived thousands of miles away,

didn't he? A place where men in big hats rode huge horses. It took weeks and weeks to get from there to here. On ships. Trains.

'But, how did you get here?'

He shrugged. 'Look, I need to talk to you. When would be a good time?'

Gerry's mouth opened and closed, like a goldfish.

'Guess I've taken you by surprise. Shall we give it a few days?'

Shaking herself out of her trance, she gave a weak nod.

'So, I hear you've moved house. Where are you living now?'

At that point, the ladies surrounding them, who'd been turning from Gerry to Coop like umpires in the most fascinating of tennis matches, practically fell over themselves to provide directions to Prim's cottage.

Gerry sensed them all simpering above her head.

'Well, thank you, ladies.' Coop stood up. 'You've been charming company. I'm real sorry to have spoiled your evening.'

He turned to go, leaving Mrs Applegarth and her little group still clucking and twittering like a clutch of old hens.

'How extraordinary,' Prim said. 'Did he say what he was doing here?'

'He didn't say much at all. Except that he wanted ... no, *needed,* to talk to me. You know, Prim. I don't think I can bear it.'

'Oh, he probably just wants to thank you, that's all. You know, for giving back your share of his ranch. What did you say?'

'I couldn't speak; I was dumbstruck.'

After all this time, how could they conduct a polite tête-à-tête? How would she be able to conceal how she'd felt about him? Perhaps Hallie-Lee was here, perhaps they were *married*. Oh, Lord.

It wasn't fair. She'd been doing her very best, hadn't she? Pulling herself together, getting on with things. Now, he was back. Back in her life, back in her world, catching her unawares. Asking how she was. Huh. What did he care?

She thought: something is wrong here.

'No, no, my darling. Something is very, very right.'

In her ear? Gerry looked round, startled. No, her head. Leonie. After months of silence.

Rat-tat-tat!

Gerry woke, with a start.

A knock-knocking on Prim's cottage door, loud and rude.

Peering out from the tiny bedroom window, Gerry saw the top of a man's hat. When he removed it and stepped out from the porch, she shrank back, waiting for Prim's hurrying footsteps.

No sound from below.

Another sharp rap.

'Prim!' A wild hiss. A burst of panic.

'Stay there, stay where you are!' Prim's voice floated up. 'I'll see to it.'

There followed a murmur of conversation - some polite how-do-you-dos and so forth. Then, from Gerry's position on the cold landing, she heard Prim say that unfortunately, her visitor was quite out of sorts today, and couldn't possibly be called downstairs.

Still, the conversation seemed to carry on for some time - Prim's high-pitched tone, Coop's low growl. Like the wolf, Gerry thought, at Red Riding Hood's door. She had to strain really hard to hear what they were saying - all the while, with the uncanny feeling that Coop somehow knew that she was there.

At long last, ears quivering, she heard Prim say, 'Well. You appear to be a charming man, Mr Cooper.'

'Well ... thank you, ma'am.'

'But I really think it would be best now, if you went away and charmed somebody else.'

Bang went the door.

'Look, you turnip,' Prim called up to the landing where Gerry still lurked. 'I understand why you're not ready to talk to him; I daresay you've built fantasies around him.'

An affronted silence.

'Well, I can't blame you for that. But you'll have to have a conversation with him, sooner or later; you can't *keep* putting him off.'

A thin voice, from above. 'Was it rude not to ask him in?'

'Not really. Anyway, he'd barely be able to stand upright in here.' A long, long pause. 'You're *not* in love with him, are you, Gerry?'

'Who?'

'Oh, for goodness sake! Mr Marching Through Georgia, that's who.'

'I barely know him,' Gerry said, drifting downstairs in wispy silk, the ghost from the attic.

What *was* love, anyway? She kept asking herself that question. How did you fall? Was it an unbalancing kind of thing, a surrendering? Who would ever be able to tell her?

'Well, something's going on. Even that dratted cat fawns round him.'

Igor turned away and stalked off, pretending he didn't know they were talking about him.

Gerry bicycled briskly up to the Hall. Having somehow mislaid that list of books for the library, she was hoping to find Mactaggart and get another.

Best not, she thought, *wait around at the cottage, in case Coop came by again.* She'd avoided the French Partridge, too. That must be where he was staying.

She just wasn't ready, that was all. For discussions of any kind. Would she *ever* be ready?

For once, she barely noticed the scenery. Not waist-high clouds of cow parsley and fading bluebells, nor rolling parkland. Her busy thoughts were elsewhere.

What was he *doing* here? Why had he come? For months, she'd managed to keep all thoughts of him locked away. A few times, they'd broken out and come to haunt her. But lately, not so often.

Now, they were bubbling back.

When she reached the end of the drive, she stopped dead. In front of the big house, mellow stone golden in the sunshine - was a rakish, long-bodied motor car, the biggest she'd ever seen.

Skirting it carefully, she looked around. Not a soul.

No workmen, no Mr Mactaggart, nor the Borleys. No sign of human presence, just a couple of excited fox terriers, flying out from the stable-yard as she abandoned her bicycle.

Like the Marie Celeste.

In the stillness of the house, she made her way through a sequence of rooms to the polished and panelled library. The bay window was thrown wide; ancient brocade curtains stirring in the breeze. She closed the door quietly behind her.

Breathing in the familiar smell of old books, she wandered round, peering at those dusty, morocco-bound titles that were left. Some military history. Classics. Poetry. Years ago, she would have known straight away what was missing. Now, she could only look for gaps.

If only she hadn't lost that wretched list.

Hearing footsteps crunch on the gravel, she went to the window. Two men, surrounded by dogs, were striding towards the house. One flame-haired and hatless, with weather-red face and beard. Mactaggart?

The other, oh help. No, no! The other, under his customary wide-brimmed hat and looking sickeningly fit and healthy - was Coop.

What was he doing here?

He looked at ease out there, too. Yes, comfortable. To Gerry, peering out from the library window, he still seemed an alien species. Some sort of wild animal stalking about in an English country garden.

As the men drew nearer to the house, he looked up. Had he seen her? Panicked, she stepped back behind the heavy curtain. Bother the man. She wasn't ready for this. He was here, there, everywhere.

Holding her breath, she waited, and darting to the library door, opened it a crack. For a few moments, nothing. Then her straining ear caught the tread of briskly approaching footsteps, echoing on the marble-floored hall, closer, closer.

Who? She didn't wait to find out. Heart thumping, she reached for the key and quietly turned it, staring at the door.

Someone rattled the knob. 'Hey, in there.'

A pause. Transfixed by that low drawl, unable to move, Gerry recalled advice on meeting a bear. *Look down and stay still. Don't panic. It may not be hungry.*

Dropping to all fours, she began crawling towards the window. Floorboards creaked and she bumped into a table, knocking a silk-fringed lamp to the floor. Dash it! Drat, drat.

'That you, Gerry? It's me ... Coop. Can we talk?'

Silence.

'Gerry? C'mon, open the door.'

Edging to the high window, she measured the jump to the terrace. When the door rattled again, a moment's panic. Then, hitching up skirts, she balanced on the sill and flung herself out, barely avoiding the ancient prickly rosebush below.

Wallop!

Not a soft landing. The flagstones on the terrace were hard and unforgiving. Sprawled in a wonky heap next to a huge urn, she felt hot breath on her face. A black mastiff with terrible breath stood panting over her, looking about to sink jaws into her leg.

She lay perfectly still, praying it would go away.

'Rollo! *Git* back here!'

Coop. She'd been ambushed.

The wild, black animal retreated. The taller, more formidable one stood his ground. She stared at dusty boots. Women at his feet. Well, he was used to that, wasn't he?

'Have you lost your *mind*?' She looked up to meet a well-remembered expression. 'What the hell were you trying to do?'

Wasn't it obvious? Gerry blew hair out of her eyes. Still on the ground, legs splayed under spreading skirts, she felt utterly ridiculous.

'Are you hurt?'

'No! Ow, ouch. What are you *doing* here?'

'Just ... taking a look round. Here, let me help.'

'I can manage!' Struggling painfully to her feet, she rubbed her knee. 'Where's Hallie-Lee?' She looked round. Probably round the corner somewhere, screwing knives into her chariot wheels.

'Who?' He sounded amused. 'Yeah, she visited Europe once before. Hated England. Too much rain, too many sheep.'

Perfectly on cue, the distant bleat of sheep from a neighbouring field, and Gerry felt a sudden, warm affinity with each and every one of them. 'How long are you staying?'

'That kinda depends.' Eyes narrowing, Coop considered her carefully. 'How're you doing, Gerry?'

I'm confused, she thought, resisting the urge to tidy her hair. *Upset. I'm ... just not well.*

'Oh, very well, thank you.' Then, in a rush, 'I may be getting married.'

'*May* be?'

'It's ... some things aren't settled.'

'Ah.' A long hard stare, a question behind his eyes. 'Well, your knee's bleeding. Come inside and get it cleaned up. Y'know, we need to talk. There's a lot I have to tell you.'

'Not now.' Desperate to be gone, she stepped back. 'Too ... busy.'

'Tomorrow, then. Or the day after? Saturday, Sunday?'

'The cricket match. I'm ... '

'Playing?'

'Making sandwiches.'

He offered other suggestions; she made more excuses.

Yes, of *course* she wanted to hear what he had to say. No, she couldn't *possibly* stay a minute longer, now. She had to get on her bicycle, right away, and go home. Things to do, and ... 'Is that your car?'

'Sure is.'

'It's very grand.'

'Isn't it just. Tourer, sixty-horse-power..'

Hmm, costly, too. 'Well,' she said, casting around for something else to say, 'I expect ... I'll see you ... some other time.'

'Oh, yeah. Count on it.'

At that, Gerry turned tail and headed for the hills

Pedalling furiously away, she narrowly missed a tree. Idiot! Why hadn't she stayed longer, behaved better, swallowed her pride? Why make a fool of herself, by refusing to listen to a single thing he had to say? Stupid, stupid!

He'd seemed different, too. No longer impatient and demanding. Just easy, kind. What was going on? Well, on her high horse and galloping away like this, she was none the wiser, was she?

Look, it had been a shock, that was all. She hadn't been prepared for the effect his sudden appearance would have on her. She needed time, to think.

Why are you here, she'd *wanted* to say, *why have you come?*

Perhaps she should write a note.

No. Be sensible. Go back, now.

Gerry tried out at least a dozen ensembles, before slanting the little velvet cloche over one eye, buttoning single-strap shoes and pulling on gloves to bicycle back up to the Hall - all the while, rehearsing and rehearsing questions in her head.

So, Coop. What are you doing here, I meant to ask. Holiday? A shoot?

Abandoning her bicycle at the end of the drive, she took off her hat. As she neatened her hair, trying to flatten that swoop of a side parting, a vision suddenly loomed, high on a great horse.

Hallie-Lee *Kittrell*? Yes! Large as life. Her own abundant hair neatly coiled under a rakish bowler.

Struck dumb, Gerry almost swallowed the two hairpins she'd had clamped between her teeth. Wait. *'Hallie-Lee isn't here,'* Coop had said. Hadn't he? She was sure of it. *'She doesn't like England.'* Yet here she was now, on one of those precious hunters.

Why would he lie? What *was* going on? Had they joined forces and were planning to invade middle England or something?

Impatient to be off, the huge horse struck the cobbles and stamped sideways.

'Stand!' Hallie-Lee commanded, jerking the reins. 'Geddup there!' Then, 'So nice to see you again, Gerry!'

'Oh. Yes. Are you ... um, visiting, at the Hall?'

'Mmm-hmm.' A vigorous nod. 'I'm staying here, with Coop.'

And before Gerry was able to utter another word, the other girl had turned the horse. 'Must go,' she threw over her shoulder, clattering away, 'weather's on the turn again.'

Gerry just stood, winding a lock of hair round and round on her finger. 'Ha!' she said to herself. 'I knew I couldn't trust him.'

CHAPTER THIRTY SEVEN

'Join a ramblers' club. Accept an invitation to a church social.
Say 'Yes' rather than 'No'.
A Modern Girl's Guide to Love, 1922

Long summer days. Leather on willow. Googlies and ducks
and silly mid-offs.

Gerry adored cricket.

Such a perfect English idyll, wasn't it? Ladies in wide-
brimmed hats sipping tea at the boundary edge, the slam and
slug of tree-trunk bats, echoing cries of 'Howzat!' So ... so
reassuring.

But, where would the annual cricket match be held this
year? For weeks they'd all been wondering. Since the mid-
nineteenth century, it had taken place on the Hall's very own
cricket ground, with its little pavilion, bordered by woodland.

Lord Evelyn had always organised the Lower Shepney
Market XI, mostly from estate workers, gardeners and house
guests. He'd arrive in pony and trap, wearing aged flannels,

and in spite of his workers being desperately keen *not* to run him out, was often clean bowled for a duck.

Rumour had it that when engaging household staff, his first question had always been; how fast can you bowl?

So, would the elusive new owner give two hoots for those aristocratic traditions? Well yes, according to Sully. No objections had been voiced, anyway.

The pavilion had been decked with bunting and chairs set outside.

Drifting by to find a chair, Gerry gathered up a frothy sweep of skirts. Yes, this dress *was* far too fey and floaty for cricket, but absolutely vital now, for keeping confidence up.

Tilting the brim of her Tagel straw over her eyes, she settled down to watch the match.

Coop? Hallie-Lee? She waved a wasp away. Why let them spoil this occasion? Anyway, Hallie-Lee was probably back at the Hall, admiring a diamond the size of a small field mouse on her wedding ring finger.

The day had dawned clear, blue and bright. Flaming June, for once, living up to its name. And although countrymen who knew about these things were warning of storms and thunder, no-one was taking any notice.

By lunchtime, the air was drowsy with heat, the atmosphere languid. People sprawled on grass at the boundary edge were already fanning themselves with hats. 'Who's in charge today, then?' they kept muttering.

The Vicar? Gerry wondered idly, watching him humming

and buzzing about, a bemused bee in a panama hat. No *true* blue-blooded aristocracy for miles around anymore, to present cup and prizes.

Archie was opening bat for Lower Shepney Market XI, strolling fearlessly to the crease in immaculate white flannels. No grass-stained knees or whiff of mildew there.

Modestly acknowledging the polite burst of applause, he gave Gerry a quick wink and wave of his bat. There was an approving wheeze behind her. 'What ho! Attractive bat, that Dutt-Dixon-Nabb fellow. Good medium-paced bowler, too.'

Out of the corner of her eye, she caught sight of Archie's be-whiskered pa, chest puffed out like a pigeon. Aha, she thought. Perhaps the Major will present the cup. He is MFH, after all, with a strong whiff of English gentry. Important, too. At least, he thinks that he is.

The afternoon grew hotter and stickier and seemed to be teetering on the edge of a thunderstorm.

Squinting into the sun, Gerry watched admiringly as Archie slugged the ball this way and that, making a huge number of stylish runs. Well, good for Archie. Most of the time, she really, really liked him. His parents were awful, of course. But, why *not* marry the man?

'You know why.'

'No,' she said, out loud. 'I don't.' And as heads turned, she was tempted to say; 'It's alright. I'm just talking to dead people.'

Instead, she muttered, 'It's no use talking to me now. Where have you been? Where *were* you when I needed you?'

No reply. Not from Leonie, anyway.

But as Archie's runs reached a half century, even as his stylish strokes at the wicket were being admired and applauded, someone leaned over her shoulder and with a voice like spilled syrup, drawled in her ear, 'If that's the feller you've got your money on, Gerry, it's in the wrong bank.'

She swivelled round. No chance to respond. Just Coop's retreating figure strolling casually towards the pavilion, where - ha, just look - a smug-looking Hallie-Lee was waiting under a parasol. Oh. How dare he!

After that, everything seemed to go wrong. Clouds gathered, Gerry's spirits plummeted, and Archie was bowled out. The rest of the raggle-taggle team, with so few able-bodied men to choose from, went from bad to worse.

Lower Shepney Market XI all out; Oakenford in, with runs mounting.

All around Gerry, cricket talk, cricket gossip and dressing-room squabbles. 'He's made me third man and he knows I've got a gammy leg!'

If only she could take up her own bat again. But women and cricket were now considered an unholy alliance, weren't they?

'Wimmen playing? It'd be like asking a man to knit,' she'd heard someone growl.

Anyway, she wasn't in the right mood to do much of anything, anymore. Coop's presence had set her nerves on edge. What did he want, what was he doing here? And what about Hallie-Lee?

'You should have stayed to ask him, shouldn't you? Then, you would have found out.'

Oh, shush!

'Don't be such a scratch cat, darling!'

An hour later, as the sky took on the threatening colour of a bruise, tedium set in. The last but one Oakenford batsman, a pugnacious, showy sort of fellow, couldn't be dislodged and was slamming balls all over the field.

When a new man in whites stepped up to bowl, Gerry was far too fidgety and distracted to pay any attention. Even Major Dutt-Dixon-Nabb harrumphing about 'these colonial types' didn't alert her.

It wasn't until one batsman had been clean bowled and the next was quaking at the crease, that a squinting Gerry recognised the tall, eye-catching figure pounding towards the wicket, like something out of a Boy's Own adventure story.

Coop? Well, really! The brass neck of the man, sauntering back with an heroic swagger. What did *he* know about this game, about the forty-two laws of cricket?

She spent the next few minutes, mouth catching flies, as all around, deckchairs creaked, necks craned and thrilled cries of, 'Oh, I *say*! He's *bowled* him!' and 'Well done, well done, sir!' filled the air.

Game over; all hail the conquering hero.

Then, the wind got up and the match came to a hurried end. Spectators started milling round the pavilion steps, awaiting the presentation of the cup, now proudly displayed on the verandah.

The milling went on for some time. Who and what were they waiting for? The Vicar? Major Dutt-Dixon-Nabb? Some visiting dignitary come to cast his lustre on the occasion? No-one seemed to know.

A flash of lightning, and as the Vicar stepped forward to make an announcement, his words were drowned out by an immense clap of thunder.

He waved a gracious hand towards the newly appointed giver-of-prizes, and at the next huge clap of thunder - an omen, obviously - a person stepped out of the crowd. A stranger, yes, a visitor from the New World.

Shuffling forward to watch, Gerry stared. Huh. A Texan cattleman who hadn't known a thing about this game until she'd endeavoured to explain it all to him, many months ago? At one time, townsfolk here would have run him off, with pitchforks.

What was going on? What had any of this to do with him and why hadn't anybody told her about it? It simply wasn't how things were done here.

Coop proceeded to shake hands with all and sundry, saving special congratulations for Archie. Oh, yes. Gerry looked from one to the other. They were having a long conversation, they ... oh my, they were actually laughing together. Enjoying a joke!

And suddenly, in this place where she knew everyone and his dog, and everyone knew her - she started to feel an outsider. The only thing that made her feel any better, was when

Hallie-Lee suddenly started flap-flapping, and was stung, apparently, by the most enormous bee.

'Buzz!' came Leonie's gleeful voice in Gerry's head.

Then, another flash of lightning brought the dark summer storm heaving in, over treetops. Large drops of rain began to fall and people rushed for cover.

Gerry didn't move.

As wind got up and rain started drumming the pavilion roof, Coop dipped his head against the sudden deluge and ran down the steps towards her. 'Gerry! Come inside. You're getting wet.'

Something snapped, and she said, 'What is this all about? What are you *doing* here, why have you come?'

'Look, I tried to tell you. Then later ... guess I thought you knew.' He looked slightly uncomfortable. Then, 'See, I've bought the Hall.'

Was he mad? As hard rain pricked arms and neck, she said, 'But, *why?*' It made no sense.

'Why not, I've always admired it. A real fine property. Look, let's go talk in the pavilion. C'mon, you're getting soaked.'

Stock still, in rain now lashing down, she said, 'But you've got one, already, you've got a house.'

'Well, I ... was in the mood for something different. A fine old house, with y'know, a lake, a rambling garden.' He waved a hand, expansively. The Lord of the Manor, welcoming house guests to his country pile. 'And a ... what is it? A ha-ha. That's right, yeah. I kinda fancied a ha-ha.'

'Well, that's just ridiculous.' How dare he tease and make

jokes? She felt more and more indignant.

'Beg pardon?'

'You live thousands of miles away. You have commitments, you have ... cows. All of those ...'

'... head of cattle? Look, I had the money. You wouldn't expect Lord Evelyn to have me chased out of town with sticks now, would you?'

'Yes, and what *about* that money?' She pushed wet, and now Medusa-like hair from her eyes. 'I signed my share of the ranch over to you, without taking a penny farthing! I came home with ... with huge debts, to save you having to let the drillers in.'

'I know, yeah, I know you did, Gerry, and I-.'

'Have you any idea how *hard* that was?'

'Yeah, it was pretty impressive.'

'It felt impressive, until it started to feel stupid. Because now, I find out what you did with all that money. You *bought* the Hall, behind my back. Why? Why would you play that sort of game!'

'Look, I tried to tell you. The other day ... I wanted to, but you wouldn't talk, wouldn't listen to me!'

Torn between anger and distress, Gerry stood, shivering and dripping and soaked to the skin. Rain plastered hair to her head and trickled down her neck. All those foolish dreams she'd harboured about this man; the feelings that had been tugging at her, since she'd come back to England. They meant nothing.

She'd been duped. He'd made a fool of her. And she was

not going to cry in front of him, was *not*. Another great, operatic roll of thunder made the scene seem like something from Tosca.

'Trust me, Gerry.'

Trust! She shook her head.

'I can explain.'

'No!'

'Aw, c'mon.' His hand closed round her wrist, as he tried to cajole her. 'Get down off that high horse and let me tell you about it.'

A moment of paralysis. Acutely aware of his damp hair, that stain of stubble and the scent of his skin, she started to remember how they made her feel. She held his eyes for as long as she could, then thought - no. I can't *bear* this.

'Look at me, Gerry, listen to me ...'

Shaking free of his hand, she turned blindly away and ran off, head down, through the heavy curtain of rain.

CHAPTER
THIRTY EIGHT

'An old maid is only an old maid when she makes up her
mind to be one.'
Heart-to-Heart Column, 1922

No stopping, no looking back. No thinking. Gerry's feet found
their own way along a familiar path. From childhood right up
until the time around Leonie's death, her place of escape and
solace had forever been the same. The island. On the lake. In
these grounds of the Hall.

That same Hall and lake now owned by Coop, the traitor.
Rain and tears mingled on her face. Not only had he stolen
her heart and her money - now her hiding place belonged to
him, too.

The rain was so heavy that she could barely see more than
a few feet, but she knew the way, by heart.

Dark ancient woodland fringing the lake offered some protection from the rain, but the jungle of ferns and undergrowth
was already lush and damp, hart's tongue and spleenwort

hugging the shade.

Several times Gerry stumbled, slipped and almost fell on the winding, hidden path to the water, setting wood pigeons fluttering.

On, on, under the old trees, heart bumping.

No birdsong here, just a steady drip, drip through the green canopy. The smell of wet vegetation and once, a stink of fox. But, as ever, under trees of oak and beech, that gentle lapping water and air of mystery somehow always managed to soothe her.

Slipping down towards the stillness of the lake, she covered the ground quickly, like a ghost.

Would the little boat still be there? Must be at least a year since she'd seen it. Yes, there it was - hooked to a stump at the water's edge, next to rotting planks that made up the jetty. Rocking gently, paint peeling, but both oars still inside.

She stopped. Since Leonie's funeral, she hadn't been anywhere near the little island, had barely been able to think about it.

On *that* day, the dreadful funeral day, a treacherous sun had been out, hadn't it? And the flotilla of little boats, filled with Leonie's friends and lovers and decorated with ribbons and floating streamers, had bobbed over to the island.

A few maudlin minutes, then no more hesitation. Hitching up sodden skirts, she clambered in, took up an oar and pushed off. Rain now pouring down in bucketfuls, lightning flashing across the water, she rowed blindly across to the little island, coots and swans and water lilies rocking in her swishing wake.

It wasn't far, but the water was deep. She'd done this many, many times before, though. Day time, night time. Summer, winter.

At the island, climbing out and trying to tether the little boat, both hands were icy. When she tripped, tearing the hem of her aunt's diaphanous tea dress, it brought more choking tears, more sniffs. *Oh, Leonie.*

Shoes oozed mud and she was shivering violently.

But, but ...

She looked around. As ever, she felt safe here. She had the boat, she was untouchable; no-one could reach her. As a child, she'd always put up a flag and used a telescope to spy on invaders. Her own private kingdom.

Inside the tiny folly of a temple, she sat down, with a bump, on cold stone. The little statue of Aphrodite stood behind her, silently observing. The goddess of pure and ideal love? Ho, ho, ho!

Between downpours, the rain eased. All around, the air was densely green, surrounding the temple in mysterious green light.

Flapping her arms, Gerry tried to warm herself. Thoughts racing, the taste of the lake still on her lips, she turned things over and over in her mind. Such inner mess, such muddle.

What had Coop been plotting? Crossing the seas to buy the Hall and estate like some swashbuckling pirate, for goodness sake. It seemed such a hostile thing to do.

Why, in Texas he'd seemed an almost noble character.

Someone with values, trying to exorcise his own demons, fighting for the survival of his ranch.

She'd admired that, hadn't she? Respected it. She'd wanted to help, for goodness sake. Wasn't that why she'd given away her share of her inheritance? How could he have behaved so badly?

Oh, what had she expected? There were no white knights anymore, riding to anyone's rescue. He was human, fallible. And what of Hallie-Lee? *Were* they married now? They must be. She pushed away the pain of that thought.

What would Hallie-Lee and Coop talk about, on hot summer nights under the stars? Would he tell her about the constellations? Perhaps, from time to time, they'd even speak about Gerry.

How dull I must have seemed to them, Gerry thought, *how strange and Anglo-Saxon.*

Still, Coop coming all this way, to a tiny corner of England, to buy the Hall did seem particularly odd. How could she have been expected to deal with that? Too much, too soon.

Silence. Just the steady percussion of rain dripping from overhanging trees and a few solitary quacks from the lake, all adding to her misery.

She sat, utterly alone and very cold. Perhaps she'd stay here for ever, eventually turning to stone, like Aphrodite. No-one would find her. After all, how would they get here? She had the boat.

Thankfully, when some spark of reason returned, she remembered the old box, behind the statue, where rugs were always stored for picnics, and pulling out a dusty, moth-eaten mat, wrapped it round herself, gratefully.

Rooting round, she found more treasures. Some battered tin cups, a bottle of brandy. Her old telescope! All brought back vivid memories of visits with Leonie.

Once, they'd carried the wind-up gramophone and some records here in the little boat, making it rock precariously. Wearing wide-brimmed hats, they'd sung and danced - black-bottoming around a stiffly appalled Aphrodite - and then cooked little fish over an open fire.

Leonie, Leonie. I miss you so much. Where *are* you now? I need your help.

Silence.

She shook herself. Come on now, pull yourself together. In time, you'll get over this. You will, you will.

And slowly, very slowly, after a few tots of brandy, the heat of anger cooled and Gerry started to feel a tiny bit embarrassed for the way she'd behaved. She'd used all the wrong words, hadn't she? Said the wrong things.

Still a whisper of rain, but the storm had stopped rattling and was moving away. No sound. Just the breeze stirring leaves. More rain, more drips.

All of a sudden, a huge splash.

Duck?

She peered out into the gloom. No. Something bigger had just hit the green water. Otter? She fumbled for her telescope.

A long, sinuous shape was cleaving a path through the water lilies. Fish, fowl? She held her breath. No, wait. A *human* form. It kept disappearing beneath the water, then surfacing again, its hair sluiced back. Sinking? Drowning! Yes, yes, going under.

Alarmed, Gerry dropped the telescope and rushed through long grass and stinging nettles to the water's edge. Far deeper than it first appeared, this lake was thick and heavy with weeds. In the past, people had dived in on hot summer days and had to be dragged unceremoniously from its murky depths.

She raced up and down, shouting, bracing herself. What kind of fool would risk swimming in these conditions? Should she row to the rescue?

Several hysterical minutes later, the figure neared the shallows, stood up and waded out, water streaming from his clothes. Limp with relief, Gerry stopped dead in her tracks.

What sort of fool? Ha! One with a cool nerve and the most outrageous effrontery, that's who. Someone sent to plague her.

CHAPTER THIRTY NINE

'Always in love, always some shining star on the horizon.'
Leonie Alexandrina Bent, Diary 1919

'Oh! That was so ... *stupid*. You could've drowned!'

'Nah.' Coop shook weed and water from his head, like a dog. 'Haven't you taken it in yet? We Texans are a superior race.'

'But ... what are you *doing* here?'

'Desperate times, desperate measures.' He stripped off his shirt, wrung it out. 'Buddy boy back there, that Dee-Dee-Nabb feller ...'

'Archie! Here ...' Shocked by this sudden intimacy, she passed him the rug and he rubbed head, iron-hard abdomen and muscled shoulders, vigorously.

'Yep, called me 'old boy' and said you often come here when you're upset. You *are* upset, I take it?' Pause. 'Uh-huh, thought as much.'

Barefoot and now bare-chested, the rest of his wet clothes were clinging to that athletic body, and Gerry's gaze veered away, uncomfortably aware that every one of her nerve endings had started to tingle.

That powerful, physical magnetism, the blood-red vitality. He looked like a ... gladiator. Oh, for pity's sake!

Archie? She wrapped her arms tightly round herself. *Archie* had told Coop to come here? Why in the world would he do that?

'That strange cat kinda led the way. Yeah, the big, black one. Showed me the path, when I was trying to hack my way through to the water.'

And while Gerry tried to absorb that nugget of information, he looked towards the temple and whistled. 'Wow. Quite some place.'

'And I suppose you'll soon want to make changes to all of this, too.' Even her vocal cords were quivering.

'Why the hell would I do that? It's magical, a sanctuary. I can see why a person would love it. Anyhow, I haven't made changes to anything, yet. Just repairs, y'know.'

Silence.

'Well,' he drawled, at last. 'Here we are, together again.'

'We are not together. You're in my special place, and I'm not enjoying it.' A pause. 'Why did you follow me?'

'To try to get a lick of sense into your head.'

Ah. So, he was the one acting in an underhand manner, but *she* was supposed to hang her head and shuffle feet. How had that happened?

Apparently reading her expression, he went to the boat and held up the oars. 'Listen Gerry, I've tried gentlemanly restraint and asking nicely. But so help me, if you're planning to high-tail off again, I'm going to throw these out into the lake.'

'No, no, don't! No, I'll listen, I will!'

'Promise? Don't play dare with me, now.'

A stiff shake of her head.

Trailing back to the temple, busily rummaging in the box for another rug and tin cup, she tried hard to put on a show of being perfectly at ease, and in control. She poured Coop a tot of brandy, but resisted one herself, even though she was all ghost-pale and goosepimply. Her head was spinning too much.

'Brandy?' he said, stretching out full-length and leaning back on his elbows. 'To cure whatsoever ails us. My, you've thought of everything.'

So polite, so good-mannered. Any minute, she thought, he'll start discussing the weather, or the batting average in today's match. The tension was unbearable.

Her dress was still uncomfortably wet and clinging limply to her; in places, it was almost transparent. She pulled the scratchy rug more tightly around.

Back there, at the water's edge, there'd been a moment when she'd been aware of his slow gaze, looking her carefully up and down. As if he'd been taking off all her clothes and putting them back on again, in the right order.

What had *really* shocked her then, was how much she'd wanted him to touch her. The strength of that feeling had made her panic. Danger, danger! Down, down that slippery slope to ruin. The last twitches of a frustrated spinster.

Oh, stop! How could she understand passion? She'd no experience of it. Except in literature, poetry. Brahms, Beethoven. A passion for clothes, perhaps. But really, she knew more about the workings of a sewing machine than her own body.

Presently, having tossed back his brandy, Coop asked about Aphrodite, in that smoky Southern drawl - a voice seductive enough to woo goddesses. 'Wasn't there some story,' he said, 'about a feller swimming out to see one of Aphrodite's virgin priestesses?'

Pushing back damp twists of hair, Gerry stared.

'What? Still think I'm some hick from the sticks with no idea about culture?'

'No. No, I ... Hero and Leander. Hero was the priestess and he swam out to see her.'

'Aha. Kinda like me, then. So, what happened to old Leander?'

'He drowned,' Gerry said, with some satisfaction.

Minutes ticked slowly, painfully past. She turned her face to the sky. The rain had almost stopped and a watery sun appeared low over the horizon. Then, a rainbow, and light shining through the leaves turning them a mythic, hazy green.

An omen? Augury. Of what? Gerry wondered. The talk they were surely soon to have?

'So,' he said at last, eyes on her face, assessing her.

'What?'

'What's all this about, that's what! This skittering away, refusing to talk to me. I'm getting kinda tired of having to fight the War of Independence over and over.'

Silence.

'Are you pouting?'

'I don't *pout*.'

'Well, seems to me we're pretty much back where we started. Only this time, you're doing the shouting.' He frowned. 'I mean, I know we've had our issues, some bigger than others, but -'

'I hadn't heard a word from you for months,' Gerry cut in, avoiding eye contact. 'Then you arrive out of the blue and announce that you've *bought* the Hall. How did you expect me to behave?'

'You didn't let me explain.'

'Explain! You've made a fool of me, humiliated me.'

'Hogwash. It wasn't-'

'Then why not tell me? You could surely have written. I had no warning.'

'You're right, yeah. Shouldn't have taken you by surprise like that, it was stupid.'

Their eyes met.

'A mistake.' He shrugged. 'Guess I messed up.'

Messed up? In the yawning silence that followed, Gerry irritably waved away tiny flies that had started flickering over the tall grass. There was no way that she was going to forgive him for that.

Then, 'On the other hand, Missy, what about you leaving *me* all those months ago? Without a goodbye wave or word of explanation? There were consequences to that, y'know.'

'Consequences!' A shifty sidelong glance. 'Such as you

spending all of my money?'

'Hey, I didn't touch a cent of your money. Is that really what you think of me? That I'd take your inheritance and get on with my life without a backward glance?' He pushed long hair back from his face. 'Do you know how that makes me feel?'

'Well -'

He held up a hand. 'My turn. See, I actually thought we'd reached some kind of understanding back then, a chance of something good between us.' A dry pause. 'Okay, we had a ways to go, perhaps. Were there still some things I wasn't ready to talk about? Yeah, guess there were.'

Her head still spinning, Gerry barely took that in. 'Well, if you *didn't* take my money, how in heaven's name could you buy the Hall?'

'Black gold, oil. Rode out onto the prairie and asked Frank what I should do, just like you told me. Yeah, and it felt pretty damn silly at the start, I can tell you. But after shouting at the sky and listening to the wind for a while - reckon I got my answer.'

Gerry pictured that big brassy sky, hot wind, and felt a pang.

'So,' he said, 'there you go. They drilled on the Circle-O's borders, hit some gushers and hey ... now I'm one very, very rich cowboy.'

A stunned silence.

'But, why come all this way, just to buy the Hall? It seems ridiculous, so lavish. Almost ... careless.'

'Oh, Gerrygerry. I'm not doing so well here, am I? You still don't get it.'

She shook her head.

'See, the thing is, I was missing you. And I kinda hoped ... well, that you were missing me, too.' A pause. Trees breathed and sighed over and around, and there was a tiny shift in intimacy as he inched towards her. 'How do you feel about that?'

'I ... a little confused.' Wait. 'What about Hallie-Lee?'

'What about her? You want me to take her a message or something?'

'I understood ... that you two were married.'

'Where the hell did you get that idea?'

'I think ...'

He was no longer a comfortable distance away. Eyes still on her face, he eased closer, shrugging off his blanket, and she caught heat coming off him and scent of soil, wet leaves and something else, something warm, intoxicating, potent.

There was a moment of stillness between them, like water before it slides over a precipice. Leaves stopped rustling, birds, insects fell silent.

'I love that parting in your hair.' Coop traced a path from forehead to eyes to cheek with one finger. 'Love your lips, the shape of your mouth.' Rubbing his thumb gently across those lips, he managed to strike some very erotic sparks.

Her stomach turned over; heart was thud-thudding.

'Forget what you think, Gerry,' he said, softly. 'How do you *feel*?'

Not a muscle moved. No word from her, just a quiver of

breath and rush of joy as he moved hands to her waist, pulled her hard against him and kissed her open mouth.

Drawing back, they held each other's eyes. Neither blinked.

'Still confused?'

Arms tightened around, the blanket slid from her shoulders, and with the tingling, electric sensation of damp skin on skin, he drew his tongue along her lower lip, then his mouth came down on hers and Gerry moved her hands to his hard back and hung on, with all her strength, and kissed him back.

A brief flash of a smile as he slowly drew away. Taking her hand, he kissed her knuckles. 'See? I'm bewitched. Buying the Hall was my collateral. That's property pledged as guarantee for repayment of money, if you'd care to know - I looked it up. In other words, payback. I did this for you.'

'You bought the Hall for *me*, that huge, huge house?'

'That's right.'

'But, why?'

'To give us a real chance to get to know each other better. See, I want to know everything about you, hopes, dreams. Family history.'

'Why didn't you just *tell* me how you felt? Was I supposed to guess?'

'You didn't give me a chance, just high-tailed back here, without a word. Scoot begged and begged me to ask you back, but I didn't want you to come to Texas until you were sure that's where you wanted to be. So, I'm telling you now. Right from the first time we met, there was something going on between us. For me, it started when I first clapped eyes on you.'

She stared. 'You could have said something.'

'I could have, but I didn't. Anyway, you weren't listening.'

'You were so rude, you said-'

'Yeah, I know.' Reaching out, he pulled a leaf from her hair. 'Bad of me, bad, bad. I'm unpredictable. But you weren't like any other woman I'd ever known. You brought me back to life, Gerry.' A slow shake of his head. 'I didn't think anyone could ever do that.'

'So, Hallie-Lee?'

'She followed me here, sure; with no encouragement, I have to say. Look, I can't deny there've been plenty of women. From time to time, I've even thought about marrying one of them. But never, ever Hallie-Lee. She's like some annoying kid sister.'

'For that matter,' he said, after a moment, 'what about that Archie fella? Y'know, we country boys don't stand no messin' around with our wimmen folk.' A pause. 'Are you crying?'

'It's just ...' Was this really happening? The sweet release of all the joy and desire she'd held back for so long. Hadn't she imagined this? Pictured it, dreamed of it. But never ever, in a million years, expected it to happen. A passionate declaration of love?

Would someone pinch her in a minute, and wake her up?

Taking her face in both his hands, Coop's lips brushed eyelids, cheek, throat and Gerry leaned in closer, closer to catch the flame.

'So.' Coop eased back onto his elbows. 'Tell me the story of your life, Gerardina Chiledexter.'

They talked and talked until night crept in over the lake, coaxing stories from each other, swapping hopes, dreams. Then, as fingers of inky cloud parted and moon lit up the temple, they lay on their backs looking up at the stars.

His voice drowsy, Coop said, 'Y'know, this place really is magic.'

She nodded. 'There's always been something fairytale and other-worldly about it. There are ghosts here, you know, spells.'

'You really believe in all that stuff, don't you?'

'Oh, yes,' she said, feeling the faintest breath of something on her cheek, a secret whisper, barely a puff, a trace. 'I really, really do.'

She thought, *who do you think led you here?*

And to her aunt: *'All right, Leonie. You can stop pushing!'*

'Want to tell me about it?' he said

'Mmm. Another time.'

'Strangest thing,' he said. 'I sort of started to feel Frank pushing me to come over here, too.' A pause. 'Why didn't he and your aunt make it, d'you think?'

Gerry shrugged. 'I don't know. Bad timing, perhaps? Sad, isn't it. Lost love.'

'So. What do we do now?'

She ran a finger over his stubbled chin. 'We could stay here forever, eating nuts and berries. Be castaways.'

'Tantalizing as that sounds, guess we'd better head back.

There's your reputation to consider.' He nodded towards the lake. 'I don't much care for the look of that old rust bucket, though. It's pitch black out there.'

'Oh, the boat's quite safe. And look, a few stars out now. I'll use celestial navigation.'

'Well, hey, Galileo! Guess it's better than swimming back.'

'And I am *definitely* going to row.'

'Aye, aye, Cap'n.' He gave a mock salute.

'And you, matey, must promise to do just as I say for a change, and sit absolutely still.'

Moments later, as a cock pheasant shot out in front of them, Gerry said 'For heaven sake! I was *sure* I'd secured it.'

They peered out into deepest shadow. No wind, just the cool, sulky slap of water, the glimmer of the lake. But the little boat - nowhere to be seen.

'Now what? We better swim.'

'No, no. Too cold, we'd catch pneumonia! Anyway, that water's higher than usual, after all the rain. Deeper.'

Then, as the moon sailed out from behind a cloud, a dark shape, splash of oars. 'Nice night for a rat hunt. Care to join me?'

Sully - their grizzled rescuer, their knight errant - in ear-hugging hat that moths had clearly gnawed right through, and moonbeams shining all around him.

A week later. The question was asked. And yes, she said yes, she said yes.

'So, we need two weddings.'

'Two!'

'One here and one in Texas. What d'you say?'

'Mmm. And, who will I be? Mrs Coop-er?'

'O'Rourke. Frank adopted me. I just never got round to using the name.'

'Gerardina O'Rourke? Makes me sounds like a prize-fighter!'

Just past the dreamy point of midsummer, and one week before the village wedding, a parcel arrived from Paris. Inside, swathed in reams of tissue - a heavy length of veil, made from rare lace with caplet of pearls and leaves to secure it. It looked medieval, Italian, and when Gerry held it up, it took her breath away.

'Where's it from?' Prim said. 'Who sent it?' Then, 'Oh, Gerry! That *perfume*!'

'*Mitsouko*,' Gerry whispered, and they clutched each other.

As Coop and Gerry left the cool stone of the little church, accompanied by Mrs Pratt-Steed's muted Mendelssohn and floating clouds of rose petals from a cheering crowd, Archie rearranged the trailing veil.

'Be happy,' he whispered.

'You, too, Archie.'

'I'm going out to Kenya, darling. Wish me luck!'

After the wedding breakfast and dancing under the stars, they slipped away to the water's edge, where the little boat, lined with white velvet and swansdown, waited.

And as Coop rowed them across the shining silver skin of the lake to the island, Gerry caught her breath.

Under a lantern moon, the temple had been draped with drifting white muslin, and a hundred and twenty dotted flickering candles cast a soft glow.

While a summer breeze sighed and shushed through surrounding trees, Coop gathered her up out of the boat, carried her to the bed, plumped with silk cushions within the drapes, and set her down.

'So, Mrs O'Rourke,' he said, turning her round and starting to loosen a hundred tiny pearl buttons from their looped fastenings. 'Where exactly were we?'

Overhead and far, far above them, the stars aligned for a spectacular horoscope.

Because, oh yes. Leonie *always* got what she wanted.

ACKNOWLEDGEMENTS

So many wonderful people have put up with me in the of writing this book. I'd like to thank them all, especially the fantastic Kearns family, my own particular branch, and all other off-shoots, too. You know who you are. Then, there's the Clancys!

To Christophe, Carolyn and Tom L for professional, artistic and moral support.

To the ever-patient Jane Dixon Smith for cover design and formatting, and the hugely talented Christian Eldridge, for the fabulous 20's figure on the front cover.

To my excellent proof reader, juliaproofreader@gmail.com

To Amanda Grange, author of 'Mr Darcy's Diary' who having started us off on this journey, has been hugely supportive and encouraging, and also **The Romantic Novelists' Association** for their support, expertise and friendship.

Lastly, to my fellow authors, greatest supporters and friends: Mags Cullingford, Lizzie Lamb and Adrienne Vaughan - **The New Romantics 4**

ABOUT THE AUTHOR

June Kearns has always been a daydreamer. As an only child, she used to spend a lot of time staring into space and making things up. Now, with quite a few children of her own, she's still doing it!

She wrote *An Englishwoman's Guide to the Cowboy* after far too many hours spent watching cowboy loners bring order west of the Pecos.

Her second novel *The Twenties Girl, the ghost, and all that jazz*, was inspired by the style and fashion of the 1920's, and a time in England, after the Great War, of crumbling country houses and few men.

June believes the best romantic relationships involve great conversations, argument, and plenty of humour, and that's what she aims for in her novels!

A former teacher, June lives in Leicestershire with her family.

Also by June Kearns

An Englishwoman's Guide to the Cowboy

The American West, 1867

After a stagecoach wreck, well-bred bookish spinster, Annie Haddon, (product of mustn't-take-off-your-hat, mustn't-take-off-your-gloves, mustn't-get-hot-or-perspire Victorian society) is thrown into the company of cowboy Colt McCall – a man who lives by his own rules, and hates the English.

Can two people from such wildly different backgrounds learn to trust each other.

Annie and McCall find out on their journey across the haunting mystical landscape of the West.

Available from Amazon in paperback and Kindle format. viewbook.at/B009XRRU2M

Some reviews for An Englishwoman's Guide ...

'Witty, sparkling and romantic, this is a fabulous read!'

*'This funny, charming, delightful book! I hope it gets
the grand audience it deserves.'*

*'Whoooeeee! Hot Dawg! What a great read!! If the hot outlaw,
the bitchy sister or the don't-mess-with-me-attitude doesn't draw
you in, the Southern drawl will.'*

*'A charming, historical romance that brought
the 1860's West to life.'*

'What an unexpected delight this book is.'

*'Ms Kearns has returned to the tradition of decency, honour and
rough-diamond gallantry. Hip Hip Hooray!'*

Check out all the novels published by the **New Romantics 4** – available from Amazon in paperback and Kindle formats.

Tall, Dark and Kilted

&

Boot Camp Bride

By Lizzie Lamb

Last Bite of the Cherry

&

Twins of a Gazelle

By Mags Cullingford

The Hollow Heart

&

A Change of Heart

By Adrienne Vaughan

Printed in Great Britain
by Amazon.co.uk, Ltd.,
Marston Gate.